THE IMPOSSIBLE BIRD

TOR BOOKS BY PATRICK O'LEARY

Door Number Three
The Gift
The Impossible Bird

THE
Impossible Bird

PATRICK O'LEARY

TOR®

A TOM DOHERTY ASSOCIATES BOOK
NEW YORK

THE IMPOSSIBLE BIRD

Patrick O'Leary's homepage:
http://people.mw.mediaone.net/patri10629/newindex.html

"The Summer Day" from *House of Light* by Mary Oliver. Copyright © 1990 by
Mary Oliver. Reprinted by permission of Beacon Press, Boston.

This book is printed on acid-free paper.

A Tor Book
Published by Tom Doherty Associates, LLC
175 Fifth Avenue
New York, NY 10010

www.tor.com

Tor® is a registered trademark of Tom Doherty Associates, LLC.

ISBN 0-765-30337-X

First Edition: January 2002

Printed in the United States of America

0 9 8 7 6 5 4 3 2 1

To St. Jude, Gene Wolfe, and Kathe Koja—friends indeed

Acknowledgments

"Well, I'm back." Heartfelt thanks to all the usual suspects whose guidance was so essential on this arduous journey. My friends in the Detroit Writers Guild: Anca, Anthony, Carol, Claire, Jane, John, Melanie, Olivia, Peggy, Robin, and Suzanne—you know your last names. Faithful readers: Ken Ethridge, Kathe Koja, my agent Susan Ann Protter, Moshe Feder, and especially my editor David G. Hartwell. My beloved first reader, Claire, who knows what it cost me. Family who did without: Lochlan and Colin. Overdue thanks to Nancy Dougherty for critical help on *Door Number Three*. Thanks to Sphene and June, and Gloria Frank for hummingbird tips. Thanks to Patrick Swenson, editor of *Talebones*, where a section of this work appeared, as we all do sometimes, in a different guise. To Nick Lowe for the title. To friends who kept asking "How's the bird?" To Gene for believing in me though he had no reason to. And to the readers who will make a home for this story. It doesn't have one without you. Peace.

P.O.

*"If two [subatomic] particles have ever interacted with each other,
from then on anything that is done to one of them
affects the other in the same way no matter where it is
—with absolutely no connection between them."*

DAVID LUNDE, *UNCOMMON PLACES*

1962—We're in This Together

Danny and Mike were brothers.

They grew up in a big white house outside of Saginaw, Michigan, surrounded by fields: corn across the dirt road, green fallow to the west and, on the other side, beyond their next door neighbor the widow McNulty's, endless rows and rows of sugar beets. It was a fair hike out through the backyard garden of vegetables, past Uncle Louie's bomb shelter, over the cold, cold stream they were just old enough to leap, up the hill of dry weeds, and through the apple orchard where they used to catch fireflies, to the golden field of ripened wheat—where they lay, side-by-side on their backs, as if they'd fallen from the sky. Watching the white clouds slide by slowly in the perfect blue of a late summer day.

"You ever think about dying?" Danny, the eight-year-old, asked.

Mike, the ten-year-old, answered, "Sometimes."

"I been thinking about it. Ever since we caught the fish."

Two weeks before, they had found a sucker in the shallows of the stream. They put the slippery silver fish in the rain barrel under the downspout behind the back porch. It only lived a few days.

In the distance they could hear Mr. Schlitbeer threshing in his combine. Taking in the harvest. The golden stems swayed above them. The patch of bent stalks they lay upon was soft and dry and comfortable.

Mike was chewing on wheat—he'd press his hands together as if in prayer and rub the kernels between his palms to shed the chaff, then pop them in his mouth and crunch away. They tasted like sweet cereal, and they expanded as he chewed.

This was gross to Danny—the more careful of the two. He wasn't putting anything in his mouth. "Gort."

Mike smiled. "Barrada."

"Nikto," said Danny.

"Your world will be reduced..."

"To a burned-out cinder."

Then they did their best to mimic the theremin theme of the famous black-and-white movie they'd just seen on TV: the music they played whenever the robot was going to kill somebody. They lay there, humming the same mechanical ghostly whine through their noses. It ended in a fit of giggles.

Mike said, "I still say the soldiers didn't feel it."

"They were disintegrated!" said Danny.

"Yeah, but they didn't scream."

"The deathray was too loud. I betcha they screamed."

"I was watching their mouths," Mike assured him. "They didn't scream."

"That doesn't mean it didn't hurt," Danny said.

"Maybe they were shocked," Mike said.

"In shock," Danny corrected.

"Same thing."

"No. Remember when we touched the cow fence?" Danny asked.

It was a dare. To see if it was electric or not. And, of course, Mike had taken the dare. Mike, taller, stronger, faster, with a head of curly blond hair. A joker. The one kids always picked first for kickball. The first suspect whenever there was trouble at school. An average student with the exception of art: he had a talent for drawing. His favorite thing: girls. Mike touched the wire and felt the numb tingle slide up his arm. And jerking away, he had touched Danny and passed the shock on.

Danny wouldn't have touched the wire if you paid him. He knew better. Danny, shorter, rounder, quieter, short brown hair. His faintly bucked front teeth, his thick lenses that made his eyes seem bigger than they were. A model student. His report cards recorded his scholarship and conduct as impeccable. His favorite thing: books. Still, Danny was glad Mike had shared the shock. And passed on the knowledge secondhand.

They had screamed, then laughed. Then rubbed their arms.

"I bet aliens do it different."

"It's a movie, Danny. It doesn't have to make sense."

"Heinlein makes sense."

"Oh, shut up about your damn books."

"You shouldn't swear. It's not polite."

"Crap. Piss. Butt. Dick."

"Stop it. I was just saying: his stories—you believe them." Mike was silent, chewing. Danny continued, "Like he writes: 'The door dilated.'"

"What's *dilated?*"

"Like an eye. You know, when the iris closes 'cause it gets too much light."

Mike had studied that. "So?"

"So it's not just tricks. It's the future. It's on a spaceship and a round door makes a better airlock."

"Airlock?"

"In case there's an accident. Like a hull breach."

"What the hell's a *hull breach?*"

"Mike..."

"Mike," he mocked, doing a perfect imitation of his brother. "Shit. Poop. Nipple. Tit."

Danny sighed. There was no stopping him. "A hull breach is like a leak. Except not water but vacuum."

"Vacuum?"

"That's like nothing."

"Nothing?"

"No air to breathe. That's what space mostly is. Vacuums."

Mike tried to imagine that much nothing. He couldn't. The universe had to be made of something. How could it be mostly nothing? He hated it when his little brother knew stuff he didn't. "That's nonsensical," he said, using Dr. Klinder's word.

"No, it's not. It's science. Anyway, books make more sense."

"But they're boring," Mike said. "Give me a movie anytime."

"You can reread books."

"You can see pictures again."

"Yeah, but you have to pay another quarter. Library books are free."

"Screw the library."

"Mike."

"Hey. Wouldn't it be great if we had our own theater? And we could watch our favorite movie over and over."

Danny thought about it. "And we wouldn't have to pay."

"What if it was, like, small like a TV." The idea excited Mike. "And you could watch it all by pressing a button. And reverse it in case you didn't get a part."

"Or go forward to the end. Real fast. Skip the boring parts."

"Yeah, and freeze it if you had to pee," Mike said. "And move the camera to see the things you want to see. And talk to the actors. And look for the boobies."

"And turn the sound up real loud," said Danny.

"*Gort!*"

"*Barrada!*"

"*Nikto!*"

"And all the popcorn in the world," said Danny.

In the distance, they could hear Mr. Schlitbeer's combine coughing, then stalling out.

The stalks of wheat around them calmed and stilled as if someone had taken all the wind out of the world. They did not return to their upright and locked positions; they leaned. But there was no wind.

Some 200 yards above them, a round object oozed into their line of vision. It made no sound. A silver dot surrounded by a haze of white, hovering in the sky like a gigantic staring eye.

For an infinite moment they were treated to a bird's-eye view of two boys lying in a golden field. Two tiny dark stick figures side-by-side. Abandoned. The picture would stay with them for the rest of their lives. They never talked about it. But the images they retained in their separate minds were identical, as if they had two copies of the same photograph.

As easily as the object appeared, it passed beyond their sight.

Neither boy moved a muscle; they couldn't even look at each other.

"Let's go watch it!"

"You first," Danny said reluctantly.

"I can't move," Mike said. "I wanna move, but I can't."

"Me neither. Mike. I'm scared."

"How come we can talk if we can't move?"

"Deathray," Danny said.

They both lay there in the wheat field. Frightened, but curious too. Not wanting to miss their deaths.

They never heard the motor on the combine restart. But after a time, the stalks around them straightened up and leaned once again in the gentle breeze.

"A saucer."

"Or a Frisbee," Danny said.

"Too high," Mike concluded, still looking up.

Danny said, "Maybe we just made it up."

"Bullshit."

"Mike . . ."

"Dick. Wiener. Gina."

Danny asked, "What's a *gina?*"

"That's what girls got instead of wieners."

"Really?"

"Jeez, don't you know nothing? That's where the babies come out."

"I thought they had an operation. On their bellies."

"Naw, they come out between their legs. Or they're adopted like us. Didn't Stinko tell you yet?"

He shouldn't call him that, Danny thought. He asked for the whipping. "Uncle Louie told you?"

Mike nodded. "Gimme some Juicy Fruit."

"Haven't got any." Danny rolled his eyes. "You know, it wouldn't kill you to say *please* every once in a while."

"Why?" asked Mike.

Danny sighed.

They lay in the wheat thinking: Deathrays. Little movies. Heinlein. Wieners. Ginas. Dilate. And where the babies come out.

They found they could turn their heads. There were dark bruises around both of their eyes, as though they had been fighting for an hour, both of them giving as good as they got, until finally exhausted, they'd collapsed beside each other. A draw.

Danny giggled. "You look like a raccoon."

"Look who's talking," Mike replied.

Silence as they both remembered, or tried to, the missing time, the time they spent without each other. Danny in the hospital with trench mouth. Mike in Buffalo, "visiting relatives." The first time they'd ever been apart.

"I missed you," Danny said.

Mike was quiet for a time. "It wasn't that long."

"It felt like forever."

"I don't want to talk about it."

"Me neither."

The wind breathed in the wheat.

"I thought we were dead," Danny said.

"Me, too."

"Maybe we're dead and we don't know it."

"That's nonsensical."

They turned to look at each other then. The wheat shushed above them.

Danny put his hand on his brother's heart and felt the rhythm. "You're alive."

Mike did the same to his brother. "You, too."

They kept their hands there. On each other's hearts.

"If I die," Danny said, "will you die, too?"

"Sure."

"Promise?"

"Sure."

"Swear?"

"Cross my heart and hope to die."

"Stick a needle in your eye?"

The wheat waved back and forth and back.

"Sure," Mike said finally. Though it was the same word he had said twice before, it sounded different.

A pause when everything seemed settled.

Then Danny said, "You won't leave me?"

"Don't worry about it," Mike assured him. Then, "Nobody's leaving anybody." Finally, "We're in this together."

And it was settled.

Their faces were so close they could feel each other's breaths.

Mike sat up and they discovered they could stand. They stood and watched the skies for the silver disc, but it was nowhere to be seen. Then they saw they had been lying in a small square patch of dying khaki wheat. The rest of the field around them had been harvested.

They walked home through the empty field over stubble, dead chaff, and dirt. The sharp, rotting tang of autumn in the air.

2000 — The Magic Word

Y ou couldn't blame him if Daniel Glynn didn't know he was dead. He had never been dead before. And in matters of this sort he was always the last to know. As far as he was concerned he was merely reading a fantasy by the fire, a professor looking for something to assign his 300 class next year: Literature of the Fantastic, a man who had paused to look out the window. Actually, it was a long pause.

Daniel was thinking of his brother Mike when he heard the child scream.

"Dad!"

He had lost himself in the snowfall over his Detroit home. The flakes were yellow under the porch light. He was watching them collect on the silver hood of his spanking new Volvo. Daniel could see his own reflection in the living room window—a portly, balding middle-aged man in a blue robe sitting in a chair, wearing John Lennon glasses, holding a book. His slightly bucked front teeth hanging in his open mouth. Then looking past his image, Daniel caught a glimpse of the quantum world. His body was full of snowflakes—subatomic particles, a roiling mass of separate things that created the illusion of solidity, like a field of dark matter momentarily illuminated by some as yet undiscovered instrument of science—thick as fog, dawdling in lazy random orbits. *As if they existed in their own time frame and had found a compromise with gravity.*

He'd been thinking, before the scream had startled him out of his trance, how fairy tales all begin in normalcy. They only sound exotic to us because they're usually set in a past remote from ours. But the convention actually was to start in a mundane reality: a sort of setting-your-bearings real world before the adventures and miracles kicked in.

Miracles made him recall something his brother Mike had said on the last of his infrequent visits—or "intrusions" as he and his wife (but she wasn't here) had come to consider them. Mike was more of an intense, disruptive presence than a person, actually. An award-winning hot-shot director of commercials. He was so rich he lived in hotels all the time. Yet he was the sort of person who stole towels and shampoo from his suite: "They're included!"

Mike demanded. He exhausted. He disturbed. As the act of observing the subatomic disturbed the fabric of reality, changed its building blocks from particles to waves and back. As if some god, long dead, unseen or indifferent—as Daniel had come to regard him—could change everything merely by politely paying attention, could, if he chose, transform the falling snow into drops of peppermint.

Now that would be a miracle.

Since childhood Mike and Daniel's lives had been one long argument. There was something between them that would never be settled, that always had to be hashed out, worked over, brought up and beaten down. But, the odd thing was, if you had asked them what they were arguing about—they couldn't say. The true subject of their dispute was never made explicit, but always expressed in code. It was as if they were circling around a forbidden word, a word so terrible it could not be spoken. For, once said, there was no unsaying it, and it would hang there in the air above them like a hatchet stuck in a ceiling beam, that might, at any moment, dislodge itself, plunge down and do one or both of them harm. Wasn't that an old folk tale or something? So powerful was this unsaid thing, so dark, so unmentionable its secret, that it created a vortex and a vacuum around itself—a suction that drew them in, drew them back together and held them in their tense orbit—unable to break loose, unwilling to risk its declaration. And, over the years, as their perpetual debate ran on and reconvened at intervals, they came to know it as a constant companion: the one who may not be introduced, the one who wasn't there, the one who would never leave them.

"Life is an accident," Mike had said haughtily on his last visit. "Miracles are only parts of reality that haven't been explained yet."

"But that's most of it," Daniel had offered.

Explaining Miracles. That would make a good title. He'd try it out on his Contemporary Mythologies in Science Fiction class next winter. As an associate professor with tenure, Daniel was enjoying the fruits of his first sabbatical.

The details of the arrangement were hazy, like trying to see through the fog of snow outside his window. Apparently a lot of it was handled by phone. He seemed to recall the old dean assuring him that a full year at 60 percent pay would be no problem. Take as much time as he needed. He was an invaluable member of their team. They would wait. And meanwhile he might even finish that long work on Faulkner he had been promising for years. No pressure, of course—just a thought. It might even help the transition.

Transition. That was the pretty word nurses and doctors used for the last stage of childbirth.

Transition. It meant pain.

The details of the transition were cloudy. Well, in his present state that made sense. His mind was adrift. He had to remind himself to do the simplest things. Like dressing in the morning. One academic year off. January through January. To grieve. To mend. To research. To publish after his wife had perished. He seemed to recall the chair of his department had suggested on the phone that last year's grant proposal, which they thought brilliant but didn't get funding from the NEH, would serve as his sabbatical proposal and justify the extended break beyond the normal bereavement period, which at his enlightened university was considered a little shy of the six-week maternity leave: seven days. Have a baby: Take a month and a half. Lose a spouse: Take a week.

But, amazingly, the gears of academia must have turned greasily for his department, then the grant committee of the college, then the provost's approval, and it was done. Daniel was officially grieving. He could throw himself into his scholarship for twelve months. Twelve months at 60 percent pay and the expectation that he would have something to show for it when the normal period of grieving ended.

Normal. Period. Ended.

That was—what? A week ago? He couldn't remember. As far as he knew he'd been sitting here reading, watching the foggy snowstorm for days.

And he hadn't written a word.

"Dad!"

Daniel was halfway up the stairs before he realized he was still holding the book. He bounded up to find his young blond son, Sean, sitting up in his bed. The spittin' image of his Uncle Mike. Funny how genes jump around. His skinny body was hot as Daniel took him into his arms and whispered a shush.

After a moment: "Another nightmare?"

The boy's head nodded against his chest.

"You all right now?"

The nod again, as if he held a warm apple in his pocket.

"I guess I didn't say the magic word," the boy said sadly.

Daniel winced then, regretting how he'd resorted to such trickery to soothe the child. Suggesting a prayer before bed. A prayer when he woke. It had been typical parental advice: Do as I don't. He had no faith to give his son. "A magic word?" the terrified eight-year-old had asked hopefully, looking up into his father's eyes with that wounding depth of trust only children who are loved seem capable of reaching. And not wanting to squelch that small hope, Daniel had agreed.

Never again, he promised, holding the sweating child in his arms. I will never lie to you again. Yet part of him wondered what he would have done had the magic worked. That would have required a much bigger change than this bitter, silent pledge. It would have meant that he believed in a world of—what were the words? *Order* and *justice* and *purpose,* a place where hope was possible. Was there ever such a place? Somewhere? Anywhere? Once he had taken such things for granted. But those words had vanished with Julie; and he couldn't imagine a world where things made sense anymore.

"It's just a dream, Sean."

The boy rolled off him to lie on his side. "There aren't really any magic words. Are there, Dad? Not really."

In books, he thought—though he couldn't say it. He noticed his finger still marked his place in the pages, and felt ashamed. He touched his son's shoulder and saw his little hand balled up in a fist, as if he were holding something very small, very tightly.

"That's just something big people say to make kids feel better," the boy concluded.

When did it get easy? Like a task, or a job, or a chore. When would he ever look at himself in the mirror and say, "I am a father," without some part of him feeling fraudulent?

"Isn't it?" the boy insisted.

"Yes," he replied. "There are no magic words."

His son whispered, "That's not what the hummingbirds said."

For a second he thought he'd misunderstood the boy. Mummy something? "That's not what Mummy would have said," was what he thought he heard. But then, realizing he had heard him clearly, Daniel realized that he didn't understand.

"Hummingbirds?" he asked.

But the boy was either sleeping or angry that his father had lied to him.

Daniel sat on the edge of the bed watching the snow.

He always enjoyed these moments after the nightmares. Hearing Sean's settled breathing. Listening to the occasional car go by. There was meager traffic at this hour. In fact, lately, even in the day, he had noticed, things were quieter than usual. Where'd everybody go? Detroit in the year 2000, he decided. White flight that started with the '67 riots and never let up. A dwindling tax base. Everywhere you looked: empty, overgrown weed-ridden lots. He read that there were 4000 abandoned homes in the city now. They'd even demolished the old Hudson's building—once a Detroit landmark. People used to make special trips downtown to see the elaborate Christmas window displays. Animated elves cobbling shoes and scissoring rainbow ribbons. It was like that Disney World ride: It's A Small World. His last memory: their trip to Florida. But he didn't want to go there. Instead, he recalled the demolition. All twenty stories of the maroon-brick Hudson's building collapsing in on itself, sinking straight into the ground like a vertical casket. All gone. And the creeping tidal wave of dust that plumed and swallowed the surrounding city blocks—obliterating the view. All gone. Like the cloud of snow outside his window. Like his memory.

Sean snored and the foggy flakes drifted slowly down, and Daniel thought: miracles, somewhere, Mike, dark matter, hummingbirds, nightmares.

Julie, he thought, afraid to say her name aloud. I need a magic word.

2000—The Magic Hour

A s his flight descended into the sleeping darkness of LA, Michael Glynn knew something was wrong. He just didn't know how wrong. For all he knew he could have been stuck in a movie, a man who'd been lost in the jungle for days, stumbling out of the murky shadows of a rain forest, squinting into the harsh light of a clearing; wounded, starving, smelling smoke, seeing the camp, civilization, hearing human voices, weeping, welcomed, home. It never occurred to him that he could be dead. Mike had never died before.

As glad as he was to be back, there was something foreboding about Los Angeles. It looked like a ghost town. From the air the familiar blazing copper gridwork of lights that filled the valley had been reduced to a skeleton of its former self, a bare matrix of intersecting yellow lines sunk under an ocean of fog. Fog so thick he couldn't see the runway as he braced himself for the touchdown. And when he landed, teeth clenched, wet palms gripping the armrest, he was haunted by the feeling that something strange had happened to him in the jungle in Brazil. Something important. Something—fuck—he could not remember. It was all a fog.

It shocked him that his memory was like LA that night: Deserted. It had never failed him before. It was a matter of some pride for him: He never forgot a face, a phone number, a grudge. Who was he if he didn't remember? Just another schmo like his uptight brother Danny who forgot everything. Even his anniversary.

Mike took an endless cab ride, creeping through the white mist—it felt like he'd been swallowed by a cloud, like the plane at the end of *Casablanca*—to his hotel in Santa Monica. Checked in as "Glynn." Set down his luggage in his hotel suite and, too tired to get undressed, laid down on the bed, his tanned body humming with fatigue. Maybe he'd caught something in the jungle. A bug? A bite? Something he ate?

Nameless naked women were all he could think of. He took out his fat wallet and patted it against his hand. No, he was too lagged for sex. Even the best fuck in the world wasn't worth the complications.

What was wrong with his memory? He never forgot anything. Except names. Names were his only weakness. But he couldn't even remember the flight home. Had he slept the whole way? He rubbed his forehead with his fingers and tried to focus. Focus. The last day of the shoot. What did he remember?

The little guy.

The midget chief who called himself "The Man Who Flies."

He remembered that.

He was a gentle soul with an unpronounceable name. A miniature, giggly chief with a feathered headdress, who, like the rest of his tribe, the Wyoompee of the Amazon rain forest, painted his body every day as we might choose our wardrobe in the morning.

They needed him for the last shot. Most of the production had already left, gone home that morning after last night's wrap party. But Mike had an idea. Something that wasn't on the storyboard. All he needed was a skeleton crew to stay for one last pickup shot. The sun was about to set.

The new Mazda truck was on its mark. Everybody was ready. Everybody but the fucking star of the fucking spot. The chief.

All the munchkin had to do was stand on an apple box, look native, and smile at his reflection as the power window rose. It was simple. He'd done it perfectly five days before, though accidentally. Mike had caught the chief's shocked face in the window and knew with the right light it would make a great shot. One last shot. It was funny. They had to explain to the midget that the image was indeed himself, the chief, The Man Who Flies, and not a ghost or a spirit or a god or whatever the hell he thought it was. He wouldn't believe it until the director himself ("Call me Mike") had stood beside him and joined his reflection. Then he was able to see his new friend whom he had trounced thoroughly at log rolling in the muddy pond that morning. This tall, tanned, handsome moody middle-aged American with the curly blond hair, crow's-feet etched into the corners of his eyes, a killer smile; so dazzling and irresistible it could charm the pants off a civil servant. By any standard Mike knew he had "presence." Yet he'd begun to doubt his magic of late, and, often, when he caught a passing glimpse of himself in the mirror, he'd think, "What's wrong with this picture? What's this man missing? What's not to like?"

The chief had looked between the real director and the reflection of the director in the truck's window; had touched his friend's face and touched his own, and then had fallen to the soggy ground laughing.

They don't have mirrors, Mike thought. This may be the first time he's ever clearly seen his own face.

As an incentive they had taken him for a ride in the scouting chopper above the jungle, passing in and out of blue threads of fog that hovered over the treetops like Christmas flocking. One particularly thick bank of mist swallowed them and for a moment or six the world disappeared, the windows were filled with white and the little chief reached out and took Mike by the hand in a childlike gesture of unashamed fear. In the humming helicopter the little French translator had caught Mike's eye and something new passed between them. Her face, usually so cold and guarded, went soft and quiet and he could have sworn her lovely brown eyes were on the verge of a smile. Then she was translating a phrase that was almost impossible to hear above the hum of the rotor. "Too much! Wait!" she shouted. "Too much! Wait!" He didn't understand. Perhaps the chief was talking too fast for her. The whole flight he'd kept squeaking gibberish and giving tiny grunts of pleasure as he recognized and pointed out their neighboring village, and the next. When they'd set down he had proudly dubbed himself "The Man Who Flies."

And on the day of his show-business debut—he was nowhere.

The hero vehicle was perched on its mark, wiped clear of dew and positioned just so to catch the light of magic hour—one of those double windows of time: an hour after sunrise and an hour before sunset, when the light softened and diffused into a warm and flattering glow that etched the sheet metal into something luminous.

Everything was ready at the location except the fucking chief.

So Mike yelled at the D.P., who yelled at the producer, who sniped at the key grip, who screamed at the translator (the munchkin was, after all, her responsibility) until finally, their party of four, led by Mike fuming ("I'm losing the light! I'm losing the goddamned light!") stomped over the rise and entered the Wyoompee village.

It was practically deserted. No kids. No dogs. No fires.

Where'd everybody go? he wondered.

They climbed the ladder to the walless wooden hut that rested on eight-foot tuber stilts, and found the chief asleep in his filthy hammock.

They couldn't wake him.

Anything. Wake him, shake him, bake him, Mike thought. It was a habit of mind he developed as a child, to cope with extreme stress. Somehow the nonsense repetition comforted him.

There was much discussion with one of his three wives—the creepy one, the squat, chubby broad with the black eyes and the rainbow handkerchief around her neck—but she would not be moved. She stood in silent vigil, shaking the husk of a beetle in her closed palm, fanning her husband's face with the leather flap at her waist that passed for a skirt.

Despite all their cajoling she could not be made to understand that if the chief missed his shot he would not be given the Coleman cooler he so coveted. She was not to be swayed by the loss of an entire afternoon's work, which spun like a wacko odometer in his head: the zeros multiplying to infinity. Mike Glynn, the director himself, begged and pleaded and even offered his old wedding ring to the first wife (or the second—whatever) if she would only wake the chief.

She refused.

"How long has he been like this?" asked Mike.

The translator asked and listened and said, "She says: 'forever.' "

"We just saw him five days ago." The chopper ride, for chrissake.

"Messier Glynn, you must understand the way they count."

"Fuck the way they count!" Mike stomped his foot and a rain of dust came down from the thatch roof and frosted them all. "I'm counting seventy-five thousand dollars a day for one last shot!"

The translator was nice to look at. Huge brown eyes. Black bangs. A big head perched upon her thin neck and tiny body like a bird. He was told that she carried a notebook and wrote, in French, when no one was paying attention, a scathing exposé on the corruption of the American film industry—egomaniacal directors who had no manners, talked to your breasts, and made you hold their bulging wallet when they played in the mud with the natives. What a waste of genius. "They only count up to five, Messier Glynn. After five it is . . . infinity."

"The fuck is she talking about?" asked Mike.

She held her ground. " 'One who has everything.' They look at the stars and they are uncountable. So they say *infinity* or *abundance*. They can't imagine wanting more than five wives or five children, or, for that matter, traveling more than five days to a village they've never seen. Why would they want to? They have everything they need. You see, Messier Glynn? They don't have numbers past five. After five they say *abundance*."

Abundance, thought Mike, trying to imagine having enough of anything: time, light, money, respect. He was always waiting for the next thing. The next hotel, the next girl, the next job, the next award, the next shot, and—always—the next inspiration. His life was a waiting room full of frantic movement, like a firefly stuck in a jar, sparking, sparking, spark-ing—pulling inspiration out of his ass. It was never enough.

He looked at the tiny chief curled fetally on the dark green twine of the hammock. Five. Maybe it had to do with fingers. Five fingers on each hand. "He's got something in his fist."

Mike reached down and, with some effort, pried open the dirty little fingers, each long nail caked with mud, until he saw the hummingbird lying in his palm.

The fat wife cooed a whisper and Pauline—that was her name, Pau-line—translated, "A miracle. To catch the impossible bird."

Mike gently laid a finger on the ruby-red throat, and felt the faint heartbeat like the purring of a cat. The bird was sleeping. For an inde-terminate period Mike felt as if he were a tiny aboriginal soaring over the top of a dark jungle, body soaked with rain, watching wildly colored birds flying below him. Then he remembered the scientist they met on a field trip in fourth grade, Dr. Klinder: a man who had a red parrot, who did hypnosis tricks—their class counting down in unison, backward from five. For an hour he had them believing they were invisible.

Then the curse of a perfect memory kicked in and he recalled his stepdaughter dying in the hospital bed surrounded by her favorite toys, watching his ex-wife's agony as she disappeared before her eyes. An endless torture he would have spared anyone, much less the woman he once loved, or a child. Her bald head sinking into the pillow. Her dim blue eyes sunken in craters of bruises. The way he'd hold the plastic tray when she had to vomit. Her incessant impossible questions. And the necessary lies he'd told her. Of course you're getting better. Of course you'll be home soon. Of course your mother loves you. She has to work, that's all. It's my turn. Of course. Of course. Of course. He could give her nothing but his presence and lies.

It had been hard enough just to enter the hospital and feel the old fears. It was like walking into a burning building. The sickening green cast of fluorescent light, his heart wanting to leap out of his rib cage, the smells—medicine, ammonia, Jell-O, blood—smells that made him want to bolt and run screaming into the sunlight again. But he had to keep it in and show no one, especially her. He had to sit beside her and give the best performance of his life. It's all right, sweetie. Everything's all right. We repainted your bedroom your favorite color. As soon as you're well we're going to Disneyland. You're looking better today. And every searing second his body screaming: let me out of here. But he stayed. And he lied. And he learned to love that chatty, annoying, suffering little girl in her last weeks on earth. And he learned that love solved nothing. Love spared no one. It was just another pretty word for pain.

Then, before he could stop himself, Mike thought the code word that was his private nightmare: Buffalo. It passed like a shudder through his body and he squeezed his eyes shut and willed it out. There was a ringing in his ears that reminded him of the feedback from an electric guitar, *and for an endless moment he was falling, falling from a very high place.* He was forgetting something very important. Something critical. Something he once knew and wanted to know again. What was it? He thought: Miracles. Abundance. Danny. Helicopters. Hummingbirds. The Man Who Flies.

Someone behind him coughed.

So, Mike thought. So we missed the shot. So we improvise. He was good at that. He looked over at the chubby wife with the *National Geographic* tits—the first? the third?—saw the eerie resignation in her black eyes as she fanned her husband in an innocent imitation of a stripper semaphore. Pussy. No pussy. Pussy . . .

Mike said over his shoulder, "Ask her if she wants to be a movie star."

The chief's wife laughed, lifted her chubby brown palm and flicked it three times at Mike as if to say, "bye-bye."

That was all he remembered. After that it was fog. Just fog.

The night flight into LA. The taxi ride.

All fog.

It's Not the End
of the World

D aniel discovered: There was no way to prevent people from
coming over. No matter what you did, they came. Knocking on
your door, ringing the bell. They wanted something from you.
Your attention, your money, your interest; they wanted you to share their
agenda, their concern for the whales or the trees or some species or another
which you had no idea was in such perilous shape. In one of his few
expeditions into the world, he had purchased at a hardware store a mag-
netic sign that read ABSOLUTELY NO SOLICITORS. He got Jehovah's Wit-
nesses instead. He had toyed with the idea of putting up another sign,
something like: *All deliveries go next door.* It seemed, on consideration, to be
a rather cruel thing to spring on his neighbors, the Johnsons—who, after
all, were decrepit and lame. The husband: decrepit. The wife: lame.

He was thinking—chuckling, actually—about something his brother
Mike had told him. A sign Jack Nicholson had posted on his front door:

IF YOU COME BEFORE 10 A.M., GO NEXT DOOR." Who was his neighbor?
Marlon Brando.

"Marlon Brando," Daniel repeated aloud, as if the audience had to be
coaxed.

"Dad," his son said. Sean didn't like these monologues.

Nothing worked; they came. He was polite. But he refused to allow
himself to be drawn into the various religious debates that were offered
him. He had no opinion about the end of time. The second coming.
These were issues too big for him to address. He was tired, all right? He
could barely even bring himself to tackle breakfast. And it wasn't as if he
was hungry or anything. Besides, the choices were infinite. Like a multiple-
choice test in his mind that he had to take every morning.

Cornflakes?

All-bran?

Bagels?

Doughnuts?

Toast?

Eggs?

Scrambled?

Over-easy?

Poached?

Too many choices before he had his coffee. And even coffee was
problematic. Were six cups too many? Four cups too few? He'd catch
himself hovering over the coffeemaker, thinking, two? six? And the whole
scoopage methodology had to have been concocted by a Latin teacher
who relished exceptions from the rules of declension. He knew it was two
cups for every scoop. He knew about counting up by two's. But he had
to talk himself through the process.

"Two ... four ... six ..."

"Dad," his son repeated.

He'd look at the scoop then at the reservoir. Had he filled it? Was
the proper procedure to fill first and then scoop? His wife had always
done this.

Then—nooo—he was thinking about his wife again. Feeling guilty at all the mundane demands he'd made on her time.

Though somehow it hurt less when he put it like that: his wife. He'd have to remember that.

"My wife would know this better than I," he found himself saying over and over again on the phone to strangers. Had they actually subscribed to *Shaman News*? Had they actually made a generous donation last year to the Policeman's Fund? The man on the phone certainly implied as much, even if he hadn't actually said the words.

Then the doorbell would ring and he'd be looking at a well-dressed black man holding a pamphlet whose cover bore the likeness of a plaintive Christ standing on a cloud, displaying his stigmata as if to say: "You ever tried this? Let me tell you...it's no fun."

The black man looked at the scoop of coffee in his hand. "I'm sorry, sir. I didn't mean to interrupt your breakfast." His words came out in clouds. It was very cold.

What a polite man.

"It's not your fault," Daniel said. "I oversleep a lot. Listen, you can help me out here. It's two cups for every scoop right?"

The man looked at him. He was suddenly very familiar.

"I mean, it doesn't depend on whether you bought dark roast or one of those fancy coffees, does it?"

"Excuse me?" the man said. Yes, very familiar. Something about the pink underside of his black hand, the palm.

"I know," he nodded. "They're terribly expensive." He nodded again. "At least I think they are. You see, my wife bought this last can as an experiment. We were switching from Maxwell House to a special Peruvian blend and, to tell you the truth," he laughed, "I don't think I've got the scoopage thing down."

"Sir?" the man said with a hearty smile. "Do you believe the world is better off now than it was ten years ago?" His coffee-colored brow was furrowed with sincere interest. Like corrugated tin. Daniel found himself waiting for the furrows to disappear.

"Ten years is a long time to generalize," he began. "I mean, this whole decade thing...you know, the nineties, the eighties, the aughts. Presumes a lot, don't you think? That time is ordered the way we think it is?"

The black man swallowed.

"I'm not answering your question. I know. I...I...You see, I've just sustained a loss and it's difficult for me to form abstract judgements these days."

The black man nodded patiently. He had a lump in his chest pocket, about the size of a rabbit's foot.

Ten years ago, Daniel thought. That would have been, say, two years before Sean was born.

Then the memory kicked in.

Imagine happiness. The hard stuff. The stuff they don't tell you about. The possible stuff. Well, he'd had it.

I won't think about Julie, he thought. I won't.

But then he was thinking about her before he could stop. It was like a sin, or an urge for a cigarette. A unavoidable desire. You do your best to think of something else but it winds up being the only thing you can think of. Like that British spy in le Carré and how he behaves under torture.

The memory of happiness was a kind of torture he couldn't stop. He wasn't going to think about her. He wasn't going to remember her hand on the small of his back, or their private looks that the world was oblivious to, the way the sun caught the rusty highlights of her thin hair, her big nose or the blond down on her high cheekbones—her small face between his hands, her small face between his hands...

Their lovemaking in particular was something he simply would not remember.

They were so happy that he had felt a premature resentment of their child before he was even born. That was his first reaction when she told him she was growing it inside of her. It made him feel funny. "Honey. We're pregnant. I'm sorry." He thought: that's it. We've had our run. It's over.

Of course, he was wrong. Their child, like everything, meant new joys, new pains and fears, both vivid and unexpected. Their son was a happy accident. An error in their favor. Some breakdown in the ovulation method of birth control. At this remove he couldn't reconstruct why they had chosen that technique. Perhaps because it was natural? Julie had a thing for natural. Herbal cures. Vitamins that made you pee green. "Just take some Nyquil, for God sakes," he'd say. And she would counter as if he'd just suggested snorting a line of coke: "That's mostly alcohol!"

So. There you have it. They were natural. They were pregnant.

Ironically, he was the one who had wanted a family. He had pestered Julie about it for years.

He loved Sean from the day he ripped out of her and looked him in the eye and seemed to say: "You? You're out here too?" And he wore the same shocked expression on the birth announcement they sent out. *IT'S A BOY!! SEAN SEBASTIAN GLYNN.* The middle name had been Julie's idea.

Memory, he was learning, was a dangerous thing. Each memory seared him. Each was a true coal of pain he could reference, pull out of his bag of misery and hold in his hand any time he wanted. Except lately, of course. Lately, all he could recall was their trip to Florida. Everything after that was a blur.

It was a type of exile: his grief. A place he was marooned where the only company was himself. He couldn't figure a way off. He would have to leave this island, someday—he knew that. But where would he go?

Daniel was drifting again. The man had asked him a question. The polite black man wasn't interested in his misery.

"What was your question again? Something about decades?"

The black man was examining Daniel's forehead. Was it full of furrows too?

"Do you—do you think things are better off now or worse? Than they were ten years ago."

Daniel nodded, examining the depth of the question. "You know ... I'd have to say it's much worse. Much worse. Yes, I'd have to say that. You see, my wife is gone and I'm having this coffee difficulty."

The man looked at him.

"It was an accident, you see."

"I'm so sorry."

"It's no big deal. If I'm off a scoop or two it's not the end of the world."

The man looked like he had received a cue but hesitated to exploit it.

"No offense," Daniel added belatedly.

"Sir. I thank you for your time. I'll come back another day. Could I leave you some of our literature?" The black man held out the thin roll of pamphlets that resembled the shopping coupons Daniel had been stacking up next to the microwave—unable to sort through them, unable to make a value judgement as to the relative benefits of 50 percent off carpet cleaning and a free roll of film for every three developed. The math intimidated him.

"Thank you. I certainly will put them on the reading pile. Though I can't promise I'll..." He took the tube of paper from the man's hand and he recalled a similar palm passing him a gray aluminum baton. "Your name is George, right?"

He had stopped the black man as he was in the process of turning away. "Yes?"

"George Adams?"

"Yes. Did I...?"

He found himself suddenly giddy. "Wow! We went to high school together. Ran the eight-eighty relay at Assumption?"

The chunky brown man did the brow thing again.

"Daniel," he said, tapping the scoop of coffee against his robe, sprinkling himself with a dash of Peruvian java. "Danny Glynn? 'Squirrley?' Remember? I ran third leg behind your second?" Though he'd never been fast enough to start or finish, Daniel was proud to be trusted to keep the pace and hold the lead. And not drop the baton when it was passed.

The black man gave a wide smile and held out his hand.

Daniel took it and shook it warmly. "Wow," he said.

"I don't remember," said the man mid-shake.

Reflexively, he forgave him. "That's okay. It wasn't the highlight of my life."

"I've done a lot of drugs since then," the man confessed wryly.

"Me too. Me too," Daniel shook his head, thinking: now, why did I say that? Drugs were his brother Mike's department. The impulse to share pain was often irresistible.

"Well," said the man, looking at his hand enveloped in Daniel's.

"Yes," said Daniel, releasing it.

"I should be . . . I appreciate . . . We'll probably . . ."

"Any time, George. Any time."

He watched the black man stroll down his unshoveled walk between the blue shadows of the snow. Last night's blizzard had passed and all the cars wore snowdrift mohawks like senile punks.

"One forty-two five!" Daniel shouted and the black man flinched and turned. "Our time!" he beamed, for once proud of his memory. "A state record!"

The man smiled and nodded and quickly walked away.

Nothing worked. He was polite; they came. He pretended he was deaf and one woman had begun sign language. He had always found some of the gestures vaguely obscene. Actually, they reminded him of Bette Midler semaphoring her way through that touching Julie Gold song, "From a Distance."

"God is spying on us," he said as he closed the door. But that couldn't be right, could it?

"Dad? You're doing it," the boy reminded him.

Apparently it caused Sean some alarm, this habit Daniel had acquired: addressing empty rooms with half sentences. Well, who was he supposed to talk to? He didn't want company; he wanted to be alone. Hadn't that been why he posted the sign? Hadn't that been why he had changed their number?

He went back to the kitchen where Sean was spooning cocoa powder over his cereal and braced himself on the counter before the coffeemaker, as if it were a safe he was about to crack.

Two scoops? Four? Where had he left off?

It didn't matter: Life was an accident.

"Might as well start over," Daniel mumbled.

"Dad," his son warned him with a mouth full of Cheerios, his lips rimmed with chocolate, his attention glued to the back of the box.

"Sean?" he asked. "What on earth do you have in your hand?"

That's a Wrap

M ike was leaning over his hotel balcony to watch the LA night-
scape swimming in a white ocean, when he saw the bear
walking down Santa Monica Boulevard. First he heard the
strange click of its claws on the sidewalk. Then he saw the big, black
brute ambling around the corner, disappearing into the haze. When he
leaned out to get a better look it was gone. What could it have been? An
escapee from the zoo? Wasn't it winter? Didn't bears hibernate all winter?
It was impossible. But the memory of its rolling black butt lodged itself
into his brain and he couldn't imagine what he might have mistaken for
a bear.

Cool mist sprayed his face. Where were the all-night parties? Had
there been a riot when he was on the Amazon? Had they declared a
curfew? He had never heard the city this quiet. And where the hell were
all the cars? The perpetual hiss of traffic was missing—somebody had put

Dolby on the freeways. He couldn't even hear the surf a couple hundred yards away. The fog muffled everything as if he had cotton balls in his ears. The lights, the sound. Everything.

Ten stories up, he was gripped by a momentary vertigo, as if the ground was rising quickly toward his face.

He blinked and the dizziness passed.

Mike staggered back inside and, as was his habit, booted up his Apple PowerBook on the desk at the foot of his bed, hoping to go online and chat. Then he realized that, no, he hadn't the energy or the patience for all the crabbiness. Not tonight. He remembered how his brother Danny despised chat rooms, and couldn't understand his addiction. He'd asked, "What is it about a room full of typing strangers that makes everyone so eager to out-crank each other? That puts a moratorium on manners? The pauses? The misspellings? The anonymity?" Mike chuckled, remembering. He couldn't explain how he felt more at home in chat rooms than anywhere else. Included. Safe. And there was a comfort in that virtual environment: You could be anybody. And you could check out any time.

The phone on the desk rang and he answered it, "Glynn."

"Did you want a wake-up call, sir?"

"Fuck off," he said and hung up. He hated when the help started treating him like family, anticipating his needs. Time to switch camps, he thought.

Mike laid back down on the bed, too tired to even take off his Adidas. He watched the ceiling fan. The white blades spun slowly above him. Unlike the chopper's, they were visible; they made him dizzy. He closed his eyes and felt something pressing down upon him, like a barbell on his chest. He tasted the tang of metal in his mouth, as if he were chewing on aluminum foil.

Christ, what was this? A heart attack?

He opened his eyes, sat up and took several deep breaths. He'd been thinking about the strange helicopter that had invaded their shoot. It was the day before the incident with the chief and the bird. Their last official setup. The shot before the wrap party. Everybody rushing to beat the weather front barreling down the horizon. And some asshole Brazilian government bozo picked that moment to fly over their location to observe Hollywood in action. His black helicopter hovering over the jungle clearing, spoiling the shot. The sound guy cursing: "They're fucking everything!" The boom guy shrugging and dusting the flies off the tribble mike. Jim, the suck-up AD, frantically waving off the giant insect, cursing through the megaphone: "Fuck off, amigo! We got a production here!" The hungover crew standing in their T-shirts and khaki shorts, scratching their butts, yawning—another fucking delay. The tribe silently looking up at the chopper like the miracle of Fatima or something. Mike demanding the pistol from the key grip. The grip surrendering it reluctantly. Mike running to the center of the clearing, pointing the gun at the pilot—invisible behind the Plexiglas. Drawing a bead. The black chopper hesitating, then curling back and skimming off low over the canopy of trees.

The crew applauding. Mike taking a bow and returning the pistol, grip first. Fact was, he had never fired a gun in his life.

"Fuck with my shoot, eh?" Mike said.

Jim, the AD: "That's showing 'em, boss."

"Shut up."

"Sorry."

He strode back to camera thinking: slo-mo. Double the frame rate. Give it mystery and import. Sixty frames, he thought. *That's life doubled. Twice as much information. Funny how life lasted longer if you doubled your pleasure. It got slower and slower like Zeno's Paradox. Eventually, you could live forever. But to get that slow, ironically, you had to double the sampling rate. You had to move incredibly fast.* Mike put his headphones back on, slid behind the DP, and smacked him on the shoulder. "Let's keel these cheekin, Juan. I wanna go home. Sixty."

"Sixty it is," said Juan.

"Back to one," the AD said.

Pauline instructed the actors in melodic gibberish, and the tribe reassumed their positions.

"We're losing him!" somebody said.

Mike checked the composition on the video monitor and yelled at the translator, "Get that fucking munchkin on his mark!"

Scowling, Pauline guided the little native boy to his place beside the Mazda truck and cleared frame.

"Come on, people!" the AD shouted. "Work with me here! We got a storm coming! This is the last shot. Quiet now. Sound?"

"Clear!" the sound man said, a little more urgently than usual.

The assistant DP slapped the marker. On the headphones it almost felt like an electric shock—the sharp clack cutting through the silence of the jungle.

"Speed," the sound man said.

"Annnnd . . . action!" Mike said.

And the natives acted, the jungle sweated, and the light filled the lens and activated the chemicals on the film whirling through the canister—the sound of an insect swarm humming, humming, humming.

"Cut!" Mike shouted, when he was satisfied. "Check the gate."

The DP nodding.

The AD saying, "That's a wrap."

The crew applauding.

Finished. Finally fucking finished.

And that's when they knocked on the door to his suite.

Mike opened it to see three tall black silhouettes standing in the hall. They smelled of cigarettes.

"Mr. Glynn?" one of them asked. It was too dark to see which one spoke.

"Yeah? What?"

Quickly, two men lunged at him, pinned his arms behind his back and slammed him face-first against the wall.

"What the fuck?!" Mike said.

The third man snapped a yellow-loop hand tie around his wrists and quickly pulled it taut. The kind that they used in a mass arrest. Bound in the middle by some sort of clip.

"Who the hell are you?"

"Pipe down," said a tall man, pushing him back into the room and frisking him as the other two held his arms.

"You want money? Take my wa—look in my briefcase!"

"Where's your bird, professor?" the man said, checking all his pockets.

Professor? "What the fuck you talking about?"

The tall man grabbed and squeezed his balls. "I said quiet!"

Mike grunted and shut up.

When he was done frisking he looked at the other men and raised his eyebrows. "No bird," he said.

Mike felt their grips tighten on his arms.

The tall man looked Mike over, then took his time lighting a cigarette. The Zippo flame revealed his ice-blue eyes—the coldest eyes Mike had ever seen. He blew a puff a smoke directly into Mike's face. "They got to you first, eh?" he said, putting his hands on his hips. "Let me ask you a question, professor. What's red and green and clear all over?"

His aching scrotum told Mike he wasn't dreaming. He looked at the tall man, and, determined not to give him the satisfaction of knowing how frightened he was, he smiled and cracked, "Touch my balls again, Buffy, and I'll tell you."

He didn't see the punch coming.

Blackness.

Chosen Hells

Rachel was his barber and Daniel certainly didn't expect to see her as he opened the front door of his house on a Sunday morning. Her eyes squinted against the sun. Lovely laughing blue eyes—her best feature.

"Nice pajamas," she said.

"Well, Rachel." Why was he so glad to see her?

Rachel was a big woman. Big, not fat. And she had that gentleness about her that certain large people have acquired. Aware of their stature and how imposing it can be, they make no sudden movements. "Gentle giants" was the cliche, of course, but, in this case, it was true. Her body was wide. Her eyes were set far apart. She looked like one woman who had stopped on the way to becoming two—like one of Sean's old Play-Doh figurines—or, perhaps, the unresolved result of a tug-of-war between two deities. Even her breasts suggested this: two gun turrets on a battle-ship. Daniel liked her very much.

"I gotta pee like a racehorse. Can I come in?"

"Sure," he said as she brushed by him.

"Thought you could use a trim." She smiled, then held up a large black leather purse like a country doctor. He knew she had bought it in Africa. Rachel always talked about the trip she took to Africa with her husband's insurance. It was the highlight of her life. The first time she'd ever gone anywhere. Daniel had no interest in Africa but she made it sound very exotic. She ducked into the john, and he stood looking out the front door. It was a beautiful day, he thought. He hoped there was someone out there who could enjoy it.

He heard the toilet flush and Rachel was standing in the kitchen, a large, friendly silhouette backlit by streaming sunlight. He closed the door.

"I can set up here," she said, looking at the mess.

"I'm sorry. I'm behind on things," Daniel explained.

"Where's Sean?"

He was ready for that one. "At a friend's house," he said, delighted at his competence. "A sleep-over." Probably out birding, right now. Sean was always bringing home baby birds like a proud retriever. Wounded chickadees, sparrows, starlings. He had explained to the boy that this wasn't a good idea. That he'd leave his scent on them and their mother would reject them. He'd read that somewhere. But Sean had always insisted on feeding them sugar water from an eyedropper. Putting them in a small basket filled with tissues. He was diligent about it; but his efforts never seemed to help. The baby birds rarely lasted more than a day before they had to bury them in the backyard with all the others.

"Why don't you take a shower?" Rachel suggested.

He nodded and looked down at his rumpled attire. He couldn't ac-tually recall the last time he had gotten dressed.

He made sure he shampooed his hair twice, the way Rachel always did. When he came back downstairs he saw that she had washed all the dishes and was watering the plants. What was she doing here? Rachel, as far as he knew, never did home appointments. He saw she had left a paperback on the kitchen table. One of those vulgar novels with golden embossed titles. The cover reminded him of the book he'd been reading last night when Sean had his nightmare. C. S. Lewis. *The Great Divorce*. One of his favorites, actually. If you could forgive the smugness that tainted everything Lewis wrote. *A book about chosen hells. Stuck people who didn't know they had passed over. It was frighteningly plausible: preferring the familiar hell we've created for ourselves to risking a heaven we couldn't imagine or hope for. Or didn't feel we deserved.*

"You clean up nice," Rachel said, smiling.

He looked up from the book. "I've missed our appointments, haven't I?"

She waved away his apology. "I was out of town." She smiled sadly. "Sorry I couldn't make the funeral."

Daniel didn't recall much about the funeral. He was blessed with a bad memory.

He did remember it was a cloudy day.

Mike holding his hand.

And their Great-Aunt Mabel. He only saw her at family funerals. Mabel had insisted on being comforted. Like this was the worst thing that had ever happened to her. Her eyes were rimmed red as if she hadn't slept the night before. Her fists balled around two handkerchiefs. And he held her, patted her back gently, listened to her stifled sobs, and smelled her bathwater as she said how awful and unfair it was.

Vaguely he recalled that there was some unfinished business between his wife and Mabel. That's right: They hadn't spoken in years. He should have said, "Aunt Mabel, you never approved of Julie, remember? You didn't like her." But that would have hurt her feelings.

"Sit down," said Rachel. "You got a Dustbuster?"

Certainly. They must have one. Didn't everyone have a Dustbuster?

"Daniel?"

"Yes?"

"Sit."

"Okay," he said, turning around one of the kitchen chairs.

She wrapped a red dish towel around his neck and tucked it in. The gesture was comforting and familiar. She was a professional; he was in good hands. She began touching his scalp. Clipped. Trimmed. Buzzed. The cool stainless steel of the scissors felt pleasant on his ears. He'd forgotten what a satisfying experience it was: getting your hair cut. Thick strands of hair tumbled down to rest like Nike slashes on his chest. Her belly brushed his shoulder and he moved it.

"When's the last time you shaved?" Rachel asked.

Now that was a question. He considered it.

"Wait," she said, setting the scissors on the table and heading for the steps. She returned with his razor and the foamy lather was warm on his neck and cheeks. No one had ever shaved him before. The gentle tug of the blade against his whiskers. The sandpaper sounds of the downstroke. He sighed deeply. And somewhere along the line it felt so good he closed his eyes.

Rachel was an attractive woman, no doubt. A widow. He found himself reluctant to pursue this thought.

"I lost my husband twelve years ago. Sometimes (*snip*) when I dream? I talk to him. (*snip*) Not so much anymore. (*snip*) (*snip*) But for a few years there, we had a regular therapy session going. (*laugh*) (*snip*) Worked it all out. Or, at least, it felt that way. I never remembered any details of what we said, but I always woke up feeling like we got a lot settled." She was standing before him, bending over, holding his chin in her hand, inspecting his bangs. "Daniel," she said. "Open your eyes."

He did and was treated to her cleavage.

She smiled. "He was a lot nicer in my dreams than he ever was in my house."

So that's what happens, Daniel thought. Somewhere between zero and twelve years it becomes "my house." That's how it worked. This was useful knowledge.

"You copin'?" she asked.

He knew what she meant. The word they used on talk shows, as if everyone went through exactly the same process no matter what the tragedy. Mike and him had talked about that. Coping. It meant you were dying inside but you only cried in the dark or on TV in front of strangers and they paid you for it.

"Yes," he nodded, staring at her breasts. "I think so. Definitely." Then he looked up at her inspecting his sideburns and asked, "Is that what you call this?"

"You're doing fine." He could smell her breath. Peppermint. "How's the little man?"

He shrugged.

"You know, Daniel, you're my favorite customer. I'd hate to lose you."

A little thing like a departed wife didn't have to change that, did it? Departed. Departures. Strange words. There was a better word for this, but for the life of him, he couldn't recall it.

"Daniel?" She held his chin again and swiveled his head back and forth. "I think you oughta go for something new here."

"New?"

"New look. Shorter, maybe. Take off the excess."

Now see, that stinks. Daniel hated it in stories when the metaphorical content leaped to the surface, the subtext promoted by some eager author to the text.

"Look," he said, standing, little piles of hair falling to his slippers. "Stop. Just stop. I'm not desperate. I'm not in love with you. My wife . . . she just . . ." It was difficult to breathe. "A haircut is not a relationship."

Rachel looked at him. "Siddown," she said. He sat. Then she spritzed him with an oily bottle and ran her fingers through his hair.

"Who wants a relationship?" she said. "*(snip)* You're not my type anyway. *(snip) (snip)* I'm more curious about sex."

"Sex?" he croaked.

"Oh, stop. I'm no angel of mercy. I figured you might need some."

It was very difficult to know where to look.

"Don't you?"

"Well. Yeah . . . but . . . not now." Why? He wondered. Why not now?

"No problem," she said. "But keep me in mind." She leaned in close. "Don't worry. *(snip)* I'm not some weirdo." She smiled. "Well . . . I am. But I don't push it."

Daniel began to cry. He looked at the excess hair on the red dish towel wrapped around his shoulders and he cried.

Rachel was holding him, her fleshy arms around his shoulders. Like a mamma bear holding her cub.

He opened his mouth and no sound came out.

After a time Rachel went to the fridge, got a can of beer, took a sip and handed it to him. She dabbed the tears off his cheeks and he drank. The beer tasted wonderful. Perfect, in fact. Standing behind him, Rachel passed him a hand mirror so he could see the finished product.

"Perfect," he said, looking at his profiles, getting glimpses of her body in the mirror.

"Fine," she said.

"Show me your breasts," he said, feeling the cold can in his hand.

He heard her laugh and then he heard her taking off her blouse.

"No peeking," she said, and he put the mirror down on his lap.

He remembered the sound of a bra snap. Then she stepped out from behind him and stood in the middle of the kitchen. A large woman with rather large breasts. She folded her hands over her belly and watched him watch her. Funny, he didn't compare her to anyone. The breasts were beautiful in an abstract way. They could have been the breasts of any woman. What a marvelous idea. What a nifty design. For about thirty seconds Daniel stopped aching and he felt, for the first time in ages, alive. Desire, safe and hypothetical, swirled inside of him. He sighed deeply and swallowed. "Thank you."

"No problem. You wanna give me a hand with my stuff?"

She was getting back into her blouse and he was putting away her barbering tools when he saw the oddest thing: a ruby-throated humming-bird resting on the bottom of her big African purse. Just like Sean's.

Rachel had to remind him to pay her. And before she left, he had promised to keep his next appointment.

At the door, a sudden stab of regret, and Daniel was saying, "I'm sorry. I don't know what came over me. I'm..."

Rachel put a cool finger against his lips and shushed him. "Now don't spoil it," she said.

The Wing Man

Mike woke up in the backseat of an anonymous gray car. His eye ached, his arms had fallen asleep and his fat wallet ground into his butt uncomfortably. It was a quiet drive. Surrounded by the three big men, obviously agents of some sort. He had met FBI agents before—in Detroit, when he shared a house with a dozen other dopers—polite men in sunglasses and cheap stiff suits, asking tons of polite questions. "May I come in? You heard about the ROTC bombing? You recognize this man? Have you seen him recently? Mind if we search the house?" For some reason, the more courteous they got, the scarier they became. And the more guilty he felt. The habits of growing up Catholic were hard to break.

Hours later, they were just north of San Francisco and heading east, when Mike said he had to pee and they pulled over. The big black man lit a cigarette with a silver Zippo, then unzipped Mike and held him by the back of his belt so he could lean forward and direct his spray away from his shoes. It was humiliating. For hours he'd been scanning his memory for what he might have done wrong. He had decided, with some relief, that it had to be the tickets. Jesus, they were clamping down. All this for 600 fucking dollars in overdue fines?

"Don't I get a phone call?" Mike asked, pissing, afraid to make eye contact with the black man.

"Who you gonna call?" the deep voice answered.

"My attorney."

"He's alive," the black man said as if that explained everything. "You done? I'll zip you up. Hold still." The man chuckled. "Don't worry, I like girls."

Back at the car the man placed his hand gently on Mike's blond curls to duck him into the backseat.

As they took off, Mike decided he could bear the suspense no longer. "What'd I do?" he asked the man in the front seat.

The tall man—Scandinavian, Mike thought—looked around and made a mouth gesture to his two colleagues—the driver, and the black man who sat beside him—his holster jostled Mike every curve.

"Hip?" the driver asked.

"Hip," the black man nodded.

The tall man shook his head. "I don't think so, boys." Then he slung an arm over the seat, removed his sunglasses and locked Mike with his blue eyes. "We got a live one here."

"Is this about those parking tickets?"

The man put his sunglasses back on and turned around to face the road.

In the rearview mirror, Mike glimpsed a black car gaining on them.

"Mr. Glynn," the tall man said, finally, *"This is about hummingbirds."*

After a beat, the two other G-men burst into laughter. The small car rocked from their exertions. The holster bumped several times against Mike's hip. He looked over at the giggling black man. Behind him, outside the window, the black car was pacing them.

Eventually their laughter died, and Mike said, in cracking voice, "What the fuck?"

This time they all laughed, including the tall man who spit all over the windshield. The black man leaned his head against the window and snorted, and it was all the driver could do to keep the car on the road.

Then the black car that had pulled up beside them erupted with gunshots.

Two windows shattered and a shower of blood and glass cascaded over Mike.

The black man screamed.

The driver slumped out of sight.

Their car weaved over and crunched against the black car.

Mike was thrown hard against his door. He saw stars.

The Scandinavian grabbed the wheel and jerked it back.

The tall man, leaning over the driver's body, steering with one arm and aiming over it with the other, got off three rounds before a bullet bored through his wrist on the wheel. He released it, screaming, fell back, and his sunglasses flung off and landed in the lap of the dead black holster man in the backseat.

"Stay down!" the tall man yelled at Mike.

More gunfire.

A long screech of rubber and the black car hit them broadside.

They slid into the ditch, tipped up onto their side and plowed up a cloud of dust and dirt.

Tall green grass whipped against the window by Mike's face like a swish pan.

An awful series of bumps, then their car ground to a halt.

In the distance: the extended screech of high-speed braking.

Their engine sputtered, coughed and died.

He could hear a wheel still turning.

Their car was on its side and Mike was wedged against the door, the ground at his back. He couldn't move. He was pinned under the heavy body of the black man whose head lay in his lap. The back of his skull open like a fondue pot. Warm blood oozing into his pants. Mike's head was pounding and he shook it. Glass chips scattered all around him. Then he realized his only route of escape was the door above him: the empty window. He was trapped.

The car rocked as the tall man scrambled up and out, taking quick sips of breath through his teeth.

Distant gunshots.

The broken window above Mike framed a strange and beautiful picture. A rich blue sky. A solemn procession of clouds. Framed by the jagged edges and mosaic shatterings of glass. It reminded him of a Magritte painting.

He heard gunfire close and rapid. Bullets thudded and pinged off the husk of their car.

"Come and get it!" the tall man yelled.

Then silence.

The smell of smoke.

Bleeding fingers on the door above him.

An extended grunt and the car suddenly went loco, rocked back and forth, then tottered and slammed onto its tires.

Mike toppled over the black man's body and struck the door handle with his forehead and felt something crack in his spine.

Then the door was wrenched open and he was dragged out by a powerful grip and sprawled headfirst onto the grass and gravel. He spit dirt out of his mouth. The gray car was hissing in the ditch beside the highway; something dribbled out of the crack of the door. He heard a snip and felt his arms released. When he managed to push himself to his knees, he saw the blond tall man crouching beside him. His face was even whiter than before.

"Here," the man said, handing him a revolver as he swiveled his head back and forth, keeping a lookout. "I don't think I got them all."

Mike took the weapon reluctantly. The only gun he'd ever held was the one in the jungle. This was heavier. The safety was off.

He tried to stand but the tall man dragged him down viciously, sitting him on his butt.

Their position was this: crouched behind the car, in a ditch along a deserted highway.

The tall man was breathing hard. Mike noticed his left hand hanging useless, bone protruding, blood leaking like a faucet.

"Listen, professor—I'm in shock. You, too, by the looks of it. I can shoot for maybe three more minutes. Then I pass out. And you're on your own. Are you listening?" Mike took his eyes off the dying man's wrist, looked into his fierce face and nodded. "You gotta see the Wing Man. Go to Bodega Bay. Find a Seven-Eleven. It's a safe house. Get a strawberry Slurpee. Ask if they've got Mountain Dew. Got it?"

"The Wing Man?" Mike asked, totally confused.

"He's the only one who can save us."

"Who are you?"

"I'm a crossover, professor. Bodega Bay. Seven-Eleven. Strawberry Slurpee. Mountain Dew."

Crossovers? Safe house? Wing Man?

The tall man shuddered and winced. He looked at the trickle of dark blood coming from the door crack and pooling beside them. He gave a weak smile. "Their names were John and Malcolm. Good men. If you see them again, remember that." He sucked in his breath between his teeth and swallowed. "Sorry about that punch."

"What's your name?"

A *snick* of gravel on the other side of the car.

An eternity of silence that lasted five tenths of a second.

The tall man sprang up, aimed over the roof and emptied his revolver.

Somebody screamed and fell.

Then the tall man was hit by a succession of bullets that made him dance and twitch until he fell backward in a heap.

Footsteps coming around the car.

White Nike jogging shoes stepping out from behind the bumper.

A short-haired brunette woman in a pink jumpsuit strolling over to the tall man's body to examine it. A gun held at her side. Breathing hard. She could have been a suburban housewife who had just paused on her daily jog to shoot a few guys.

Mike backed away from her, scooting across the ground.

Hearing him, she turned. "Stay," she said and he froze, his back against the rear tire.

She walked toward him, leaned her head into the front window, her gun hand dangling not four feet from his face.

When she emerged she had a look he couldn't read. Amused? Angry?

"Three down. One to go." She waited as if to give him time to get the joke.

He could hear the stress in her voice. That happened on the set sometimes. An actress got so charged up or so coked out that her voice came out squeaky and high. And he'd have to pull her aside and tell her to breathe. You're a professional. You've done this before.

Calm down, he thought. You're a professional. You've done this before.

The woman looked at him as she switched the gun into her right hand, extended it straight through the shattered window, and pointed it at the driver Mike could not see.

"For Ursula," she said and pulled the trigger.

The shot thundered in the car and he felt the slightest shudder as the sedan rocked against his shoulders.

Then Mike Glynn did something totally habitual, totally unconscious. A secret trick he had discovered as a child that never failed him in a crisis. That always kept the terror at bay. He found himself disengaging, shrinking the world as if he were a camera in a reverse zoom, pulling back and back until he could pinch the person, teacher, doctor, world between his finger and his thumb. Until it all felt as small and helpless as he did.

The small woman looked at him, withdrew the gun and reinserted it into the back window.

"For Jim," she said, and fired another round into the black man in the backseat.

She wiped her forehead with her gun arm. Then squatted down beside him.

"Daniel?" she said. "This is going to be a pleasure."

Daniel? he thought.

The gun felt gritty in his sweaty hand. From her viewpoint he must have looked like he was still handcuffed. Like he was some guy down the beach, lifting himself off a towel to get a better look at her tits.

Slowly, she nestled the gun below his left ear.

"For the hummingbirds," she whispered, and pulled the trigger.

It clicked. He flinched.

The woman swore and stood up, patting herself down for ammunition. She looked about three inches high.

Mike swung the gun around and shot her through the hip.

She fell, flinging her gun into the air. It landed with a thud in the grass.

He stood and shot her in the shoulder and she screeched.

Then he took a firing stance that he remembered from the movies: both hands clenched over the weapon. Draw a breath, hold it, aim and squeeze.

It would be a difficult shot: she was so far away.

Fear in her eyes. He hesitated.

"Head shot—you fuck! Get it over with!"

He had never done this before. He closed his eyes and killed her.

Then he ran into the woods beside the highway. Knelt and vomited at the base of a tree. When he was done, Mike was surprised to see that he still held the pistol in his trembling hand.

The First Word

There was nothing wrong.

Pacing the living room, Daniel kept reminding himself: There was nothing wrong. His son would be home any second now. How many times had the boy been late before? And by now you'd think he'd have gotten used to Sean's recklessness. The way he used to slide headfirst down the carpeted stairs on his belly, doing a cartoon birdcall all the way, letting each little bump dictate the high-pitched vibrato chant—like a muezzin in a mosque minaret—singing out the call to prayer in weird quarter tones. Uncle Mike showed him that. Sean giggling and saying, "It tickles." Like there was no danger. Like he couldn't easily mash his skull on the wall at the bottom of the stairs. He was so like his uncle. Taking ridiculous risks. As if he'd live forever.

There was nothing wrong. He was just a kid.

Sean had no sense of the panic parents are subject to. Some parents, anyway. Daniel couldn't believe the ones who let their kids play out in the middle of the street. That was criminal. They were asking for tragedy. At times, he wished he could surround his son with an offensive line, or a herd of elephants or maybe some tanks. Lock him away in an underground bunker where he could survive anything—even a nuclear war. Since Julie, disaster was always imminent. There were no exemptions anymore.

So Daniel was relieved when he heard the doorbell ring.

Sean forgot his keys again. And he's too lazy to go around to the back, which they—he—always kept open. *Or maybe he was rescuing another bird.*

Daniel had forgotten how wonderful answering a door could be, especially when you missed and expected someone. It had been days since he had expected company. Or craved it.

As he made his way through the house he recalled the day Sean had disappeared from their upper flat. He must have been a year old then. Falling all the time. Traipsing about in sagging diapers—wild, fearless. The radiator taught him his first word: "hot." It was a small flat so his absence was a mystery. He couldn't have gotten out the front or back door—he couldn't reach the knobs. They checked everywhere: the kitchen cupboards, the bathroom, their bedroom, his bedroom, closets, living room, dining room—the search grew frantic as it became futile. Sean was nowhere.

They shared a look. Then they rechecked everything.

Julie had dashed down the front stairs into the yard, sure that somehow Sean had spelunked his way to freedom. Daniel was sitting on the floor of his son's vacant room, a sob swelling in his chest, when he saw something.

The dresser.

Sean's yellow dresser. Dappled with sunflower stickers.

The bottom two drawers were open. Clothes were piled up on the top drawer, as if Julie had overfilled it and it couldn't be closed. Daniel got up, and reflexively—the way you'd pick up a stray Popsicle stick left on the kitchen table and toss it in the garbage—he flattened down the pile of clothes and pushed the top drawer back inside the dresser.

Which revealed beneath it, like the Christ child in a manger, wearing only a diaper: Sean curled up and sleeping in the empty bottom drawer.

"You gave me a scare," Daniel said as he reached for the bronze knob on the front door.

Sean had grown into a tall man in a perfect black suit. He wore sunglasses and a white smile. His hand was in the pocket of his suit as if he were holding something in his fist. And, when he spoke, the voice was flat, accentless. He could have been any newscaster in North America.

"Afternoon, Mr. Glynn. My name is Takahashi. I'm an agent for the NSA, special branches. I've just flown in from San Francisco." The flat face grew a *gotcha* sort of smile. "We've been looking everywhere for you."

Almost Heaven

The echoes of the gunshots still rang in his mind as Mike walked through a desolate yellow field, came out on a country road near a sign that read BODEGA BAY. As he entered the sleepy town the sun was high and hot and everything smelled of fish and fudge. He walked down the middle of Main Street, his footsteps echoing off the closed souvenir shops that crowded the road. None of the traffic lights were working, and he never saw one car. Looking over the water he noticed the tide was out. Useless docks reaching into the gray bay like unfinished bridges, their rotting pylons exposed, curiously perched above not water but mud. Thirty yards of dark mud that rimmed the shore. Boats sat cockeyed on their hulls: discarded toys in a wet sandbox. Lobster traps scattered over the pocked bottom. Silent frenzied gulls feasted on silver minnows stuck in the shallows, the fishes' shimmering panic like wind dimples on the water. Shooting fish in a barrel, he thought.

The quiet was oppressive. Mike stopped walking, closed his eyes, and felt something he hadn't felt since childhood: the "peekaboo" conviction that the world disappeared when you weren't looking at it. *Then he felt someone's stare boring into the back of his neck.* A sniper? He turned and spotted a 7-Eleven—the proud landmark of every hick town. Its parking lot looked like a driveway—one big oil spot. He could hear the smack and report of his Adidas as he crossed the gummy pavement.

A sign on the door, handwritten in black Magic Marker: NO SHOES, NO SHIRT, NO BIRD, NO SERVICE.

Entering, he was engulfed by a wordless Muzak version of John Denver's "Take Me Home, Country Roads," which, unfortunately, didn't prevent him from a mental sing-along: "Almost heaven..." Shut up, he thought, passing a glass oven where several mummified hot dogs were rolling, and a gaudy counter display of pick-me-up vitamins and hangover remedies.

Mike was alone in the store except for a longhaired teen in a T-shirt at the register, and the obligatory camera, peering over his shoulder. Strolling by the ice cream he caught his reflection in the fridge's glass door. Tiny dots of blood on his face. A spray of dandruff on his gray sweatshirt turned out to be flakes of glass. His soggy black jeans hid the blood pretty well. This, he thought with a shudder, is a man who is lucky to be alive.

The boy was doing a drum solo with a pencil, watching him. Red hair and ponytail. An athletic Robert Crumb woman on his chest. "Help you find something?"

Mike recited the instructions of a dying man. "Slurpees?"

The young man pointed the eraser at the machine in the corner.

Mike pulled down the strawberry knob. The sickly sweet scent as the frozen ooze snorted into the cup—a vaguely disgusting process.

"One-oh-two," said the boy, holding out his hand.

"Do you have Mountain Dew?" Mike asked.

The boy's open hand hovered in the air.

"Mountain Dew?" Mike repeated. It sounded like something he may have heard in Morocco. One of those rare melodious phrases that rose above the gargling nonsense, usually from the mouths of beggars who had honed their craft of persuasion into lovely, irrefutable questions: "Help? Please?"

Placing both hands on the white counter, the boy leaned over and inspected the icy treat. Mike got a close-up of his many freckles.

Mike said, "Strawberry."

"Sis!" the boy called.

An annoyed voice replied from the back office, beyond the open door. "What?"

"We—we got Mountain Dew?" he asked, never taking his eyes off the stranger.

Relax, thought Mike. You've done this before.

In the back room something dropped and jangled on the floor. By the sound of it: a bag of empty cans. A round woman came out of the office dressed in a red-and-white 7-Eleven bowling shirt over blue jean cutoffs.

She saw her brother pointing at the Slurpee. She looked at Mike. He nodded, hoping he was playing this right. He had no more passwords.

She reached up behind her and unplugged the video camera. The red light went off. "Bobby. Fetch me Charlie and Kyo, would ya? And go rewind the tape."

The boy stared at Mike as he left.

"When's the last time you had a shower?" she asked.

Mike frowned. He honestly couldn't recall.

The woman crossed her fat arms over her chest. "Do you remember yours?"

"My what?" he asked.

The woman tilted her head to one side and smiled. "Bobby? Charlie."

"I got him," said the boy as he exited the office carrying a silver handgun and a black cell phone.

Mike backed away as the boy handed the weapon to his sister. She held it on him as she walked around the counter and directed him down the aisles to the entrance of the coolers. It was a stainless steel door that opened to a gap behind the frosty glass. A sign read, CROSSOVERS ONLY. And beneath it: NO DEPOSIT. NO RETURN.

"Get in," she said.

Once inside Mike felt the chill and got a can's-eye view of the 7-Eleven. Bobby was on the cell phone by the pretzels, gesturing frantically. Then she poked the barrel into Mike's back and marched him to the rear of the dark cooler. This seemed to be his day for guns. There was a door with a vertical freezer hinge handle. He opened it at her command and they entered an alley. The cooler exhaled streams of cloud into the air. With her gun she indicated a pyramid of blue-and-red plastic milk crates. "Siddown."

There was nothing to see in the alley. The woman was not talkative. The smell of chicken grease wafted over from the KFC next door. For a second, Mike felt he was lost in an art film, waiting for the next subtitle. But this was life. He thought: I am sitting in an alleyway with a strange woman holding a gun on me. Now what?

There was a crunch of gravel as the black Jeep pulled into the alley. A man stepped over the ledge and strutted over. He had his hand tucked in the pocket of his black suit like Christopher Walken in the movie *The Comfort of Strangers*. Tall man. Late thirties? Thin. Asian. Flat face. Some sort of official. Mike thought: Do all government agents look this obvious? Was there some genetic screening process they had to pass? Chiseled? Check. Heroic? Check. Repressed? Check.

"Hey, Rita," the man said with absolutely no hint of an accent.

She nodded. "Hey, Kyo."

Mike registered a mental flinch when he heard the name Kyo. But it passed as the man stood before them, put his hands on his hips, and looked him up and down. "You're packing," he said.

Mike lifted and dropped his sweatshirt, letting them glimpse the gun tucked into his pants.

"Jesus," the woman said, disgusted with herself. "I thought it was his—"

"—It's okay, Rita," Kyo said without looking at her. "We're all friends here. You better go calm Bobby down."

Rita slunk back into the cooler and the man held out his hand. "Kyo Takahashi."

"Mike Glynn," he said, shaking. He had heard that name. He was sure of it.

"Ycnacavon?" the man said.

Mike frowned. Yc-na-kavon? What was that? Russian? There was something familiar about the agent's eyes. Black intent eyes in an utterly expressionless face.

"Where's your bird?" Kyo asked.

That question again.

"You don't have one, do you?"

That one wasn't any better. Mike held up both his hands and closed his eyes. He couldn't take any more stupid questions. Sooner or later somebody had to make sense. It might as well be him.

"Listen," he said, feeling a sudden urge to confess, as if he had just witnessed an accident, and had to tell someone. "I was kidnapped by some weirdoes who called themselves Crossovers. They knocked me out. We were ambushed. They had guns. Everybody's dead." He felt himself choking up on this last word. "Everybody."

The Japanese man grew very still. "You killed somebody."

"Yes," Mike said, stifling a gag at the image of the brunette's head. "How'd you know that?"

"You said the magic word."

Kyo reached into his pocket, pulled out a black pager, pressed a few buttons, then handed it over. "Here's your lifeline, Mike. You keep this on you at all times. It's as good as two in the bush. We can track you with it." Kyo put his palms together and opened them like a beggar. "Don't worry. You're in good hands."

The weirdness of the exchange was slight compared to the relief Mike felt when the stranger handed him the pager. It embarrassed him, this childish, aching gratitude. Mike had grown into a man who expected nothing to be given to him. To take what he needed. And bitterly he had discovered that taking was not the same as getting. That, as much as he took: pleasure, money, fame, power; the very act of taking seemed to deplete the object of desire of any satisfaction.

"Take my Jeep. Keys are in the ignition. We'll be in touch. Meanwhile lose yourself. Disappear. Can you do that?"

Mike nodded and felt the pager pulsing faintly in his hand.

"They called me professor," he said. "I think they thought I was Danny. What the fuck is going on?"

The man reached into his suit coat pocket and got himself a cigarette. Salem. Took his time lighting it with a Zippo. Finally, he said, "Under what name did you check in at your hotel?"

Mike frowned. "My name."

"How did you sign the register?"

He remembered the blue pen. "Glynn."

The man rubbed his eyes with one hand. Irritated, apparently, by somebody's fuckup. "There you go. Simple case of mistaken identity. Happens all the time. Those people who tried to kill you? They're Correctors. Renegades. They're after your brother. They want him dead."

"Why?"

"They think he's got the code."

Code? Code?

"He's a dangerous man."

Yeah, right.

Agent Takahashi slowly exhaled a cloud of smoke. "We been waiting years for you guys. Scanning records. Bills. ATMs. A name pops up and we send out the hounds. We were tracking Daniel in Florida. Then he disappeared. Any idea where he is?"

"He lives in Detroit."

"He's home?" the tall man asked, puzzled.

"How should I know?" Am I my brother's keeper?

"If Daniel's in Detroit, I'll find him. But, like you, he's got no bird, so as far as we're concerned he could be anywhere. Listen. If the Correctors find him first, he's a goner. We could use your help."

Mike almost laughed. Crossovers? Correctors? Danny is dangerous? If this was a film pitch he would have tossed them off the lot. "You guys kidnap me? Put me in danger? Mix me up with some sort of bullshit conspiracy and you want *my help*?"

"I did ask nicely, didn't I?"

"I'm supposed to—what? Find my brother? Turn him over to you?"

"Exactly."

Mike laughed. "Or you'll what?"

Agent Takahashi straightened up. "Rita," he called, without turning his face from Mike.

The young woman stepped out of the cooler door. "Yeah?"

"You still on one?"

"Yes."

"Your turn."

"Really? Jesus. Thanks, man." She called inside. "Bobby? I got the go!"

The boy emerged from the shadows of the steaming doorway. He looked at Kyo and Mike.

"Okay by you?" Takahashi asked.

"Sure. I'll catch up with you, sis." He gave his sister a long hug. "I still don't remember the robbery," he said, apologetically.

She took her gun out. "That's all right, Bobby. I do."

The boy turned to Kyo. "Listen, I don't have to, like, *look* at her, do I?"

The tall man shook his head. "You don't have to look at her."

The boy nodded, then turned around and put his hands in his back pockets. Mike read the back of his T-shirt. *Boy Howdy!*

The woman hesitated for a second. Then lifted her gun and put a bullet into her brother's head.

Mike leaped back and screamed.

The woman dropped the gun to her side, staring at her dead brother with a strange, exalted look. Then she turned her eyes to Mike and smiled. "Two down, one to go."

Mike looked to the ground.

"Rita loved that boy," Takahashi said quietly. "She doesn't give a damn about you. Do you understand what you're dealing with here?"

"No," Mike admitted in a hoarse voice. "I don't understand anything."

"You ever hear the story about the man who was dead and didn't know it?"

"No."

"You will." Kyo laid a hand on his shoulder—a gesture that was somehow both menacing and kind. "You want to live, Mike? Find your brother."

People Do Not Disappear

I s there something wrong?" Daniel asked, looking over the broad shoulders of the tall man, scanning up and down the street. No sign of Sean.

Agent Takahashi held up a black leather wallet and flopped it open in his palm to reveal an ID card. His thumb covered his first name. "I just have a few questions."

He was staring at the pile of newspapers in their yellow plastic bags that been stacking up beside the door. Actually, Daniel had meant to cancel their subscription. He had stopped reading the paper when he'd seen the headline EVERYTHING SWELL. That was journalism? He'd been tempted to write them a note. But he didn't want to get anybody in trouble.

"Mr. Glynn?" the polite man asked. "Shouldn't take but a minute."

The agent waited for him to sit in his chair before he sat on the couch. His black shoes were the shiniest Daniel had ever seen.

"You say you've been looking for me?"

"Yes."

" 'Everywhere'?"

"Yes."

The absurd implication was that Daniel had been eluding them, hiding even. "I'm right here. I haven't gone anywhere."

Agent Takahashi sniffed a sarcastic laugh. "First place we should have looked, eh? Mr. Glynn, have you had any recent contact with your brother?"

Daniel's eyebrows rose. He had to retrieve his mind from another track altogether; it took a moment. "Mike?" He shook his head. "Not for months."

The man cleared his throat. "We think he may be in grave danger."

Daniel's right foot twitched in his slipper. It was too much. After Julie, it was too much.

"Wish I could go into more details. But it's classified."

He must have expected this conversation for years. Grave. Danger. The way Mike lived, it was inevitable. Crazy special-effects shoots. Explosions. Diving helicopter shots over Angel Falls. Like he was asking for it. But you can't brace yourself for tragedy on a regular basis. Wait a second. Classified?

"Classified?" Daniel asked.

"Mike is one of our most valuable operatives. We've lost him. Actually, we have reason to believe he's been compromised."

Compromised? Oh, please. If this was one of Mike's jokes . . . "You're telling me . . . my brother works for the government?"

"Yes."

It was hard to keep a straight face. This was very amusing.

"You don't mind my saying so, Mr. Glynn, you don't seem particularly shocked."

Daniel leveled his gaze at the man. "You met me three minutes ago. You have no idea what I feel. What's this about?"

Agent Takahashi started nodding his head like a salesman, hoping to batter you into agreement. "It's a deep cover double agent counterterrorist–type thing. Top secret."

Daniel thought: How top secret can it be if he's telling me?

"Did your brother send you something recently? A gift perhaps?"

"No."

"You didn't pick up your paper today. Maybe you forgot to check the mail."

"No, I checked." It was how he acknowledged the world outside the dark house. But there was never any mail.

"Federal Express, then. When it positively, absolutely has to be there overnight." The agent smiled. "They leave those sticky things on the door."

Daniel looked blankly at him.

"It wouldn't have to be a big package. Maybe as small as a pack of cigarettes. A book, maybe? A videotape?"

"I told you: nothing." Daniel was looking out the window again. Checking the street. Why couldn't Sean come home when he was told to? He knew the rules. Home when the streetlights come on. In bed by nine. If he went anywhere off the block it had to be in the company of an adult.

"Mr. Glynn? We need to find your brother. And we'd like you to help us."

Daniel's face did several things, one after the other. Finally, he asked, "Wouldn't *your* people be better equipped to handle this?"

"We have reason to believe his friends are protecting him. We also suspect you know more than you're telling us. That could be very unwise."

Daniel went through at least four possible replies, before he arrived and settled on, "Is it your policy to harass people?"

"Mr. Glynn. People leave messages. They check in. They tell their colleagues, their friends, their family. They don't just disappear."

Disappear.

His brother's words came back to him: Something about vibrations. Something Mike said on his last visit. After the funeral.

He remembered: They were sitting in the same positions in the living room as the agent and he, only reversed. Mike was in his chair. He always sat in Daniel's chair. He was thumbing through Daniel's copy of *The Caloreum Fortune*—a gift from a student. A New Age feel-good novel. It was still a bestseller two years after its debut.

"You read it?" Mike had asked.

"Not yet." Actually, he had no intention of reading it.

"Don't bother. I'll give you the treatment. There are ten steps to enlightenment. Number ten is you get so enlightened you vibrate at a higher frequency, and then you disappear."

Daniel smiled.

Mike smirked. "People do not disappear, Danny. They die, they rot, and *then* they disappear."

"There's faith," Daniel offered.

"I call it paranoia." Mike held up the book. "Paranoia's what we got now instead of God. UFO abductions. Government cover-ups. Conspiracy theories. We can't abide a meaningless universe so we've substituted a malicious one. Who needs God when you got the CIA?"

"Mr. Glynn?" the agent said, calling him back to the present.

After the funeral. That was the last time he'd seen his brother.

Maybe it was the agent's suggestion that Mike had a secret life, but the more Daniel remembered it, the more his fond recollection of that last visit took on sinister overtones. It was as though Mike was acting out a pantomime for the hidden tape recorders. On one level he was simply debating with his brother, on another, he was conveying a host of clues about a mystery Daniel wasn't even aware of. A mystery that emerged like those images hidden in magic eye 3-D stereographs. One minute you're staring your eyeballs off, trying to make sense of these deranged fractalized pictures—visual nonsense until something weird happens— your brain says: "Oh, I get it now," *and suddenly a new dimension emerges—a swarm of hummingbirds form a rainbow heart*, psychedelic dolphins float on the page, a mermaid waves coyly from a rock, a school of sharks bears down

on you, an Escher flight of geese suck you into their impossible formation—you're in.

Takahashi was saying, "Mike hasn't debriefed us since he got back
from his jungle operation. Plenty of time for him to roll over some very
compromising material. I can tell you this much: He has access to some
pretty serious codes."

"Codes?"

"To certain parties that material could be worth more money than
you can imagine. They will do anything to get it. Anything. I'll be honest
with you, Mr. Glynn. We've come up dry. We need your help."

Daniel rolled his eyes. "Excuse me, but, this is really stupid. What the
heck do I have to do with all this?"

"Well, frankly, Mr. Glynn—it has to do with your son."

Sean's tardiness began to buzz again in his head. "My son?" he said.
"What are you talking about?"

"We have him. He's safe. But he's ours."

Daniel's mouth opened but nothing came out. He found it very difficult to breathe. His rimless glasses were fogging up. He took them off
and used the belt of his blue robe to wipe clear the condensation. A
trickle of sweat slid off his brow, curled into the corner of his eye, paused
briefly, then continued as a tear. Until that moment Daniel had never
understood why people kill people.

The agent held up a hand "Now, take it easy."

Daniel put his glasses back on.

The agent said, "Take a few breaths through your nose and let them
out slowly."

It seemed like good advice. He took it.

"Your reaction is natural. But if you were to act on it, I can promise
you: I would hurt you very badly. Your son is safe."

"Where is he?"

"Quiet now ... we got him in protective custody."

"Go on."

"That's better. The breathing helped, didn't it?"

"Go on."

"We want you to find your brother, Mr. Glynn. You find him, and we'll return your son." The man stood. "Don't tell anybody. Don't call anyone. You're on your own. Just you."

He didn't have to say: Or you'll never see your son again.

"Here's my card. If anything should arrive . . . don't open it. Call me immediately."

Daniel examined the agent's card in his hand. Black type over a golden seal.

Agent Takahashi said, "Do you keep any birds in the house?"

"Birds?" Daniel said, thinking about the graves in the backyard.

"Pets."

He didn't suppose the buried ones counted. "No."

Agent Takahashi nodded as if that settled a nagging final concern. "We'll be watching you, Mr. Glynn," he said and turned for the door.

"Excuse me," Daniel said, standing. "How do you pronounce your first name?"

The man turned back. They stood in the living room. The pudgy father and the tall agent. A body length of space between them.

"*Kee-oo.*"

"Kyo," said Daniel, flicking the card against his fingers. "Kyo Takahashi. NSA. Special branches."

After a moment, the agent said, "That's right."

Daniel stopped flicking. "If anything should happen to my son, Kyo, I will hold you personally responsible."

The agent was quiet for a long moment. Perhaps he wasn't used to being threatened. Perhaps he was surprised that a man like Daniel would risk such a thing. Or perhaps it was something else.

"Find your brother," Kyo said, finally.

When he was alone Daniel went up to his son's bed and laid down. He could smell Sean on the sheets. He recalled that Julie had left her scent behind as well. In their bed.

He slept for a time.

He woke in a panic, sitting up, swiveling his head back and forth. For an awful second he did not know where he was. Then he recognized his home.

He sat in Sean's bed and rocked back and forth, back and forth.

He noticed that he still held the agent's card in his hand. It was like his last connection to reality. And for a moment he feared that if he let go of it, he would disappear.

A strange thought occurred to him. This was, he thought, like being in a mystery-thriller novel—a type of fiction he had always condescended to. The complexities of life reduced to a trivial formula: Who dun it? Where's the bomb? Who's the traitor? "Comfort literature," he had tagged it. But Daniel discovered, to his amazement, that it was an entirely different matter on the inside. When you're inside a mystery, you experience the thrills firsthand. You get caught up. Your life suddenly has a plot.

The card was evidence. Marching orders.

Oh good, Daniel thought, as something broke inside him and the world outside the window looked, for the first time in days, really, really real. He was filled with a fantastic sense of purpose. And he made a mental list.

He would find Mike.

He would rescue his son.

He would hurt anyone who tried to stop him.

Daniel realized that he had wanted to do that for a long, long time.

The Buddy System

s Mike drove the black Jeep away from the body behind the 7-Eleven he noticed it was hard to keep a grip on the steering wheel. His hands were slick with sweat. And for the rest of the drive south down Highway One he kept up a manic running monologue like a rookie comedian bombing on his first night at the microphone, looking for a punch line that never came. For as much as he babbled he couldn't keep the image out of his head for long.

The memory was stuck there, looping over and over in slow motion like that Vietnam street execution: the first on TV. The clenched face. The flicking head. The spray of blood jetting out in the opposite direction—a red arch. The young man's body crumbling. The body twitching on the gravel, then stopping. The Boy Howdy T-shirt.

His sister smiling at Mike, holding the gun.

It was absurd. A pitch with a ridiculous plot. Why would anybody

THE IMPOSSIBLE BIRD 77

want to kill Danny? Danny was "dangerous?" Depressed maybe, but dangerous? Danny was too boring to be dangerous. Too responsible. Danny's kind of people had nervous breakdowns or heart attacks; they didn't go postal. It was all a very bad movie, he thought. No credibility. No character arc. No plot. Just random explosions and killings to keep your nerve endings jumping. Puberty stuff. It was like half the screenplays he read. He'd been looking to make the transition from spots to features, so his executive producer, Mel, had started passing him scripts. Boy, did they suck. Every one was a sequel or a prequel or a remake of a lousy sixties TV show. *The Revenge of Ms. Kong! Godson—The Last Godfather! Petticoat Junction 2000!* Or star vehicles with the high concepts as their punch line. Hanks is Lincoln! Whoopi is pope! Jackie Chan is president and he's kicking China's ass!

Find your brother or you're a dead man who doesn't know it.

What the fuck?!

It took him most of the long drive back to Santa Monica to calm down. He told himself: he wasn't afraid. He could handle it. He had a plan. And he had a gun.

Mike made a pit stop to buy new clothes and toiletries on the Third Street promenade, and paid cash. He parked Takahashi's Jeep in the underground lot and checked back into his hotel. They'd never guess he'd be hiding there. Lightning didn't strike in the same place twice.

Still, he changed his name on the register at the front desk to "Kringle." The man who pretended to be himself. Had a bellhop transfer all his stuff from his old room. Tipped him heavily. Told them he was under no circumstances receiving visitors.

"Yes, Mr. Glynn."

"My name is Kringle."

"Yes, Mr. Kringle."

Mike concluded it wasn't hard to hide. You just disappeared. You talked only to strangers, only when necessary. You never gave your name. Never went out. Ordered room service, squelched any eccentricities—you blended. Hit the mattresses. Laid low.

They'd never find him.

The hotel was a quiet yellow stucco place on Ocean Boulevard. A lima bean–shaped pool in the courtyard. As he walked to his room he saw two little black kids splashing in the pool. Where were their parents? he wondered. Christ, what kind of person would let their kids swim unsupervised in a pool?

The boys looked at him as they treaded water.

"Where are your parents?"

"They're not here yet," one of the boys replied.

"Well," he said. "It's not safe for you to swim in the deep end like that."

"We use the buddy system," said the other black boy proudly.

"That's smart," he said, standing. "Still, you better get out until they come."

The boys shared a look of relief. Then they swam to the ladder and climbed dripping out of the water. One found a large fluffy white towel and they wrapped themselves in it. It reminded him of a scene from Morocco. Two beggar boys squatting in the hot square, sharing the shade of a white sheet.

"Have you seen her?" asked the littler one who was immediately elbowed by his older brother.

"Who?" Mike asked.

"Mom," the boy replied.

Something hungry and worried in their eyes. "Maybe she's in the room."

This got no response.

"Your room," he said, hoping to clarify the matter.

There was a noise from across the courtyard. Mike saw a Latino pool cleaner, loaded down with a skimmer and a bucket of chlorine. The effect of his presence was immediate. The kids scampered out of the nearest archway. He was amused as the man finally noticed the dropped towel and trail of wet footprints leading away from the pool. As he climbed the stairs to his room he heard the hurricane fence rattling as they scrambled over it.

Mike smiled. Danny and he had done the same thing: Pool hopping when their neighbors were on vacation. They used the buddy system too. Except Danny was useless. He was the one who was always rescuing Danny. Yelling him out of the deep end. Loosening his jeans when he got stuck crawling through a barbed wire fence. Dragging him out when he broke through the thin ice into the ditch—freezing water up to his waist. Helping him down from the tree when he was too afraid to jump. Stepping between him and Uncle Louie whenever Shithead put his sights on Danny. Taking the whipping. And here he was again: bailing him out. Some things never change.

Well, it was the least he could do.

Yeah, hiding was a cinch, he thought, lying on the bed and flicking through the channels with the remote. You watched old black-and-white movies on the Turner channel. They were playing all his favorites. *Harvey. Psycho. Miracle on 34th Street.* The old guy who left his cane in the corner.

Then the images flashed in his mind again. Three in a row.

The black chopper hovering over the clearing like a sci-fi metallic dragonfly. It was just a helicopter—why did the image freeze his soul? Then in quick succession: the hummingbird in the chief's palm. The translator's mouth, her pretty black lipstick lips saying: "Too much! Wait! Too much! Wait!"

Something had happened in the jungle. Something he couldn't get a fix on. It was like his memory kept butting up against a wall. Like trying to see in a fog. He wanted to tell Danny. Danny might get it. He was always analyzing things. Coming up with stuff that nobody else saw. Breaking the codes of books that most people didn't even notice. Overthinking everything. Such a sad life he lived. Boring academic with a mortgage, a son, and a beautiful, unhappy wife. A perfect immune existence that Mike had always snickered at (though never to Danny's face). So straight. So dull. So comfortable.

Well, not always comfortable.

It had hurt him to see Danny so broken up at Uncle Louie's funeral. His last visit.

Uncle Louie. Big, tough Uncle Louie. He recalled the rank smell of his breath: glue and beer. Stinko was one of his nicknames. Shithead was the other.

And that cloudy day beside the grave, surrounded by tearful strangers and half-remembered relatives from their past. He had stood beside Danny—the only reason he had come. Aware of Julie, distant and polite beside their eight-year-old son. Then Mike did something so casually it brought him right back to their childhood. He reached over and held his brother's hand. It was cold. And together they watched the green metal casket descend into the hole as the priest talked on about passage into a new world, a better world, where all our sorrows will be washed away, where all our dreams come true, and all the struggles of this veil of tears were replaced by magic *F* words like forever and forgiveness and fuck that shit.

No magic words. He wanted no magic words. Not over this grave.

"We're finally free of the old shithead," he had whispered.

"Shut up," said Danny. "He was all we had."

For as long as they lived they could never agree.

Did others have a similar bright shadow in their lives? Mike wondered. That necessary opposite. Danny was the wall that set the boundaries of his self. The white sheep who made him feel black. And their incessant arguments were like those two escaped convicts chained at the ankles, Tony Curtis and Sidney Poitier sharing a shackle, rivals locked in an inescapable, unresolvable debate. Often, when they'd reconvene after months apart, he'd catch himself competing, raising his level of discourse, goosing up his diction to impress the professor. But they couldn't even agree on their history. Their childhood—raised by their Uncle Louie in a farmhouse south of Saginaw, Michigan—had been brutal and boring, or adequate and forgettable—depending on which brother you asked. Remember? he'd say at their reunions. Remember, Danny? But his brother never did; he relied on Mike to fill in the blanks. There were a lot of them. Their past had been full of secrets. Where was Dad? Where was Mom? Why did they leave? Why didn't anyone talk about it? She was gone by the time Mike was four and Danny was one. But, unlike Danny, he remembered her. He could picture her face. Hear her laugh. He recalled her sweet smell and gentle touch. Her long red hair. He had gotten used to her. And, like his brother, he had been left behind. The difference was: Mike knew what he was missing.

His whole body flinched when the phone rang. Reaching for the receiver he thought: maybe he hadn't calmed down. Maybe what he was feeling was something closer to shock.

"Mr. Kringle?"

"Yes."

"This is the front desk. You have a message."

"Yes?"

"Shall I read it to you?"

"Sure."

"Just do it."

"What?"

"It says: 'Just do it.' "

All Your Wishes

D aniel's life had been reduced to two simple questions: Where was Sean? Where was Mike? Yet they were like the last questions on an entrance exam in a bad dream. A test he hadn't studied for.

How do you find a missing person?

He called Mike's production house. Everyone but the old secretary was out: Mrs. Van der Tuin. Hadn't he said she retired for heart reasons? She said Mike was on vacation—not to be disturbed. Daniel said he was his brother and it was an emergency. She gave him his new cell phone number. No answer. He called his ex-girlfriend—a toothy model who had dropped him for an actor. Mike said she snorted heroin. She said she couldn't care less where the bastard was. He called the Director's Guild, who referred him to several of Mike's favorite crew: a D.P., a key grip, a gaffer—whatever those were. They all said they hadn't seen him since the jungle. Then he recalled Mike's favorite editor—Adam Brady, an old chain-smoker who joked about his triple bypass. On the phone he said he had a "rough cut" to show him on the Amazon spot, but Mike hadn't checked in. They were like everybody in LA: charming, friendly, self-absorbed. Useless.

Mike had disappeared.

He thought of hiring a real detective, but he knew Agent Takahashi would nix that.

This was stupid. How the heck would he know where Mike was?

Daniel decided that the difference between life and books was that books left out all the boring parts. Thrillers were all suspense and propulsion. Mysteries were neat and dramatic. Life was a detour—frustrating, messy, endless. Well, not endless—it only felt that way. Much to his dismay, Daniel discovered that he wasn't as bright or perceptive or brave as those heroes on the pages. Actually, he was bad casting. He wasn't suited for the tedium, the cul-de-sacs, the damnable trivia that refused to become clues. In books the hero's innate character gave him an edge, charged him with a zeal, and the enemies would topple, the doors would open, and the evidence would fall into his lap.

Frankly, his lap was empty. It had never been emptier.

Still he dialed. Information. Libraries. Old friends. Nothing. The only positive result of his futile investigation was that it kept his mind off Sean. But by the end of the day his ear was numb, his fingers aching from punching the phone, and he had nothing to show for all his work except a migraine.

At a strip mall drugstore he was frowning at two different bottles in his hands, comparing milligrams, when a young man in a blue druggist lab coat said, "You take that shit?"

His nametag read *J. Cross.*

"I don't usually buy this stuff myself. My wife actually—" Daniel began, but couldn't finish.

"Might as well eat candy," the young man said. Dark ponytail. Kind black eyes. Horsy face. Holding a fat, black briefcase.

"I haven't got a prescription," Daniel admitted—blood worming through his temples.

"You look like you got a class-one migraine."

"You're a doctor?" Daniel asked.

"Christ, no. Look." The man took the bottles from his hands and reshelved them. "None of this over-the-counter stuff is what you need. I got something at my place that'll do the trick."

Daniel raised his eyebrows. "Legal?"

"Sure, legal." He smiled. "Most of it."

What a helpful man. The headache was at the vise-grip stage; someone had bolted his skull like Frankenstein's monster. Daniel was willing to try anything.

The druggist's house was within walking distance, but Daniel drove him.

"Aren't you wearing your seat belt?" the man asked as the Volvo started.

"Sorry," Daniel said, buckling up. "Bad habit of mine." One he wished Sean wouldn't emulate so often.

"Nice car," the druggist said. "What's this button?"

It was a round blue button with no handy label. A dealer-installed-option-type thing. A special theft alarm or something, Daniel assumed, but he never bothered to read the manual. "Don't touch," he said. "That's the armageddon button." The druggist smiled and Daniel felt proud: his first joke in ages. "You touch that, and—"

"—I know, I know," the druggist said. "The world ends. How stupid do I look?"

They laughed.

Daniel could smell the patchouli as he entered the druggist's upper flat. A hippie's bachelor pad: yellow shag carpeting, a yellow beanbag chair, yellow plastic end tables, a *Yellow Submarine* poster on the wall. They sat in the yellow-tiled kitchen at a yellow table and the man opened a yellow drawer and pulled out a small green ceramic frog. It was almost a relief.

"Kiss the frog. Turn into a prince." The druggist laughed as he held it on his palm for display. One those exotic Amazon frogs. Red stripes on its sides. And a scoop in its back. "It's a pipe, for chrissake, what'd you think it was?"

"Will it help?" asked Daniel, rubbing his forehead.

The druggist snorted. "Oh, yeah." He opened the freezer and got out a baggie—a lid—and a slim corked vial half full of white powder. He took a pinch of green dope, tamped it into the hole, and sprinkled a tiny bit of white on it.

"Next stop: oblivion!" he announced, clicking open his Zippo and flinting the light in one motion. The frog's back glowed orange under his attentions. He held the smoke in his lungs and passed over the pipe.

It was warm in Daniel's hand and he smirked at the necessary hole in the frog's mouth. His first toke in many years. He sucked up the hot smoke and looked from the man's smiling black eyes to the tree outside the kitchen window.

The man watched Daniel's face. "Five-four-three-two—"

"One," said Daniel, exhaling. The smoke slowed as it exited his mouth, like a film running down until the frame freezes on the screen.

BAM—just like that he could see every wrinkle on the gray bark of the maple outside, every crevice, every black crack and smooth flake. It was like the first live pictures he'd seen of the moon. The auditorium in junior high: all the students assembled to watch a TV on stage showing the radio-delayed black-and-white images as the unmanned craft descended to the lunar surface. The craters getting bigger and bigger until they were like the bark of the tree. Blackout when it had crashed. The kids erupting with applause as if that were the best part.

It felt like he was touching the tree with his eyes. It had become a thing of FASCINATION. Life capitalized. He studied it as if it contained prodigious content. Though what that was exactly he couldn't say. Daniel remembered: this was getting high. "Petrified into the now," he used to call it. Nothing hurt anymore. He had no worries. No stress. No bills. Time had ceased; there was no tomorrow, and somebody else was on duty, watching out for him, taking care of the details.

It was like being a kid.

Daniel was reminded of their mysterious custodian. The one they called "All Your Wishes."

Every Christmas Eve they got a phone call from Santa's favorite elf: Aloysius.

It was an occasion of rare formality. They wore their starched Easter best. They blew their noses. And as they huddled head-to-head on the scratchy purple couch, sharing the receiver, inspecting their shiny black Sunday shoes, Mike and Danny knew they were lucky. They knew none of the neighborhood kids were patched into the North Pole like this. And they kept it a secret. Years after they ceased to believe in Santa Claus, they still held Aloysius in awe and eagerly anticipated his uncanny phone call.

They didn't know then that this would be his last.

Aloysius always wanted to know if they had been "good boys." And every year they assured him it was true. This was a sincere holiday amnesia. They avoided the topic of who pilfered the pagan baby fund from the can on Sister Schaberg's desk, who painted the lions red on Mrs. Crabtree's porch, whose slingshot took out Mrs. Campbell's bay window, who decimated the Scarfones' pumpkin patch, who slammed the door on old Mr. Gregory's legs when he lay belly down and whisking out his Edsel, who defecated in Mr. Ambrogio's rosebushes, what sadistic midget shaved Robin Watson's poodle bald, what mad barber clipped off Peggy Stack's pigtails during church, or who could have possibly liberated the population of Mrs. Vlasopolo's goldfish pond when she was vacationing in Romania. Their long and checkered annual sheet of venial and juvenile sins remained unwitnessed and unrecorded and therefore, their characters, come Christmas, were unblemished when Aloysius took his moral tab.

As usual, his voice on the phone was garrulous and slurred—like an adult after three manhattans. He admitted it had been a most trying season. A most troublesome year. The elves were singularly uncooperative. Never properly braiding the straw tails of the wooden buffaloes—ahhh, ponies. He meant ponies. Oh, those elves. Careless with their sewing needles. Constantly distracted. Humming all the time. Oh, the headaches he had to put up with. The nonsense. The messes the reindeer left. The reams of rainbow ribbons that had to be imported in gigantic rolls from Central America, the perpetual hammering of the cobbling elves that left poor Aloysius with a migraine.

"What's a migraine?" Mike asked his brother—who shushed him.

The only consolation this burdened elf ever enjoyed was the daily dose of hot chocolate Mrs. Claus delivered personally to him after the day's work was done. Renewing, Aloysius called it. The sweetest, most intoxicating brew you ever tasted. Steaming and coated with star-shaped marshmallows that shed clouds of fine sugar powder into the air, which tickled his nose. And Mrs. Claus beaming at her favorite assistant—a fine woman, an ample woman of stature and bearing and flaming red hair. Whose touch was so soft and kind and ardent that the elf would blush and his white forelock would, for a brief embarrassing moment, stand at attention. So, gently, she would lick her dainty fingertips and stroke it down into place upon his crimson head.

"What's a forelock?" Mike asked—only to be shushed.

Well, he had to go now. There was still a sip or two of cocoa left and it was criminal to neglect such a treat. He'd be calling again next year, same time. And he assured the boys that he would be watching them—wherever they were, wherever they went—he'd be watching. He might be two hundred years old, but his eyesight was perfect. He never missed an "instigator" or a "snitch." He was particularly displeased with instigators and snitches. They were something he could not abide.

"What's an instigator?" Mike asked.

"You," Danny whispered, puzzled. The only time he'd ever heard that word was in the confessional with Father Otto. "Good boys tell, Daniel. They do not protect instigators."

And perhaps, Aloysius continued, the boys might consider that goldfish were some of Santa's most favored creations—each the product of a special frozen fire that only burns at the North Pole, and when the tongues of flame were trimmed with a golden pair of scissors, they fell into the crystal goblets of the fire-tending elves and were shipped to pet stores all over North America, to be given to good boys and girls everywhere.

Mike and Danny looked at each other aghast.

"Good stuff," the frog man grumbled in a high voice—he had surprised his vocal chords.

"Uhm," Daniel grunted, realizing they hadn't been speaking for quite some time.

"Make it a double?"

And after a moment their laughter spittled out. It was like being offered a blow job after the best sex of your life.

Then he drew his attention from the gray bark and noticed the nest. *A bird's nest on a branch. A Day-Glo orange silk hanky woven into its wall of sticks and stuffing. There was something creepy about it. The nest was empty, abandoned. A home that nobody lived in.*

And then, the images came again, flashing against his mind. First, the one that always made him flinch: a boy's arm breaking; an *I* becoming an *L*.

And then: the hurtling picture of a gray tree trunk, like the one out the window, falling toward him. A collision course that always stopped just before impact, as if the camera had run out of film.

Daniel reeled and steadied himself. Paranoia, he thought.

He wondered if this was what the end of life would be like. A slide show of memories fast-forwarding past your mind's eye.

He was going nuts. He must be going nuts. Why was he sitting here getting stoned with a stranger? Where had all his bravado gone? What about his mission? The missing persons. Why wasn't he hunting for them?

He was a coward.

He imagined the trusting face of his son, needing him, sitting alone in a room somewhere, surrounded by strangers, waiting for his father to come.

I'm sorry, Sean, he thought, his chest aching. I'm a coward.

Wrenching himself out of that painful train of thought, he asked, "What's your name?"

"Joe."

"I'm Daniel."

The man held out the pipe. "Another?"

Daniel shook his head. "You been a druggist long?"

Joe smiled. "Who said I was a druggist? I'm in pharmaceutical supplies."

"Oh." Daniel felt stupid. "You like that?"

"Fuck no! But it gets me free samples." Joe stood in the center of the kitchen and looped the frog about like a kid's airplane doing infinity eights. It left a strobing green glow in its wake. "I used to like a lot of things. Used to read a lot. American history mostly. I got bored around Eisenhower. Anyway, it doesn't matter. All the yearbooks stop at Ninety. The year our friends pressed SAVE."

Ninety? Friends? Save? This guy was out there.

"They're right, you know," Joe continued. "History just repeats itself. So I figured, fuck history, I'll try science. I read lotsa science. But I got bored after quantum. After quantum you realize that nobody knows nothing and it's all crazy, so what's the fucking point? You know Heisenberg's last words before he croaked? 'Why relativity?... Why turbulence?' " The man held up the frog and looked it in the eye. "The father of uncertainty didn't have a clue." He kissed the frog. "So I gave up on books. Did a little sex. Got into the stupid twelve-step church for a while. Fucking bird nuts. Now I smoke."

Daniel had never seen a man with such empty eyes. "That's all?"

Joe smirked. "What do you do?"

Daniel stared at the yellow floor. "I'm looking for my son."

Joe cocked his eyebrows. "Really? Why?"

"I lost him."

"I never had any kids," Joe said, holding the frog before his face, slowly turning it back and forth. It was as if that subject, like everything else, was closed.

It was sad, actually. Daniel felt bad for the man and what he had missed. Then he realized he was wasting his empathy. He wasn't real to

Joe. He was just a dope buddy. A stranger who'd shared a frog with him on a cold winter's night. Apparently Joe wanted as much nothing as possible. Something important without content. Daniel decided he didn't want to go there.

His headache was gone.

"Thanks, Joe," he said, standing.

Joe continued staring at the space he had just left. "You're leaving?"

"I got things to do." He paused by the door. "Am I safe to drive?"

Joe set the frog down on the yellow table. "Just stay the limit and follow the yellow line."

Daniel could do that. He felt sure he could. He gave Joe a thin smile and reached for the door.

"Find your brother yet?"

Daniel froze. He felt every muscle in his body recoil at the quick unexpected braking. The dope. It had to be the dope. "What?" he asked, turning.

"Let me explain something to you," said Joe. He walked over and punched Daniel in the mouth.

Daniel fell to the floor. His jaw was throbbing. Not necessarily an unpleasant sensation, he discovered—dope enhanced everything. Joe was speaking fiercely. "Your brother. Remember? He's the one you should be looking for. He's the one. Clear?"

Daniel was looking at the yellow tiles on the floor when he felt a shoe laid against his ear. That was not pleasant.

"Clear?" said Joe, louder this time.

"Clear," he mumbled through a mouthful of blood.

"Find your fucking brother and we'll give you your fucking son."

As Daniel walked down the stairs, holding his aching jaw, each step sending jolts of pain up his spine, he recalled Agent Takahashi's words: "We'll be watching you."

Out into the chilly street.

Silent black birds streaked by overhead.

His breath frosted above his upturned face.

The keys jangled as the Volvo turned over. For a moment, just a moment, his brain fixated on the mysterious blue light on the dash. The armageddon button. Daniel imagined it would cue a jettison pod that would thrust him out of this reality clear into safety.

For several seconds it was all he could do not to press it.

The First Letter

Find your brother or you're a dead man.

Okay. Fine. No problem. Couple phone calls. A few questions. Bingo.

But on the tenth ring of the twentieth call Mike slammed down the receiver and said, "Shit."

Had they turned off their answering machine? Changed their number? Were they on vacation? Kyo had said something about losing him in Florida. But Danny had always been the most reachable of people. He had two numbers and an e-mail address. People like Danny didn't disappear. He'd check his voicemail. He had one residence and the same job for twenty years. Mr. Predictable. Where the hell could he have gone? His secretary hadn't a clue. His dean couldn't be reached. His old neighbor with the pacemaker said he hadn't seen him for days.

The one time he really needed to get ahold of him and he was no-where.

Danny, where are you? That was the question.

Mike wasn't afraid of questions. He usually savored them. He didn't understand people like Danny who surrendered their doubts and settled for mystery. Who gave up debating the big questions they had studied in college. Maybe it was because Mike had never gone to college, was never fed the canon and intimidated into believing that better minds than his had considered it all and come up short. As far as he was concerned, the big questions were still on the table. And he constantly pressed his brother to reexamine his assumptions, to break out of his safe routine.

Danny, where are you? That was the question.

He booted up his Apple PowerBook and checked a few of his favorite chat rooms—boring. Went to AltaVista and searched for Missing Persons—depressing. Searched for Faulkner and Daniel Glynn. Lots about Faulkner, nothing about Danny.

Then he recalled the words of a dead man: "Mr. Glynn, this is about hummingbirds."

He searched for *hummingbirds* and found lots of birders, obsessive tips on feeders and one weird fact: *"Hummingbirds are one the few birds that can hover like helicopters. During courtship their wings beat up to 200 times per second."*

Something else the dead man had said. "You gotta see the Wing Man."

Mike thought an almost-thought. A harmony of connections that weren't quite connected yet.

He typed *hummingbirds, helicopters,* and *the Wing Man.* Then pressed search.

And found an article by Dr. Joel A. Klinder titled "The Impossible Birds."

Mike stared at the screen for a full minute, his mouth hanging open.

Then he followed the link to the Crossovers homepage and discovered what seemed to be a sermon set in a pretentious cursive font against, of all things, a tasteless scroll background. Holy Writ.

My fellow Crossovers,

It is a time of great crisis. Violence. Doubt. Bloodshed. Terrorism. As we face these most trying times it is good to recall that every great spiritual movement is tested. Especially when it is young. And our wisest course is to reembrace our first principle: radical acceptance of the gift of eternity which is the heart of our creed.

I am your Wing Man not because I am qualified to accept this mantle. But by virtue of the authority entrusted in me by our superiors, the impossible birds. I accept this burden. Faith. Trust. Acceptance. Cling fast to these, my friends. Fortify yourselves against the forces without and within, heathens and heretics who would destroy or contaminate our sacred steps.

To those who would topple our stronghold of faith, we grant no mercy. To those who have lost their faith, we say: There are no alternatives to the truth. There are only dead ends.

Creepy. That sure didn't sound like the man he knew. Had Klinder gone guru?

A strange menu of links below the sermon at the bottom of the page:

The 12 Steps. What We Believe. A Brief History. Who Is the Wing Man? Our Enemies.

Mike recalled Agent Takahashi's words about Danny: "They think he's got the code."

The dead man who said, "He's the only one who can save us. The Wing Man."

Mike coughed out a big puff of breath as if someone had socked him in the stomach. He didn't breathe in for fifteen seconds.

That dead man at the shoot-out had thought he was talking to Danny. The professor.

He was telling him to go see Klinder. The Wing Man.

The intuition rang like a gong in his chest.

Klinder has Danny. He was sure of it.

Mike followed a link to Klinder's homepage, where he got his address in Berkeley.

Jesus, Danny. What the fuck have you gotten involved in? Some kind of cult? Don't you know Klinder is bad news? You dip. Why do you trust people so easily?

Then Mike stood before the mirror and heard a voice in his head—a voice he hadn't heard in years. The voice of a woman whom he had loved ten years ago. A woman who may as well have been dead. She was saying, "He's a truster. He doesn't understand when people hurt on purpose. At first he doesn't believe it. Then it shocks him."

Mike remembered. It used to be that way for him. And he remembered where it had all changed.

Buffalo.

He pulled out his wallet and removed the yellowing pages of stationery that had acquired flexible creases over many rereadings. He sat on the edge of the bed and read again the first letter—and the last she ever wrote him, the one with the black handwriting. He always hoped that one day he would understand it. How someone in their right mind could choose to be unhappy. But as many times as he had read it—in hotels, airplanes, limos—it never changed. It never made sense. Her choice. Her reasons. The end of the affair.

2:30 A.M., FEB 4, 1991

Dearest Michael,

I've tried and tried to think of a way to form the words so I could tell you. So I could look in your eyes and know you understood and forgave me. I can't. I am a coward. I

roar and show my claws but inside I'm quaking. And when things get tough I run off with my tail between my legs.

Do you remember the last time? Yes, the last time. The day after the nursing conference we drove to Mt. Tam and had too much wine? The wind was up at sunset and we could see the Golden Gate silhouetted, coming out of the fog like two black pillars, a mile apart but connected under the surface of the fog, strong and fierce like guards at a gate, each knowing and trusting the other so well—no words needed. They'd never fail each other, never stop keeping their promises, solid in their secret love.

It was so beautiful and cold and neither one of us wanted to move. You kept me warm in your jacket and I wondered what pictures you would make here, how you saw it with your artist's eye—how did you get it? How do you keep it? It's something I always wondered, wanted to touch in you and understand what it was like to see the world that way, to pick up on the beauty and be able to share it with everyone.

I was weak. Too cowardly to get out of a marriage that held so little joy. Was so safe and predictable. I loved your smile. And you were the most fascinating creature I'd ever met. So I teased you and shared what little time I had to spare. I never expected you to really love me. I thought I was done with love.

I remember shivering and the breakers far below us, those golden hills and the cliffs and the white foam dripping off the rocks and I recall wondering why we couldn't hear anything. And then that bank of fog coming, a fat white cloud with tints of blue at the edges, so quietly, so fast, like a dream and before we could say anything it swallowed us. And I could barely see your face in the chilly mist, and I didn't want it to end. I could have stayed inside that cloud forever. But then it was too late. I lost something in that cloud.

I knew you loved me and I knew I could never leave him and love you the way you deserved and some sick part of me felt I was going to be your muse. At least I would have that. You'll laugh but that's the way we think—people who aren't creative, who can't make something out of nothing. And I wondered if some day you'd make a movie and I would see myself on-screen. I know, I know—it's embarrassing. But I'm trying to be honest.

Honestly, I love you. Honestly, I can't do it anymore. I can't do it to him and I can't do it to you.

You deserve better than me. Someone who won't give you the leftovers. Someone trustworthy and someone who won't take all the time. I was greedy. And you thought it was flattering.

So I can't. I just can't. I can't look at myself in the mirror and think I am a liar and a cheat and a coward. And the price I was willing to pay for a little charge, a little light in my life. And not so many books. And talk about books. And talk about people who talk about books. And the politics of an English department and the life of a professor's wife. I can't. I tried, my sweet. I can't.

You deserve better than me.

This hurts you, I know, but I can't do it anymore and it would hurt worse if I kept this up, the deception, the late hours, the nursing conferences I didn't really have to attend. The leftovers. I can't live like that. Maybe you can. I'm sorry.

I'm so sorry. I'm so very sorry.

So when we meet at the next family thing—God, they are so awful, Aunt Mabel giving me those dagger looks. I still can't believe she saw us in that restaurant. And me

smiling and nodding and pretending an affection and disapproval when you tell your wild stories when all the time
I'm thinking, God I want you; I want your hands all over
me, and I want to swallow you and keep you deep inside
and all the time I'm listening for a phrase, a few words,
something, some hint of the private language we've shared
in our many beds, thinking, that's Michael, that's my lover,
that's who I love. It'll be hard, I know. But we have to do
it. I have to do it. I can't live this way. I'm not made for
it. Maybe you are.

This all would be easier if we didn't love him.

What he says about the importance of courtesy? It
shames me. He expects so little of me. That's the least I can
give him.

He's a good man and I can't do this to him anymore.

Love,

Julie

Mike remembered that when he first read the letter he wasn't sure
which hurt more: her change, her new loyalty, or her rejection.

And eight months later he got another mailing that was no less shocking. For when he opened this one, Mike knew, even though the question
wasn't answered, the issue was closed. He understood that all the com-
pelling arguments he had offered her in his mind were not valid in the
real world. It was not debatable. All his hopes for a relapse on her part
were nonsense. It was over. And all his trust in their connection was
misplaced. It takes two to love that way. One isn't enough.

And reading the words set in beautiful golden script he had understood
something else. For the first time he understood what he had done to his
brother. Before then he had always justified it as love. Love happened.
Like an accident. You couldn't control it or direct it. Choose it or create
it. Those were the words, weren't they? *Falling in love.* You fell. You fall.
But after the love was severed all that was left was the betrayal. He had

cut off his closest bond on earth. Truly broken the family link. The trust. All that was left was the biggest mistake of his life. And a debt he would owe Danny for the rest of his life.

IT'S A BOY!
DANIEL & JULIE GLYNN
ARE HAPPY TO ANNOUNCE THE ARRIVAL
OF THEIR FIRST CHILD!
SEAN SEBASTIAN GLYNN.
BORN 9/13/91
8 LBS, 5 OUNCES.

Sean's squat little Buddha's face agog at the camera flash. Like he couldn't believe he was here.

*What the Fuck's
a Miracle?*

ind your fucking brother and we'll give you your fucking son."

Joe's words were like a wake-up call to Daniel. He was back on track now.

Shaking and terrified, but back on track. He was on the case and he wouldn't stop. He would find them if it killed him.

He sat down at his desk determined to organize his thoughts. This usually meant making a list. Daniel was an habitual list maker. His desk at the university was covered with yellow stickies. Lists helped supplement his dreadful memory and counterbalance his tendency to drift.

Missing?

Lost?

Hiding?

Secret agent!!??

Ten steps to enlightenment.

Vibrations.

Trash talk shows.

Diary.

Miracles.

He put down the pencil.

He was trying to reconstruct Mike's last visit. Their strange, convoluted conversation. He believed now that Mike had been trying to tell him something critical. But what? What had he said? There was nothing unusual about Mike's visit. It was mostly his typical editorial comment.

"We've become a nation of tattletales," Mike had said, his blond curls trembling as he shook his head. "Tell-all and tell 'em off. Losers spilling their guts in public. For what? For the privilege of being told off by an audience member with microphone access. Yeah—that's freedom of speech. Tell 'em off. Call her a ho. Call him a fool. Roast that dufus! He let Roy bang his best friend's sister while sleeping with their mother."

Daniel laughed. "Maybe it's comforting to know there are people who are more screwed up than you."

His brother smirked. "Nah, it's their five minutes of airtime. Their one shot at immortality. It's like confession without the God stuff."

"Immortality. Huh! That's what bugs me about Christians," Daniel said. "The nonsense. 'Once upon a time there was a man who didn't die. . . .' "

Mike laughed. "Yeah. Easter always gave me the creeps."

"I know. You like Halloween."

"My favorite holiday. Oh. You're remembering—"

"—the way you used to wake me up wearing that bum mask with the drooping eyeball."

Mike beamed. "Scared the shit outta you."

"You were so bad," Daniel said, chuckling.

"One of us had to be."

Daniel shook his head. "We were talking about Easter."

"Why doesn't anyone believe in the second law of thermodynamics anymore? Life is an accident, Danny. Immortality is bunk. We rot, we die, and we disappear."

Daniel smiled.

"Pay attention," Mike continued. "This is important. I can't rewrite that old diary I kept when I was ten and call it a diary anymore. You can't have it both ways. You can't be a parent and a pirate. Life is choices. Sacrifices. Choices have consequences. Consequences are fatal."

"Maybe that's why Christianity is so popular. A whole philosophy based on that ugly idea of sacrifice, and something no one's ever seen . . . a miracle."

Mike said, "What the fuck's a miracle?"

"I'd know one if I saw one," Daniel said.

Mike scoffed. "Miracles are only parts of reality that haven't been explained yet."

"But that's most of it," Daniel said.

Miracles. It was a word from their childhood. The secret promise at the heart of all religion that never came true. It meant saying the rosary on Good Friday with Uncle Louie. Three hours of excruciating silence commemorating Christ's entombment. A holding pattern till the miracle landed. No sweets for forty days of Lent. Fish sticks on Friday. Confession every Saturday—Uncle Louie seemed addicted to it. Kneeling and standing and sitting in church—that Catholic choreography that hadn't struck him as weird until he'd abandoned his faith. And absolutely the worst music in the world. Catholic hymns were a type of aesthetic torture. Caucasian rhythms wedded to arch lyrics that never quite scanned. "PIERCE US WITH THY NUPTIAL BLESSING, HAPPY VIRGIN JESU'S BRIDE! LAZARUS BLESSED BY HIS REDEMPTION, TWICE TO LIVE AND TWICE TO DIE! FLAMES OF HELL WE DO EMBRACE THEE, BURNING ON THE STAKE OF LOVE!"

Oh, the torture.

But chiefly, it meant boredom. That was, Daniel concluded, after a childhood of devotion, the true miracle of Catholicism—that anyone could stand the boredom.

Miracles. That was the last time he saw his brother.

Was it after Julie's funeral? Why couldn't he remember her funeral? It was a foggy gap that filled him with dread, like a rule he had forgotten. An important rule that could save his life: *When you go into a skid, turn in the direction of a skid.* Why couldn't he recall the burial of the most important person in his life? He must have blotted it out. He must have.

There was something about Mike's blue eyes when he mentioned his diary. Some intensity that suggested he was trying to convey more than the words spoken.

"I can't rewrite that old diary I kept when I was ten and call it a diary anymore."

He was saying you can't change the past. But he was also saying there was truth there. A truth he couldn't change as much as he wanted to. What did he mean?

In a chilling moment he remembered that Mike had dropped off a briefcase of his belongings on his last visit. Said he was making a clean sweep. He was going to the jungle to shoot one more fucking Mazda spot, then he was taking some time for himself. He'd been working 200 days a year for the last ten and he had had it—no more. He was thinking about buying some land. Getting out of Hollywood. Doing documentaries. Fuck it.

The yearning behind his eyes, as if Mike needed his approval. That had surprised Daniel.

And then he handed Daniel the old brown briefcase full of "junk." "Pics, birthday cards, memories, my old blue diary. Stuff like that."

Daniel stood straight up and recalled Agent Takahashi's words.

"He has access to some pretty serious codes."

"It wouldn't have to be a big package. . . . a book, maybe? A video-tape?"

The diary. It was in the attic.

Daniel found the briefcase in a dusty corner beside Sean's stash of mint-condition *Star Wars* action figures—unopened and unplayed with. An "investment" whose worth, his son insisted, would accrue exponentially over time and eventually put him through college. As he carried it down the ladder from the attic Daniel remembered the night he was packing for his trip to Nevada. He'd laid his empty suitcase on the floor while he stacked his clothes on the bed and counted his underwear. After a minute he turned to find Sean curled up like a fetus in the open suitcase on the floor. To show that he could fit too.

Daniel unbuckled the briefcase and dumped the contents on his bed. Mementos from Mike's past. Notebooks full of sketches. Some pictures of his ex-wife and stepchild. A small black chess knight. And a blue silk book locked with a tarnished golden buckle. *My Diary* embossed in gold flake on the cover. It smelled old. From another era.

He cracked it open and a dozen black-and-white snapshots fell out. Each dated 9/13/62. They showed a boy in baggy trousers and a T-shirt with horizontal red stripes. He was holding his white cat, Sebastian, then dropping it. Technically it was Mike's cat. He had named it. But he couldn't be bothered with feeding Sebastian or changing his litter box. He left it to Danny, the boy in the picture, who never took his eyes off the camera. Mike was the photographer. He had stolen Uncle Louie's Kodak to determine whether cats always landed on their feet. Mike was really bossy about the whole thing. Danny could never get the timing right. And the photos revealed some of his frustration as his brother directed him. Until they finally settled on a working method. A countdown: "Five, four, three, two, one . . . action!"

For as long as Daniel could remember, his brother had been obsessed with how things worked. This particular experiment was about gravity, which Mike had labeled "nonsensical." Funny how each photograph was a variation on the same action. The white cat, at different levels of descent, tense paws splayed outward, corkscrewing its spine to achieve an equilibrium. The only constant was the way Danny stood, sideways, smiling at the camera, eager for approval, his hands open, his black tennis shoes untied. He noticed how Mike had cleverly composed the shot against the white horizontal slats of their garage, so that the progress of Sebastian's fall could be charted against a frame of reference.

The test, he seemed to recall, was inconclusive. *Gravity may or may not exist.*

Cradling the diary in his hands, Daniel sat down on the bed, ready to crack the code.

He read, "This is my diary and my name is Mike. And if you are reading this Danny I will kill you."

He had to close the blue book and laugh for thirty seconds before he could go on.

Dreamland

Mike was amazed at how lax the security was at the airport. No X-ray belts. No bored guards with their stubby metal-detector Jedi swords. It was like nobody cared anymore. His gun, which lay heavy in his coat pocket, waltzed onto the plane with him. He couldn't wait to see the look on Klinder's face when he pulled it out.

The flight to San Francisco was extraordinary. The airplane food was delicious—even by first class standards. They served him all his favorites: lima beans, breaded veal, garlic-whipped potatoes—and the rolls—Jesus, the rolls were to die for.

Mike had always loved flying. He never turned his cell phone on when he flew. He relished the time-out between places when nobody called, no one could reach you, and nothing happened. It was the landings he hated. That spongy sprong or the rudely clanky touchdown. Then the yawing tip-down until the front wheel bit the runway and took hold. It always made him shudder.

Midway there he needed to stretch his legs so he got up and strolled to the back of the plane. There was a strange little woman in a florid muumuu standing by the lavatory. She smiled at him. Creepy black eyes under thick black bangs. She reminded him of the little chief's stubborn fat wife in the jungle—except he'd never really seen her with her clothes on. There was something comforting about her: a childhood scent of chocolate graham crackers washed down by a cold glass of milk.

He read the door. *Vacant. Occupied.* And an unexpected third option: *Free.*

"Free?" he asked her.

"It's up to you, Tin Man," the small woman answered in a low purr.

Tin man? Hoookay. He turned around and headed back to his seat, thinking: Well, it is a flight from LA.

His seat was remarkably comfortable. It had a massage button. He pressed it and twin serpents coiled and uncoiled under the leather—the best backrub he'd ever had. And he was amazed to find that TV in the armrest played erotica, which he clicked off, embarrassed, when a little girl was escorted by the Hawaiian woman to his row and sat across from him in the aisle seat.

He let out a long breath. For a moment there he thought she was going to choose the empty seat beside him.

Just eight or so. Holding one of those pink toy purses. A golden set of wings pinned to her red blouse. He hoped she wasn't a talker. Kids get talking and they never stop. Still, he felt a pang of sympathy for her traveling all by herself. What kind of parent would leave a little kid like that to fly on her own?

Looking out the window, Mike noted, as he had on previous flights, the old hieroglyphic serrations that marked the desert below—long stretches of plain and valley scored with what could only be human-made residue—roads that went nowhere, geometric blocks and outlines whose purpose was obscure. Failed subdivisions? Or maybe Dreamland. That's what a retired government man had called it on *60 Minutes*. Dreamland: home to top-secret bases, defense engineering research labs, experimental underground facilities. But wouldn't this be restricted airspace?

Through the sparkles of condensation on the glass he saw *a round shadow on the ground: creeping parallel to his plane, a shadow as big as a petroleum tank. Oddly shaped: a dark dot in the hollow of a pale circle.* Peering up as far as he could see, checking the angle of the sun, Mike could find no trace of aircraft or balloon—nothing that could produce this round, fuzzy figure that moved deliberately as a stingray, sliding over the sand, curling over the sage dotted hills, clinging, as only a shadow can, to the surface, adopting the geography into its undulating form.

What, he wondered, had he seen? A cloaked aircraft? Do satellites throw shadows? Surely, they were too high.

"I hate flying," the little girl across the aisle confided in a whisper.

Her fear was so raw Mike wanted to lay a gentle hand on her soft brown hair. "It's okay. We're safe."

The girl inspected him, looking up through her thick glasses. "How old are you?"

"Forty-eight."

She paused for a bit of calculation, then caught him with her wide brown eyes and concluded, "You're half-dead."

He chuckled silently.

"When you're older . . . does time go faster?"

"Much faster."

She nodded. "When you're older . . . are you still afraid of needles?"

"I am," he admitted. "I don't think it's about age." Her questions were starting to make him nervous and he tried with his posture to say: That's enough now.

But she continued to stare at him. And he felt he had to leave her something. "It does get better, you know. Lots of . . . wonderful things happen when you grow up."

"Like what?" she asked.

Boy, that was a tough one. Nothing really came to mind. Everything he could think of was kind of boring. "Swimming," he said finally.

"I can swim," said the girl. "I can hold my breath underwater. I was teaching the baby in the tub."

He swallowed. There had to be something. Would any answer satisfy her? "Cable."

"We got cable," the girl said.

"Love! All right?" he snapped at her. "Love and kissing—oh, never mind." Jesus—kids, he thought. There was no pleasing them.

He covered his eyes with his hand and recalled the impossible questions his stepdaughter had asked him in the hospital. Am I getting better? When am I coming home? How long do I have to stay here? They were breaking up when she got really sick. And for a time it kept him and his wife together. But the worry and the waiting wore them out. After she died they couldn't look at each other without remembering. It was too painful. And years after that Mike would never share an elevator with a child, sit beside one at a restaurant, walk next to one on a sidewalk. He couldn't bear being that close to a child again.

"You mean sex," the girl across the aisle said.

He looked at her.

"That's what Mommy likes," she added with a nod, curling her lips into a comic downward *u* and puffing out her cheeks.

Mike smiled in spite of himself. "She's right."

She looked back at him. "She's dead."

And her face was so unguarded, so open in its sorrow that Mike wanted to excuse himself and exit to another reality. A reality where children didn't have to look like that, didn't have to carry such burdens. "I'm sorry," he said.

The girl twisted her mouth as if she'd just been told to eat her broccoli. "It's not your fault."

He went to sleep with the turbines humming in his ears.

And dreamed a lovely dream.

He met an old girlfriend in the white fallout shelter Uncle Louie had installed in their backyard—their favorite play place. Stinko had given up on it when fallout had been explained to him. There was a submarine hatch above them, a painted white-steel wheel with spokes. Canned goods were shelved from floor to concaved ceiling. A cot curved to conform to one section of the round wall and, under it, a stack of old yellowing newspapers, as if it were necessary to maintain some continuity after history had been wiped out. The shelter was well lit by an unknown source: he expected dangling lightbulbs, but saw none.

In fact, he only had eyes for her. His true love. They embraced as if they hadn't seen each other in years.

Mike realized he was twelve and she was much older. Practically a young woman. It crushed him: this impossible love. Like the day he understood that Haley Mills was a teenager and he was a child. The mixture of grief, relief, and rightness was profound. It was as if his life's purpose had been revealed. Safe within her arms, he had a hazy residue of context—past meetings, chance encounters, letters, afternoons making luxurious, unhurried love on golden sheets. It didn't matter that she was a different woman with a different name each time they met; it was always her. He recalled that obscure Mark Twain story, one of Danny's favorites: "My Platonic Sweetheart." Same story. Then he worried about how he was going to explain to Danny that he couldn't kill him, but that he had to go with this woman. Anywhere she took him. He would never be left behind again.

"Don't worry," his old-new love said. "He'll understand."

Of course he would. Danny was very understanding.

Mike was taken by a sudden fear and held her tighter. He understood that he was dreaming; it was one of those lucid dreams. But this knowledge did not comfort him. If anything it made him feel more powerless. "We have to stay here," he said. "Don't let go. If you let go, I'll know I'm dreaming and none of this is real and I can't let that happen."

She pulled back. It was Pauline, the French translator. The woman who had disappeared. He'd forgotten how beautiful she was. The way she almost smiled at him in the helicopter when he held the chief's hand.

The way she made his simple words music in other tongues. He wanted to pick her little-girl body up and swing her around in circles. He wanted to tell her that he really wasn't an asshole and that he'd been waiting for her all his life. But her face, though sympathetic, was stern as well, as if she were dealing with an impossible demand from a child. "It doesn't work like that, *mon ami.*"

"Please," he said. "We have to stay here."

She let go of him. "No, my sweet, we have to change. One cannot stop." She held up a finger. "The leading cause of hummingbird death is sleep."

"I'm not talking about hummingbirds," he said irritably.

She hugged him gently. "Of course you are, Daniel."

The thought that his true love might have mistaken him for his brother horrified him. "That's not my name!" He pulled back and she had changed. "I will always love you, Daniel," Julie said.

"My name is Mike!"

"And I will always love him too."

The muumuu lady took him by the arm. "Michael Glynn," she explained, "the logic of dreams is impeccable. Do not attempt to correct it."

"She knows everything," his little brother on the cot added. "There's a big word for that."

"Listen to him," the woman he loved said. "He was your brother."

"And she is my wife," said Danny.

The landing in San Francisco jolted him out of the dream. The girl beside him was coloring on the tray table. She looked at him and giggled. "You snore like a bear."

The Whole Schmear

This is my diary and my name is Mike. And if you are reading this Danny I will kill you. I live in the country near Saginaw with my little brother who is a dope. My uncle was a fireman who didn't put out fires. He worked for the C&O railroad which stands for Chesapeake & Ohio. They're the train with the cat on the side. Cats are boring. They call him fireman because he shoveled coal. He doesn't work anymore on trains because there were accidents. And now he sells mail order packages for the seed and flower catalogs which look like Kool-Aid and sound like maracas. Like that cookie lady on TV. Maracas are an instrument of music from Mexico which once grew on trees. Gourds they are called and when the seeds dry up you can stick a stick in them and shake them and they sound just like Ricky Ricardo.

I am advanced for my age but my uncle says not to put that in so ok.

My favorite things are TV, Rock and Roll and Science like how do they make it so when you jump up in a plane you don't fly back and smash your brains out on the back wall?

My mother was an unsuccessful actress but she died.

This is the longest I've ever written.

We surely thank you for your business!

Mike Glynn

ALL THE HOT DOGS IN THE WORLD

The best day of my life was the C & O picnic. It's where everybody who works there brings their family to a park and has a ball! They got gobs and gobs of pop by the gazebo and you can drink all you want totally free! It was so hot the bottles were slippery. This is due to the fact of condensation. I had two colas, blackberry, three orange, and a root beer and it was so hot I never even peed. This was due to the fact of evaporation which means the pop comes out your pores and not your wiener. All around the gazebo they got grills made out of barrels cut in half and all the hot dogs in the world! I had six, and two and a half bags of chips which were no charge too. They had horseshoes for the parents and races for the kids and I won the potato sack race and my prize was an Eliot Ness Machine Gun Squirt Gun that shoots twenty yards! This is due to pressure. Two dads got drunk on Stroh's and got in a fight till their wives came and pointed two fingers with a cigarette in the middle and called them fools. That was cool.

I was kinda woozy at the picnic so I laid down and watched the clouds through the trees. Clouds move faster when you stop and look at them. This is due to the fact of atmospheric winds. You do not fall off the earth because of gravity which Dr. Klinder says is "nonsensical." Anything you can't taste, touch, smell, hear or

see is nonsensical. Ergo gravity is nonsensical.
This happened on the field trip. The day we got invisible.
We surely thank you for your business!
Mike Glynn

LATIN IS THE ROOT OF ALL LANGUAGE

Ergo is a Latin word I learned in Advanced Learning. Latin are
root words. Latin was the language of the Romans who were very
smart even if they did feed us Catholics to the lions. Equis is a
root word. Aqua is a root word. Ergo is not a root word. Ergo is
a word you reason with. Like if I started the picnic with two
quarters in my pocket and Jimmy Schlitbeer didn't believe me and
said can I see them so I give them to him and he runs away then
Jimmy Schlitbeer is Ergo a stinking thief. I was going to tell his
mom but he's in sixth grade and he would pound me.
We surely thank you for your business!
Mike Glynn

FISHING

Saturday Uncle Louie took us FISHING by the stream. I hate
fishing so mostly I teased Danny. He reads in the car all the time.
I don't know how he doesn't puke. Danny likes the books with
the golden rocketship on the side. I think it is stupid. They got
sputniks and mercurys but they'll never put a man on the moon.
We found a garter snake as big as Danny's arm and bashed its
brains out with a rock. We found a sucker. Danny wouldn't touch
it so I put in the rain barrel.
We surely thank you for your business!
Mike Glynn

DR. KLINDER. SMARTEST MAN IN THE WORLD!

I got invited to Dr. Klinder's hotel with another kid from my Advanced Learning class. He picked us special from all the students on the field trip. Uncle Louie dropped me off and made me take a bath before. The room was full of cigarettes and bird books. There was a woman in a white bathrobe. I called her Mrs. Klinder and she smiled and said, No, Honey. I'm just Gale. Gale smells very nice. She said she used to be Dr. Klinder's student too. This was a long time ago ergo she wouldn't be so big like the lady in the calendar. Dr. Klinder taught us chess. Chess is a very long game but very logical. They gave us memory tests. Gale gave us Vernor's ginger ale. Dr. Klinder says I may be the smartest boy in my school but that's between him and me. When he said it my cheeks felt very hot like when you're looking down the toaster till it almost burns your face off. I got sleepy. When Uncle Louie came to pick me up Dr. Klinder gave him a fat envelope.

We surely thank you for your business!

Mike Glynn

THAT'S DEBATABLE

When I told my uncle that Dr. Klinder believes there is life on other planets he said, He's for the birds. I believe this is debatable. If you disagree with someone like when they say Rocky Colavito is a lousy left fielder you can say "That's debatable." This means they are stupid. Debates are arguments only you use reason and wear ties. We are going to study reason next week. Greeks invented it. There were only 10,000 Greeks. They wrote plays and wore towels but they laid the Foundation of Western Civilization. Their slaves did the laundry.

We surely thank you for your business!
Mike Glynn

MY FAVORITE 45s

So my favorites are The Lion Sleeps Tonight, Runaway, and
Traveling Man. I have a photographic memory and I remember all
the songs because the radio I invented is next to the bed. But I
have to listen very hard because if it's too loud Stinko bangs the
wall and says turn that noise down. This is ignorant. Dr. Klinder
says ignorant means you don't know and if you don't know you
shouldn't say.
We surely thank you for your business!
Mike Glynn

WE INVENTED RADIOS

We invented radios in school out of toilet paper rolls which if
you don't believe me read the News because a reporter took our
picture. We took toilet paper rolls from home and Tommy
brought one with all the paper on so our science teacher Mrs.
Brown says: We just need the inside Tommy. Ha! The cool part
was wrapping copper wire around the roll and dipping it in a
Maxwell House can of varnish. The tricky part was welding a
tiny transistor that looked like a nut with some silver paste in the
middle. Then you hook a safety pin needle so when you lean it
on the copper wires you get the music. We surely thank you for
your business!
Mike Glynn

THINGS I FOUND IN UNCLE LOUIE'S WALLET.

A 1909 S BVD Penny only Lincoln has no beard.
A balloon wrapped up like an Alka-Seltzer.
A little green feather.
A C&O employee card.
Seeds.
The corner of an ace of spades.
5 hundred dollar bills. Benjamin Franklin.
A ticket to the world series.
Aloysius' phone number.
A silver tuba.
47 bare naked ladies in Hong Kong.
A time machine.
My mother.
We surely thank you for your business!
Mike Glynn

WHY I LIKE NATIONAL GEOGRAPHIC

Tits.
We surely thank you for your business!
Mike Glynn

IMMEMORIAL

My uncle says I think too much about girls. That's debatable.
First they got boobies and we don't. Second they smell. Third
Roger Troutman says if you put it in their hole you gotta get
married. I don't know. But like Dr. Klinder says: A scientist must
explore all options. Who wants to put it in their hole if that's
where the pee comes out? And how can they pee when they got a
baby stuck there? These are mysteries of time immemorial. That's

what my favorite TV show says but I don't get that word. I asked Danny. He knows the big words. Danny says: I think it means you can't remember. Maybe that is why it is a mystery. Mysteries are not very logical. Logic is where you use your mind until it hurts. Roger Troutman says sex is when you use your wiener until it hurts. These are not good options but I am a scientist.
We surely thank you for your business!
Mike Glynn

STUFFED.

We found a fawn stuffed in a Purina dog chow bag in the ditch by our dirt road. A fawn is a deer before it grows up.
We surely thank you for your business!
Mike Glynn

I DO NOT BELIEVE IN DREAMS

My best friend is Gerry Light only he punched me in the stomach and moved to Detroit which the green signs say is 72 miles away. Lonely is when your best friend is someone you hate. I do not believe in dreams. I believe our minds are making them up. And I don't believe everything my mind says.
We surely thank you for your business!
Mike Glynn

THE WHOLE SCHMEAR.

I am a failure as an altar boy. I hate the dresses. However I like the Latin singing especially the Kirry ay. I'd give it an 80 if it had a beat. Father Otto is a new priest who wears a black dress and is

unhappy. I think there is a connection here. If he wore red like the Bishop who came and slapped those 8th graders on Confirmation day I bet he would be happy. Except the dress part. Father Otto talks a lot about faith, faith, faith. I do not believe people who repeat themselves. I do not believe in faith. I believe in proof. When I turned ten I prayed to see a naked woman. Not the bottom or the top. The whole schmear. God answered! I saw Mrs. McNulty getting bare naked in her bedroom out the back window when it was dark. It looked like an armpit. She is our only neighbor. She plays the piano. The rest is fields. She's always yelling at me and Danny like when we stomped the mole tunnels on her lawn. Uncle Louie says Mrs. McNulty has a bad temperament. She looks pretty good to me though.
We surely thank you for your business!
Mike Glynn

ALL THE DIRTY WORDS I KNOW

Buffalo.

NEEDLES

Uncle Louie says, "Only chickens are scared of needles."

I AM A CHICKEN MY BROTHER IS A RACCOON AND
UNCLE LOUIE IS A RICH SHITHEAD

Any questions?

I HAVE A PHOTOGRAPHIC MEMORY

I will sell it to you for free.

I DO NOT BELIEVE IN GOD ANYMORE

He can kiss my ass.

I WANT TO DIE BUT I DECIDED IT IS NONSENSICAL

That's debatable.

WHO SAYS AMERICA IS GREAT?

Danny says: Just because we won the war and everything doesn't
mean we're so great. We dropped two bombs on Japan. Danny
says.
I say: They were the enemy. What about Pearl Harbor?
He says: We didn't have to drop the other bomb.
I say: One bomb, two bombs, what's the difference? They were
asking for it.
I'm thinking about the boy I met in Buffalo. I don't like thinking
about that so I say if we didn't have the bomb the Commies
would annihilate us. Danny gets mad and says: You don't even
know what that means.
I say: It's from the Latin Root Word Nihil, you dope. Which
means Nothing. Which is exactly what happened to those stinking
Japs.
And which is exactly what your brain is full of. NIHIL!
He's quiet for a long time. And I see the tears.
Kids, he says. Like you and me.
What a crybaby.
Mike Glynn

I THINK ABOUT DYING AGAIN BUT DON'T WORRY

Sister Schaberg says death is an illusion.

Our faith tells us we will live forever in heaven with God and the
angels.

If we are good.

I think that is asking too much.

(There was as line crossed out in blue ink: illegible)

Mike Glynn

DOCTOR KLINDER HAS TO GO

I am sad because Dr. Klinder has to move to California. He rubs
me on the top on the head. He smells like cigarettes. He calls me
brave. He says to remember my promise. I'm good at secrets, I
say. I would never tell. He smiles and gives me a buffalo nickel
and black knight chess piece and says: Acceptance is the key to
survival.

I don't want to survive if Dr. Klinder is gone. I say I will
remember him forever and asked him to sign my diary on the
next page.

Joel A. Klinder, Ph.D., to my favorite student Mike, 8/15/62

WHO MADE THE DAMN WORLD?

God made the damn world.

Why did he make it?

So we could be happy.

What is happiness?

Knowing God's Will and doing it.

What is God's will?

That we love him with our whole heart and our whole soul, obey the church law and love our neighbor as our self.

Does that include my little brother?

Yes.

Even when he is being a stupid jerk?

Yes.

Even when he reads all night with the lamp on in the down bunk?

Yes.

Does God want me to be happy?

Yes.

Then why did he make Dr. Klinder go away and why doesn't he kill my little brother?

We surely thank you for your business.

Mike Glynn

Stay Off the Wings

The diary stopped there.

August 30, 1962.

Daniel smiled, remembering. The diary had given him a clear picture of the boy inside the man Mike would become. He was still there: scowling, wild, disarming everyone with his winning smile. Drawing people into his orbit of influence—followers he accrued as naturally as a star gathers paparazzi. Bossy, yes, but the kind of kid who exuded personality and made everyone around him appear half-baked, lesser somehow, dull foot soldiers eager to be led into battle, take his orders, join in his pranks and schemes, bask in his approval. Life was more exciting around Mike. And he was always saying he was going to kill him. Of course he didn't mean it.

Still, he was back where he had started. As far as Daniel could tell, there were no codes. The diary was clueless. What had he expected?

He'd expected fiction. Something he could interpret. That was his job, after all: Dredging up the subtext that the clever author had left like a map to a buried treasure. But this was a diary. This was life. People were always confusing life and books. If a book was deemed life, it was valid, valuable. The question journalists always asked authors: "Is this autobiographical?" Just once he'd like to hear some writer say: "No. None of it's true. I made it all up." But once a book forfeited its face as fiction, it lost the power of gossip. Life is boring, he thought. Give me fiction.

"Codes!" he said disgusted, and threw his brother's diary across the room.

Then he recalled the only line in the diary that had been struck out. He retrieved it and reread the pencil-scrawled journal of a ten-year-old boy until his eyes fell upon a line that had been thoroughly crossed over by a blue fountain pen. Daniel turned the page to look at it from the other side. Still illegible. Then he held it up to the light to make out Mike's words under the ink. They glowed like a silver rope against a hedge of blue. They were backward. And it took him a moment to translate what he was reading.

"If god loves us so much we don't die Dr. Klinder then why would he let you do that to us?"

Then Daniel turned the page and saw the signature and tribute. The one line written by an adult. The handwriting slanted extremely to the left. Written with a blue fountain pen.

Joel A. Klinder, Ph.D., to my favorite student Mike, 8/15/62

Everything else in the diary was written with a pencil. Except those lines.

Klinder.

Klinder had crossed that line out.

Why? Why had he crossed it out?

What was he hiding? What had he done?

He paged back through the diary, faster and faster until it was confirmed. The man's name must have appeared at least a dozen times.

He was the most important character in the text.

Maybe that's what Mike was trying to tell him.

Maybe Klinder knew where Mike was.

It was pure intuition but it rang like a gong in his mind: find Klinder. Find a man who'd taught grade school in Saginaw in 1962. How hard could it be?

It took him ten minutes on his computer to search and find Dr. Joel A. Klinder. Professor of psychology at Berkeley. He printed out the number and address and packed and in two hours he was on a plane to San Francisco.

The nose tipped skyward and the jet sprang off its wheels. Daniel had never seen Metro Airport so empty before. And his flight had so few passengers that they declared open seating. Strange for a prime-time flight. Where'd everybody go?

"You grunted," said the young man in the seat beside him. Rough beard. Short, greasy bangs. He smiled. "Scared?"

"I hate takeoffs," Daniel said.

"Sweaty palms? Butterflies?"

He nodded. It felt like the plane was never going to achieve the air. And when it did, it was like a vortex sucking him up, wrenching him away from his home, his life, everything comfortable. "Doesn't it bother you?"

"Dude, I am *so* not scared. I got a system." The young man bent closer and whispered, "My uncle's a pilot? I call him before every flight. I tell him the make and he tells me the safest seat. This is a seven sixty-seven. Nothing in the rear. Stay off the wings. They tear out on impact and take the windows with 'em. First thirteen rows is your safest bet. Aisle seat." He patted the armrests.

"Aisle seat," Daniel said.

"Right. Imagine trying to climb over a couple of hysterical passengers with sprained wrists in a cabin filled with smoke."

"But *I* got the aisle seat," said Daniel, looking around at all the empty seats.

The young man smiled painfully. "Late booking." He did something with his hands, as if he were trying to conjure up an argument. "See, airplanes are like living. We know we're going to crash—we just don't know when. We don't think about it. Dude, if we thought about it? We'd go crazy."

Daniel thought about it. He looked at the *No Step* on the wings.

The young man said, "They say it happens mostly on takeoffs and landings."

Someone behind them pressed the steward button. There was a loud *ding*.

"Landings never bothered me," Daniel admitted.

Later the pilot came on and in a thick Spanish accent said that they were ahead of schedule due to prevailing winds.

"Damn," said the man.

"What?"

"That's another thing."

"What?"

"My uncle says never fly with a pilot whose first language isn't English. Universal language of air traffic. And the best flight schools."

Daniel saw the arm of a passenger ahead of them press the steward button. There was a loud *ding*.

"So. I'm a student. What are you?"

"Government work."

The young man looked at him.

"I'm a teacher," Daniel said.

"You teach government?"

"No. English. But right now I've got a consulting project for the CIA." Daniel enjoyed saying this; it gave him focus.

"Really. Cool. But, dude—isn't that, like, secret or something?"

"Yes."

"So why you telling me?"

"I have questionable judgement."

The young man laughed. "So if I told anyone, I'd be blowing your cover?"

Daniel smiled. "And I'd have to kill you."

The young man raised his eyebrows and laughed again. For a second, Daniel thought he was looking at himself in the mirror. Then Daniel laughed at the idea of him killing anybody.

The plane bucked and the air made pockets and Daniel grunted again.

"Doppler is an inexact science," said the young man.

Someone else pressed their steward button. There was a loud *ding*.

They ate. They flew. They slept.

Daniel dreamed.

He was living in Venice, reading an Italian paper in his white robe, scanning the personals for the ransom instructions. They lived in a beautiful marble house with paneless windows, ancient coiling columns that opened onto balconies, walls covered with old maroon and golden tapestries. A perfect pink sunset over the brown canal two stories below. The water smelled of cork and sewage and chocolate graham crackers. It was the most beautiful house Daniel had ever lived in. This saddened him. Because he realized he'd have to sell his home in order to pay the ransom and rescue the boy.

Daniel heard a fluttering noise.

A flit of rainbow arched out of the dark mouth of the large marble fireplace and disappeared over the balcony. A hummingbird. Daniel had read somewhere that a bird in the chimney meant someone was going to expire. He wanted no bird in their house.

Hey, I'm dreaming, he thought. One of those lucid dreams. That means I can do anything. I'm free.

He could hear the docked gondolas beating together, hull to hull, like lovers. Daniel strolled to the warm balcony and looked down. On one of the rocking vessels he saw a strange gondolier standing in the bow. A small, round woman holding an enormous wooden pole. She wore a brightly colored Hawaiian housedress—he forgot what they were called. She had a strange teardrop tattoo between her black eyes—like the ones

Mike had seen in Morocco. And her posture was somewhat comical—a Buster Keaton burlesque of balance—the way she grappled the long pole horizontal, like a runt Wallenda. She looked up at him under the thick black bangs of her Prince Valiant hair. Her face was ruddy and cheerful, amused and slightly embarrassed by her predicament.

He wanted to encourage her, give her advice. But he realized he knew nothing about the matter. This did not stop him. Like men who are asked directions and feel compelled to adopt an expertise they do not have. "I would get in the middle of the boat if I were you."

"You are me," she said.

In the logic scheme of the dream this made perfect sense to Daniel. Apparently she had no existence without him. Well, it was *his* dream. "I know you," he said. "Why don't I remember your name?"

"I have a lot of them," said the boat woman. "No one remembers them all."

Suddenly the balcony's graying white marble was cool on his palms. Daniel was overcome by a wracking grief, or rather, a gathering of griefs that smothered him so totally he felt as though he had been jamming them like towels into a linen closet for years, bracing shut the doors until, finally, they had all burst out together. He cried. And he cried. It felt like he hadn't cried for ages. But if you had asked him what he was crying about, Daniel couldn't have answered. And he wondered if such dream tears counted in the waking, or if the whole painful process would have to be endured again.

That's when Daniel woke up, his eyes streaming with real tears.

The engines were humming. The young man beside him was asleep—his headphones blaring something by the Doors.

Hummingbirds and Venice. The small, round boatwoman with many names. What good were dreams if they only made him sad?

When the jet landed in San Francisco a crowd of tourists up front applauded.

His aislemate leaned over as he made ready to go and, smiling, said, "Germans, dude. They always do that."

Somebody Else's Sun

Nothing could have prepared Mike for the shock of seeing what thirty-eight years had done to his favorite grade-school teacher. Dr. Klinder had turned into a fat, white Michael Jordan.

A large, bald, fussy old geezer who wore a strange brown sweat suit that seemed to be made out of paper, holding up one fat finger and talking in a soothing voice. "One second. Let me clear a place for you." The old man scooped a pile of paper off a blue chair opposite his pale wood desk, then sat down heavily in a swivel chair to face Mike.

His office was mesmerizing. Like a furniture store display: dust-free, exquisitely artificial. The walls were full of mementos and his desk was laden with golden picture frames; each held a different type of humming-bird. The only evidence that a real human being used this imaginary space was the crystal ashtray full of butts.

"So." Humor sparkled in Klinder's eyes. "My favorite student. You're looking great!"

"I'm all right."

"And you say you're searching for someone?"

"My brother."

"How can I help?" He folded his hands together.

"I was hoping you might be able to tell me where he is."

Klinder's eyebrows rose. "Me? Hell, Mike, I've never even met the man."

It was obvious to Mike that he was lying. He couldn't say why. He felt it. "Doctor? Can we please cut the crap? I want to know where Danny is."

The doctor lit a cigarette with a Zippo, took a long drag, and blew the smoke in Mike's direction. A challenge? "*Daniel?* Is that his name?"

Mike showed him the gun and the doctor's body language changed.

"Goodness! What do you intend to do? Pistol-whip me?" He was leaving Mike the option that all this might be a bad joke.

Mike pointed the gun at the doctor's computer. And fired one shot. Klinder jerked back in his chair as the bullet shattered the monitor, sent glass shards onto his perfect desk. A small puff of smoke drifted upward and random sparks danced inside the dark orifice.

"Christ!" The doctor looked like he had just witnessed the death of his best friend. "Are you out of your mind?"

"Yes. Let's say that. Let's say I'm a desperate, crazed man." He pointed the barrel toward the doctor's ample stomach.

Klinder held out both his hands. "Don't!"

Mike had his full attention now. "Where's my brother?"

The doctor wiped his mouth with one hand. "Would you believe me if I said I didn't know?"

"I might."

"I swear to you—I don't know."

"Okay," said Mike. Then he fired one bullet into his perfect crystal desk clock. It shattered and bounced onto the floor.

"Someone will hear!"

"I don't care." Mike pointed the gun at the doctor's stomach again. "Tell me what you know."

"I will, I will," the doctor said. "Just—please. Put down the gun."

"No. Where's my brother?"

"Please. I honestly don't know."

"That's not what I want to hear," said Mike, drawing a bead between the doctor's eyes.

Klinder held up a fat finger, squinched his eyes and said, "He's near."

Everything changed. It was like the perfect shot: The happy accident of prep and nature and you're looking through the lens and you can't fucking believe how beautiful it is.

I gotcha, Danny, he thought. You're safe now. Nobody's killing anybody. We're going home.

"Please." The doctor chanced opening one eye. "He just got here. I'll tell you everything I know. But—I warn you—you may not believe me."

Mike said nothing. He was enjoying this.

The doctor sighed and collapsed into the squeaky swivel chair. He looked like a condemned man who had nothing to lose. Then he laughed darkly and stubbed out his cigarette. "It's a long story, but you're not going anywhere." This pissed Mike off slightly, and he toyed with the idea of plugging Klinder's diploma on the wall. But then the cornered man proceeded to tell him the most preposterous story he had ever heard, and he lowered his gun.

"The first law of thermodynamics is that matter and energy can neither be created nor destroyed—only changed. The second law is entropy: things run down. Do you see? They contradict each other. The first claims immortality; the second death. Which is true? For they both can't be."

"This is all very interesting, doc . . ."

"Wait. Let me tell you a story. Life, when you chunk it down, is simply patterns. Repeating subsystems. Heartbeat. Digestion. Thought. Memory. Sex. Complex patterns that have evolved."

"My brother?"

Dr. Klinder held up a meaty index. "Trust me. It doesn't make sense without the preamble."

After a few seconds Mike sighed through his nose and nodded for him to continue.

"Patterns. Imagine if someone discovered a way to duplicate those human patterns and store them in a another medium."

"Like . . . cloning?"

"That just copies the body. I'm talking about the whole schmear. Body, mind, soul, spirit."

"If you're getting mystical on me, I'm gonna get pissed."

"*Mystical* isn't the right word. *Magical* is closer. *Miracle* would be our best equivalent. It's about reality. Imagine . . . if you could copy reality. Like a hard-drive copy of analog tape. One is a pattern of magnetized metal particles on plastic tape. One is binary code: zeroes and ones. Same data. Same pattern. Different mediums. Now think about memory. Specifically, the memory of a song. That's a whole different medium, isn't it?"

Mike nodded. This better be leading somewhere.

"But how can sound—vibration patterns of air—be transformed into the mind? That's thrice removed from reality, you might say. The song sung. The analog dub of the song. The binary remaster of the song. The memory of the song imprinted on the neurons of the brain." Klinder paused, then continued. "What happened was this. The aliens—"

"—hold it," Mike said, lifting up his gun.

The doctor stopped mid-sentence, his mouth open, his eyes focused on the barrel.

"Aliens," Mike said. He tapped his fingers on the arm of his chair. He thought: Secret agents. Kidnapping. Black helicopters.

Okay, then—aliens.

But part of him was disappointed. Why did it have to be something so . . . dumb? It was like half the fucking scripts he'd read. Written by some twenty-five-year-old wannabe who'd never read a book in his life. Who grew up watching TV and regurgitated the plots of old sci-fi sitcoms that were done better forty years ago. He sighed. The doctor watched him. He wasn't sure he wanted to hear the rest. Klinder could quite simply be any one of the kooks who claimed the privilege of extraterrestrial in-knowledge. If my life were a movie, Mike thought, this is where I'd walk out.

"Aliens?" he asked.

The doctor shrugged sheepishly. "I know. Believe me, I know."

"Spaceships? Invasions?"

"Hey, it's not *that* weird. The Apollo mission."

After a moment Mike said, "Your point is?"

"We invaded the moon in a spaceship in 1969. We were aliens to everything there."

Mike frowned, turned his head to the side, then looked at the doctor under his brows, blinked two times, then looked at the floor. He'd never thought of it that way.

"So . . ." Klinder checked if it was okay for him to go on. Mike nodded wearily. "The aliens found a way to copy reality. The whole schmear. The human experience of being alive. They dubbed it. And stored it. And created a collection of patterns maintained by a self-running program and evolving through internal feedback. In short, a different reality constructed in a neural network."

After a moment, Mike asked, "What was the storage medium?"

"Hummingbirds."

"Oh, fuck!" Mike said, disgusted.

Now Klinder switched into the high enthusiasm of a true birder. "Birds are the most successful terrestrial vertebrate. There are three hundred billion of them—nine thousand living species of birds, compared to forty-one hundred species of mammals. How come nobody ever told us? Birds own the earth. *We're* the minority. What makes us think the aliens would come to us first?"

Of all the absurd things Klinder had said so far, this was the weirdest. And, strangely, it made the most sense to Mike. If there was an invasion why would they come to humans first?

"Hummingbirds are like their Olympic champions. They can do it all: hover, fly upside down, backwards. Their brains are amazing. The perfect medium for a virtual reality."

Mike almost laughed. He'd heard of bird-brained ideas before but— fuck. "That's where we are?"

"Yes."

"A neural network?" He looked around the office. "That's what this is?"

"Yes."

"I'm a copy?"

The doctor smiled. "Well, actually, you're dead."

Mike coughed a laugh. "I'm dead?"

Klinder blinked twice when Mike said the word. "Yes . . . yes. Sorry to be the one to break the news." But Klinder didn't look sorry at all. He looked like a magician about to spring a card on him.

Mike decided to humor him. "Okay. Where's my body?"

"Probably where you died. Or buried by now."

"Doc?" Mike objected. "This doesn't feel virtual. *I* don't feel virtual. Wouldn't the dub know it was virtual?"

The doctor shook his head. "Does the dreamer know he's dreaming? There are the occasional anomalies—sometimes the feedback will create dissonances, glitches. Grass might turn momentarily blue. Seen anything strange lately?"

"I saw a bear," he admitted reluctantly. "Walking down the street one night."

"There you go," said Klinder. "It takes them a while to get the program up to speed. But, luckily, there are continuity reflexes in the brain: Aeons of evolution have taught us to ignore our blind spots, to create necessary illusions, to guess what we can't know, to bind loose ends together and create coherence. The mind thrives on excuses. Have you had any memory lapses recently?"

How would Klinder know about that? He recalled flying back from the jungle. Struggling to pull the last day into focus. Feeling like he was forgetting something important. "Yes," he said, beginning to feel a bit uncomfortable. "Right after I got back from the jungle."

"Do you remember a fog?"

In the chopper with the chief and the translator. They had flown through a bank of fog above the jungle. "Too much! Wait!" she had said. "Yes. There was a fog."

"That's them. That's when they saved you. And that's probably where you bought it."

"Doc, I don't remember dying."

"That might be a good thing, you know. And it's usually harder your first time. Took me weeks to remember my first death."

His first death, Mike thought.

"Amnesia is not uncommon among accident victims. Meanwhile, the hummingbirds are working overtime to help you adapt to your new world. Life goes on but sometimes there are . . . gaps. Unexplainable gaps. And there are several stages of transition. Like grief, denial, delusion . . ."

"Come on! Nobody's that gullible," Mike insisted. "Somebody must be able to tell the difference between here and there."

"There's really only one big difference, Mike. Death. The aliens don't believe in entropy. They've mastered it. In fact, it's an obscenity to them."

The light was coming through the windows golden and Klinder looked much like he did on that field trip thirty-five years ago. He'd lost his head of black hair. He was a lot fatter and he had jowls. Wore weird paper pajamas. But there across the room from him was the same man. The same gleeful, slightly crazy man who had showed them a glass display case of tiny stuffed birds. Their claws tied together with wire, and under each a label neatly typed: *Chickadee. Wren. Sparrow. Swallow.* He had brought along a big red parrot with a white splotch on his crown who, perched on a wooden cross, would repeat everything Klinder said: the perfect pupil.

Klinder. The man he had loved more than anyone, though he'd only met him twice.

The man who hypnotized his whole fourth grade class into believing they were invisible. Leading them in a chorus countdown in the Saginaw Museum's science wing.

"Five! Four! Three! Two! One!"

And suddenly the beautiful feeling of being safe. Truly safe. Nobody watching. Nobody seeing. His science teacher Mrs. Brown and the field trip chaperons, lined up by the frosted glass door. Their eyes closed, their smiles benevolent. All his classmates quiet and crowded together, smiling guilty smiles.

Mrs. Brown slowly licking her lips, remembering a private pleasure.

One boy touching himself through his corduroys.

One girl reaching out and holding the hand of the boy in front of her.

Mike looking at Peggy Stack's red pigtails. Finally free to stare without shyness at his secret crush: her freckled face and blue eyes. Mike smelling Peggy's scent: peaches. Dr. Klinder speaking, and though he stood across the room, it felt like he was whispering in his ear. "You look like you want to kiss her, Mike. Go ahead."

Mike hesitating.

"Go on. She can't see you."

And Mike leaning down and tilting his head toward the little girl in pigtails.

Contact: the electric warm smoothness of her lips.

His open eyes taking in the white down on her freckled cheek.

The tip of her tongue gently parting his teeth.

His first kiss.

Klinder's red parrot giving a wolf whistle that echoed off the high ceiling of the science wing.

And the huge tear trickling down her face, interrupting the kiss.

Her sad eyes and her one word. "Daddy?"

Mike looking puzzled at Dr. Klinder standing proudly with his arms folded before his case of dead birds. "It's all right, Mike. It's perfectly fine. She won't remember anything. Neither will you."

But he did. He remembered everything.

Klinder. The man who left Mike with the worst memory of his life: Buffalo. The word that froze his blood whenever his mind allowed it in.

Don't trust this man, he thought. Don't make that mistake again.

Apparently, Klinder didn't notice the change in Mike. "It's a great gift they've given us, Mike. All we have to do it accept it."

"You know, I'm really bored with your bullshit. I think I might just kill you."

"You can't kill me, son. I'm already dead. I died in a plane crash nine years ago. And I've been killed several times since."

Mike laughed. "Then why are you so afraid of this gun?"

"The pain," he said. "They got pain here. And joy. And pleasure. And everything. Everything but death. You hungry?" the doctor asked. "The Chinese stuff here is amazing. It's as good as you can imagine." He smiled and added, "Your brother is safe, Mike."

He better be, he thought.

"He's at the compound. That's our nerve center. It's not far. I'll drive you. But first..." Dr. Klinder leaned over and opened the top drawer of his desk. He reached in and pulled out a fist. He held it open for Mike to see the sleeping hummingbird.

"What's that?" Mike asked, remembering the tiny chief.

Klinder smiled. "That's me."

And for the first time, Mike had an inkling of the strangeness, the futile pressing of human thought against the barrier of something truly other. *A mind born under somebody else's sun.*

The Twelfth Step

D r. Klinder was delighted to see the brother of his long-lost student. He had often wondered whatever happened to that bright boy, Mike.

"I'm looking for him, actually," Daniel said.

"Me too!" said Klinder. Then he lifted one fat finger as if he'd just had a great idea. "Hey! Maybe we can pool our resources!"

Was Daniel hungry? They could have lunch at the compound if he wanted. It wasn't far. He looked sleepy. Was he sleepy? It was all right. He must be jet-lagged. His eyelids could barely hold themselves up. It was all right. It was such a long flight. And nobody could blame him if he wanted to lie down right here in the office and take a short nap.

What a polite man, Daniel thought. He was nothing like he had expected. A fat, bald man in paper pajamas with a soothing voice and a mesmerizing smile.

Klinder drove like a madman in his green Beetle from his offices to the university. Two tires bit air on every corner. Good thing there was hardly any traffic. Where were all the students? Daniel wondered. Was everybody on winter break?

The "compound" turned out to be a modern wing of Berkeley University, which overlooked a blue San Francisco Bay. It seemed to be a bunker of sorts. Several security stations. Armed guards. Thumb-print IDs.

"Stupid government regs," Klinder said, chuckling. "The price we pay for being on their research payroll. It's a miracle anything gets done."

After they issued Daniel a visitor's badge, Klinder said, "You've got to go through the process. Shouldn't take long."

An elevator door hissed open, revealing mirrored walls and two burly men in lab coats.

"I'll meet you on the bottom, okay?"

"The bottom?" Daniel asked.

"Don't let him out of your sight," Klinder barked at the lab men. With a jolly wave, he disappeared around a corner. From then on Daniel was never without an escort.

Twelve buttons on the elevator identified the possible destinations. One red button marked with a white X. A tall man got on, his hand stuffed in the pocket of his black suit coat.

"What's going on?" Daniel asked.

Agent Takahashi smiled white under his dark sunglasses. "You cracked it, didn't you?"

"What?" Daniel asked, totally confused.

The elevator doors hissed closed.

Their descent between floors seemed to go on forever. Daniel sensed that they were deep underground. About halfway down, he turned to the large man behind him. "I've done nothing wrong."

He turned to the other man. "I don't know anything."

He turned to the agent. "Please," he said.

The man looked down at him. He removed his hand from his suit pocket and pressed the red button. The elevator stopped.

Takahashi took off his glasses. Daniel was surprised to see the fear in his eyes. "Okay. Listen, Mr. Glynn." When his name was spoken, Daniel saw something in the mirrors: the two big men in lab coats became very still. "We're not gonna hurt you, so relax. You pass security and you can see your son."

The world was a beautiful place again. Julie, he thought. I've got him! I'm getting him! Everything's going to be just fine.

Agent Takahashi pressed the button and their descent resumed. "And I'm sorry about that shit I told you about your brother."

"What?"

"That he was a government agent."

I knew it! Daniel thought. This was getting better and better.

"Normally, I don't lie but . . . Klinder's orders."

Daniel shrugged. "Everybody lies." Benevolence cascaded over him like a warm waterfall. "Don't sweat it."

"Hip," said one of the men behind him with a smirk.

"Hip," replied the other.

"Shut up," said Agent Takahashi. "He's not the only one."

Daniel couldn't have cared less what codes they were talking in. He only had to wait now.

He was led through a series of rooms.

In a circular room with tinfoil walls he was told to strip and given a type of fencing mask to wear. Then he stood on a red X in the middle of the floor. There was a flash of light that make him squinch his eyes, followed immediately by another flash of light and heat. When he opened his eyes and removed his mask, Daniel smelled the sick scent of burnt hair and saw the wisps of smoke curling off his arms. He was covered in ash.

Outside his escorts assured him that his epidermal hair had been singed off. "The body's a filthy thing," said one of the men. They never gave him back his clothes.

He was led naked to a small shower where he used a type of blue soap that made his whole body tingle. The whole floor of the cubicle was a drain: a steel grate. When the water turned off overhead blowers turned on and dried him. Afterward he smelled of incense. He was given paper pajamas and booties. They were brown like seared marshmallows.

I'm coming, sport! he thought joyfully as he dressed. I'm coming!

A dark room made of glass. He stood on a round platform and spun like a ballerina in a music box.

"Lift one leg," a voice said from a hidden speaker.

"Which one?" he asked.

"Lift one leg," the voice repeated in the exact same tone, so that he understood it was a digital message that would loop until he obeyed. He obeyed.

"Walk backward until you touch the wall." He did. "Spread your arms." He did. "Flap your arms." He did. "Faster . . . faster . . ."

Daniel flapped until he felt a trickle of sweat run down his ribs. He laughed, thinking, I'm coming, Sean! I'm flying!

The ceiling flickered on above him. The door opened and his escorts waved him out. Agent Takahashi met them in the hall. They all wore brown pajamas. It was like a slumber party for adults.

"I want to see my son," he said.

"Patience," the agent said. "It takes a tough man to make a tender chicken."

Daniel thought about that till he was led to a green room with a gray Formica table. Three men with pens and notepads. In brown pajamas. Daniel looked at them and immediately thought: scholars.

"Where's my son?" he asked.

"Soon," Agent Takahashi assured him.

One of the professors—and this gesture made Daniel realize he was their leader—laid a handwritten letter on the gray table. Written with a blue fountain pen. They watched Daniel read silently.

The Wing Man was bathing in a spring. And there he was visited by a strange bird. And the bird spoke with a forked tongue with many voices that only the Wing Man could understand. And the disciples watched as the bird floated before his face like a petal in the wind. And when he was done the bird flew away and he explained. He said the bird's name was "Puffleg." He had foretold the coming end and how all would be made new. But his disciples did not understand. And the Wing Man said: "The Father's Plan is a mystery to all his sons. And not all endings are the same. Blessed is he who knows the impossible bird and hears what is missing."

Not a translation, Daniel thought. It sounds like a modern imitation of one of the gospels.

"What do you think, professor?" the leader said. "Authentic?"

"I have no idea," Daniel said. "The last lines sound like one of the Apocryphal gospels. Thomas? The rest seems like a pastiche to me, but I'm no theologian. Or Biblical scholar."

The men exchanged glances.

"Professor, if you were to analyze a text rumored to be from the hand of a famous author—a newly discovered manuscript, mind you—what would you look for to authenticate it?"

"Who?" he asked and they looked at each other.

"Well," the tall man said, "Suppose that was the question? 'Who's the author?'" The others nodded.

"First, I'd want to know the source of the rumor. Then physical stuff: circumstances of the find, carbon dating if possible, handwriting analysis. I'd read it once for historical context, look for naive mistakes. Then I'd read for themes and style and quirks and voice. Compare it to his accepted work. Textual motifs. That sort of thing.... can I see it?"

They didn't answer.

"Do you have the text?" he asked.

"Assume it's totally convincing and you could prove it. What would you do?"

"Do? I'd publish an article. Give it to a library."

"Suppose it was . . . scandalous? Reflected badly on the character of the author?"

"I don't follow you."

"What if you found something that undermined the divinity of Christ?"

Another man added, "An original manuscript, predating the Sea Scrolls."

For some reason, everyone in the room started to giggle, as if the man had cracked a joke. Hands covered mouths. Men looked away.

Daniel raised his eyebrows. "What's so funny?"

"Sorry," the man said, collecting himself. "I mean, suppose it was one of the original drafts of a gospel. What if it revealed private things about its author and his subject that had far-reaching consequences? Shocking implications," the man said, mysteriously. "Something that might nip Christianity in the bud."

No, not scholars, Daniel thought: priests. He shrugged. "I'd publish my findings."

This seemed to upset one man. "Even if that meant he'd be targeted for unjust retribution?" he asked vehemently. "Even if it meant a stellar reputation and career would be ruined?"

Another man added, "And his enemies could use it as propaganda!"

"Like a what?" Daniel asked. "A diary or something?"

Nobody in the room moved.

"So this author is still alive?" Daniel asked.

Nobody answered.

"There might be libel issues. Depends." Daniel shrugged. "But if it was a matter of honoring history, and ethical scholarship, I'd tell the truth, of course." He turned to the leader. "Where's my son?"

He was led quickly away and escorted down a long, white hall by a man with three gold stripes on his bicep.

"Where's Klinder?" Daniel asked.

The man looked at him. "You know him?"

"I just met him."

"I've worked here eight years and I've only heard of him. You're a lucky man."

"Why?"

"He's the Wing Man. The one that made contact with our friends."

"Friends?"

"The birds. Mister—where have you been? The world ended ten years ago." Then the sergeant leaned in close and whispered, "Who won the Stanley Cup in 1993?"

Daniel looked at him.

"I don't get out much," the man whispered sheepishly.

Daniel thought: Red Wings. Avalanche. Sabres. He could never keep the names straight. "Sorry, I don't follow hockey."

The sergeant looked like a child who had just been told he wasn't going to get his favorite toy for Christmas. After a reflexive sympathy, Daniel felt suddenly annoyed. Why do people constantly confide in me? Dump their trust on me? Is it something in my face? I wish they'd tell someone else their problems.

They went down an endless, arching hallway, like a particle accelerator. Every thirty yards there was a laser beam of blue light at ankle height. How stupid: anyone could jump over it. Daniel jumped over one and there was a deafening alarm. The sergeant smiled. "Took you long enough. Most people get it after the first hundred yards or so." Then he smacked his hand against an intercom on the wall, whispered a word, and the alarm stopped.

Daniel held up a hand and said, "Hold it. Just hold it. I demand to see my son!"

"It's the process, all right?" the sergeant said. "I didn't write it. I just follow it."

Finally Daniel was led into a dark room with a wall of glass. There was a party of sorts on the other side of the glass. Cocktail chatter and people laughing. A shadow approached him out of the darkness: Takahashi. "We got your profile now. Moral leanings. Psych. Health. Reflexes.

We even got your DNA. Took a blood sample," he said, holding back a laugh.

"Why didn't you tell me it was a test?"

"It wouldn't have worked then."

"Where's my son?"

"Shhhh," the agent said. "This'll all be over soon."

Daniel ground his teeth and turned his attention to the people in the room behind the mirror. It could have been any number of parties. The dean's yearly bash—bad wine in clear plastic cups. Or a good-riddance party—everyone cheerfully wishing bon voyage to a man they never really liked much. The only thing missing was the only thing that had made these parties bearable: Julie.

"They can't see us?" Daniel asked.

"No," said Takahashi. "Two-way mirror."

"Then why is that woman staring at me?"

The agent turned to look and Daniel was going to point her out but apparently she had left. The tiny woman with shiny black eyes who wore a Hawaiian dress. She had smiled at him as if she were in on the joke.

"What woman?"

"She's gone," Daniel said.

"Glitch," Takahashi said with a smirk. "The relentless pursuit of perfection."

Someone was talking behind the mirror. "That's the tragedy of my life. I will die a man who will never dunk."

Laughter spiked and buzzed on the speaker system in the watching room. A child's giggle rang high and sweet above the chuckling adults. Daniel looked for the child behind the glass, but his view was blocked by the men and women.

"I'm dying for a cigarette," someone said.

More laughter. Where was the child?

A woman's voice: " 'Dying' is the operative word."

Giggles everywhere.

Daniel turned to Takahashi beside him and asked, "What's going on here?"

"R and R. They just got back from a mission. Bagged a few Correctors and they're celebrating their first kills," Takahashi said. "They're letting off a little steam."

"They're using the *D* word," a child's voice explained from behind him.

For some reason, Daniel was afraid to turn around. A tiny, cold hand gripped his. "It's okay. Really. It's okay."

Daniel turned to his son. He looked comfortable in his paper pajamas.

Sean said, "What took you so long?"

"Sean?" Daniel held the boy's face in his hands. "Is it really you?"

"It's me."

Sean's face looked strange. It glowed as if someone had lit a lightbulb behind his eyes. And there were bruises all around them.

"What happened to your eyes, sport?" Daniel asked. "Did you fall down?"

Sean looked up at Agent Takahashi, then nodded sadly.

He hugged the boy for the longest time, thinking: it worked. He had searched for Mike and found his son. The thriller was over. He had won. Life made sense again. Then, braced by the waves of impossible joy that engulfed him, Daniel confessed his second deepest fear. "I thought I'd never seen you again." Then his first. "I thought, I thought . . ."

Takahashi said, "You thought he was dead?"

"Yes," said Daniel, the word spilling out in a sigh.

"I am. It's okay. We all are."

The Correctors

"Where is everybody?" Mike asked, struck by the emptiness again. Where were the car pools? The lawn men? The shoppers? The kids?

Klinder shrugged. "Ten years of dead people don't take up much space. Do the math."

He wasn't about to do the math. His mind got tired just thinking about it. Klinder was driving Mike to the compound, the doctor smoking like a fiend behind the wheel of his green Beetle. The only thing making it bearable was the mint-green deodorizer in the shape of a hummingbird hanging from the rearview mirror.

Finally, he saw a pedestrian. A homeless woman pushing a shopping cart full of returnable cans. She wore the strangest multicolored muumuu and her puckered lips suggested whistling even though he couldn't hear her. They watched each other as they passed. Her eyes: shiny, black. And

Mike could have sworn he'd seen her before. Close up she didn't look all that decrepit. She seemed more like a cheery hostess at some cheesy resort, the kind who hovers over the guests, checking their pineapple drinks to see if they need refills.

"Pay no attention to her," said Klinder curtly. "She's a glitch. One of those anomalies I mentioned."

What'd he say? Mike thought, feeling hazy and strange.

"Let me ask you something. I'm told you have an exceptional memory. Exactly how much do you remember about the day we met? That field trip in grade school?"

Mike looked at him and lied. "Nothing."

Klinder smiled. "Good." He patted Mike gently on the thigh. "Good."

"How's Danny?" Mike asked.

"He's doing fine. He's going through the process. His son's here too."

The process? Sean? It had been months since he'd seen his nephew. They had never connected. It was like the boy smelled something on him.

No. He couldn't have possibly known about Julie.

"Sean's the only one the birds talk to," Klinder said. "And I'll be honest with you—I have no idea why. But now that we have Daniel, we have the code breaker."

Code breaker? Mike was finding it hard to follow the doctor. His mind kept sliding off to take in the passing scenery. "I saw you on the Web. Since when did you get religious?"

"That's just packaging." Klinder smiled and exhaled a cloud of smoke. "I've never been religious; I'm a scientist. But people here need something to believe in, Mike. Someone to follow. I provide it. I give them structure, and hope." He chuckled. "It isn't easy being dead."

Even in his confused state, or maybe because of it, Mike felt there was something appalling about Klinder's giddy pride and casual sense of entitlement. It was as if he'd said: "These suckers actually elected me pope! Can you believe it?" He felt a repulsion at his immense ego and cheerful phoniness. He was like some of the ad guys he'd met. Slick, soulless, and charming as hell.

And Klinder also reminded him of someone else. Someone less easy to discount.

"You okay?" the doctor asked.

Mike nodded and swallowed down a gag.

Klinder cocked the rearview mirror, grimaced, and inspected his teeth. "I'm surprised you haven't seen me on the tube, son, I'm our resident expert."

"On what?"

They stopped at a red light.

"On everything. The camera likes me. I ever tell you I used to be in the movies? It's how I met your mom. I was like the original Mouseketeer."

Mike tried to remember the Mouseketeers. All he could think of was Annette and her tits. What did he say about his mom?

"This was in the early forties. A prototype of the Mickey Mouse Club. I was the host. ARE WE HAVING FUN YET?"

Mike flinched at the shout.

"Sorry. That was my line to open every show." Klinder's eyes seemed to get misty as he recalled. "Happiest time of my life. Curtain calls. Standing ovations. You get the stage bug in you and it's fuckin' hard to get rid of."

Yeah, Mike knew exactly what he was talking about. And the knowledge shocked him. That was who Klinder reminded him of: a carny barker, a cheerful con man. Someone glib and gifted. Someone who never questioned the privilege of his position in the spotlight, or the power he wielded. Someone who spent his life directing others like chess pieces, devoting his talents to prettifying and promoting ideas he had no investment in and no commitment to. With a great wave of nausea he realized: it was like looking into a mirror.

Klinder reminded him of himself.

The doctor went on, oblivious. "They shot a few episodes, tried to sell it as a newsreel. But it didn't catch on." He smiled. "Then they Ebsened me."

"Ebsened?"

"Yeah, I got ugly when my hormones kicked in."

Damn, this is a long red light.

"I was a whiz on the banjo." Klinder's fingers crawled in place on his ample belly, plucking and grinning over invisible strings. "But I was deep into puberty. Didn't you ever notice what happens to child stars?"

Didn't Klinder ever shut up? God, how this man loved the sound of his own voice.

"They're so fucking adorable when they're kids. And then they hit puberty. And their cuteness goes sour, turns into something grotesque. That was me." Klinder chuckled.

It was true, especially the Beaver. Damn, this was a really long light. "Ebsened?"

"The original Tin Man. In *The Wizard of Oz*."

A black car pulled up and cut in front of them to make a turn. It turned on its blinker, but it didn't move.

"He had an allergic reaction to the silver makeup. Sicker than a dog. And Jack Haley took his place. Buddy must have been pretty depressed at the time. Jack became a star. Peak of Ebsen's career was dancing with Shirley Temple."

He remembered that. "She didn't get ugly."

"No, she became the US ambassador to Mali or something."

"And Buddy struck oil in Beverly."

Klinder smiled. "Hills, that is."

"Swimming pools," Mike said.

"Movie stars."

Klinder clawed his fingers again, and just as their minds were about to begin the Flat and Scruggs banjo break, a blast of buckshot took out their back window. Glass showered over their heads and shoulders.

"Jesus Christ!" said Klinder.

As Mike ducked down he saw a fat Chinese man sticking a shotgun out the back window of the black car that was pulling up close beside them. The car in front of them backed up until their bumpers touched.

Shit, he thought. Here we go again.

But Klinder was fearless and steaming. "Do you fuckers have to do that?" He reached out over and started pounding on the blacked-out window of the black car that had pinned them in. There were beautiful diamonds all over his shoulders, like sequins on Michael Jackson.

"Who is it?" asked Mike, tucked under the dash.

"The Correctors," Klinder said. "Who else? They're just trying to scare us."

Mike sat up and the window on the black car rolled down. A brunette woman wearing large sunglasses smiled. Between her eyes there was a type of tattoo. An X. "Morning, doctor," she said.

"Fuck you! Haven't you idiots got better things to do?"

"We want to talk."

"So call me."

"Not to you. How ya doing, Mike?" the lady said. "Kept the pager, didn't you?"

He nodded, wondering how she was connected to Takahashi. The Asian with his hand in his pocket.

"They gave you a pager?" Klinder sputtered, "Do—do you have any idea who these people are?"

"Not really," he admitted.

"Textbook sociopaths." He held up one finger. "You stay clear of them."

It amused Mike that Klinder assumed he would obey him the way he used to. "Why?"

"Why? *Why?* They kill people, that's why!"

"I thought you said everybody's dead."

The driver of the black car whispered, "Jesus."

"Everybody *is* dead," said Klinder.

"How the hell can they kill dead people?" Mike asked.

Klinder rolled his eyes. "They just can, okay? Take my word for it."

"Are you with him or us, Mike?" the brunette woman asked.

Klinder or the Correctors? Was that the question? Mike looked at the woman with the mark between her eyes. Forty. Short, dark hair. Good bones. Her voice reminded him of a young Lauren Bacall: smoke and gravel. Then he looked at the bald, overweight Klinder in his paper jumpsuit. The man who had hypnotized him when he was ten.

"Whatever happened to Gale?" Mike asked him.

"Gale?" Klinder said, frowning.

"The woman you used to live with?"

"Oh. Gale." The doctor licked his lips. "I dunno. We split up. She was kinda uptight. She didn't approve of my methods. And she never got along with the aliens."

"The aliens suck," said the woman.

Klinder snickered. "Boy, there's a rich philosophy! No wonder you guys got so many converts."

The choice was over before he was even aware he'd made it. Relief flooded through Mike as he got out of Klinder's Bug. It felt like he had been trapped in a cage with a python. The question, he decided, was: Who threatened Danny more? Klinder or the Correctors? It was a simple choice. Klinder was a coward. He had seen the Correctors kill. He would explain to them that they got the wrong guy. Danny was not a dangerous man. He was a professor, for Chrissake. They would take him off their hit list, and this crazy business would be over.

"What are you doing?" Klinder called.

Mike walked to the rear of the black car.

"Get back here!"

The woman said, "Shut up, doctor."

"They got guns, Mike."

"So do I," Mike reminded him.

The woman smiled. "We've got a lot in common."

"I've got one question, Klinder," Mike said, leaning on the bumper of black car. "If they got guns, why am I not afraid of them? Why am I afraid of you?"

Klinder didn't answer. He wiped his forehead, which had gotten very sweaty, very quickly.

"Tell him, doctor."

"Any number of explanations. The stress is affecting your judgement. You're maxed out. You're in denial..."

Mike laughed.

"Or you're hypnotized," said the woman.

Mike smiled. "Or I'm hypnotized. Didn't you think I'd remember that thing you did with your finger and your voice? How could I forget that, doctor?"

The woman started to count backwards. "Five . . . four . . ."

"Shut up, you bitch," said Klinder.

"Three . . ." the woman said.

"Shut up!"

"Two. One," Mike said, and snapped his fingers.

The transformation was immediate. The light around him changed: grew warmer and deeper. The woman in sunglasses was much prettier than he had noticed. The X he'd seen between her eyes was gone. And there were shards of glass all over Klinder's shoulders.

"It's a dead end, Mike. You can't beat the Hummingbirds."

"Light's green," Mike said.

The black car in front of the bug turned the corner.

"Listen—acceptance is our only choice."

"Doc?" He waited till he was sure he had Klinder's full attention. "Tell Danny I'll catch up with him."

Klinder let out an exasperated sigh as if he had never heard anything so absurd. "Come and see me when you want the truth." The doctor popped the clutch and sped off.

The shattered rear window of the green Beetle disappeared around the corner. Mike realized he couldn't have taken Klinder's company for another second, that the hypnosis must have been the only thing that had made that prick bearable.

The woman in the black car had a handgun on her lap.

Mike said, "Correctors, huh?"

"That's us. Get in."

The fat Chinese man with the shotgun opened the door and slid over in the backseat. Mike plopped down beside him.

"My name's Dot," said the brunette woman up front. "This is Wu." The driver, a tall, skinny man, apparently had no name.

"How'd you guys know about the pager?" Mike asked.

"Takahashi gave it to you, right? He's one of us."

"I got the impression he was with Klinder."

"He is. Kyo's a double agent."

That name again. There was something about that name. A double agent? That meant the woman and the boy at the 7-Eleven were double agents too. That meant they were Correctors. It was all very confusing. After a moment Mike said, "Takahashi said you guys were trying to kill my brother."

"We were."

"Look. Danny's with Klinder. The Crossovers, right? So you can call off your hounds."

"We know," Dot said. "We got the codes now."

Codes, schmodes. "Listen. It's all some huge misunderstanding. Danny's not a dangerous man."

"He is to you, Mike," Dot said.

The driver said over his shoulder. "I'll do him for you, bro. You just say the word."

Mike leaned against the door and spoke to everyone in the car. "Let me make something really clear. Anyone who touches Danny is a dead man."

"Fuck," said the big Chinese with delight.

"I told you," said Dot, beaming at him.

"He's the one," said the driver, smacking the steering wheel with the palm of his hand.

Mike took out his gun and pressed the barrel against the ear of the fat man beside him. "You think I'm kidding? You think this is a fucking joke? Try me, fatso."

"I *like* him," said the Chinese man, chuckling. He slapped Mike on the thigh. "Maybe I kill *you* someday, aye?"

The Crossovers

T he man placed the blue pamphlet gently on the table in front
of Daniel. One of Klinder's "priests." A lump in the front pocket
of his lab coat like a roll of quarters. "This is the handbook. It
explains everything."

Sean sat on Daniel's lap and rolled his eyes. "It's so boring."

The way it was presented to him, solemnly, as if it were holy writ,
reminded Daniel of one of Mike's favorite shots: the library in *Citizen Kane*
where the reporter, in search of Rosebud, is presented Mr. Bernstein's
sacred memoirs. But this room, deep in the bowels of the compound, had
none of the majesty of that library, no marble, no columns, no gigantic
steel vault, no shafts of light. It was a conference room as plain and white
and functional as any at his university.

"Is this the one they wanted me to analyze?"

"Sir?" another man asked, puzzled, from the far side of the long brown table.

"Jeez, doesn't anybody talk to anybody around here?"

Sean squirmed on his lap. Daniel shushed him and opened the thin blue book.

THE 12 STEPS OF CROSSOVER
by Joel A. Klinder

I. HAUNTING

CO's (Crossovers) linger at the point of entry. Unable to unloop from their past, connected unconsciously to the remnants of the Previous.

2. DENIAL

CO's go on as if nothing has happened, finding excuses for any discrepancy between their reality and their past.

3. DELUSION

CO's constrct elaborate explanations for their present circumstances. They often fixate upon a past mythology or gravitate toward extremes of the delusional spectrum: from paranoia to paranormal.

4. BARGAINING

To ward off overwhelming feelings of displacement, CO'S adopt any number of ritualized obsessive/compulsive habits (See "Magical Thinking" and "Fandom").

5. GRIEF

The loss of mortality is not easily adapted to. Every framework the CO has used to comprehend their existence was dependent on the lens of time—a vision which has been suspended. In a world without deadlines, consequences, endings—a world without the clock—

CO's have no consistent paradigm with which to judge their actions, decisions and self-worth. After previous coping strategies prove futile, they experience their loss.

6. BLAME

CO's become stuck in complexes such as revenge, misdirected hostility, existential rage. They seek a scapegoat, an object they can blame. Which can lead to...

7. VIOLENCE

A brief, useless aberration, which, thankfully, few CO's do more than entertain as a thought (See "Correctors").

8. CATATONIA

Exhausted by the preceding stages, CO's are vulnerable to an odd psychic paralysis. They choose not to move, talk, or engage in anything remotely human. They choose nothing. Avoid these people. They are deceptively powerful vortexes of negative energy.

9. CURIOSITY

In a world without bills, appetites repressed, unnecessary suffering and fear, CO's are free to pursue hitherto untapped realms of diversion and leisure. This can be a rewarding process: unexplored territories are charted, unexpected possibilities are investigated. Hobbies become full-time occupations.

10. ECSTASY

CO's experience a suffusing happiness. They become "Relishers" and their company is much desired. They party; they laugh; they joke; they sex.

I I. ACCEPTANCE

You're dead. You're going to be dead for a long time. Welcome
aboard.

I 2. REUNION

The experience of reencountering your previous acquaintances and
loved ones can be a renewing moment that all CO's live for. The
shock of the experience is not to be underestimated.

Daniel closed the book. Sean had fallen asleep in his lap. "This is the
most insane thing I've ever read."

The lab man said, "denial."

"Surely, surely there must be a better explanation than this?"

"Delusion."

Daniel opened the pamphlet again. "Twelve steps. Why is everything
twelve steps? Just once I'd like to see a thirteenth-step program."

The lab man was silent.

"*Construct* is misspelled," Daniel added.

"Bargaining," the man said.

"Stop it! I read the book! What the hell is a Crossover?"

"One of the newly initiated dead."

"You're telling me that everybody here is—" he struggled to find the
absurd word—"I can smell my son's hair! I can feel his heart. What about
Rachel? What about—I just talked to my old high school friend, George.
You're telling me . . . cadavers go door to door?"

The lab man cleared his throat and sat down opposite Daniel at the
table. He pulled a handheld computer from his coat and pressed a few
buttons. "Rachel?"

"Rachel Lindsey. My barber."

"Detroit, I assume?"

Daniel nodded.

The man typed with his forefinger. "Rachel Lindsey. Denial. Dead of
cancer a month ago."

Daniel looked at the man. The man said, "George?"

"George Adams," he said weakly. "We ran track."

Tap. Tap, tap, tap, tap, tap. "George Adams. Delusional. Died of a drug overdose. Eight years ago. They're all dead. They're all here. Anybody who's died in the last ten years is here."

Sean opened his eyes and said, "Since 1990."

The other man added, "That's where all the crowds went, in case you're wondering."

"You—" It was all Daniel could do not to swear. "What have you done here?"

"Chill," Sean said.

"Blaming," the man said, and Daniel wanted to smash his face in. "You probably want to smack me."

"Shut up!"

"Anger and violence. You're making great progress."

"I broke things," Sean admitted.

The other man slid something across the table. It stopped right next to Daniel's hands: a silver Zippo cigarette lighter taped to a pack of Salems.

"Welcome aboard," the lab man said.

Daniel felt suddenly weightless. As if at any moment he might float up to the ceiling, and hang there like an escaped balloon at a mall. He clung to his son then as if he were ballast. He felt Sean's warm head, his impossibly smooth cheek. This would be—what?—catatonia? Knowing what he was feeling didn't make any difference. He felt nothing. Sadness. Hunger. Pain. His body had lost all appetite and desire. It could have been anybody's body.

"Turn to refusal," he thought. That old engineering phrase Uncle Louie had used once when they were fixing the postmark machine. "Use the seven-sixteenths and turn to refusal," he had instructed. That's what it was like. The bolt wouldn't get any tighter. There was no turning it.

"We should sleep," his son said. It was a distant voice, a memory from another time. As if he were in the next room and not in his arms.

Sleep sounded good. Sleep sounded very good.

The door opened revealing Klinder and Takahashi arguing in the hall, the doctor sweating with his fat hand on the doorknob, his pajamas sparkling like Michael Jackson.

"Get him back, dammit!" Klinder said. "We'll work on the book."

Rebuked, Takahashi nodded and walked away.

"What stage?" Klinder barked, entering the room.

"Nine," said the lab man.

"Excellent work." Klinder walked over and stood before Daniel. His sleeves and shoulders were covered with glimmering diamonds. "Daniel? I've got some very good news. I'm going to count down from five. Then I'll snap my fingers and you're going to wake up. Ready? Here we go. Five, four, three, two, one."

Snap!

Daniel blinked. He noticed Klinder's shoulders were covered with tiny shards of glass.

"How do you feel?" Klinder asked.

Daniel yawned. "Tired."

"You've just been hypnotized. It accelerates the stages of crossover."

"Hypnotized?"

"That's right."

"But I remember everything." They were asking him about Mike's diary. The men in the green room. He knew that now. They were pretty subtle about it. Why were they so worried about the diary? What was the scandal they were so afraid of? Daniel rubbed his eyes and yawned again. "You said something about 'good news.'"

"Yes, I did," said Klinder, nodding, sitting on the edge of the brown table. He lit a cigarette with a Zippo lighter, relished the inhale and the pause. His words came out with the smoke. "Your wife is alive."

It was like a balloon of confetti had exploded in his chest. More than relief, more than pleasure, more than joy—he hadn't known he could feel this good and this incomplete at the same time. Or maybe it had been so long since he felt anything like pleasure, it had overwhelmed him, filling the vacuum inside like a draught of pure oxygen. There was hope. She was coming.

But how was that possible?

Klinder said, "Ecstasy."

"What?" said Daniel.

"All you have to do is wait for her. Can you do that, Daniel? Can you wait?"

What a stupid question, he thought. *This was much better than waiting for nothing.*

Klinder said, "It's time I introduced you to your mother."

How the Cookie
Crumbles

⁓   ⁓   ⁓

Mike felt like he was in a presidential motorcade.

Two big, black Lincolns in a row. Tooling down the 101.
First time he had ever driven it when it wasn't gridlocked.
The hulking Chinese man named Wu, who held the shotgun in the back-
seat, asked for Mike's beeper.

Mike handed it over.

Wu crunched it in his fist and tossed it out the window. "Welcome
aboard," he said.

"Where are we going?" Mike asked.

"Sacred Heart."

Sacred Heart turned out to be an abandoned Catholic high school.
There must have been a hundred people there, all dressed in funeral black.
It seemed like a hive for the depressed; everyone moved with grim purpose.
Some were carrying guns to and from classrooms. In the gymnasium cots

were laid out all over the basketball court. A stage at the far end for
assemblies. In the corner, a firearms demonstration was in progress. Wu
waved over at a young woman with long, blond hair who was drawing
on a blackboard: the outline of a person in white. She smiled at Wu, then
continued her lesson. Her black T-shirt lifted and exposed her belly button as she reached up to chalk in the head.

Turning to her class, she asked in a sweet southern accent, "Now
who's gonna tell me where the three clean shots are?"

A man raised his hand. "Behind the ear."

The blond woman nodded.

An old woman raised her hand.

"Yes, Kay?"

"At the base of the neck."

The woman nodded. And waited. "Anybody?" She sighed and said,
"Come on, people! Through the heart!"

The small group snickered and looked embarrassed to the floor.

The blond woman put her hands on her hips. "Now, where's the
heart?"

Rebuked, everyone put a hand over their left breast.

"*Super!*" the blond woman said.

A tall, thin man sat reading a black Bible. A man in a black T-shirt
was showing a few women how to clean a rifle. Dot led Mike to a big
aluminum coffeemaker sitting on a table covered with a white paper
tablecloth, a tray of Oreos beside it. She served him a cup and looked
at him.

"What?" Mike said.

"Who taught you manners?"

He had no idea what she was talking about.

"I just gave you a cuppa joe."

"So?"

"So what happens when that happens?"

Strange question. Mike thought about all the cups of coffee the PAs
would deliver on the set. Took him one loud minute to train his team

how he liked it. After that they never forgot: double cream. No sugar. He liked that. Hell, he needed that. Twenty-seven setups a day. An actor who did great in the audition but couldn't hit his mark and had one line reading and one reading alone. The cloud bank threatening to throw them all into shadow, fucking continuity to hell. The agency producer looking at her watch, the rain machine on the fritz—he had so much to think about on a shoot day he took it for granted that someone was taking care of his coffee.

"Not following you," Mike said.

"Hmm," Dot said as she poured herself one from the tap and wrapped a few Oreos in a napkin.

They took their cups and snacks to some folding chairs in the corner. Light was coming through the tall windows covered with heavy steel mesh—protection against bouncing balls. Under the stage and the thick maroon curtains he could see a type of shelving similar to the fold-out benches in his high school gym, benches that collapsed back into a filing cabinet. The musty smell of sweat and dirty socks. A discarded pom-pom in the corner—maroon-and-white. Banners hung above the stage. CITY CHAMPS 1987, 1988, 1989. Someone had painted a modern crucifix on the brick wall. A hippie Christ with a neatly trimmed beard, planes of color on his robe. Sort of a cubist thing. The four stigmata very tasteful.

"Why'd you choose this place?" Mike asked.

"It doubles as an armory. Pretty much unlimited ammunition."

"You're shitting me."

"Right under the chapel's sacristy." Dot shrugged. "You want the story?"

"Sure."

"Did Klinder tell you anything?"

As he ran down the doctor's wild-assed theory, watching himself reflected twice in her wraparound glasses, he wondered what color her eyes were. He noticed there was a lump in the pocket of her black dress. Tissues? A gun? When he had concluded, he said, "It was the dumbest story I've ever heard. Hummingbirds. Aliens. A virtual afterlife."

Dot washed down her Oreo with a sip of black coffee. "It's true," she said.

Mike looked at her.

"Every word Klinder said was true."

"Then why aren't you on his side?"

"We don't follow the Wing Man," she said, snickering. "He's a phony."

"But you just said you believe all this hummingbird shit."

"It's like the scriptures. We interpret it differently." She smiled and crossed her legs. "How's your coffee?"

He stared down at the plastic foam cup. He hadn't tried it yet. "Fine."

"No, really. How is it?" Coffee freak, he thought. How would the little French translator do that one? One who relishes? One who is a snob? Connoisseur? He missed her voice. "It's good," he said.

She leaned forward. "Michael. Maybe you think I'm being a gracious host. I'm not. I'm asking you a serious question."

Well, then. He took a sip. He swallowed. He looked into the cup and saw his nose and eyes reflected in the dark brew. It wasn't a good cup of coffee at all. It was, perhaps, the best cup of coffee he'd ever had in his life. "It's . . ." he exhaled and searched for the right word. "Superb."

Dot leaned back and smiled. "Best you've ever had?"

"Easily."

She held out an Oreo. "Try this."

He took it, smelled it, and nibbled. The cocoa exploded in his mouth. The crunch was wonderful, not too dry, not too hard. The sandwiched vanilla was a swirl of subtle delights. It felt like the first time he'd ever had ice cream. Like he was a kid again. "Jeshush," he said around the cookie.

"Like it?"

"It's amazhing."

"Best you've ever had?"

He looked at her and swallowed. "What are you guys? Gourmet chefs moonlighting as assassins?"

"You haven't eaten much lately, have you?"

It was true. After the jungle he had lost his appetite. He couldn't recall his last meal. This bothered him somewhat, but then food had never been a priority. "No. Why?"

"It's all like that."

"All your food? No wonder you get so many followers."

"No. Not our food. All food. Every peach. Every hot dog. Every bowl of soup. Take one bite of a strawberry shortcake and you'll think about it for hours."

That was hard to imagine.

"You don't believe me?" She smiled. "I see you haven't had sex recently. I could prove my point, but it's even better with someone you like."

"I'm missing something here."

"It's all that way." She looked around the gymnasium. "Every day. Every sensation. Exquisite. It's like our tastebuds have been perfected. They're trying to give us everything we want. Trying to see to every one of our needs. They can't abide want. You never noticed any of this?"

"No," he admitted. "Klinder said the aliens took away death."

"We're bringing it back." Dot said. "We're at war, Mike. We are a guerrilla force in occupied territory. We're Killers."

"Why?"

"It's a perversion. The Hummingbirds are just feeding on us. We're their Oreos. Their snacks. We're their favorite cookie. And we want them to starve."

"So you kill?"

"Killing is the only weapon that'll stop them. We're trying to create a paradox. We kill enough people, bring enough suffering into this little utopia, and it won't be paradise anymore. They'll have to kick us out."

"They will?"

"They will. That's why our ranks are thinning. This gym used to be full. Every person we kill, we get closer to freedom. We started with each other. Then we moved onto loved ones. Then strangers. We're going random now."

"Random."

"Anybody, any time."

"Jesus, you mean it."

"You think we're crazy?"

"No, of course not. It's a great plan. Shoot everybody at random; the aliens get ticked and boot you out of paradise. Jesus, why didn't I think of that?"

"It's a little trickier than that. There are rules, you see. To get booted—erased, we call it—takes three kills. A stranger. Someone you like. And a relative."

Mike almost laughed. He didn't want to think about the implications. The implications were sickening. "How long did it take you guys to figure this out?"

"Years."

"So what happens to the people you kill?"

"They come back."

Finally he couldn't help himself. He laughed for a good long minute. People around the gym looked over, wondering what the joke was.

"You don't recognize me, do you?"

She took off her large sunglasses, and Mike stopped laughing.

"Head shot," she said.

It was the woman in the pink jumpsuit. The woman he had killed. She had no scars.

Mike swallowed several times. Of all the scares he'd had recently that was the worse. He found it nearly impossible to look her in the eyes.

"Ever wonder why you can say that word?" Dot asked. "Death? Not many people can. Klinder can. Some of us. It's the bird's deep programming. A sort of taboo." Dot put her sunglasses back on. "You can say it because you killed."

After a minute he said, "you thought I was my brother."

"Yes. Sorry. We fucked up."

"You were gonna kill him."

"Yes."

"Why?"

"We were trying to save you."

"From whom?"

"Him. He's going to try to kill you."

"Why would he do that?"

"It's the only way the Crossovers can win."

Mike held his head in his hands. His mind had reached the limits of adhesion and thought slid away like an egg off a Teflon skillet. It made no sense. Takahashi had said: If you want to live, find your brother. Why would he send me after Danny if he thought Danny was going to kill me? And Christ—Danny wouldn't harm a fly. Didn't they know that?

Eventually, Dot said, "Mike? You asked what happens to our victims, but you never asked what happens to the killers."

His mind was stunned and reeling with dread. "What?" he asked, reluctantly. "What happens to the killers?"

She called across the gym. "Wu?"

The large Chinese walked over like a weightlifter, as if he had a pillow under each armpit.

"Wu? Which mark are you on?"

"Two," he said proudly.

"Tell him," she said.

Wu pulled up a chair and sat on it backward, crossing his meaty arms over the back. "A guy roller-skating on Venice Beach. My wife." He saw the look on Mike's face and added, "Clean kills."

Dot said, "He means little or no pain. Tell Michael what happens when you kill someone you like?"

He smiled. "I'm off-duty. Erased."

She handed him her gun. "Take your pick."

His eyes went wide when he got it. "Really, miss? Oh, thank you! Thank you very much."

Wu dashed through the gymnasium like a boy who had just been told he'd won a trip to Disney World, going from group to group, talking excitedly.

"He's looking for volunteers?"

"Yup."

"Someone he . . . likes?"

"Right."

"This is sick."

"Dot!" Wu called. He was holding up the arm of the thin blond woman who had drawn on the blackboard. "Dawn!"

"Bring her over."

Mike had seen this before. At the 7-Eleven. Rita and her brother. He couldn't remember his name.

The young couple stood before them, all smiles. Like they were about to be pronounced man and wife.

Dot said, "You sure, Dawn?"

" 'Course I'm sure. Wu's my bro."

"Go ahead, then."

Dawn lifted her baggy black T-shirt and pulled out a snub-nosed 38. Another glimpse of belly button. She held it out for Wu. "Use mine, sweetheart. I just cleaned it."

"Cool!" He accepted it and spun the chamber slowly with his thumb. Then handed Dot back her pistol.

"Now, don't you miss," Dawn teased.

"Wait," said Mike standing, and they all stopped to look at him.

"Who's this?" Dawn asked.

"Mike Glynn," Dot said. "Dawn Jacobs."

Mike said, "You don't have to do this."

After a moment Dawn said, "I know. We want to."

"Yeah," said the large Chinese man. "We want to."

"They want to," said Dot, then nodded at Wu.

"Wait!" Mike said.

The blond woman closed her eyes and the large man shot her in the side of the head. The report echoed through the gymnasium like a cymbal crash at band practice. The woman fell on her face. The spray of blood made an arc on the polished wooden slats. Like a crescent moon. She lay on the maroon paint. Three-second violation, he thought.

Mike looked at the large man smiling crazily, holding the gun.

Exalted. Quivering with gratitude. He could have sworn there was a shimmer all over him, as if he were coated with dew. Mike smelled something awful: burning hair. Their eyes locked and Mike saw something he never wanted to see again.

Wu's eyes. The dark pupil—a hollow dot resting in the center of a brown ring, braced by two white wedges—radiated outward. The black ink seeped quickly into the iris, absorbing its color. The round black wave spread outward, saturating the margins of the eye until it was wholly empty—a bulging slit of glistening darkness.

Wu's eyeballs had turned black.

Then his teeth turned black.

And then he disappeared.

The pistol fell on the gym floor with a hollow clunk.

The gymnasium erupted with applause. People were standing on cots clapping wildly. Somebody yelled, "Erased!"

The tall man who had been reading the black Bible strode over like a hillbilly undertaker and laid a white sheet over the woman's body. He stood and clasped his hands before him, holding the Bible, and began to recite.

By the rivers of Babylon, there we sat down,
Yea, we wept, when we remembered Zion.
For there they that carried us away captive required of us a song:
And they that wasted us required of us mirth,
Saying, Sing us one of the songs of Zion.

How shall we sing the Lord's song in a strange land?
If I forget thee, O Jerusalem,
Let my right hand forget her cunning.
If I do not remember thee,
Let my tongue cleave to the roof of my mouth;

Remember, O Lord,

The children of Edom in the days of Jerusalem; who said,

Raze it,

Raze it, even to the foundation thereof.

O daughter of Babylon, who art to be destroyed;

Happy shall he be,

That rewardeth thee as thou hast served us.

Happy shall he be,

That taketh and dasheth thy little ones against the stone.

Bobby, Mike remembered.

At the 7-Eleven. The boy's name was Bobby.

Dot bent down to retrieve the gun. She offered it to Mike but he just looked at her.

"That," she said, "is how the cookie crumbles."

The Cocoa Graham
Cracker Girl

〜　　　〜　　　〜

My mom's here too?" Daniel asked, stunned.

"I'm afraid not," Klinder said. "She died before the saving. But we've got some archives that'll answer a lot of your questions."

The doctor led them down a long, white corridor to a conference room. A big screen at one end. Stainless steel pitchers evenly spaced around the table. The room was very clean: it smelled of Lemon Pledge.

Sean sat on Daniel's lap. He had decided he would never let him out of his sight again.

Klinder in his paper pj's grabbed a clicker off the far end of the table. The lights dimmed. The show began.

It started with a bad fifties movie. A trailer, actually. Weird melodramatic orange type sliding onto the screen. THE INCOMPARABLE

ESTHER WILLIAMS! A buxom blond in a yellow one-piece suit strutting to the edge of a diving board.

"Now, that's a lot of woman," said Klinder.

THIS TIME FOR KEEPS. The title, apparently.

"Shot on Mackinaw Island," said Klinder.

SHOT ON LOCATION AT MACKINAW ISLAND!

The doctor flushed briefly at his gaffe, then carried on. "They had to heat the pools for Ms. Williams."

GLAMOUR! ROMANCE! HEARTBREAK! A couple kisses in the moonlight, the sparkling Straits of Mackinaw behind them.

"Years before the bridge was finished, of course," said Klinder.

"I wish he'd shut up," Sean said.

HER GREATEST PERFORMANCE YET! High board diving. Wom en doing synchronized swimming. Blue underwater shots. Esther's amazing Olympic stroke and bod. Pretty risqué stuff for its time, Daniel thought. But Klinder was a showman who couldn't bear sharing the spotlight.

"She must have waterproof makeup," Klinder said.

"You wanna pipe down?" asked Daniel.

"What?"

"We don't need your running commentary."

"I thought I was amplifying. It doesn't help?"

"Shut up," Daniel explained, and his son gave him a priceless smile.

A nightclub. Swirling couples in black tuxedos and dresses like beach umbrellas. A SPECIAL APPEARANCE BY XAVIER COUGAT'S OR-CHESTRA! At the microphone: a mustachioed round man in white tux and tails, wearing a fez and holding a bald doggie in his arms. His red turbaned orchestra on risers behind him. Cardboard palm trees in the background against a painted backdrop of a starry sky.

FEATURING THE COMIC GENIUS OF JIMMY DURANTE! "The Schnoz" falls into a wedding cake, mugs and exclaims: "Aye-Yi-Yi-Yi-Yi!"

FOUR NEW ORIGINAL NEWMAN AND BAUM SONGS! Some fey Robert Taylor type in a blue monogrammed silk robe, smoking a cigarette, looking dreamily over a balcony, and crooning over eighty thousand strings.

"Does he suck or what?" said Sean.

"Is there some point to all this?" Daniel asked.

Klinder froze the film on a nightclub scene. "Third row, orchestra right. That's your mom...." He stepped up to the screen and pointed. "The redhead playing violin? One of the fiddlers was sick that day and they needed a stand-in. They taped the strings together so they wouldn't make a sound."

How could he know that? Daniel squinted at the scene. That was Mom, all right. He'd seen pictures of her. He felt a deep aching, as though someone were pressing their palms against his chest. He remembered Mike's diary entry: "My mother was an unemployed actress but she..." What was the rest of it?

"She was in a commercial," Daniel said, trying to pull the memory out of some dusty corner in his mind.

Klinder smiled. "The Cocoa Graham Cracker Girl. Did a little hootchie-coochie dance in a tutu. Shook the cookie tin like one of those Latin seed things. She told me it was the high point of her life: being on TV. But it was a live commercial, before dubbing. Otherwise, we'd have a copy."

"I never saw it," said Daniel. But he recalled the tins. He once thought everyone had them. Blue tins of chocolate-covered graham crackers stacked in the breezeway. They'd melt in the summer heat and freeze in the winter. The company must have given her a private stash. He and Mike were forever raiding them until, one day, Uncle Louie threw them out in a hungover rage.

A jump cut. Esther Williams and Peter Lawford arguing. Reflections of water playing on their faces.

"Your mom's an extra poolside," Klinder noted. "The redhead in the blue one-piece? Her only official on-screen appearance. Let's go in."

The film got grainier as they blew up and looped the sequence of the redhead crossing her legs. Tilting her head back to the sun. "Do you see it?"

"What?"

"Look closely."

There was a small bit of shadow hovering over her head. A leaf? A pine cone? The frame slid up slowly to reveal the source: a tiny hummingbird above the woman.

"That's 1953," Klinder said. "A year before you were born."

Next slide: a black-and-white snapshot. The happy mother holding a newborn wrapped in a blanket, walking down the steps of a church. "St. Bart's. Downtown Saginaw. That's your baptism."

"Who took this picture?" Daniel asked.

"I did. Notice the shadow on the wall behind her?"

Before Daniel could ask why on earth was Klinder at his baptism, he noticed a small, dark shape like a half-eaten banana, the peel flaps hanging. Then he recognized it: a hummingbird shadow.

"Like an angel," Sean said.

Next slide: Two boys pointing pop guns at each other. Mike and Danny dressed in short shorts. Scowling. "Nineteen fifty-eight. Your fourth birthday."

"I remember the picture," Daniel said. He remembered the guns.

"Look closer."

At the edge of the frame a smear of bird hovering over them. Its wings frozen, pointing to the sky. It reminded Daniel of the memorial cards you get at funerals. The white dove—a stand-in for the Holy Ghost.

"You were living with your Uncle Louie then, right?"

"He never told us about Mom."

"She was one of the first contactees. With me. We were inducted. She died in a facility much like this one. In Buffalo. When you were very young. Cancer. She was a fine woman, Daniel."

"I'm sorry," said Sean.

"Why weren't we told?"

Klinder lit a cigarette. "It was a top-secret project. Kids weren't in the loop then."

"We are now," Sean explained. The proud nine-year-old.

"You were well taken care of. The government provided a handsome stipend for both of you. And your uncle retired from his mail-order seed business."

Must have been when he started drinking, Daniel thought. Uncle Louie had always liked having his own business. "No bull. No clock. No bosses. Direct mail cuts out the middleman." He recalled him working in his tank top T-shirt and striped boxers. His hairy shoulders bent over the dining room table, stacks of shoe boxes stuffed with seed packets like Kool-Aid. The rubber stamp he used to sign off every letter: *We Surely Thank You For Your Business!* The address labels he typed on his old Remington. Licking hundreds of them. His tongue yellow and his breath smelling of glue. That was before the green government checks started coming in.

Next slide: Mike and Danny tumbling down the Sleeping Bear Sand Dunes on Lake Michigan. He remembered: one of his favorite vacations with Uncle Louie. He seemed happy when he told them, "I'll never have to work another day in my life." His breath changed after that. Soon he did nothing all day but drink beer. Stinko, Mike used to call him.

"Look at the shadows," Klinder said.

There was a gray cloud shadow behind the boys, rippling on the pocked yellow sand.

"A flock. Quite a rare formation."

Next slide: Daniel in his purple graduation gown. This time he didn't have to be told to look for the birds. There was one in the background—plain as day, ruby throated, mid-flight, just over his head.

Next slide: wedding photo. Him and Julie. Outside the church. Beside a rosebush, squinting into the hot sun. He smiled, remembering. When Julie first got the ring she used to go to the produce section at Kroger's just to admire it—the same lights that flattered the avocado, the rutabaga, and put the freshest face on the endive lettuce, gave her diamond the full, dazzling spectrum of light. She admitted to its distraction on the steering wheel on the commute to the hospital and once or twice or maybe three times she ran a red light while basking in the reflections of her engagement. Later, she swore she had gotten tendonitis from looking at her ring. She loved being married.

"I remember the roses," Daniel said.

"Actually, those aren't roses," said Klinder.

Daniel saw they were actually perched hummingbirds. A bouquet of them scattered throughout the bush. You'd think they would have noticed that.

"That's enough," said Klinder, and the lights came up slowly.

For a long minute Daniel sat, overwhelmed.

This history lesson explained something that he'd had an inkling of all his life, but had never understood. *The feeling of being watched, being wide open, as if, literally, someone else was thinking his thoughts as they formed, some silent reader, sharing his voice, turning the pages of his life in a library.*

"My whole life? Why?"

Klinder smiled. He sat on the edge of the long table, curling one leg back; his paper pajamas made a crinkling sound. He lit a cigarette with his Zippo. "There's something you should understand, Daniel. You are dead."

Daniel sighed. Sooner or later this nonsense had to end. "Prove it."

"What's Arthur Miller's most famous play?"

Daniel raised his eyebrows.

"I'm serious," Klinder assured him.

Daniel thought: the one with Willy Loman, of course. Lee J. Cobb. He sold stuff. "I am well-liked." Weird. Why couldn't he remember the title? It was a classic. He was an English professor! "I can't recall," he said.

"Death of a Salesman," said Klinder.

Daniel nodded once, feeling extremely stupid.

"An old man falls in love with a young man. Sort of an infatuation. The young man represents ideal beauty. Aesthetic perfection. It's a famous novel."

"Something in Venice."

"That's right—what's the title?"

"I told you."

"No."

Klinder waited.

"I don't recall."

Death in Venice.

"Of course." Daniel nodded, embarrassed.

"What's a word that starts with *D* and means mortality?"

Daniel laughed. It was like studying your whole life to be a guest on *JEOPARDY!* and forgetting who wrote the Gettysburg Address. He was a word man. He knew this was an important word. An obvious word.

"Deceased?"

"No."

"Departed?"

"No."

His frown was starting to make his head sore. Finally, he admitted. "I don't know."

"No. You do know, but you can't say it."

"Say what?"

"Death," Klinder said. "Unless you're a Corrector. Or you're me." He smiled proudly. "I can say it any time I want."

" 'Corrector?' "

"Killer."

Daniel tried to shake away the nonsense with his head. "You're telling me I can't say..." The word wouldn't come. His mouth couldn't get around it. "I can't say..." He bobbed his head a few times trying to force the syllable out. He had to say this word. His life depended on it.

He tried to sneak up on it. "Doubt."

"Dorothy!"

"Desk!"

He tried shouting. "Debt!"

That was as close as he got. Sean, on his lap, started giggling.

Daniel took off his glasses. Held them in one hand and rubbed his eyes with his finger and thumb. It reminded him of the first time he heard the word *fuck* on the radio, during some NPR pledge drive. Mike used to tease him about it: pledge drives had always been a guilty pleasure. Daniel loved their polite cheerful begging, their flattering presumption that he was one of them; liberal, generous, enlightened. He recalled some hippie-poet forgot broadcasting protocol and spilled the obscenity on-air. It had surprised him, because he realized that most censorship was habitual, self-enforced, unconscious—something everyone takes for granted. Like a button somebody pushed whenever you felt the impulse to swear. He wondered if there were other words like that. Words everybody knew but nobody could say.

"You're right," he said wonderingly. "I can't say it."

Klinder spread his hands wide as if he held an invisible accordion. "Welcome to eternity. It gets weirder from here."

Life Is a Take

Had the world ever been this empty? Mike wondered as he crossed the courtyard with Dot.

If anything confirmed the virtual nature of this reality it was the unearthly silence. You could look down a street and see no cars, no people, no pets, no birds. It was like the aftermath of a neutron bomb blast. A land bleached of all noise and clutter.

Life had never been this barren. Surely, that was a clue.

Even this Catholic high school, which should have been teeming with kids, was so deserted their footsteps echoed as they walked the halls. He'd see the occasional semi-full classroom, or the odd young "newbie" mopping floors. But it felt like some of the soundstages Mike had shot on, after the cast and crew had wrapped and gone home. The false walls buttressed by a matrix of two-by-fours. The overhead grid work of hanging lights, shut down and waiting to be redirected for the next scene. He felt that if he looked up he would see it: the skull beneath the skin.

Yet he still couldn't bring his mind to accept it. A neural network?

How was that possible? He could feel his heart, hear his breathing, smell the scent of tobacco coming off Dot's black suit, aware of her body and the way it moved. She directed him down a dark hall to a bright locker room. Sun streaming through the grated windows. Smells of damp towels and unwashed gym clothes. Rows and rows of gray lockers—lacking, strangely, locks.

Things had been very weird since he had gotten back from the jungle. He had killed a woman and she had risen from the dead. He had seen a man disappear. He couldn't deny that. But aliens? Dead people who lived? Carbon copies? His brother was going to kill him? He'd been hypnotized, after all. Maybe he still was. Maybe that's why the cookie and the coffee had tasted so amazing. Maybe that's all that happened to Wu. It could have been a trick. And it would take more than magic to convince him it was all true. It would take a miracle.

In one corner, a shimmering mound of discards, like a heap of parade props swept aside the morning after Mardi Gras. A pile of sleeping hummingbirds. It reminded Mike of a pyramid of doused charcoal with rainbows in the seams, or the vivid jungle rot of the Amazon rain forest: an embarrassment of colors. It smelled like shampoo.

"That's us," Dot said, standing with hands on hips.

There must have been a couple hundred birds in the pile. "Amazing colors," he said.

"Illusion," she said.

He looked at her.

"Their colors. Their necks and breasts are actually clear. Little air bubbles in the feathers create the colors by refraction. Like all of this—it's bullshit." She smiled that "I'm available" smile. "I used to be a zoologist. You want to touch it?"

He looked at her. An attractive woman who had once tried to kill him.

She pointed. "The pile."

Oh. Mike bent down to examine the heap of birds. He reached out to take the one with a red collar in his hand. For a moment he felt the miniature thundering of the sleeping bird's heart.

And he got his miracle.

It was a new type of shock that danced through his fist and up his arm and shot straight into his brain. A flash of nightmare. The fact that it only lasted a second didn't make it any less horrifying.

He was in a woman's mind.

A woman trapped inside a broken, smoking car.

Dying and in great pain.

Her view of a cracked windshield. Engine steam.

A plastic Big Bird toy lying on the seat beside her.

Thinking about her baby.

"Please," was the only word she said, before he dropped the bird.

It rolled to the bottom of the pile and Mike was on his knees breathing deeply.

Please. Ease. Keys.

My god, it was true. It was all true.

"See?" Dot asked. "You see why we hate them? They're collectors. We're their private collection of snuff films."

After he caught his breath he said, "That was . . . horrible."

"You wanna make your deposit?"

Mike swallowed a mouthful of bile. "What?"

"Add yours to the pile?"

Oh, he thought, she doesn't know. He shook his head.

"You don't have one, do you?" she asked, delighted, looking up and down his body. "Kyo told me, but I wouldn't believe it till I saw you myself."

Again, the name sent a shiver of dread into his brain. He couldn't understand why. "Believe what?"

Her eyes glimmered with something like lust. "You're the one."

Mike closed his eyes and sighed. He wanted to be away from this abrasive woman who kept shoving these ugly things in his face, things he had no desire to know. He wanted out of here. He wanted his life back. A life where people didn't talk in riddles. His life had turned into a sequence of accidents and mistakes. Like that new fad at the end of movies: outtakes. Everybody blowing their lines, tripping on furniture, bursting out laughing. His life was a series of outtakes.

Wait. Wait a second. There *are* no outtakes in life, he thought.

Life is a take.

"Can I be alone for a while?" he asked.

"Sure . . . you want to stay here?" Dot asked, indicating the pile as if it were something obscene.

"I'm not touching it again, don't worry." Even the thought made him shudder.

"I could find you some place more comfortable. Or we could get some sleep."

He looked at her. Sleep. It wouldn't be the first time he'd slept with someone he didn't like. But that was the last thing he wanted to do. "No, thanks."

He watched her leave, her butt rolling in that beautiful infinity swirl. He hadn't told Dot the worst of it. The worst of it was: The woman in the wreck had reminded him of Julie. The worst take of his life.

The way she said, "Please."

Please

Two deceased men and a deceased boy sat in the auditorium of the Crossovers' compound.

That's what we are, Daniel thought. That is what is happening. He had to hold on to that impossible thought, as tightly as he held his son on his lap, or he felt he would disappear.

Klinder said, "It's a long story, but you're not going anywhere. The aliens invaded in 1945. They tried to communicate with us. But nobody understood them."

"Nobody?" Daniel asked. "Why?"

"They're *aliens*, for pete's sake! All our ideas about invasion were based on human projection. We were prepped for an enemy. Centurions, Barbarians, Nazis—we could handle those. We expected death rays and monsters. We couldn't deal with something truly other." Klinder put out his cigarette in a copper ashtray and immediately lit another. "We weren't ready for gods."

Daniel said, "I thought you said they were hummingbirds."

"They're aliens using hummingbirds. No one's ever seen what they really look like. We don't even know their names. And the only people they talk to these days are kids."

"Kids." Daniel looked at Sean. "They talk to you?"

"Yeah."

"What do they say?"

Sean looked at Klinder, then looked down. "I can't tell."

Daniel laughed. "Hey, sport—You can tell me. I'm your father."

Sean squirmed on his lap, his set mouth holding back a sudden sadness. "No."

"Why on earth not?"

"I promised."

"Sean ... there are promises, and then there are promises."

"That's what they said you'd say. They don't trust big people."

"Why not?"

"You lie."

Daniel was silent for a long time. He couldn't think of an answer to that.

Klinder continued. "Here's what we do know. The aliens are infinitely more powerful than we can imagine. And they have no desire to reform us, or conquer us. But they've sampled us for decades. And ten years ago, in 1990, they made a miracle."

"The *D* word," Sean said.

Klinder nodded. "They took away death. They created a different earth. A virtual earth where everything was recognizably the same. The only major differences were that no one could be hungry ... no one could age ... and no one could die."

"You mean ... ?" Daniel couldn't get his mind around it.

"Everybody stays the same age they were when they died."

"That's stupid. Why don't they just reincarnate people in their prime?"

"They say they can't."

"Why not?"

"They can only do copies of existing forms. The process only works at death, during the transition. Like steam. You can't make a copy of steam if it's water or ice."

Daniel thought about that. There was something very disturbing about that. He couldn't say what. But a dread rose in his belly and the back of his skull began to tingle. "How do they do it?"

Klinder laughed. "Good question. They actually explained it to me once. Know what? I am one of the smartest people I know. I have three degrees: psychology, physics, and medicine. And I'll be honest with you. I didn't understand a word."

Daniel was about to ask a question. Then another. Then another. None of them quite did the situation justice. And the dread was rising. "What do they want from us?"

"That's what we're trying to find out. That's why you and Sean are so important."

"They like us," Sean said.

"Why?"

"They like the way we taste."

Daniel felt a revulsion. "They're eating us?"

"No," Sean said. "It's like they're tasting us."

"Tasting?" Daniel had a memory of a friend's golden retriever licking his fingers and nuzzling a spongy black nose into his palm. His whole body was tingling with dread now, for he realized that there was still one question that he had forgotten to ask: the most important one.

"I can't deal with this," Daniel said. He gently set Sean down and walked over to Klinder. Klinder stood.

"You said my wife was alive."

"You're relapsing. Denial."

"You said she'd come. When is she coming?"

"Daniel."

"When?"

Klinder looked down. "I don't know."

"Tell me!"

"Nobody knows. She's alive. She'll get here when she gets here."

"I have to wait till..."

"Till she dies."

Daniel felt all the blood drain out of his face. It was like he had lost her twice. "That could be years."

"Yes. I'm sorry."

Daniel balled his hands into fists. "I want to see her now."

"Son, try to calm down." He held up one finger. "You look a little sleepy."

Daniel slapped his hand away. "Stop it! I want to see her now!" He shouted to the room. "I want to see my wife now! Please!"

"Don't," Sean said, embarrassed.

The word tore out of him in a scream. "Please!"

They came from under the table. Wisps of color pouring upward like rainbow smoke. They swirled around the center of the long brown table like a cyclone of ribbons. The flock of hummingbirds condensed and formed a figure. A naked human. A woman who stood and hovered six inches above the table, undulating. Her body formed out of shivering lumps of feather. Her muffled reflection in the polished top. Upside down.

It was Julie.

Daniel fell to the ground sobbing, covering his head.

Sean was kneeling beside him, rubbing his back. "They're trying, see? If you ask nice, they'll try to give you anything you want."

"But they'd have to kill her to bring her here," Klinder said. "And they won't kill anything. That's one thing we do know, Daniel: they hate death. That's why we're here. That is their great gift. And all we have to do is accept it."

Daniel sat up, sniffling. Reluctantly, he lifted his eyes to the long, empty table. The horrible apparition was gone. But the squirming sculpture of a woman made of birds turned in his mind like the memory of a lynching. The dangling feet swaying slowly back and forth, back and forth.

It was truly the most grotesque thing he'd ever seen. And it was the first time she had ever repulsed him.

"That wasn't Julie," he said disgusted, his voice deep and froggy.

"Yeah," Sean agreed, rubbing Daniel's shoulders and doing his best to share his irritation. "Mom wore clothes."

The Last Time

Mike sat near the pile of hummingbirds in the locker room and remembered their last time together. Julie and him lying in the golden, windswept grass of Mount Tam. He had shot several car spots there. The winding roads and ocean vistas always flattered the cars no matter how dull Detroit had made them. In the distance, on the horizon: The twin towers of the Golden Gate and San Francisco, like a row of black teeth sticking up out of the fog. Fog everywhere. Curling in rogue wisps that oozed up and down the mountainside. It was like flying above the clouds, and in the blank breaches, getting glimpses of the slate bay below, the breakers on the rocks, the seals like pepper dotting the surf. Her lips, he remembered, tasted of merlot.

"Please," she said. "Don't."

"What?"

"Please don't spoil it."

They were lying side by side in the tall grass on the hillside, hidden from view, from the road. They hadn't even taken off their clothes.

"You're thinking about him," she said.

How could she know? He nodded.

Mike had been recalling the first time he'd felt attracted to her. It was the day after Thanksgiving when they had snacked on chocolate graham crackers and ice-cold milk in the kitchen while Danny was tucking Sean into bed, reading him a story. Doing the dirty work. He was upstairs a long time and he and Julie sat next to each other at the table and, though he was stuffed from the leftovers—the turkey, dressing, mashed potatoes and gravy, cranberry sauce—he couldn't stop eating the cookies. Washing them down with milk. One after the other. Talking. They hadn't talked that much before. He told her about his first and only pet: that old cat, Sebastian. Then she had asked about his stepdaughter; Danny had mentioned it and she was surprised: She hadn't known Mike was a father. And, for some reason, he had told her the story. She was, in fact, the first and only person he had told about the whole ordeal. The child who had taught him how to love again—that useless, agonizing knowledge—a child who, like everyone else, had left him behind. And something changed. Julie was looking at him in a new way. As if the brother-in-law she had known for years had transformed into a different person before her eyes.

Then she wanted to know all about the commercial he had shot in Morocco. A place she always wanted to go, she'd said. One of the many places she'd never been. "You'll have to take me along someday," she said, innocent, teasing. And as he talked she listened, really listened, and he saw it: behind her eyes, that new, hungry look. That available look. It had surprised him, after so many years of amused disapproval. Then innocent Danny had come downstairs yawning and both of them were suddenly aware of how close their faces were. Julie caught herself and leaned back in her chair. He saw her posture change to cool, and the wife mask slide back safely over her face.

The chilly wind off the bay blew a strand of hair into her eyes and she squinted. "Michael? Stop it. Men are so serious about sex."

"I always thought it was the other way around."

"No. We don't think about it as much. We're more in our bodies than you. You make lists."

"Lists?"

"Best dunks. Most homers. Lowest ERA."

"You know about ERAs?" he asked.

She slugged him on the arm. "You're so worried about comparisons."

Mike raised his eyebrows and adopted that familiar, befuddled face and sincere voice, "Actually, now that you bring it up—"

"—don't!" She glared at him, "You know I hate it when you imitate him."

That was stupid. Why did he do that? To prove he hadn't lost his touch? That he still had Danny down? Or because, Mike thought guiltily, he still has what I don't. "I hate the thought of sharing you."

"Most steals. Best slugging percentage. Highest score. It's all a competition for you." She snickered. "You and your heroes."

"There are no heroes anymore," Mike said. "They've been replaced by stars."

Finally, she smiled.

He thought: The real stars understood that fan love was phony and fickle. Which was why they were so protective of their public image. They knew they were one scandal, one stretch away from rejection. The lies they tell you about love. That there is somebody out there who will take you and cherish you as you really are, who didn't demand your best profile, require the best makeup and lighting. Whenever Mike saw couples fawning over each other, he didn't register jealousy; he merely smirked. Oh, stop it, he wanted to say. Just stop it. You aren't that happy. Wait'll you know each other. Wait'll they see your other side. Wait'll the day the sex stops and you're stuck with someone who hurts and bores you. Then talk to me about love.

"I feel rotten," he admitted.

They were silent for a long minute.

Julie said, "He'll never know. We wouldn't hurt him like that."

"Of course not."

"So let it be." She sat up and looked over the ocean. "He's a good man. But he doesn't know me, okay? He doesn't *have* to know me. He thinks I'm still that girl in the graduation picture he carries all the time. He doesn't know about the men . . . or my past."

"I do. It doesn't matter."

"That's why I need you," she said.

He couldn't quite bring himself to ask the painful question: Why stay married to him? What he asked was, "Why did you marry him?"

After a long while, she said, "He was the first man who didn't treat me like crap. I didn't believe men like him existed. He was kind and smart and gentle." She looked at him. "Good enough?"

"Hey."

"Then stop it."

"What?"

"Please, stop the jealousy."

He realized that he didn't know her. No matter what she said. She was a mystery to him. Had he thought that sex might change that? Mike closed his eyes and thought again of how the pleasure with Julie was always local—like having sex with a stranger. Never what he expected. And as good as the sex was he never felt any closer to her than he did before. How was that possible? Wasn't lovemaking supposed to draw you in? Open new doors? But with Julie it always felt as if there was a wall, impermeable, impenetrable. Like she only let you so far in. He always found himself wanting more. And was always surprised when she never gave it to him. Then the longing got the better of him and Michael wished a childish wish. Please. This is all I'm asking for. This is all I want. If only there was some tangible proof, something that he could hold onto, that would cement their connection, fill this gnawing, aching gap he felt whenever they had loved and love was not enough. Something he could name and point to and say: see? That's ours. That's us. And nobody can take that away. Please.

"Look," Julie said.

Mike sat up.

And almost before he saw the bank of fog approaching swiftly, it swallowed them in a white that was so immaculate and pure it hurt to look at it.

Then a cool mist breathed over him and in a moment he could barely see her. There was nothing but a ghostly white cloud sliding past. Sometimes it lightened, sometimes it darkened, and the shadows were blue. And though he couldn't see her, it didn't feel like they were alone. It felt like they were together for the first time, truly one. In the absence of shape and shadow he reached out and took her hand: damp and cold. He closed his eyes. When he couldn't feel the soft spray on his face, he opened them. It was like a dream. The cloud had passed and Julie sat beside him—her lashes and thin, brown hair speckled with tiny crystals that sparkled, and her open windbreaker revealed her breasts; they had a fine sheen of jewels. Like the breasts of hummingbirds whose true color was clear.

Emerging from the memory, Mike felt, oddly, as if he had just shared his thoughts with another mind, as if he were sitting in a dark theater with a stranger beside him, screening the dailies of his life. The producer? The clients? Someone who had final cut. "N.G." he'd always think. *No good.* That dolly move is late, the focus is soft, the light too harsh, the timing off, the performance pitched just a little too sharply, as if the actor were playing for the crowd like a cat in heat—always the biggest temptation of actors: they wanted so much to be loved. The compulsive need to be on and interesting. This feeling of being watched. He knew it well.

He was back on Mount Tam. Stunned by the beauty of Julie. Her body glistening with fog drops. He wanted her again. And when she turned to him and opened her eyes he saw a great, unguarded sadness in her face—which she quickly covered over, as if he were a stranger she had just met, as if they hadn't just made love.

"I'm sorry," Mike said. The words felt curious on his tongue. He couldn't recall the last time he had apologized for anything. To anyone.

"Shut up," she replied. And, grasping his head with one hand, she guided his mouth to her wet, cold breast. For the last time.

It Was a Given

D aniel wasn't well. They'd put him in a plain white room with a bed.

He had refused sedation and hypnosis. He wanted to be alone. Alone, he thought, staring at the ceiling. Alone and the whole bed to himself.

He slept and dreamed of waterfalls. There was a man behind the curtain of water; he could almost see his face. "Who are you?" he asked.

When he woke he noticed, on the middle of the white bedspread, his keys and pens and brown wallet.

He reached for the wallet, laid back, opened it and looked at her photograph.

And his mind spun out a monologue like a runaway sled.

The picture's edges were frayed by being jammed in there for so long. He noticed that her portrait had been superseded by the photos of a growing Sean. Each school picture from preschool to third grade. Sean changes slightly each year. Some days he doesn't know what to do with the camera. Then gradually there is a dawning apprehension that this is for history. And he assumes the subtlest poses. You can see his mind working its way into his face, consciousness fighting to creep into his features. Then about second grade it arrives. He wears that *What am I doing here?* face. Then in third grade, he's posing, holding himself back from sticking out his tongue, holding back a laugh, proud of his new haircut, his new shirt.

Meanwhile, as her son grows over her, like cards stacking over the queen, Julie remains the same—the same high school sweetheart accumulating surface wear. Her thin, rusty brown hair that she was always apologizing for. Her sharp, hurt eyes that always looked as if they'd just stopped crying. Eyes guarded and wounded, wondering and afraid. Her almost smile, no teeth, just two slight curls at each corner of her lovely lips. And the nose that she was so mortified to wear, that large, turned-up elfin protrusion, permanently flared nostrils sniffing out rejection—a nose, she once said, that belonged on somebody else's face. It had always been too big for hers. The thing, she called it. "The first thing," she winced, "that anyone sees." Daniel thought it was the nose he fell for.

Beauty is so relative. There is no standard. What triggers desire in some is invisible to others and will not pronounce its magic. The heart can't help itself. It loves what it loves in spite of all evidence and standards, and that is its curse and gift. Actually, he thought, that's one of the most merciful things about desire—there seems to be someone for everyone.

Julie was beautiful in a way that made him feel protective. It took him years to accept that no matter how many times he'd make love to her, praise her, gift her, touch her, profess his desire in every way he could think of, she could never bring herself to believe it. Something dark and slivered had staked itself into her heart and wouldn't let go. It was as if her whole body was a mask for something terrible, something she didn't dare let out, but something too she couldn't allow to go unmentioned.

Who taught her that? That deep-down dismissal of anyone who tried to give her more credit than she thought she deserved. That reflexive dodge of joy. It made him love her more, and despair that he would ever find a way to pull out that stake, to convince her that she was—for him at least—the most beautiful creature he had ever seen. Perhaps his desire was so unqualified she couldn't trust it.

"You're the truster," she said once. "You're the one who believes people really mean the best."

It was an issue they could never agree on. So they let it pass. And as the surface of her sepia-tinted graduation photo took on age and scratches in his wallet, the face in the picture never changed: She would always be that high school girl who would never be good enough, smart enough, pretty enough for anyone to love. "That's okay," her picture said, "I'm nobody."

But she wasn't. She couldn't have been if she tried. She was everything he wanted. And it seared him that she didn't feel the same.

Sometimes Daniel wished there was a rewind button on life. If he could, he would go back to those moments when life had gone awry, taken bad turns, and play Cassandra to himself. Wait! He'd say to his doomed predecessor, you're too young for that. Don't drink that third martini. No, the answer is C you idiot! Don't correct that bully; he'll kick your ass. No, the interviewer doesn't want your candid admission to being less than up on Victorian literature, he doesn't admire self-deprecation; he's a fraud and he's threatened by honesty. Why the hell are you voting for McGovern? He's a loser! Microsoft, you dip. Buy Microsoft. And especially, he would pound on the steamed-up windows of that old brown Ford and warn that young teacher making out with the young nurse he'd met while giving his regular blood donation: "Stop! You're marrying the wrong woman! You're marrying the wrong woman! You're marrying the wrong woman!"

Of course, life only moved one way. It couldn't be corrected or reversed. It had to be lived forward.

It was a given.

The door opened to the dark room. He saw the black silhouette of a boy in the doorway. Silently, Sean moved to him and gently took his hand. The same way he'd come to the boy when he was caught in a nightmare. The thought amused him: a miniature of himself comforting his grown son. Sean turned on the nightstand lamp and looked around, taking in the mess Daniel had left all over the bed. He thought: If he was me he'd make me straighten up my room now. Daniel watched his eyes darting over the strewn items. Keys. Glasses. Wallet. School photos spread out on the blanket.

"Hey! Those are me." Sean scooped up the pictures and lay belly down beside Daniel and started leafing through them. "Yuck," he said, and Daniel knew he had discovered second grade: bad hair day.

Then he got to his mother.

"She used to sing to me."

Daniel closed his eyes.

"I liked her voice," said the boy sadly.

Please, don't sing, Daniel thought.

"Hey. Where——?"

Suddenly, Sean was frantically searching the room. Looking under the sheets, checking under the bed.

"What the heck you doing, sport?"

"I can't find it!"

"What?"

"Where'd you put it?"

"What?"

"You can't lose it!" the boy hissed angrily.

"Hey, hey, hey," Daniel said, sitting up, taking the child by his shoulders. "Take it easy, now. What are your looking for?"

"Your bird."

Daniel looked bewildered at the boy's desperate face. "What are you talking about?"

"Everybody's got one."

"I never had a bird." The look on his son's face horrified him. "What?"

"Everybody's . . ." The words faded with a breath. His son stared at him.

"Sean," he said sternly. "Calm down now."

The boy was crying.

"Sean?"

"You don't belong." He reached into his pocket and pulled something out, then presented it in his palm: a ruby-throated hummingbird. "You gotta have a bird!"

Daniel had no idea what was upsetting him so. "So? What's it mean that I don't have a bird?"

"You're a Corrector!

"But, but . . ." he tried to reassure the boy. "I can't even say the *D* word!"

His son fell sobbing into his arms.

Daniel's face was frowning so hard it ached as his hand gently rubbed the shaking little body. What kind of world is this? he wondered. What kind of world have I fallen into?

The Unsuccessful
Kamikaze

Mike was looking at the rainbow bird pile when he heard footsteps.

He turned to see the man from the 7-Eleven, the tall, dark Asian who resembled that Hong Kong shoot-'em-up star. Agent Takahashi. Still dressed in his perfect black suit. Smiling, he tossed something to Mike and he caught it: his wallet.

"What the fuck?" asked Mike. "That's my personal—how the fuck?"

"Wu. When you were in the car. We're gonna miss that guy. He was our best pickpocket."

Mike looked furiously at Takahashi.

"Hey. Chill. It's procedure. Come on." He crooked a finger and led him to the showers: a long, green marble room with round drains every three feet or so. Kyo turned on the wall spigots one by one. The hissing grew louder and the room filled with steam. Then he started to undress, setting his shoes on a wooden bench. "Better take your clothes off. This can get messy."

Mike shook his head.

"Your funeral," the man said.

He sat on the bench as Kyo took off his suit coat, tie, and shirt. Though there were deep lines at the corners of his eyes, and weathered hands below his perfect white cuffs, on close inspection Mike noticed that the man was younger than him. Takahashi checked his watch. "Five minutes to reentry."

"What?"

"You better brace yourself. First time I nearly lost my cookies."

He was struck again at how familiar the man looked. He had at the 7-Eleven too. He never forgot a face. But he couldn't place Kyo. "Where are you from?" Mike asked.

The man smiled. "Tokyo. Grew up in Frisco after the war. I am the son of one of the few unsuccessful kamikaze pilots on earth."

" 'Unsuccessful?' "

"He lived." Takahashi was removing his pants. Red boxer shorts. "You really ought to take off your clothes. Your shoes, anyway."

Mike was removing his Adidas when he heard a whimper echoing through the showers like the wail of a ghost. He froze. "What the fuck was that?"

"She's coming. Hand me those towels." Mike reached over and grabbed a few of the pink towels stacked on the windowsill and tossed them over. Kyo laid them over his forearm like a waiter at a nudist colony.

Mike waited, but Takahashi offered no explanation. Finally he asked, "What happened in the war? Your father missed?"

"He was twelve. By then Tokyo was pretty much rubble from the bombing. The first waves of pilots were all lost. Their best men. Fathers. Older brothers. Only oldies, kids, and women left. Mostly. Kamikaze was a grand idea only the Japanese could have concocted. A last-ditch heroic sacrifice. Your life for the emperor. Very spiritual. They were down to boy pilots near the end of the war. My father said they trained in little wooden

planes, like soap-box derby cars. No wings. Had a joystick throttle." Mike
got very still when Takahashi placed both hands before him as if he were
holding an imaginary baseball bat. He leaned back and forth. "Left. Right.
Dive. Playing army. Father said they had a great time but they couldn't
show it. Very solemn. Ritualized. On their first run they wrapped rising-
sun bandannas around their heads. He had his first sake. Saluted. Was
marching toward the plane—no parachute, of course—when the loud-
speaker at the base announced the emperor had surrendered. The war was
over. Japan had lost. None of them could believe it." Kyo looked at his
watch, then up at the ceiling. Mike looked up too. "Imagine a group of
six boys, ages twelve to fifteen, standing tipsy in their new uniforms in
the middle of the runway. Their commander sitting, weeping on the tar-
mac. Looking at each other, thinking: 'We've been robbed. We had a
chance to prove our loyalty, our manhood. And they robbed us.' My father
said some of the boys were ashamed to look at each other. Some were
angry. Some were just lonely kids wanting to go home. He told me: 'I
was willing to die for a person I'd never seen. A man who said he was
god. That's a mistake I'll never make again.' "

Jesus, what a story, thought Mike. He'd have to use that. "What did
he do after the war?"

"Advertising," said Kyo. He sang horribly, *"Rice-a-roni. The San Francisco
treat!"*

Mike looked at him.

"Father wrote that," he said proudly. "Commercials. That's how I
learned English. Father used to say—"

There was the horrible smell of burning hair and a naked woman was
suddenly thrashing on the floor of the showers. Screaming. Convulsions.
A thick jet of piss streaming from her pussy, spraying everywhere like a
loose fire hose. Takahashi knelt beside her, held her down by the shoulders
and hissed at Mike, "Get her legs!"

Just a Copy

⁓ ⁓ ⁓

Daniel had never heard himself snoring before. But there he was, watching a videotape of himself sleeping: a green night-vision image taken from a high corner of his bedroom. A man sleeping on his back.

He was in the compound. Back in the long conference room again, watching the tape with Klinder in his perpetual paper pajamas, smoking as usual, the sleeves dotted with tiny little burn holes. The long tabletop was shiny as a mirror; it bisected Klinder neatly in the middle, doubling his image upside down, so that he resembled a face card: a fat jack of diamonds holding a cigarette.

There was a flutter of movement on the large screen. *A bird with invisible wings entered the frame. It hovered over Daniel's sleeping head. Then scooted closer, and coiled itself back like a bent prong and jabbed its needle nose into the corner of his eye.*

"Jesus!" said Daniel, his hand involuntarily covering his face.

It went on for a long time, its feeding. Then the bird left the frame as quickly as it had come, and Klinder stopped the tape. "Now you know why I didn't invite Sean."

Daniel shuddered and touched first one eye, than the other. They didn't seem any worse for the wear.

"That was last night," Klinder said.

Daniel moved to the water cooler in the corner. It glugged and beluga bubbles rose to the top of the clear, plastic bottle. He lifted the paper cone and drank. Then crushed it in his hands. Darn good water, he thought.

"I've got some rather shocking news. You better sit down."

Daniel tossed the cup in the trash and sat.

"They've been doing it all your life."

If the video of that one intrusion was creepy to Daniel—and it was—the thought that it was not an exceptional event was horrifying. His glasses were rimmed with beads of condensation and he removed them and wiped them clear. "What are they doing?"

"Updating."

"Updating?"

"Your thoughts. Your DNA. Your body. Your emotions." He spread his arms wide, as if to include the whole virtual world. "The whole schmear. We're all samples, Daniel. I know. It's a lot to swallow."

After a time, Daniel said, "I'm not me?"

"No."

"I'm a sample?"

"You're a copy." He smiled. "A carbon copy. We all are."

"A clone?"

"Close enough. But you have all your memories."

Not all of them, Daniel thought. I still don't remember the accident. He closed his eyes and made a mental list of answers.

Alive?

A sample?

Not alive?

A copy?

Who am I? That was the question.

It was like the brutal, unrelieved self-consciousness of adolescence. A desolate country of caste and cruelty, uncertainty and desire, a place he had never wanted to visit again. But here he was: questioning everything like a teen. The way you walked. How you looked. Your words. Your cracking voice. The feeling of being incomplete, knowing you were between selves. No idea who you were or what you were becoming. Your face erupting with angry, red volcanoes—every morning in the mirror: a new horror, something else to hide, something that marked you as undone, a changing thing, stuck in somebody else's body.

Maybe that was the secret of the diary. How quickly people changed. There was Mike before Buffalo and Mike after Buffalo. Two totally different people.

Daniel had discovered early on that people couldn't be trusted to be one thing. There was the happy Uncle Louie, drunk and cleaning the brown trout in the kitchen sink, singing Bing Crosby as he eviscerated the fish. And there was Uncle Louie hungover in the morning, growling and ready to backhand you at the breakfast table. You had to watch carefully. Why didn't Mike get it? He never got the timing down. Never understood that you couldn't contradict Uncle Louie before 10 A.M. Or talk back. Or disobey him, ever, never. Mike paid the price. Danny would bring him ice cubes in Saran Wrap and find him laying down in bed holding a hand to his bruised cheek. And no matter how many times he tried to explain how he was at fault, how he could avoid the hand the next time, Mike never heard him. "He's a shithead," he'd say as if that explained everything. "No," he'd try to tell him. "You just got to pay attention. You gotta know which Uncle Louie you're talking to."

Julie used to call Daniel "predictable." She didn't know how hard he had to work at it. How many selves he battled daily. How he never developed the habit of being one thing, one person. How it was always a choice. It was a lesson he had perfected under Uncle Louie's roof—he could never quite call it *home*. "Who do you want me to be today?" was always the question. And he knew all the answers. Quiet? Sensitive? Thoughtful? You want another beer? Can I get your Chesterfields? Hoe the garden out back? Well, all right. He'd do it. He had become a master at reading his uncle's moods, and adjusting accordingly. But somewhere along the line, Daniel felt he had lost something precious. He had no idea who he was. That was why it was so important to be what other people needed, he supposed. That's what defined him. Not his predictability. But his constant adaptation. That was his secret. He wasn't just one thing. He could be two or three people as easily as one. It depended on what was needed.

"Daniel?" a distant voice said.

Consequently, he had always felt like he was the most forgettable character in someone else's story. Jesus' brother. The second man on the moon. Oswald's invisible partner on the grassy knoll. The sidekick to Mike's leading man. An extra who made no visual impression. Just another pot-bellied, balding guy with glasses. Old friends whom he hadn't seen in years could never remember him. Even Sean knew it. He had written a description of his family once for school, and after lines and lines about his mom and her face and her hair, he had summarized him like this: "My Dad is Good." An odd thought occurred to Daniel. He was missing something Sean used to say all the time, usually when he was embarrassed by him. The word "Dad." Ever since he'd arrived at the compound, Sean hadn't called him that.

No doubt about it, Daniel concluded: He was a nobody.

Perhaps that was why he so desperately needed the mirror of love. Maybe that's all marriage was. Julie was. Someone to remind him who he was.

"Daniel?" a voice said.

Because when Julie had left, he couldn't remember anymore.

"Son?" Klinder said, standing over him. "You've been sitting there for fifteen minutes." He laid his hand on his shoulder. "Daniel?"

"Don't call me that," he said, finally. "I'm just a copy."

Reentry

Mike was reaching for the kicking feet of the screaming pissing woman in the showers, trying to pin her ankles down, when he caught a good kick to the jaw. The marble walls of the showers reverberated with her screams. Takahashi had a towel under her head and straddled the spasming blond woman. Mike finally had her legs.

Still she screamed.

Takahashi tossed him a towel. "Put it under her rump," he ordered. Mike did and the urine quickly soaked through.

Rump. Pump. Hump.

"Full bladders when they reenter," said Takahashi. "Go figure."

The woman's screams grew softer, hoarser, as if she had broken something in her throat.

"Shhhh," Takahashi whispered as he held her arms against the marble floor, careful, Mike noted, not to sit on the writhing woman.

"Swabo!" the woman screamed. Her first intelligible word. Intelligible and nonsensical.

"Shhhh," Takahashi whispered.

"SWABO!"

"Take it easy, Dawn. I got you."

Dawn? Mike thought. Then he recognized her. The blond Wu had shot. There was something in her fist.

"Swabo!"

She was shuddering now; it took a lot to hold her down.

By the time she had calmed and lay whimpering, Mike's clothes were soaked and his body drenched with sweat. In a cloud of steam they held her up under the shower and rinsed her body.

"Shouldn't a woman be doing this?" Mike asked, not embarrassed at all, but wondering if Dawn might be.

"Takes two men. Most women aren't strong enough."

"Shut up," Dawn said, her eyes still closed as Mike shampooed her hair and Takahashi soaped down her body.

"Feeling better, eh?" Takahashi smiled.

"Where's Swabo?" she croaked, her southern accent echoing off the walls.

"He's alive, remember? He survived the plane crash. You didn't."

"Right," she said. She cried for a time. "Shit, I miss that boy."

"I know, babe. He'll get here."

"I don't want him *here*, you prick."

Takahashi smiled at Mike as he rinsed her hair. "Much better," he said.

As he turned Dawn gently, directing her body toward the spray, Mike watched the soapy water and urine circling into the drain.

Later, they were sitting on a long bench that ran between the lockers. Mike, Dawn, and Takahashi. Wearing white bathrobes. One of the spigots wasn't all the way off and its dribbles echoed in the showers next door. Dawn, quiet now, smoking a cigarette. She offered Mike a drag and he shook his head.

"How many times you done this?" Mike asked her.

"Six? Seven? I forget." She looked at Mike. "Oh, you were there. You tried to stop us." She turned to Takahashi. "Did Wu make it okay?"

Mike shuddered, recalling the black eyes, black teeth.

"Erased," Takahashi confirmed.

She nodded, sighed, and took a long drag. "You joining us?"

"He's thinking about it," Takahashi said.

Am I? Mike wondered.

"I could sleep a million years," Dawn said. Dark circles under her eyes. Her skin very pale. She yawned. Big teeth in a little mouth. Like a singer whose name he couldn't recall.

"Thanks for the smoke, Kyo."

"No problem, sis."

"And thank you, Mr. Glynn," the woman said. "First time?" He nodded. "Must have been scary." He nodded. She smirked. "Imagine how I felt." She saw his bruised jaw and touched it gently with her hand. "Me?"

"Yeah."

"Sorry." She gave a faint smile as her fingers stroked his jaw. "Aren't you a sweetheart for helping out."

Mike tilted his head away toward the showers and asked, "That's what happens to all of you?"

Dawn looked at him.

"The dead dead."

"Jesus H. Christ," said Dawn. "Didn't this fella just get here?"

"Yeah," Kyo said.

"How'd he get his count so high?"

Kyo laughed. "Ancient Chinese secret. Would you believe he killed Dot?"

"Holy moly." She regarded Mike again. "You must be one tough hombre."

Mike asked, "Everybody ends up in the showers?"

"We do. This is our home. *Showers* is sort of like our password."

Mike remembered the woman at the 7-Eleven asking him, "When was the last time you had a shower?"

Kyo said, "I know people who've died twenty times. Klinder's died at least nine times. We died together once."

"So we just keep dying?" Mike asked, trying to get his mind around it.

"Well, kids," Dawn started to say, then stopped. She turned to Kyo and asked intently, "Is he the one?"

"Shhhh," Kyo said.

"What happens to kids?" Mike asked.

"They never come back," explained Kyo. "They only die once."

"Why?"

"Don't know," said Kyo. "Maybe the birds cut them some slack."

"There's not many of them, anyway," Dawn said. "Most of them missed out on the deal. Lucky bastards."

Kids, Mike thought. There was the girl on the plane. And Klinder had said Sean was here. And Danny. That meant they were dead. But how did they get here?

"Time to make my deposit," Dawn said, standing.

"You should see this," Takahashi said.

As they followed the woman in the bathrobe, Mike saw the wet tail feathers of a bird sticking out of her left fist. Dawn walked to the corner of the locker room, to the pile, and tossed the hummingbird on top. "For Wu," she said.

Mike wondered how the translator would handle this ritual. He doubted she could find a word for this. Strange that she had left so suddenly. Where'd she go, anyway?

"What's it like?" he asked Dawn. "The showers?"

"Well . . . it hurts like a sonuvabitch. Like needles all over." Mike shuddered. "Then, unless it's your first time, you remember how you bought it."

"First time?" Mike asked.

Dawn looked at Kyo. "Should I be telling him this?"

Kyo shrugged. "Sooner or later, he's gotta learn."

"Okay. Yeah, your first time . . . apparently it takes them a while to transfer all the data. It's harder to remember the first time. There's like . . . a fog over everything."

The fog, Mike recalled. The jungle. The flight into LA when he couldn't remember. *The flashes of memories: falling. Falling from a high place.*

"Then, if you hold on tight, make a fist, you remember the rest of your life. Then the longest piss you've ever had." She yawned. "Then . . . you're really, really horny." She smiled that toothy smile at Mike. "We should get together later."

Kyo smirked. "Dawn. The other white meat."

Dawn laughed and smacked Kyo on the shoulder with the back of her hand. "He's got a million of 'em."

Lucinda Williams. That's who Dawn reminded him of. That lanky and fragile country singer with the honest, sexy twang. Who always told the truth. He loved her songs.

"Was it worth it?" Mike asked.

She didn't hesitate. "For Wu? Every fucking second."

The Hospital

It's the early fifties. I'm finishing medical school. Up to my eyeballs in debt. An old prof of mine recruits me for the government. Says, 'Klinder? We need you.'" Klinder was leaning back in the conference room chair beside Daniel, his paper jumpsuit crinkling, his tennis shoes on the table between them. "Sensitive project," he said. Relishing his monologue. "Top secret." Rubbing his feet through his green-and-red striped socks. "UFOs."

"Why you?" Daniel asked.

"Kids and birds and hypnosis—my specialties. The aliens are everywhere: roaming our atmosphere, buzzing our cities. Impossible to track; at best they might show up as a funnel cloud on radar. The government, while officially denying any knowledge of them, of course, is trying frantically to make contact." Klinder switched feet. "Nothing worked. Until they stumbled on hypnosis. Hypnotized kids can communicate with them and relay the information. Over the years I've perfected the method."

"Kids?" Daniel asked, a sour feeling in his gut.

"Yeah, they're natural subjects. Malleable. Open to suggestion. See, the hypnotized subject is bifurcated. Two consciousnesses sharing the same brain. One acting on orders. One watching but with no volition—who will only remember later, and only with permission. *I believe it duplicates the way they share the bodies of hummingbirds.* But that's just my working theory," he added proudly.

"Kids?"

"Daniel. You gotta understand. The most important job in the world! And they were offering it to me! Unlimited budget for research. Zero bureaucracy. The authority to head up my country's most classified project: blue book. I didn't have to answer to anybody. The air force, the army, intelligence. For all practical purposes they were working for me! And times being what they were—there'd been some lean years, believe you me. But it all came together. They were handing me the chance of a lifetime. To save the planet! Tell me, what else should I have done? What was I supposed to do? Say, 'no thanks?'"

"Kids?"

"Yes." Klinder sighed, apparently disappointed that Daniel didn't share his exhilaration. "That was the bargain. We tried lots of kids. But we really hit the jackpot with you guys."

"*What?!*"

"They wanted me to do some experiments. Perfect their sampling methods—I learned later. You were perfect subjects." Klinder looked dreamily at the ceiling.

What did you do to us, doctor? Daniel thought. What?

Klinder finally seemed to notice his face. "We didn't have much of a choice, Daniel. They were like gods demanding a sacrifice. They said that it would be the end of the world if we didn't hand you over."

"A sacrifice?"

Klinder swallowed. "It was only for a month. That summer Mike stayed with relatives in Buffalo while you were in the hospital with trench mouth?"

Daniel had a coughing fit.

"That was the cover story, anyway," Klinder admitted. "That's when they took you to their ship."

Their ship.

A *month*, Daniel thought.

Jesus, was it that long?

Maybe that's where his faulty memory came from. Alien experiments. Missing time.

He was only eight.

Jesus.

It made him sick to think of it. The hospital. The images were disconnected, difficult to parse—like those refrigerator poetry magnets—separate, random words that had to be stacked like building blocks until they made sense. The shots. The nurse's feet. The doctor's steps. The doctor's white mask. The needle. The wet bed. The straps. The buckles. The distant screams of children in the next ward. The children wouldn't stop crying. And that neon sign out the window. Frustratingly incomplete. Flashing over and over. *ANCY. ANCY. ANCY.* And, years later trying to put together the missing pieces. Fill in the blanks. *Pregnancy? Infancy? Nancy?* Well, at least he had his own room, he'd thought. At least he didn't have to share a bunk with Mike. There was that. But even so, he called Mike's name, hoping he would come. Called Mike's name until his throat was hoarse and bleeding. Bleeding from the mouth, the ears, and the eyes. Blood trickling down the straw into the ice water. The only relief was those yucky Popsicles that stung, then numbed his open sores. Orange Popsicles kept chilled on the windowsill. Before room refrigerators. And the nurses held them in your mouth when you didn't want anymore.

The strange turbine humming that filled the room and nauseated him. The shots. Being woken by white nurses in the middle of the night to receive painful shots in the butt, the shoulder, the thighs, the corners of the eye—shots that left him so sore he couldn't walk by himself to the bathroom; was always wetting the bed. And they wouldn't let him out. Him kicking when he saw the needle coming. The white doctor holding up his fat finger as if to say, just one more. Just one more. Counting down to the blastoff. Just five, just four, just three, just two, just one. But no matter what the numbers said there was always more. And them buckling him down with the straps—over his ankles, thighs, waist, and chest—so taut that made it hard to take a breath. He never wanted to feel that way again as long as he lived. And one spidery rubber hand holding his head still as the needle went in.

He slept a lot. He remembered that. Or rather, he remembered the beautiful absence that was his only escape. The only time it didn't hurt. But they were always waking him up. And Danny promising God that if only he would make it stop, he would be a good boy. He would be good for the rest of his life. He would never do another naughty thing. He swore he would. He swore. But nobody visited; nobody came. Nobody except that strange, round nurse who smelled of chocolate graham crackers, and read him comics and sometimes touched her fat finger to his head, between the eyes. He could still feel the soft, cool impression as her finger left his skin. But in the haze of his fever, he could never quite pull her into focus. And the pain. And missing Mike so much. Every day. It was the first time they'd ever been apart. Missing Mike. And wanting to go home.

Stasis.

It had all happened in a moment. When they were lying frozen in the wheat field. "Barrada. Nikto." Were those the magic words? They'd laid down in summer and stood up in fall. A month. A missing moment that lasted forever.

Things were different after that. Danny made good his promise. He was even nicer than before. He became Uncle Louie's favorite. He resolved never to play the tacit accomplice to Mike's pranks. Never be an instigator. After all, Aloysius was watching them. But when Mike came back from Buffalo he was even worse: meaner, angrier. He had two black eyes—ugly yellow-purple bruises. "You look like a raccoon!" Danny had teased him.

"Look who's talking," Mike had snapped back, for, of course, Danny's bruises were identical.

And that was it. After that, Mike refused to talk about his month in Buffalo. Soon after he returned he started mouthing off to Uncle Louie. And getting smacked. And getting his mouth washed out with soap. He remembered that summer now. The summer they had found the fish.

"I remember the hospital," Daniel said in a haunted voice that retained the timbre of a child's. "That was their ship?"

Klinder nodded.

"A month!" Daniel coughed and his voice lowered. "It seemed like forever. What did the aliens want?"

"Finally," said Klinder, smiling and lighting a fresh cigarette with his Zippo. "The right question."

The Ties that Bind

They were sitting by the pile of birds and Mike was watching Kyo's eyes. Dark, shining, unreadable eyes. You never knew what was poised there under those heavy lids, waiting to spring. Scorn? Rage? Laughter? You couldn't tell who you were talking to. Sometimes he was a stranger. Sometimes he seemed a friend. When the man smiled it was with the corners of his eyes—a gift of expression in a desert of reserve.

Dawn had left. Kyo had opened a locker and they had changed into sweatsuits. Then he pulled out a can of lighter fluid from the locker and was refilling his Zippo.

"So. Are you with us, yet?" asked Kyo. "Three strikes and you're out."

Three? That's right, Mike thought. A relative, a stranger, and someone you liked. He had killed a stranger already—Dot. He hadn't met anyone he liked yet, except Dawn, maybe. And he couldn't imagine killing a relative—that would mean Danny. What a crazy equation. "How does that work, exactly?"

Kyo said, "Near as we can figure it has to do with bonds. The ties that bind. You break the familial, fraternal, and communal bonds, and you pass go. Pop, pop, fizz. Oh, what a relief it is. It's not really death, you know."

"What?"

"It's not really death, is it? If someone's already dead."

"How come you can say that word?"

Kyo smiled, and held up his silver Zippo lighter like it was a medal. "Membership has its privileges."

Mike swallowed and asked, "You ever kill a relative?"

"No," Kyo admitted. "No, my parents died ages ago. I was an only child."

After a moment Mike said, "So you're stuck here."

Mike saw he had hit the mark. For the first time Kyo's stony face couldn't hide his feelings. It was a talent Mike had acquired while directing. He could always tell when the actor was forcing it, faking it. But when they tapped into something true, something they really felt, there was no hiding it. That was the take. Mike had no doubt this was what Kyo wanted more than anything. And his casual words couldn't disguise his hunger.

"Yeah. You're my only way out. That's why I need your help."

"Why should I help you?"

Kyo smiled. "You might want to consider, Mike, that Daniel's going to try to kill you."

Mike laughed.

"That's why we were trying to kill him," Takahashi nodded. "Seriously."

"Bullshit."

"It's the only way Klinder can win."

"He had his chance. He didn't touch me."

"Klinder can't do it. Only Daniel can. The Crossovers believe if Daniel kills you then we're stuck here. All of us. That's the equation."

Did anything make sense here? "How the fuck do you know what the Crossovers believe?"

"I work for them. Klinder ordered me to recruit you and your brother. He was setting you up for a fall."

"Whose side are you on?"

"I'm on your side. I'm a Corrector."

That's right: a double agent. Dot told him that. "You don't know Danny. He wouldn't do it."

"He will when they tell him about Julie." Kyo watched his face. "I'd say that's a good reason, wouldn't you?"

The wallet, Mike thought. After a time he said, "You met Danny?"

"Yes. I found him in Detroit."

"Why didn't you kill him then?"

"I still needed a few codes."

"How's . . . how's he doing?"

"He's a wreck. Sleeps all day. Thinks about his wife."

Poor guy, Mike thought. "How did he . . . how did they . . . ?"

Kyo held up a hand and shook his head. "Trust me. You don't want to know."

After a long silence, Kyo said, "So. You with us?"

Mike stood. "You think you can show me a few miracles, a pile of birds and bingo, I'm an assassin? What makes you think I'd kill my brother?"

"We don't want to kill your brother, Mike. We want you to kill the Bird Boy."

"*The Bird Boy?*"

"Sean," said Takahashi. "He's special to the birds. He's the only one they talk to. He's their main link and Klinder's key to power. We've been planning the operation for years, Mike. We want to mortally offend the aliens, stop this whole existence dead in its tracks. We want out. And you're the one. The only one who can help us. All you gotta do is kill the boy and—what?—someone you like and you're off. Erased." Kyo smiled. "I'd volunteer, but I'm not sure you like me yet. How's that sound?"

"Like the stupidest thing I've ever heard in my life! You want me to kill a child? My nephew?"

The man hesitated, as if he were about to divulge something and changed his mind.

"Are you fucking out of your mind?"

Kyo said, "Think of it as a mercy killing."

"You people make me sick," Mike said.

"I know. It's a crazy world. We want out. And we're willing to do anything to get it."

"Even kill a child."

"Let me ask you something, Mike. What do you think they're doing to Sean down in the compound? What do you think he wants him for? You think Klinder's playing games? Teaching him chess?" He reached into the pocket of his black sweatsuit and pulled out a white knight, holding it between his finger and his thumb. "He taught me. I was his favorite."

Mike remembered the black knight the doctor had given him. When he was ten. And the more Kyo talked, the more nervous he became. Because he heard the truth. And because he heard all the things Kyo wasn't saying.

Kyo put the white knight back and pulled out his Zippo lighter, started clicking it open with his thumb and snapping it shut against his palm. (*Open. Shut.*) "Did he tell you not to tell too? Did he make you promise? (*Open. Shut.*) See, I've known him most of my life and all of my death. We died in a plane crash together nine years ago. (*Open. Shut.*) I've been his right-hand man ever since." Kyo smiled. "He was the only hypnotist on the planet who could put a whole crowd under. (*Open. Shut.*) Proved it with your class, didn't he? Do you have any idea how rare that is? (*Open. Shut.*) One day he couldn't hypnotize me anymore. I never let on. (*Open. Shut.*) And I finally saw him for what he is. Klinder is a man who isn't there. (*Open. Shut.*) That's his secret. He's whatever you want him to be. (*Open.*) He'll say anything. (*Shut.*) He'll do anything. (*Open.*) Anything. (*Shut.*) (*Open. Shut.*) I've been there, Mike. I've seen it myself."

Mike was watching the lighter. Finally, he looked into Kyo's dark eyes. "What are you talking about?"

"I was there."

Mike frowned. "Where?"

"Their ship. Buffalo."

It was all Mike could do to keep from leaping up and dashing out of the room. One look at the man's face and he knew.

Kyo had been to hell too.

Abraham and Isaac

Klinder opened a drawer under the conference room table and pulled out a brown leather book. "When we asked the aliens what they wanted, they pointed out this passage from Genesis."

"The Bible?" asked Daniel.

"They used to quote it a lot. Listen. See if this makes sense to you." He read:

> *"Give me thy only son; thy only son by Sarah, Isaac."*

Klinder paused and blinked several times and swallowed. It only lasted a few seconds, but his face in that brief pause took on an old, familiar shape. It was if he were trying to convince himself of something. Something he didn't want to believe but somehow had to. Justifying. Daniel had seen that look before. On Uncle Louie's face. After he had taken the belt to Mike. He still remembered the screams.

"Abraham and Isaac?"

"Exactly!" Klinder said, his proud smile swallowing that momentary darkness with relief. "I told them you were a crackerjack!"

Something happened to Daniel during that glimpse of haunted sadness that emerged behind Klinder's eyes when he was reading the passage. The moment had come and gone like a breaching fish. But in that moment, part of him that had been sleeping for a long time woke up. Once he remembered the hospital, other memories started tumbling out. He was putting them together even as he listened.

It had to do with a fish. What fish?

"Now here's some commentary that I'm particularly fond of. 'Abraham, being God's true and loyal servant, must not only kill his son, but kill him as a sacrifice, kill him devoutly, kill him by rule, kill him with all the pomp and ceremony, sedateness and composure of mind with which he used to offer his burnt-offerings. Must the father of the faithful be the monster of all fathers?' " Klinder sighed deeply. "Then the angel came to the rescue . . .

Do not stretch out your hand against this lad;
do nothing to him;
for now I know that you fear God,
since you have not withheld your son, your only son, from Me.
Indeed I will greatly bless you,
and I will greatly multiply your seed
as the stars of the heavens,
and as the sand which is on the seashore;
and your seed shall possess the gate of their enemies.
And in your seed all the nations of the earth shall be blessed,
because you have obeyed My voice.

Klinder closed the book.

The fish, Daniel thought. The sucker. The sucker they caught that summer by the stream. The one they put in the rain barrel.

"That was their test," Klinder said. "That's all they wanted. Radical Obedience."

"Sacrifice," Daniel said bitterly. "How could the government do that? Sacrifice two innocent kids for the rest of mankind?"

"I'd call it a fair exchange. Billions for two. But the government didn't do it, Daniel. I did. That's why it worked. They were quite literal, you see. They wanted sons."

Daniel frowned. "What are you talking about?"

Klinder sighed. "I'm your father."

Daniel was silent and disgusted.

"Mike's too. He doesn't know."

God, this man would say anything.

"I'm surprised you never recognized my voice," said Klinder.

"Your voice?"

"Aloysius," he replied, smiling. "My middle name."

Buffalo

M ike sat in the locker room with Kyo. But his mind was remembering hell.

Hell was a hotel in Buffalo with the red neon light out
the screened window that blinked on and off, on and off, the letters
backward, YƆИAƆAV OИ. Everything backward.

He was ten. In a long room. In a bed. The taut sheets pressing him
down. Unable to move. It was dark. It was always dark. The walls were
brick and dripping. No lights on the ceiling. There were children in the
beds. Many children crying. Many of them his classmates. The ones Klinder hypnotized, saying, "You'll remember nothing. It'll be a cool breeze
off a beautiful lake. A warm summer day and you're playing on the sand.
A wonderful trip to the beach. That's all you'll remember."

But it didn't work on Mike. He remembered everything. Except names.
He didn't want to, but he couldn't help it.

Nonsensical, he told himself.

A dream, he told himself.

But that never made the memory go away.

He remembered the doctor in white walking up and down the aisles. Even through the mask he knew it was Klinder. He recognized the eyes.

He had a needle. And one by one, one kid at a time, every day he'd put it in the corner of your eye. No matter how many times you begged him not to. No matter how nicely you asked. It never mattered. And nobody changed the sheets. Wrapped tight so you could see the bodies and legs under the white. The stains seeping through. The smells. And while the needle did its business, it moved in the doctor's hand. And it hummed. He never forgot that.

And sometimes it would be quiet for a while. Then the footsteps and the man in white and the kids would start screaming again.

And the mush they poured down your throat that tasted like rancid Jell-O. Turkey basters. He remembered that's what they used. Turkey basters.

And in the rare hours of quiet. He turned to the kid next to him. The kid with the worst cry. "Father, father, father." The skinny little Japanese boy on the next bed who called himself "Kyo." The youngest kid in the room, and the most frightened. "I wanna go home," he kept crying. The black, trusting eyes surrounded by awful brown-and-yellow bruises. And Mike swore. "I'll get you out of this, Kyo. I swear. Someday I'll get you out of this." And the boy, not believing him, wanting to believe him. Believing him. Crying. Thanking him.

And on that day Mike made a promise to himself that he would keep for the rest of his life. He would never trust anyone again, never give up control, never be a pawn in someone else's game. He swore. He would die before he would let that happen again.

And the clouds they pumped into the room. *And the birds. The birds buzzing everywhere.* A long, piercing hum that went on all day and night. And sometimes, he thought he heard a voice calling his name from far away.

And the needles.

That was where he learned to make things small. He could put himself far, far away, step outside the smells and cries, pass through the dripping brick wall and the red neon sign, and watch the whole thing like a bird up in the sky. A crane shot. The shrinking trick. And everyone would get so small that he could pinch them between his index finger and thumb. And no matter how close they got, they never got to him.

He was watching it from far, far away.

Like a flock of birds flying high over two boys lying in a field of wheat.

Beyond the red neon outside the window that never stopped blinking: YƆИAƆAV OИ.

Mike remembered. Kyo had said that strange word at the 7-Eleven. He'd thought he was speaking Russian.

"Yc-Na-kavon," Mike whispered and opened his eyes. "No vacancy."

Kyo was crying and smoking.

"I knew you'd come someday, Mike. I always knew you would."

"Kyo?" he asked. It was the first time he had ever called the man by name. Kyo nodded.

After a long time, Mike asked, "They're doing that to Sean?"

"Yes. It's why I'm here. It's why we gotta stop them."

"Kill them," he said. "Call it what it is."

"Kill them."

"And the boy," Mike said.

"Yes."

"So he'll be dead dead."

"Yes," Kyo said, wiping his tears.

"What happens to the dead dead?" Mike asked.

"They go home."

What a strange word that was: home. It hung in his mind like an unpronounceable name. What on earth was *home?* Home was where you did your laundry. Where you slept. He'd always lived in hotels. What was home? It was what Danny had. A wife and kid. A mortgage and a picket fence. There was no place like it. Home was where they had to let you in. With great fury Mike realized he had no idea what he was thinking about. He had never been there.

He stood and walked to the locker Kyo had opened. Took out the can of lighter fluid and doused the pile. Their feathers darkened where the liquid splashed. He pinched the cigarette from Kyo's mouth and tossed it on the sleeping birds. The flames followed the paths of the liquid, crisscrossing the pile, sometimes dropping down into a crevice. Smoke rose. The birds ignited. In a few minutes they had a real bonfire going in the corner of the locker room. Mike kept expecting to hear a crowd of people screaming, but he didn't. They took it like that Buddhist monk in Vietnam. They never even woke up.

He imagined he was burning a pile of videotapes, a collection of snuff films. Though he didn't suppose it would make much difference. The Correctors would probably be issued a new bird the next time they came back. The pile smelled like sweet, burning grass. Black smoke rose in a funnel column to the ceiling where it curled back upon itself and formed a type of cloud. Like a bad special effect from the fifties, before digital: ink clouds injected by syringe into a tank, filling the water with demonic menace or divine retribution or the frosty wake of a UFO.

He wanted to burn the whole world. He wanted to go home.

Satisfied, he turned to Kyo. "You've been planning an operation for years?"

"Yes. I've got all the codes. Whenever you're ready, we can stomp 'em. Tonight, even."

Mike said, "Let's do it."

Kyo knelt before him in an odd gesture of adoration and gratitude. "Hosanna," he said.

"Shut up," Mike replied. "Gimme my gun."

Dad?

—～～　　～～　　～～—

For a long minute Daniel stared at the man in the paper suit. The man who claimed to be his father.

"No questions?" Klinder finally asked.

Daniel decided to do the rudest thing he could think of. Ignore the question. Give the man no satisfaction. Actually, he wasn't sure he could answer; his throat was clogged and tight. But the words spilled out of him, surprising him. It seemed he had waited his whole life to say them. "Why did you leave us?"

"You're big on the *whys*, aren't you? I'm a scientist, son. I ask *how.*" He saw the look on Daniel's face. "We were invaded, for pete's sake! Under siege. Conquered. No way to defend ourselves. My country needed me. The world needed me. What was I supposed to do?"

Strangely, this made it easier for Daniel to dismiss him. Klinder didn't have an answer for the most important question of his life. That told him everything he needed to know. The doctor could never hurt him again. "Uncle Louie was the closest thing I ever had to a father. He was a real prick, but he was there."

"I'm sorry. I had hoped you'd understand. Because, frankly, I need your help, Daniel. Passages like that—our best people have been over them for years. And we've come up short. Nothing they do makes sense anymore. We thought you might coax Sean to, you know, open up the lines of communication again."

"Again?"

There was an uncomfortable pause.

"He's the only one they talk to anymore. And he won't tell us anything."

"When's the last time they talked to you?" Daniel asked.

Klinder swallowed. "Eight years ago."

"Eight years?!"

Klinder frowned and nodded

"You mean . . . all this?" Daniel spread his arms to include the complex, the process, the bureaucracy, the Crossovers' philosophy. "This, this whole elaborate program you got here is . . . guesswork?"

Klinder folded his hands before him and started clenching and un-clenching them. "It's . . . been a challenging project. We've . . . had to op-erate on assumptions and old data. But . . . we've achieved a remarkable cohesion under pretty damned chaotic conditions. And people have a lot of faith in me."

"I take it that's a *yes*," Daniel said dryly.

"We need you, Daniel," Klinder replied, twirling his hands as if he were conjuring up a solution. "A translator. A code breaker, if you will. We thought maybe you could help us there."

My god, thought Daniel. That's why they took him. The diary wasn't the code. They just wanted to cover that up to protect Klinder's reputa-tion. Prevent his followers from learning about his experiments with the children. In "Buffalo." Sean is the code. They want me to break him.

"You have a wonderful gift. Your interpretive skills as a critic. Your analytical-slash-humanities approach to texts."

"Like the diary?" Daniel asked.

For a moment, Klinder's hand, which held a streaming cigarette, froze mid-air on the way to his mouth. "The diary?" Klinder asked, making a poor attempt at calm.

"Mike's diary. When he was ten and you were the smartest man in the world."

"We've been looking for that!" Klinder said jubilantly. "You mean to say you have it?"

"Yes."

"Where is it?"

"I hid it," Daniel said. "It's private."

"Private? Son. It's an historical document. *It could unlock the whole mystery of the hummingbirds.*" Klinder lifted one fat finger to the sky. "It could be the missing link!"

"Put your finger down," Daniel said.

Klinder looked at him.

"Down," Daniel insisted, and Klinder folded it back into his fist.

Daniel leaned forward in his chair and looked Klinder directly in the eyes. "Don't. Ever. Try to hypnotize me again."

"Son . . ."

"Don't call me that. Don't ever call me that. You haven't earned the right."

"Daniel, calm down."

"You're not a father. A real father wouldn't do that to his son."

There was a long pause. Klinder looked away and nodded several times. It seemed a lot was said in that pause, though no words were spoken. Finally, Klinder sat up and rested his arms on his legs and sighed. "I see you don't understand. You may have to, Daniel. You may have to understand a lot of things. Unpleasant things. Most of us live in a world without tenure, you know. In my life I have learned that to achieve a greater good, a great sacrifice is sometimes required. Horrible choices must be made. Some men have not had to face such choices. I have."

Was he justifying it? Was he actually sitting there justifying it?

"I have some disturbing news. The Correctors have made it clear that they will do anything to get out of here. I've told you about their killing sprees?"

"Yes," said Daniel. Why was he changing the subject? Who cared about a group of terrorists? They were safe here.

"What I haven't told you is that they work. A certain combination of killings boots them out of this reality."

"Why?"

"I believe it forfeits the conditions of their stay. The aliens hate death. That's why we're here, after all. But after a few particular murders, some of the killers are released."

"Released?"

"Erased from the program, as it were. Capital punishment of sorts. They offend the birds and they're chucked out. It has to do with family ties."

"I'm not following you."

"Our intelligence tells us that Mike has gone over to the Correctors."

"So?"

"He is going to try and kill Sean."

Daniel snorted through his nose. "That's insane. Why would Mike do that?"

"It's the only way the Correctors can win."

"I don't believe you."

"Daniel," Klinder was saying. "I can only imagine how overwhelming this is for you. But I'm afraid there's more." He stubbed out his cigarette. "There's no way to break this to you gently. So I'll come right out with it. Sean's not your son."

The silence after these words went on for some time. Daniel nearly laughed until he realized it wasn't funny. It wasn't funny at all.

Klinder was speaking but Daniel couldn't keep his mind on his words; he drifted. Somehow, he had gotten the notion that Klinder had stolen everything from him. His childhood. His brother. Julie. And now he was trying to take Sean. He knew it didn't make sense. But that was how he felt. Like he had been robbed.

"Son," Klinder said, and Daniel was back. "We didn't know it until we read your DNA. Takahashi just gave me the readout yesterday. You're not Sean's father. Mike is."

"You're lying."

"I wish I were. That is not even the worst news. The worst news is no one can stop Mike but you. The hummingbirds won't allow anyone to harm Mike. He is their special favorite. You've got a choice. You either kill him. Or he's going to kill Sean."

There was a long pause.

Finally Daniel said, "Dad?"

The word warmed Klinder's face into a proud and beaming smile. It was as if he had just received the best compliment possible. "Yes?" he said.

"Fuck you."

And then the explosions started.

Fireflies

The blast took out the compound's first security post and six guards. Mike felt the heat flare on his face even from around the corner, pressed up against the wall with Kyo, guns cocked next to their cheeks. He flinched and dots of light circled against his eyelids like fireflies. When he opened his eyes a hand without an arm was smoking at his feet and Kyo said, "Let your fingers do the walking."

The Operation

⁓　⁓　⁓

A larms shrieked through the compound like ambulance sirens.

"What the hell was that?" Daniel asked.

"Plastiques," the doctor answered, then slammed his palm against an intercom on the white wall. "Status?"

Daniel said, "What's happening?"

Klinder lifted one finger to his mouth and the intercom spoke. "Break in! We're checking now."

"How far?"

"Level two's under fire."

Klinder muttered, amazed. "They've never gotten that far before." He signaled Daniel out into the corridor. "We have to find Sean."

"Can't you just ask on the intercom?"

"Somebody might hear."

"Last I saw him was in the cafeteria."

"Level eleven," Klinder said. "They couldn't possibly make it that far."

"Who?" Daniel asked.

"Who else?"

"Can't you just lock them out?"

"There are no locks. Just security measures."

"Why?"

Klinder expelled an exasperated sigh. "They don't allow locks. But they don't understand codes, so we use them."

Daniel raised his eyebrows high.

Klinder slammed his fist into an intercom at a crossing of corridors. "Status?"

"Who is it?" a nervous voice asked.

"Klinder."

"Doctor! We think we got them pinned on level three."

"Three?!" Panic rose into his features.

"They're barricaded in epidermal."

"Shit. There's at least seven ways out of there."

Further down the corridor, Klinder slammed on the intercom. "Report."

"Break-in—level four."

"How is that possible?"

"They must have split up. All entrances are damaged. We got casualties. Fires on level two."

"Shut it down."

"Yes, sir."

"Try gas."

"They've disabled our security fumes. No idea how. Sir—" Off-mike a voice said, "Jesus, Jacob! There's more of them!"

Distant gunfire. Daniel thought: Popcorn in a microwave.

Klinder: "Shut it down!"

"I can't, sir."

"Christ!" Klinder ran, sucking in breaths and hissing them out.

Daniel followed, asking, "They don't allow locks? But fumes are okay?"

They were on eleven—almost to the bottom. Alarms whooping as they dashed down the steps. Then a massive muffled explosion echoed through the stairwell and seemed to shake the whole compound. Klinder tripped and lost his balance on the steps; Daniel caught him.

"Jesus," he said, lifting the doctor to his feet.

"That was a big one," said Klinder, opening the hallway door.

"Doctor Klinder!" A distant intercom shouted. "We got a breach!"

Klinder, huffing and puffing now, ran to the speaker in the wall. "Klinder here."

"They took out the whole fifth floor. Some sort of bomb. We'll have to use escape access."

"How many?"

"We don't know, sir. Reports say they're everywhere. They must have been planning this for months."

A female voice came over the intercom. "Make that years."

"Dot," said Klinder. "What do you hope to accomplish by this butchery?"

"Me to know and you to find out. And you will."

"Kill everyone here and in an hour we'll be back at our posts."

"Yeah. So?"

"Are you all on your twos? Is this is the graduating class of Correctors? Or some sick family reunion?"

"Call it a surgical strike."

"Sir! I don't know how she hacked this channel! They must have somebody on the inside."

"Switch," said Klinder.

"You can run, but you can't hide," Dot said before the connection was cut.

A huge explosion. Distant screams.

Daniel: "That was close."

"Doctor? They're on eight. They keep coming. But the minute I vid them they shoot out the camera. They know where the cameras are!"

"Eight. That's practically a vault."

"Without locks?" asked Daniel

Klinder rolled his eyes.

The voice said, "Sir? It's Jacob. I don't want to do it again."

Klinder sighed. "You knew the price when you signed up, Jacob. You took the pledge."

The man on the intercom was weeping. "I'm afraid. It hurt so much."

"Calm down, son. It may not come to that."

"I'm going to Sean," said Daniel.

He ran around a white corner. The cafeteria was open. Smelling of macaroni and cheese. The stereo played a numbing hip-hop tune. Stainless steel serving area before the kitchen slit. Plastic trays stacked. A bin of silverware. Tables and chairs. And—oh, the relief—there, sitting quietly in the white corner: Sean. Playing cards. Solitaire. As he approached, Daniel felt a chilly draft descending from the ceiling above. Sean was sitting directly under an air duct, the frigid exhale rearranging the blond curls on top of his head. Daniel shivered and felt a cliché: his blood ran cold.

"Hey, sport."

"Hey."

He must have heard the explosions. Why wasn't he taking cover? "The Correctors are here."

Klinder was out of breath at the swinging doors. "Twelve is the most secure. We should go down."

Daniel said, "I think we better find a hiding place."

"Why?" the boy asked with unnerving calm.

"Sean, don't be difficult. They're shooting people."

"So?"

"So we could ..."

"So what?"

Daniel put a gentle hand on the back of the boy's head. "What's buggin' you, sport?"

"We better go," said Klinder.

"Your eyes still sore? You gotta be more careful on those stairs."

Sean shuffled the cards mindlessly, expertly. "It doesn't matter," he said, glaring at Klinder. "They're so phony. They call me the Bird Boy, but they don't want to be my friend. *They only want to watch.*" He looked at the ceiling. "Yes, you do. So?...I don't care...she doesn't care about me...then why did she leave?"

Daniel said, "You can hear them?"

"We haven't got time for this," said Klinder.

"What do they say?" asked Daniel.

"It doesn't matter," Sean said. "Watch this trick." He cupped the deck of cards in one palm and sprayed it all over the table. He smiled. "Fifty-two pickup."

Daniel squatted down to look the boy in his face. "You were talking about your mom, weren't you?"

The boy's mouth was a straight line. He regarded the scattered cards. "I think I reminded her of something that made her sad. I don't think she liked me much."

"Sean! That's nonsense!" He touched his shoulder. "Your mother loved you. Deeply. Adored you."

Sean looked at Daniel. It was a look of shocking desolation, a face that every parent dreads to see upon their child, for it says that they have been robbed of something precious and irreplaceable. Daniel had seen it before. It was the same face that Mike had worn after Buffalo. Sean said, "I'm not a little kid anymore."

Abruptly, the alarm stopped blaring. The shocking silence after so much continuous noise seemed to interrupt Daniel's thought just as he was about to arrive at it. He was starting to draw a comparison between his son and his brother. Something that wasn't being said. Something they had in common. Something about Klinder's specialty: kids and hypnosis.

Gunshots on the floor above them, like someone beating a pipe against the wall, jumbled his thinking further.

As did this: Klinder shouted, "Come with me!"

"Oh, shut up," said Sean.

Daniel saw Klinder pull a snub-nosed .38 out of his pocket, so he didn't comprehend the furious look Sean had given to the doctor.

The thought was lost, never to be completed by Daniel.

"Guns are okay?" he asked, totally confused. "Why are guns okay?"

"They're just tools to them." Klinder sighed. "Look. They take away bullets and guns, they might as well take away all blunt objects. Shovels. Two-by-fours. Large sticks. Get it?"

"No," Daniel admitted.

"You can make a weapon out of anything. Daniel. We gotta go. I heard them say the target is a boy."

Daniel thought: Sean's the only boy here.

He lifted Sean out of the chair and marched him out into the hall.

They were following Klinder down a narrow hidden stairwell to the twelfth floor when they heard a ricochet of bullets pinging between the cement and steel railing.

"Faster!" Klinder said.

A dash through a yellow furnace room, then a twisting corridor with spongy dirty carpet that led them to a closet. Klinder pressed a code into a keypad and opened the door. Then closed it quietly behind them.

The room was small and smelled of ammonia. It reminded Daniel of the grubby janitor's office in his old grade school. Pale-green paint. An old wall calendar stuck on June 1990. A Mr. Coffee machine that hadn't been cleaned in months. A row of gray lockers. A mop handle sticking out of a steel sink. A bucket on wheels. Green linoleum floor. Daniel walked over and settled in the chair behind a big oak desk in the corner. Sean sat on his lap and rested his head back against Daniel's chest. The chair squeaked.

"There's a gun in the top drawer," Klinder said.

Daniel looked at him. "So?"

"I suggest you use it."

He opened the big drawer and immediately closed it. "I'm not touching that."

Klinder shrugged. "Your funeral."

There was a copper ashtray on the desktop full of stale butts. And a large pad of white paper framed in a maroon leather binding, covered with doodles and notes and faces. Klinder flicked a switch and the fluorescent lights above them winked off.

Sudden darkness.

The click of an intercom button. "Report," Klinder whispered.

Silence.

"Status?"

Nothing.

"Jacob?"

Silence.

Klinder expressed an enormous fart. He didn't excuse himself. He acted as if nothing had happened.

Daniel snickered and felt the warm head and familiar shivers of the boy. Like those nights after the nightmare. He whispered, "What is it, sport?"

"What happens when they shoot you?" Sean asked in the dark. It sounded like an idea that had never crossed his mind.

"Shhhh," Daniel whispered and patted his arm. Why wasn't this question in any of the books? Surely there had to be a book on this.

"What happens?"

Daniel wanted to see Sean's face, but his eyes were still adjusting to the dark. He could just make out the faint figure of Klinder standing beside the door. The glint of metal in his left hand.

"What do you mea—" Daniel started, then he saw the boy looking up, trusting, or trying to. Should he, could he, really answer that question?

"Well," he began. "That's hard to say . . ."

He saw the disappointment settle into Sean's eyes. He remembered his words: "Because you lie."

Daniel rubbed his little back and said, "Pain."

Sean nodded, satisfied. "And after that?"

"I don't know," Daniel said, and held him closer. "Nobody does."

You know, I really don't care who the father is. I really don't.

"Damn," said Klinder, patting his pajamas. "I left my smokes upstairs."

A shout that was too close. A shot. A body dropped. The sound of running feet on carpet: *padda, padda, padda, padda, padda.*

Daniel watched the golden bar of light under the door next to Klinder's feet.

Silence.

One shadow.

Two shadows. Three shadows.

Then the golden bar was whole again.

Someone knocked on the door. Three times.

The chair squeaked as Daniel slid off it with Sean in his arms, and crouched behind the desk.

A series of finger taps on a keypad.

The door swung open.

A shaft of white light from the corridor momentarily blinded Daniel though he was in the shadows, in the corner.

The gun entered the door, followed by a large woman in a 7-Eleven bowling shirt, holding it with both hands. She was backed up by a young man with red hair and a shotgun. The unlucky lady was pointing the wrong way. The boy patting the wall for the switch.

Klinder shot the young man in the face. Then shot the woman as she turned. The woman's gun skidded across the linoleum floor and bumped against Daniel's leg as they crouched behind the desk. At each of the shots, Daniel had felt Sean flinch.

Someone stuck a mirror on a ruler around the corner. First low. Then slid it up against the doorway to eye level. One shot from Klinder's gun shattered it.

A man tumbled into the room.

Klinder shot twice. The reports exploded in the small room. After the second shot, there was a howl.

A man's familiar voice. "Come on, Klinder."

A pause before Klinder replied, "Kyo? What are you doing?"

"Come on out."

Daniel recognized the voice. Agent Takahashi. The man who apologized.

Klinder gave a moan of disappointment. "My right-hand man!" He was digging into his pockets for bullets. "How could you?" Stalling. "After everything we've worked for?"

"It ends here, doctor. Come on—you got one bullet."

"Come and get it," Klinder said, bluffing.

"Give us the boy."

Daniel's hand reached for the gun at his foot.

"He's not here," said Klinder.

Daniel whispered to Sean, "Stay down."

"We want him now," said Takahashi.

The doctor looked over at Daniel as if to say, "Watch this."

"Dead or alive?" asked Klinder.

"Dead'll do." It was a new, calm voice: a man. He said the *d word*, Daniel thought. How did he do that?

Klinder raised his eyebrows at Daniel as if to say, "Did you get that?" He had opened the cylinder and was trying silently to reload. "Mike?" he said.

"Hey, doc."

"What are you doing here?"

"I've joined up."

"I can't *believe* you're that stupid. What did they give you? Food? Sex?"

"Truth."

Daniel was listening to his brother's calm voice. Glad to hear it again. Afraid to see his face. He said it. Mike said the *D* word.

"Truth," Klinder snorted, reloading. Two bullets. Three bullets. "Terrorism is not truth, Mike. It's madness."

Five bullets. Full.

"But don't take my word for it." Klinder snapped the chamber back with a click. "Ask your brother." He nodded to Daniel, as if to say, "He's yours now."

After a moment, "Danny?"

After a moment, "Hey, Mike."

"You okay?"

"Yeah. You?"

"I'm all right."

"Where's Sean?" Mike asked gently.

"Come and get him," said Daniel, raising the gun above the desk, gently pushing Sean further down.

"Don't," Sean whispered, as if he had embarrassed him again.

Takahashi rolled into the room, crouched and fired one shot before Klinder cut him down with two.

"Bastard!" he yelled, crumbling to the floor.

A pause.

Then the agent laughed. "You'll wonder where the yellow went."

A pause.

Kyo stopped breathing.

A quick arm snaked into the room and flicked the light switch on.

Then Mike was standing in the doorway. A gun in his hand, pointed at Klinder. The doctor backed away, pointing his gun at Mike.

Mike aimed his gun at Klinder. Klinder aimed at Mike. Daniel aimed at Mike. A John Woo bit, Mike would call it. Everybody's aiming at each other, Daniel thought. Why doesn't anybody fire?

"Drop it, Klinder," Mike said. And the man practically threw his gun on the floor and lifted his arms above his head.

"Put your fucking arms down," Mike said. Klinder dropped his arms. He was breathing hard.

"I told you, Daniel," the doctor said.

Mike's eyes were taking in the crowd of bodies in the room. For a long time, he stared down at Agent Takahashi.

Sean crouched below, fidgeting.

Mike turned and aimed at Daniel. "Drop it."

Daniel straightened his arm. "You drop it."

They could have been kids again, playing cops and robbers. There was one of those long pauses that you never see in movies. If it was the movies, you'd think somebody forgot their lines.

"Where's the boy?" Mike said.

"I told you!" warned Klinder, his eyes wide and pleading.

"Step away from the desk," Mike said.

"No," said Daniel.

Mike dropped his gun to his side. "Shit, Danny."

Daniel kept his aim. "I can't believe you're doing this."

"I don't have a choice."

"Daniel," Klinder said through clenched teeth. "Now!"

"Shut up," said Mike, pointing the gun at Klinder. "This is none of your business."

"Stop it!" Daniel shouted at Mike.

"Stop what?"

"Stop acting so tough. Your hand is shaking,"

Mike smiled and snorted. "So is yours."

"Daniel," said Klinder.

"Danny, listen to me . . ." Mike said and swallowed. "I'm good at this. I promise you: it'll be a clean shot."

Daniel took a deep breath and said, "You need to shoot somebody? Shoot me!"

"No!" said Klinder.

"Shoot me, you fucking asshole! Get it over with!"

Mike was speechless for a minute. Daniel couldn't recall the last time Mike had heard him swear.

"I'm not shooting you, Danny."

"You're not shooting anybody."

"Daniel!" Klinder pleaded. "He's going to kill us all!"

Mike frowned at the shaking gun in his hand. A sort of *what-the-hell-am-I doing-here* look on his face. He gave a sideways disgusted look at Klinder. "It's not really death, you liar. You know that."

Then Mike covered his face with his hand and let his gun fall to his side.

The whole atmosphere of the room changed. It became suddenly sane.

I did it, Daniel thought.

I can't believe I did it.

I talked him out of it!

He laughed a little on the inside. If only people would talk to each other.

"Son," Klinder said. "He's a killer!"

"Shut up," said Daniel.

"He's a Corrector!"

"Shut up!" Daniel said.

"He fucked your—"

"—*Shut up!*" Daniel screamed, and shot Klinder twice. "That's my *brother* you're talking about!"

The doctor's body melted to the floor, collapsing heavily on top of Takahashi's, like a gigantic sack of flour. His head was red.

Daniel was amazed at how little he cared.

After a time, he realized that, though he was watching Klinder's body, he was still pointing his gun at where Klinder once stood. His whole arm trembled. He laughed at how ridiculous it looked, and lowered his gun.

Now it was just his family. His brother. Sean. Himself. Daniel felt sure they could work it out.

There would be no more shooting.

Daniel was crying when he turned his eyes toward his brother. "Shooting fish in a barrel," he said and giggled.

Mike didn't seem to hear him. He was looking at Klinder's body.

"Remember?" Daniel asked, wiping the snot from his nose with his gun hand. "The sucker?"

He discovered that he didn't recognize the look on his brother's face.

"Mike?" Daniel asked, though it wasn't clear to him what he was asking. No matter: It was all working out. He was handling it.

"Sean?" Mike said in a strangled voice that seemed higher than usual.

The boy stood up behind the desk, looking at the two men holding guns.

Daniel hated correcting Sean. He held up both hands in exasperation, one was empty, one held a warm gun. He chided, "Didn't I tell you to stay down?"

Daniel shook his head ruefully at Mike as if to say: kids. What are you going to do? But he saw his brother's face and instantly understood how shocking the boy's appearance must be. The little boy with eyes like that holding a hummingbird in his fist.

"Sean, you better explain those bruises."

The boy was looking at his uncle, his eyes going wide. "Dad?"

"Let's go home," Mike whispered to the child.

"It looks worse than it—" Daniel started, turning just in time to see Mike fire.

Our Way

⌇   ⌇   ⌇

Those eyes.

Those eyes—

Thought stopped in the moment Mike saw the boy across the room rise up from behind the desk like a specter from some B movie, *Night of the Living Dead*. Sean's face said it all, confirmed the terrors that Kyo had only hinted at. Nothing Mike had seen during the whole raid on the compound had shocked him like those eyes—not the explosion of glass and steel that took out the entrance, not the smoking hand, not Dot's cool marksmanship, the bodies spurting red and toppling, not even his hurried shots, the wounds blossoming as the body count rose and they descended level after level, Kyo disarming the alarms all the way down with simple magic words *chickadee, sparrow hawk, wren, crow*. Not even his old friend Kyo crumbling before his eyes, dying with one last punchline, not even Klinder slumping over him, not even seeing his sweet, innocent brother cursing and murdering someone right before him.

—but the boy with that horror-show face and those eyes. It was like looking in a mirror. He wanted to erase those eyes from his sight, from his memory, from existence. "Let's go home," he had said, and pulled the trigger.

His best shot of the day.

Thought stopped.

Time crawled.

And everything turned red: the walls, the floor, his hand—it was as if Mike had put on a pair of psychedelic glasses.

The red gun spitting a slow, red spew of flame.

The red bullet oozing out in a scarlet puff of smoke.

The red cloud expanding from the red barrel, terminating in a smoke ring.

The red bullet spinning to a halt and hovering in the red air.

Freeze frame.

Stop, the voices said.

Familiar voices. Mike felt sure he had heard them before.

Why? the voices asked.

He had a sudden memory of a boys' choir singing Latin hymns in a sanctuary full of red votive candles. Midnight mass. Childish harmonies perfectly mimicking the strange foreign words as if they understood what they were singing.

Why is this so difficult?

Across the red room his red brother was half-smiling at him, almost shrugging, in the middle of explaining something. Believing, as he always did, that words could solve everything.

Did you not know what you were asking for? "BARRADA NIKTO."

Did Danny hear the voices too? Did he see red as well? Did he remember quoting those words in the golden field that summer that they saw the saucer?

Please listen: There is another way. Our way.

Drawn by some impulse he could not explain, Mike reached out for the red bullet suspended in the air. His arm felt as though it were moving through Jell-O.

Don't, the voices said.

Mike touched the tip of his index finger to the bullet and immediately wished he hadn't. Once, when he was a boy, Mike was playing with matches. He lit a plastic straw over the sink. It was an experiment: he wanted to watch it melt. But a drop of molten straw had dribbled onto his thumb. The pain was excruciating and he screamed. He jammed the faucet on and held his burned thumb under the cold water, and screamed again. He didn't stop screaming for three minutes. The melted plastic had burned down to his nerves. It was like holding your hand to the flame of a candle.

This was like that.

It seemed to take forever to bring the finger into his mouth.

We would save you. Spare you everything.

"Go away," Mike said, wincing, sucking the finger, staring at the frozen red bullet as if it were the source of the voices.

Listen: It is possible to trick entropy, to spin it, to redirect time to a foggy space where it cannot touch you.

"Shut up," Mike said fiercely, wanting to wrench the voices out of his head. For he recognized them now. He knew them well. They had haunted him all his life. They were the voices of Buffalo, humming their terrible hymn as their nightmare spread relentlessly, filling the hotel like creeping vines, caressing and smothering the children in their mindless hunger.

This is our gift. This is what you asked for.

Why it is so difficult for you to receive it?

"I never asked for your fucking gift!" Mike screamed. "Let me out of here!"

And they did. And the red room disappeared.

No

— — —

The bullet spun counterclockwise and accelerated across the gap between the barrel and the boy. It heat trimmed and scooped off some of the fabric on the arm of Daniel's paper sleeve. Smoke rose from the gun and formed a curlicue question mark in the air as the bullet passed neatly between Sean's ribs, through his heart, deflecting off the bones in his back, trailing a narrow jet of dark fluid behind it, acquiring on its stressful course new shape and dimension. Finally, it lodged itself inside the pale-green plasterboard wall.

Daniel screamed.

The boy's body flinched, then fell sideways, making no effort to break its fall.

First the hips connected to the floor, then the elbow, then the shoulder, then the ear.

His hummingbird landed after he did with a soft thup.

Daniel dropped his gun.

Daniel looked at the boy who wasn't there.

He looked at Mike, still holding out his gun.

He watched Mike wink out and disappear.

Daniel was alone in a room full of bodies.

Daniel knelt beside the littlest body and felt.

Daniel knelt beside the littlest body and felt.

Daniel knelt beside the littlest body and felt.

He felt the word *no* echoing in the hollow of his chest.

No, this can't be happening.

No, it was impossible.

No, he had come too far to find him.

No, he couldn't lose him twice.

No, Mike wouldn't do that.

No, Sean, stop it.

No, Sean, don't look at me like that.

No. Please. No.

Daniel's memory flashed upon a little lost boy in diapers. A boy who had disappeared and hid in the bottom drawer of his dresser and had fallen safely asleep.

That was easier, he concluded.

It was easier to deal with someone missing who you couldn't see.

Behind the body, from the mouth of the bullet hole in the thin green wall, a tiny cloud of plaster dust had puffed into the room like the expulsion of some underwater plant disgorging seed pods. The cloud floated, achieved a brief vortex, then settled swirling to the linoleum.

Three Strikes and You're Out

M ike didn't remember waking up.

He was lying on a bed looking out the window of his hotel room. It was a foggy day.

Eventually, things cleared and for an indeterminate time he watched the clouds. Finally he left the bed and looked down over the winding Detroit River to the city of Windsor, Ontario on the other side, the only part of Canada, he recalled, which lies directly south of the U.S. Mike realized he was in a lofty suite in the Renaissance Center. The Westin Hotel. The sixty-ninth floor, at least.

He noticed his index finger hurt. His left index finger. A throbbing, distant pain. He must have taken something. That was smart. But why didn't he recall how he hurt it?

He was naked in the mirror and he saw his clothes washed, ironed, and folded at the end of his bed. There was his laptop on the dark wooden desk. And beside it, his gun. And he forgot about his finger.

Oh, fuck.

Oh.

Fuck.

It didn't work.

I'm still alive.

Panic rose in his belly and he covered his mouth with both his hands and thought: What have I done?

He thought it would be over. Erased. And nobody would have to deal with the aftermath. They'd all be free. Sean wouldn't have to recall his father flipping out like that and killing Klinder. The aliens wouldn't touch the boy again. Danny wouldn't have to remember anything. His abduction. His death. He was going to spare them all. Spare them everything.

Oh, shit.

It horrified and sickened him to think that Danny might still be somewhere hating him, missing his son.

He sat on the end of the bed and tried to think it through. Had Kyo lied? No, Kyo had told him the truth. He trusted Kyo. Something went wrong. He was forgetting something again. Why didn't it work? Why hadn't he disappeared like Wu? Why wasn't he erased? Had he messed up the equation? Switched something around?

Shit!

Think!

He had killed several strangers. And a relative: his nephew. That was horrible. But at least the kid wouldn't have to go through another Buffalo. At least he had spared him that.

He looked at his gun for a long minute.

That's right.

Of course, he thought.

Three strikes and you're out.

I haven't killed someone I liked yet.

Any Place Is Better
than Here

Daniel didn't quite remember leaving the compound. Something had switched his memory off. Something had died.

He had no memory at all of ascending the twelve flights, passing through the smoke and debris, stepping over the bodies, emerging into the perfect sunlight, the always perfect sunlight. He must have, though. He must have. He was walking.

After a time he noticed how tired and sore his arms were.

After a time he noticed there was blood on his hands.

Still he walked on.

After a time he realized he was carrying Sean in his arms. It seemed important that he take him somewhere.

There was a little round lady pushing a shopping cart down the sidewalk. She waited until he was right next to her, then she said, "Here now. I'll take that for you."

Daniel looked into her black eyes and saw kindness.

"Your arms are so tired, Danny."

He looked into her pitch-black eyes and trusted her.

"Are you sure?" Daniel asked. "He's heavier than he looks."

"Yes," she said, "He's a big boy. But I'm stronger than you think." Reaching under his arms, the little woman carefully took the sagging boy off his hands. She adjusted the body and gently kissed its white brow. "I've got him now. Don't you worry. He's safe."

"Where will you take him?" Daniel asked.

"Home," she said, laying Sean gingerly on the bags in her cart, and crossing his arms over his chest.

"Me too," said Daniel, his voice catching.

She turned back. "Not just yet, sweetie. You need a powwow . . . but tell you what I'll do." She touched a cool finger to the middle of Daniel's forehead. It felt wonderful. "I'll make sure you get to Detroit safely. Detroit is better than here, isn't it?"

"Yes," he concluded after a moment. "Any place is better than here."

She was walking away, pushing her squeaky cart down the sidewalk when Daniel called out to her: "Hey!"

She stopped and turned.

"I know your name now."

"You always did," she said smiling.

"Thank you for visiting me in the hospital."

"You're welcome," she said.

"Don't blame Mike," he pleaded, weeping. "He was crazy. You don't send crazy people to hell, do you?"

"Of course not." She gave him a look of immense sympathy. "Danny?" There was no response. "Daniel," she said sharply.

"What?"

"It's okay to hate Mike, you know."

"I do hate him. That doesn't mean I don't love him too."

"Oh, Danny," she said, sadly. "You're too good for this world."

She lifted her brown palm, flicked it three times: a wave good-bye.

Then the little woman and her cart and the dead boy disappeared into a white bank of fog that drifted down the street like a rogue cloud grown tired of floating.

Soon Daniel was enveloped in a cool, comforting mist.

Bowling with Yorick

Mike examined the blister on the tip of his left index finger—
where he had touched the red bullet. He recalled the pain.

Later he would try to summon the process through which
he had reached his appalling decision. He found that he could not do so.
From the outside he was just a man sitting on the edge of his bed,
examining a fresh wound. But inside of him horrible things were happening, things which had nothing to do with thought or logic. It is a mistake
to believe we understand how such choices are made. It is incorrect to
call them premeditation. It is foolish to believe we do not make such
decisions every day.

Mike booted up and went online. Looked for chat groups. Scanned
the titles: Cops Who Flirt. Praise God. The Atrocity Channel. Uses of
Immortality. Adjusting to Happiness. Stuck on the Third Step. The Perfect Omelet. Multiorgasms. The Impossible Bird.

The Impossible Bird? What on earth could that be? *Bird-watchers?* Orni-thologists? A Klinder forum? He checked in under the handle *Martyr*. And found himself scanning a nonsensical series of nonsequiturs, stacking up on the screen between the pauses like Dada blocks.

"Alert tower. Mid-air passenger exchange."

"This is an ex-parrot!"

"He's pining for the fjords."

"He'll never play the piano again."

"He's been made redundant."

"Excuse me," Mike typed. "What's going on here?"

"Newbie! Twelve-o'clock high!"

"He doesn't know the score."

"He's bowling with Yorick."

"LOL"

"ROFL"

"EXCUSE ME," Mike typed. "IS SOMEONE GOING TO AN-SWER ME?"

"He's punched out."

"HEY NEWBIE! CAPITALS ARE RUDE."

"LOL"

"Hey Newbie. What's the opposite of working?"

"Broken?" Mike typed.

"LOL"

"ROFL"

"The opposite of early?"

"The opposite of quick?"

"Don't know what you're getting at," typed Mike.

"He thinks he's ert!"

"He took a long walk off a short pier."

Then it clicked. Mike recalled a bad pun about John Holmes, the famously endowed porn star who died of AIDS. "Inevitably, the staff was downsized."

"I get it," Mike typed.

"Then dive right in, Newbie!"

"Take the plunge!"

"Uncle Mort needs you!"

"He's fallen but he can't get up."

"He's the Wicked Witch of the East."

"His property values have dropped."

"He's eating Ding Dongs."

"He's dead," Mike typed.

The pause in the chatroom was loud. No repartee. No one-liners. Nothing. The number in the upper-right-hand corner of the screen, which displayed a head count of the people in the room, began to drop precipitously, like a thermometer shoved into a freezer. Twenty-five. Twenty-two. Nineteen. Eighteen. Fifteen. Thirteen. Nine. Seven. Five. Three. Two. It stayed at two for a few moments. Then this:

"Who are you?"

"Mike."

"I'm Donna. How did you do that?"

"Do what?"

"Type that word."

"You mean Death?"

There was a prolonged pause.

"Where do you live?" she typed.

"Detroit."

"Really? Me too."

Mike smiled at the screen of his PowerBook. This was going to be a cinch. Like shooting fish in a barrel.

"Wow," he typed. "What a coincidence."

Fuck! God! Mother!

ー　　　ー　　　ー

Daniel woke in a strange bed. He felt snug and well-rested. The radio was playing a soothing song: "Cast Your Fate to the Wind." Over and over. The same song. One of his favorites, actually.

After a time he pulled down the covers and knew immediately it was a Motel 6. They all looked the same.

His clothes were clean and folded at the foot of his bed.

Daniel noted that all hotel rooms have their own climate: too hot or too cold and nothing in between. He was too cold. He dressed himself and stood in the middle of the room for an indefinite time.

He turned off the tranquilizing radio.

He opened the white drapes and he saw his silver Volvo parked out front. He recognized the street: Eight Mile Road, the borderline between the Detroit and its suburbs.

He was home. He had no idea how he got there.

The smell of coffee was coming from the tiny kitchenette. He poured himself a cup and sipped, remembering dead Sean in their kitchen—his kitchen. Staring up at his mother's shopping list. Written on the plastic board with a black erasable marker. It was still there, after Disney World. After she had left. A last-minute list of things they needed for the trip to Florida.

Sunglasses.
Sunblock.
Brakes?
Sean's Sinus meds. Non-alcoholic.
Puzzles.
Nutri-Bars.

Her last list.

He remembered dead Sean reaching up and wiping off the list till the board was clear. Sean looking down at the black on his fingertips.

Shopping. That's what Julie always did when she was depressed. Shopping always made her happy.

What if I were happy? Daniel thought. What would that be like? He decided that perhaps what he might do was pretend to be happy. To carry this big fat night inside him and walk around like all the dead people did, pretending they were alive. Shopping. That seemed like a sensible plan.

He drove to the Eastern Market. It was less crowded than usual, especially for a weekend. He used to come here with Julie. He remembered the smells. He purchased a bag of warm doughnuts and, after tasting a sample, a hunk of Swiss wrapped in plastic—damn fine cheese. He ate it as he wandered stall to stall and watched the farmers playing checkers on the tailgates of their beat-up trucks. Doilies stitched with love by the farmer's wife. Tulips potted and wrapped in red aluminum foil—a perfect display of color, scent, and cheer. And the smell of their fresh fruit, their vegetables, and the sunburned, weathered faces of people who lived off the land. But, of course the land was barren and this harvest was an elaborate set with amazingly true-to-life props. They were lab rats pressing pleasure levers until they starved themselves. Couch potatoes watching their favorite rerun over and over and over.

Stop it, he thought. You are happy.

This isn't a novel and you're not deconstructing the imbedded cultural prejudices of the text. Look at these people, he told himself. Look. And he did. And what he saw was contentment. Dead people finally doing the work they had wanted to do all their lives. These few dead farmers and dead sellers, dead shopkeepers and dead butchers, dead gardeners and dead craftsmen were here because they wanted to be. Loved their work. They choose it by habit or vocation—they loved it. Who was he to question their joy? He was happy. That woman wasn't murdered by her son. That man didn't jump off the roof of his house. Those children didn't drown in their dad's station wagon, which he drove into the Detroit River to collect their insurance.

Stop it.

You are happy. Stop it.

Everybody had a little bulge in their jeans or their jacket, he noticed. Birds, he thought. Everybody had a bird but him.

Where was his bird?

Who was he?

Who was he now that nobody needed him?

"I don't believe it," a man was saying.

Daniel looked at him.

"It's you!" the man said. "What are the fucking odds?"

Daniel looked at him.

"You don't remember me?" the pudgy, homely man said. "First thirteen rows. Stay off the wings."

Daniel looked at him.

"The plane, dude, the plane!"

Daniel remembered.

"This is so cool. This is amazing. See, the thing is, you must have been meant to find me because—you know what?—you're the only one who didn't change seats. Ha! There are no accidents. It all means something."

The man took his hand and shook it. "You look kinda woozy, dude." He eyed the bag in Daniel's hand. "Too many doughnuts?"

Daniel could not reconstruct how the young man had talked him into coming to his apartment. He seemed harmless. And he said he could sit down. Sitting down sounded nice. He was tired. And it wasn't far. A small, chilly room above a mixed-imported–nuts shop, facing Eastern Market. There was a black, unmade futon under the window that looked out over the ugliest mural of a chicken Daniel had ever seen. Bare wooden floors. Lots of candles. An ashtray full of roaches. The layout of the room suggested a focus: Everything was assembled deliberately around the stereo system in the corner. Towering stacks and stacks of cassette tapes meticulously labeled in a scrawny hand. Everything was black. The components, the shelves, the speakers. Everything except the big white parrot perched in a large golden cage in the corner. A red splotch on its crown.

The man's name was Andy. The bird's name was Al.

"Say 'hi,' Al."

"No shoot!" the bird said. Like a gargle.

"Say 'Howdy,' Al!"

"Bite me!"

"Say 'pretty bird,' Al."

"Fuck your mother!"

Andy shrugged. "He's a very good parrot, he's just not a very good pet, yet."

Andy made him some tea that seemed to clear his mind. He insisted that Daniel sit on the futon as he paced about the room and gestured while munching on a doughnut. He had a way of moving his hands as he talked as if he were pulling thoughts out of the air. The parrot eyed the doughnut hungrily.

"He's your bird?" Daniel asked.

"He is now," Andy said, examining the bitten doughnut he held. "Just got him from a midget lady at the market." He noted Daniel's face. "Oh, you mean—no. Relax, dude, I'm not a Crossover or anything. I gave up all that bird shit years ago." Andy shook his head. "Phonies and hip addicts. That's all they are. No integrity. No balls."

The bird gargled, "Whippersnapper!"

"Shuttup, Al," Andy said with a mouth full of doughnut. He swallowed and brushed the crumbs off his hands. "They're all chickens. They couldn't follow God to the logical extreme. The other side."

"The what?" Daniel asked reluctantly.

Andy nodded. He nodded. He walked over to the tape deck, ran a finger reverently down the spine of a dozen tapes, and selected one with glee. He turned and held it up. "The real stuff. Not the bullshit personas we wear every day. The evidence. Who we are. What we feel. Where we're going. I've got it all."

Andy plopped the black tape in the deck and Daniel expected music.

But it was words.

People talking. Two men and a woman. Talking jargon.

And a strange, familiar hiss their voices swam in. Didn't Andy believe in Dolby?

"Doppler's gone lulu."

"Four-eighty-six? That can't be right."

"Shear reports from Denver."

A door opening and closing.

"Coffee's cold."

"Want some more?"

"Thanks, Jill, but if I have any more and I'm gonna have to open a window."

Laughter.

"Baldy give you any more trouble?"

"Nahh, he calmed down once I flirted with his Jap and gave him another scotch."

"Asshole. Thinks he owns the plane."

"Said he worked for the government."

"Never heard that one before."

Laughter.

"Fuck you, bitch!" the bird squawked.

The woman on the tape said, "He actually called me a bitch."

"He gives you any more trouble I'll notify gate security."

"Thanks."

Andy hit the fast-forward button, smiled, and winked at Daniel.

"Descending to ten-thousand feet. Check the flaps, will you?"

"System's fine. Denver in about six minutes."

"Remember when I asked you to dance, Jill?"

"You're a lousy dancer."

"I'm better horizontal—what was that?"

A pause. A noise.

"Damn, check backup."

"Denver, this is US AIR two-twenty-four; we're having a—"

"—shit!"

"Let me do it!"

The woman: "Can I help?"

"Shut up."

"You got it! You got it!"

"No.

"Hold it. Hold it steady."

An infinite pause, during which the bird cried, "Buckle up!"

Then voices talking quickly, overlapping.

"Denver this is two-twenty-four; say again."

"Hold it! Hold it!"

"Jill? I'm sorry!"

"Hold it, dammit."

"Up! Up! You can do it!"

"Wait!"

"No!"

"God!"

"No!"

"Fuck!"

"God!"

"*Nooo!*"

A pause.

A whisper. "Mom, I love you."

Silence.

Until the bird said, "Getting sleepy?"

Daniel had closed his eyes. He swallowed a mouthful of spit. He opened his eyes when he heard Andy shut off the tape.

"That's my favorite. I play it all the time." The man smiled grimly. "Drives Al crazy. But, dude, that is *so* not even the best one! I got 'em all. Every black box recording ever made!" He folded his arms over his chest. "My uncle's on the FAA investigative unit. I get him excellent dope. He gives me these. We're collectors."

"Correctors!" said the bird.

Andy's arm swept over the wall of black tapes.

"Here's the thing, dude," he said. "Here's the thing. You know what?" He held his palms together as if in prayer. "They're all the same." He smiled and nodded. "Like a formula scenario some network hack kept rewriting over and over." He giggled. "Little variations to throw off the folks at home. I got 'em all... every last one of them." He laughed. "They're all the same!"

He did that thing with his hands. "God!"

He did it again. "Fuck!"

And again. "Mom!" he shouted to the ceiling.

The bird gave a perfect hound whistle as if a female had entered the room.

Daniel got up quickly and made for the door.

"Wait," said Andy, grabbing his arm. "I didn't mean to freak you out."

Daniel looked at his face. Hope and joy.

"Don't you see, dude?" Andy said. "*This means something!*"

Daniel bolted down the stairs and didn't look back.

Andy called down from the top, "You don't understand! It's beautiful!"

"Having fun yet?" asked the bird, his grating voice echoing down the stairwell. "Having fun?"

Daniel caught his breath three blocks away and leaned against a cage of goats. Their eyes were yellow. A blind, black guitarist stopped his strumming and said in a raspy voice, "Deep breaths, brother. Deep breaths."

Anything but Dead

There are certain faces the camera loves. The lens lingers upon them with gratitude and desire. Maybe it's the planes of skin and bone that catch the light and give a distinct sculptural satisfaction. Or maybe it's simply the rule that every director knows: big heads. All the stars were small people with big heads and exaggerated features: large eyes, huge mouths.

Mike didn't know what to expect. But the next day, when his new chat pal made her grand entrance at an Italian place on the river, he knew at a glance: Donna was a star. Ice-blue eyes under a mane of brown hair. A woman used to being watched, comfortable with the attention her beauty inspired. But, unlike any star he'd ever met, this woman exuded a feeling Mike had always associated with delusion: contentment. And she was tall.

Within the hour they were in her loft near Greektown, under pale, wooden beams joined by steel bars, tearing each other's clothes off. Making love. And as she hovered over him, his hands gripping her hips as they thrust hungrily into him, he looked into her closed eyes and said her name. It was the most amazing sex he had ever had. Dot hadn't been exaggerating. The orgasms came and came like ceaseless waves against a shore. Exhaustion finally overtook them. They collapsed, their bodies ringing with satisfaction. And just a bit of soreness.

Eventually they talked. Or debated. It made him smile: two naked strangers wrapped around each other, debating reality. Like college kids.

"Hungry?" she asked.

"No."

"When's the last time you ate?" she said, grinning, as if she knew a secret. "You can't remember?"

"No," he said, amazed. "I guess I've lost my appetite."

"You don't have one anymore. It's your choice now."

"Why?"

She shrugged. "I bet they came from a famine culture. The aliens probably asked the birds if there was one thing they could change what would it be. A world without hunger. Not a bad idea."

"There's something," he shook his head, "wrong about it."

She looked at him as if he were nuts.

"I mean, we didn't earn it. We didn't solve it. Big Daddy came and bailed us out."

Donna gave a gentle smirk. "You've never been hungry, have you?"

Mike did not have to answer.

Gently, she drew his hand between her legs. After a time he asked, "Why birds? Why not bacteria? Or bass?"

"They're aliens. They're different. Fish are *our* natural ancestors. We both came from the water. We begin life submerged, floating in the womb. Birds are something else. No wonder they identified with them. Do that again. Strange. They're the only animal capable of mimicking our speech. They're singers too. Still, birds are the true other. Imagine how they see the world."

A flash frame blinked into his mind: two dolls discarded in a golden field of wheat. Too high for any crane shot. "Barrada. Nikto." Danny and him repeating the alien phrase. Were those the magic words?

"But why'd they do it?"

She moaned softly, then said, "Who knows? It's magic. All we have to do is accept it."

She didn't know she had said it. Quoted it exactly. The Klinder line: "All we have to do is accept it." It alerted Mike, set off an inner alarm that he tried not to show. And he felt himself withdrawing from her, even as he was getting hard.

"Mike?"

"I'm sorry. But it creeps me out."

"Why? We can have anything!" She smiled and squeezed him. "We can be anything!"

"Anything but dead."

"Yes! Isn't it wonderful?"

They made love again.

Donna used to be a depressed poet, but now she didn't do anything. She relished. Food. Sex. Sunshine. She was perfectly happy. And as he thrust into her, Mike felt an impossible desire. I want this. I want it all. I want to live. I want happiness and everything. The whole schmear. I want what she has. I want. I want. I want. He caught himself imagining that he was making love to Pauline, the little Frenchwoman. The thought hurt.

"Look at me," he said as she straddled him, biting his ear.

She pulled back and looked.

"No," he said. "While we're kissing, look at me."

They kissed. She looked.

"Say my name."

She said it.

When they had finished it was beautiful. And it was awful. Whatever he wanted, he couldn't get. Not from this contented creature.

I must be a monster, Mike thought. Everything I want is outside of me. And I don't know how to get there.

Later, holding her in his arms, her heart beating faintly against his cool skin, he watched her as she slept, and decided: he liked her.

Yes, he thought, after he had checked the emotion.

He definitely liked her.

This Sweet Old World

Daniel smelled fresh-squeezed lemonade.

He sat on the cool asphalt beside the tall, blind black guitarist, his long Robert Johnson fingers gripping the chords and
strumming the strings. The creamy cataracts in his eyes. His black fedora
upside down at his feet next to his fold-up stool and jumbo plastic cup
of beer. Occasionally, someone would drop in a dollar as he sang. People
listened, stunned by the voice, the yearning, and the pictures he made,
paralyzed with wonder, their mouths open and their eyes taking it all in.

They were happy too.

The song came from his belly, and the words rose into the air as if
he made them up on the spot. Slow and aching, not quite country, not
quite folk. The man's voice soothing—cracked and haunted as he sang of
lost chances, missed joys—a song written to someone who had left their
life too soon, and didn't know what they had lost. It sounded like a letter

to a suicide. By someone who loved them. A list of all the beautiful things in "this sweet old world."

What a sad song, Daniel thought. It's a good thing I'm happy.

Listening, Daniel jotted down a mental list. It seemed at that moment the most important list he'd ever written. It was a list of all the things that made him happy. He was trying to be happy.

Julie's nose.

That one chord change in Randy Newman's song "Marie."

A midnight garden decorated by fireflies.

Tits.

Waking up Christmas morning.

Moments when you forgot who you were.

Charlie Chaplin riding the cogs in *Modern Times.*

Cold beer in a frosty can after mowing a hot summer lawn.

Any paragraph in *Lolita.*

Faulkner's *As I Lay Dying.* When they lost the casket in the river.

Ferris wheels on the way up.

The Wall going down.

Pet Sounds. All thirty-eight minutes and two seconds of it.

Nelson Mandela being released.

Meg Ryan and rice pudding.

The Beatles on *Ed Sullivan.*

A toboggan ride.

A bonfire on the beach.

Watching a V of geese fly by.

Sean's stupid jokes.

Sean saying, "Dad."

Sean, just out of the womb, recognizing him with those dark, dark eyes.

Mike laying his hand over his heart in the golden field of wheat.

Mike holding his hand at Uncle Louie's funeral.

That's right. It wasn't Julie's funeral. No wonder he didn't remember it. Julie was alive.

Daniel reviewed the list. Looking for connections. Was there a common thread that ran through all things happy? A strange thought occurred to him: They were all temporary. They all ended.

The blind man laid his beat-up instrument on his lap, and reached down carefully for his beer, finding it with his spider fingers. "What's a matter, brother?" he asked, tilting his head toward Daniel. "That song bum you out?"

"Yes. It was beautiful."

The black man toasted the air before him. "Lucinda Williams. God's gift to the blues." He took a long sip and let out a gravelly belch. "But you ain't putting no money in my hat."

Daniel pulled out his wallet and laid a couple bucks in the black fedora. He saw the logo stitched into the silk lining: a black angel. And on the bottom, covered with a haphazard stack of green bills, a dead hummingbird.

"Thanks, brother. You okay?"

"Yes, actually. I'm happy."

"Ahhhh." The black man gargled a sigh. Then gave a broad, toothless smirky smile that showed the creases on his face. "What you so happy about?"

"Oh, you know ... everything."

"Ahhhh," the man gargled again.

Daniel tried to work up an argument, shifting into his best Dale Carnegie. "Every day's a bonus, isn't it? Every day we get to live a day longer than we were supposed to."

"I know," said the blind black man. "Terrible, ain't it?"

"Yes," Daniel agreed. "But I'm trying to be happy about it."

After a time, the man said, "You know what I do? When I feel that way? I try going to the last place I was happy." He picked up his guitar and began strumming, finding his way into another song. That's when Daniel saw the scars on his wrists.

"Where's that?" he asked.

The black man smiled. "Brother, when I find it ... you'll be the first to know."

✳   ✳   ✳

Daniel had loaded all his bags into the trunk of his spanking new silver Volvo—safest car in the world—when he decided he had to go somewhere. Somewhere was better than nowhere.

He decided to go to the last place he was happy.

Florida. His last memory. Their trip to Disney World. After that it was just him and Sean in the house in Detroit. And the foggy snow outside the window. And every morning the business with the coffee. He decided that must have been when it all started. Him grieving Julie. Afraid to leave the house. Answer the door. Read the mail. The coffee difficulty. Tucking Sean in. Sean having a nightmare. Every night. The same nightmare. *Something about hummingbirds.*

That went on forever.

Before that it was their trip to Disney World. Planning it. Sending off for the brochures. Sean memorizing them. What would they see? The haunted castle. Futureland. It's A Small World After All. Getting stuck on it—no, he didn't want to think about that. Get that melody in his head again. He remembered: they were on their way home. It was raining, a terrible rainstorm that came down in silver sheets. Once it got so bad they had to pull over. Rain pounding on the roof. The windows steaming up. Disney World. Julie's idea. The ideal family vacation. He remembered now.

He would follow the memory.

Wherever it took him. To the last place he was happy.

Behind the wheel, as he entered I-75 South, Daniel glanced at himself in the rearview mirror. He was smiling. Why was he smiling? He had a purpose. A mission. A reason to live. That was, he concluded, almost better than being happy.

"I'm going to Disney World!" he shouted and sped on.

Whoopa!

The next day Mike sat at a cold, corner table overlooking the Detroit River, waiting for her in the same place they'd met: Tony's. He'd kept his brown leather coat on against the chill coming off the window. After the lunch crowd had thinned out, the air was full of pizza and beer. Waiting for her there, Mike felt like all his life had led him to this time, this place. This occasion. Not many people have ever come to a choice like this, he suspected. They've never found out what they are capable of. He would. He was willing to try anything. Anything. He wanted out.

He adjusted himself, compensating for his heavy pocket. Out the window ice floes slid by, some of them large enough for a junior hockey game. Sun crept through the gray quilt of clouds, sending spotlight shafts to play on the green-blue water. A Great Lakes freighter oozed around the bend. Mike was always amazed by how long they were. Bloated and cruising under a full load on their way to Chicago to dump off ore, and, on their empty return, riding high and fast, a wide wake streaming behind. He liked to imagine the lives of the sailors—a peaceful life between ports—lots of downtime. To read. Relax. Whatever.

It seemed, to Mike, the perfect place. In between. For as much as he relished the completion of a project—say, a difficult shoot—he had long recognized a special enchantment in the not-quite-done. *It was the place of desire. A place beyond failure's touch. In the In Between there was no disappointment, no dashed hopes, no consequences.* The phone call you were about to make could change your life. The letter you hadn't opened yet could bring the most amazing news: a prize, a tax refund, true love. The next shot could be the best shot of your career. Anything was possible.

Maybe, he thought, that's what this place is: limbo.

When she came sunlight caught her body—her long, brown coat like something out of the seventies, the gray turtleneck that appeared to lengthen her neck. Black Levis tight as her legs scissored and her hips rolled. A lovely woman who trusted him. He both cherished and resented her look; he didn't expect to see it again.

"I ordered saganaki," she said after they had kissed. "What's wrong?"

"I was just thinking how beautiful you looked with your clothes on."

She beamed and looked at him under her lovely brows. "We don't have to eat. We can always postpone lunch and go to my place."

Mike was appalled to find the suggestion arousing. He shook his head. "We've got time."

She reached across the table and took his hand. "Jesus, you're cold."

"I'm fine."

A waiter came to their table with the platter of cheese sizzling in oil. He was patting down his apron, looking for his matches, when Donna said, "Use mine." She handed him a silver lighter. He clicked it open, flicked it, and fire whooshed up into the air. A wave of heat washed over

Mike's face. "Whoopa!" the waiter said glumly, then squeezed a lemon to douse the fire. The cheese smoldered in a low, blue flame as he set the plate before them.

"Hip," the water said, and smiled as he returned her Zippo.

"Hip, hooray," she replied cheerfully.

Mike watched her put the Zippo in her purse. That's it, he thought. That's the secret of the Crossovers. That's why Klinder was on the tube so much. He was recruiting. And that's why everyone seemed to follow the Wing Man so easily, so loyally. And why no one could see through him, see him for the vile, empty, sick egotist he was.

They're hypnotized.

They're all hypnotized all the time.

Her eyes searched his face. "Something upset you?"

"What you said last night. About eternity."

"I don't recall us talking much." Donna titled back her head and laughed. Though he could not see under her turtleneck, he recalled how perfect her neck was. Creamy and smooth. Someone had told him that you can tell a woman's age by the wrinkles on her neck. A Hungarian DP he used to work with said older women had chicken necks. He'd have to use a softer focus. Rummaging through his case of filters, he'd say, "Let's keel this cheekin."

Mike squirmed and said, "I don't think we're made for immortality."

"Whatever." It was one of her phrases that reminded him how young she was. "Like anybody wouldn't choose to live forever if they could. It's a universal concept, Mike. The afterlife."

"A virtual lottery we didn't win."

"I don't see the problem. I mean, we're immortal. Why fight it? Why not just accept it and get on with your life?"

That word again. Accept. It turned his stomach. "This isn't my life. This is a mistake. Hell, I didn't even ask for it."

He realized he was engaging in a debate he had no desire to win. It was merely to delay the inevitable. He had already decided.

She grabbed a breadstick from the basket, dipped it in the soggy cheese, and bit off a chunk. "That's kind of perverse, Mike. This is a dream come true, and you want to send it back like an undercooked steak?"

He'd been thinking about this. He wasn't just angry anymore. He was offended. "I don't want a dream," he said wearily. "I want to wake up."

She shook her head. "I don't get it. You have me—what do you want life for? What's so bad about world peace, freedom from hunger and crime and—"

He said the word she couldn't say.

Donna shuddered. "I'll never get used to how you can do that."

She was living in an edited transcript. The Watergate version of life, with all the expletives deleted. How safe and simple. Didn't she know the secret? Hadn't she met anyone who could say that magic word? For a moment he was annoyed by her naïveté. Mike looked at Donna and did his shrinking trick. Made her smaller and smaller until she was far across the room in a distant booth. About three inches tall. A pretty little doll looking at someone who alarmed her.

Mike caught himself. No. Not this way. He was objectifying her. He wasn't going to make it easy on himself. That would spoil the whole point. It had to hurt. It had to be horrible. It had to make no sense.

Sense. Tense. Mense.

"Mike? Where'd you go?"

"I'm here."

"Men." She snorted. "You're always disappearing."

Mike looked over the river and saw a crow settle on an ice floe.

"I wish you wouldn't torture yourself like this. I wish," Donna sighed. "I wish this were enough." She reached out and held his hand. "You're a thoughtful man, Mike. You care."

"No," he said, steeling himself.

"It hurts you."

"Stop," he said.

"Whatever you're punishing yourself for . . . it's over. You're a different man now."

He looked at her sharply. "You don't know me."

"You're a good man."

"I've never been a good man," he said. "I'm a killer."

Donna sighed and tilted her head and almost smiled as if he had just told her he was a kangaroo.

Haven't Had a Bite
All Day

D aniel braked suddenly and his tires screeched as his past sprung forward and smacked him in the face. He couldn't believe his eyes. There up ahead he saw a patch of crisscrossing tire skids marking the narrow stream that ran under the road—sure signs of delighted, drunken fishermen discovering "a hole."

Daniel had been retracing their route from Disney World for eighteen hours. He wasn't even tired. He'd been driving the two-lane blacktop, the detour they had taken in the rainstorm. They hadn't felt safe on the interstate. In the storm. Too little visibility. Too many trucks sweeping by them, blinding them in the backwash of their wheels. So they headed easterly, through the Kissimmee Lake region. *Home to the Finest Large Mouth Bass Fishing In America!* the sign said. They were going to take the coast up. See the ocean.

Skid. That's what Uncle Louie used to do on fishing trips with him and Mike, whenever they saw a hole: skid.

He pulled over onto what little shoulder there was, turned off the engine and listened. No wind. No birds. The faint gurgle of the stream. He could smell the wild palms in the humid air. They shadowed either side of the narrow road. Tightrope walking down the double-yellow line, he felt a power and a loneliness that reminded him of his youth. No traffic sounds. Nothing. The country was empty. Cool air and a perfect blue sky above. The stream was khaki green with darker pits at the edges—where bass would hide out, basking. The perfect fishing hole. He made his way down the steep, grassy bank and sat at the water's edge. Taking in the quiet dawdle of the stream. Insects danced on the surface. Occasionally, concentric rings pocked the water but he couldn't tell if it was from the fish or the bugs.

He heard the stranger coming before he saw him, calling out a name. "Emma? Emma?"

It was an old man in green waders making his way carefully up the path that rimmed the stream. A creel basket at his hip strapped across his shoulder, over his red long-sleeved T-shirt. A few days' growth of beard. A hat decorated with flies.

The stranger wasn't surprised to see Daniel. He did something with his hand as if to say "Hi there." A brown leather tube was strung over his other shoulder—his pole.

"Thought I heard a car. Volvo, huh? Six-cylinder?"

Daniel smiled. "Right."

"Something I do to pass the time. Telling cars by their sound."

"You're pretty good at it."

The stranger smiled and sat down next to him and removed his damp waders. His legs were scrawny in his red long johns. He removed his red socks and started massaging his foot. His creel was soaked and smelled of a fresh catch.

"You live around here?"

" 'Bout a half mile upstream. Somebody's cabin."

"I could get used to it," Daniel said, taking in the lush silence that surrounded them. "How long you lived here?"

"Since they started saving us."

"Ten years?"

"Yup. Right here." The man pointed to a fallen log half sunk in the green water at a bend in the stream. "That's where I bought it."

Daniel looked at the spot.

"Doesn't look deep enough to snag a man, but it's deceptive. Current gets mean there. Watch," he said. "Watch now."

The hole erupted: a breaching bass—truly immense—a suggestion of yellow stripes and a muscular arch of spiky dorsal and then it was gone.

"Bastard," the wader man cursed softly. "He loves doing that. Taunting me."

Daniel took in the current, the bugs, the hole, which had resumed its previous calm. Finally, he asked, "Why come back?"

"My wife. I told her I was gonna crack that hole. And she being a worrier and all, warned me 'bout the current. Like I didn't know my way around here. You want to know what I said? I'll tell you what I said. I said, 'Mind your business, woman.' Just like that." The man winced. "Last thing I ever said to her. So I traipse off like a pisser and I ease my way down into the edge of the hole and wouldn'tcha know it? I trip and 'fore I can do anything, waders are full of water. Cold, I tell ya. I almost got 'em off when I had to breath it. Everything's going green and I see, you know what I see? I'll tell you what I see. I see the biggest damn bass in the world floating under a log, watching me with one eye, like he was saying, 'You lose, old-timer.' "

The man chuckled and began massaging his other foot.

"Then all I remember is waking up dressed like this—good as new. In my bed in this stranger's cabin. Still in my waders. Radio playing our favorite song. I watched a spider scooting on a rafter. Two hours later that damn song is still playing and the spider's still on the rafter and I'm still in bed thinking, 'I wish the hell somebody would change the station.' Then I realize I can. And I do."

"What song?"

"*Gonna take a Sentimental Journey...*" the old man sang poorly and knew it. "I wait for her. A couple, three nights. Not like her. Phone don't work. Only channel on the radio is stuck on that damn song, playing it over and over again, like to wanna drive me crazy."

Daniel recalled a similar agony.

Getting stuck on the "It's a Small World" ride at Disney World with Sean. Surrounded on all sides by the cheerful puppets: Eskimos, Laplanders, Mongols, Mayans, Ethiopians; all dancing the same moves over and over, all singing the same treacly, utopian hymn. They were marooned in the middle of this artificial river—a captured audience. Sean didn't mind. And for a time Daniel was distracted by the cool bass line of the song. He wondered who played that. But after ten minutes he wanted to drown himself. It took forty-five minutes for the ride to get started up again, till they were rescued from the barrage of cute. Pure hell.

"The fridge is full of everything I like. But I can't work up an appetite. After a few days I get mad that she doesn't come. What am I? Chopped liver? Then I go up and down the stream every day, hoping the next turn she's gonna be there—pissed as ever. Saying: I told you. I warned you. It's not safe out here."

"Emma?"

"Heard me, huh? She's a stubborn woman, so I figured I'd just give her time. After a few weeks I get to thinking about the last thing I said. 'Mind your business, woman.' That wasn't nice. I mean, of all the last words that could have come between us—why that? Felt bad about it. Intend to make it up to her."

"That was ten years ago."

"Yup."

"I lost my wife too."

"You don't say?"

"Car accident."

"That's a hard one. Emma's always saying you can't trust those cars." They listened to the stream. It sounded louder.

"What make?" the old man said.

"Make?"

"Model. I'm just curious."

"Chrysler Neon."

"Never heard of it. Probably after my time."

They were quiet for a moment.

"Brakes," the man said.

Daniel looked at him.

"Chryslers always had a lot of brake recalls."

"They did?"

"Yup."

The old man closed his eyes. "Two recalls. Rotors. And . . . something about the lines." He opened his eyes, took in Daniel's face, and was suddenly flush with embarrassment. "Sorry. Emma's always saying I don't know when to stop."

"She'll come soon," Daniel said, then caught himself and recognized, under his apparent good intentions, the impulse to hurt the old man as he had hurt him. You had to watch good intentions, he thought. You never know what they'll let out. A painful truth. A patronizing right-eousness. Malice. All made invisible and unconscious by goodwill. The old man hadn't meant to hurt him. And he had returned the favor with a vengeance. "I hope, anyway," he said, by way of apology.

"Maybe. Maybe not. She was a healthy woman. Lot more sense than me. Can't see her pluggin' into a wet socket."

Daniel stood and brushed the leaves off his pants. "Well," he said.

"Yeah," the old man said, massaging his pale, wrinkled foot.

"How they biting?"

"Terrible." The man smiled. "Haven't had a bite all day."

Daniel smiled, remembering: It was what Uncle Louie used to say, the obligatory fisherman's lie.

He was walking on the crisp, yellow no-pass double lines that split the blacktop and was almost to his Volvo when the old man's voice resumed.

"Emma?"

"Emma?"

"Emma?"

Plan B

The *saganaki* had stopped sizzling on the table between them.

"Look at me," Mike said to Donna. "I'm a killer. I kill people. I have a knack for it."

"That's the beauty of all this. It doesn't matter what you did before."

"I'm not talking before. I'm talking here."

She let go of his hand. Her face, which had at first expressed disbelief, made a quick pit stop at fear, then turned slowly into dread. "Why?" she asked.

He looked at her eyes. Ice blue. "It's the only way I can wage a protest vote. *Outrage the bosses. Get their attention.*"

"That's horrible," she looked out the window, then back. "Is it working?"

"Not yet."

"Then why continue?"

"I want out. I want my flight canceled. I want to die."

Again she shuddered at the taboo word. "That's how I felt, you know. Slit my wrists in a bathtub. The long way. My parents were sleeping in the next room. It was very selfish of me. But I couldn't take another day. When I first got here I wanted to do it again. I went to the top of a building. But ... I couldn't jump. That's deep programming. Some fail-safe added to the original impulse. It took me a while to accept it. This. Everything. Now I'm grateful. I've made a clean start. I've learned to relish. So we're stuck here." She smiled and shrugged. "What are you gonna do?"

"Plan B," he said.

She looked at him.

"I've decided to kill someone good. Someone who wants to live. Someone I like." He wasn't sure which shocked her more. The idea of killing, or the word *like*.

She sat very still. "Mike."

"I'm thinking," he continued, "maybe Christianity was right about that. Maybe there's something to this innocent victim idea. Sacrifice."

"Mike."

"Maybe it'll shake things up, disrupt the laws of karma. I'm hoping something ... shifts."

"That's crazy, Mike."

"It's the only alternative I can think of."

"So," she expelled a disgusted breath, and regarded him with pity. "How were you thinking of doing it? A bomb? A bazooka?"

He took it out of his coat pocket and laid it on the table.

Her eyes went wide. "I thought it was your bird."

"I don't have a bird."

"You ... ?"

"Never had one." He looked at her. It was almost impossible for her to believe him. He said her name. "It's the only way I can show them how awful this is."

"For you," she said. "Not for most of us."

"I'm not going to enjoy it."

"You fucker!" She slammed her hand on the table and the china and silver rattled. "You egotistical, self-centered dumb ass! What gives you the right?"

"I told you I wasn't a good man."

"You're a terrorist!" she said, disgusted. "A Corrector!" And she knew it was a mistake the second she had said it. The bright, insouciant, naive young woman was no longer there. This was a clever person who had dropped their favorite persona. He could see her eyes scrambling for backup, for a contingency, for a face. This would make it easier.

"Thank you," Mike said.

She said nothing.

"So how long have you been working for Klinder?"

"Who?"

She was good. "Joel A. Klinder."

"Never heard of him." She was watching the gun.

"The Wing Man?" he offered. "First Contact? The Hypnotist? Doesn't believe in gravity."

"You're talking nonsense."

He smiled. "Why couldn't it be like life, Donna? People meeting each other by chance. The wrong people falling in love and making each other miserable. At least they'd have a say in it. Why not, Donna?"

She looked at him with new eyes. The ridges under them were lined with beads of sweat. After a long time she said, "My name's not Donna."

Mike nodded. "Why are you following a liar like Klinder?"

"He's a wonderful man and he's trying to save us."

"He's dead. My brother killed him."

Mike remembered his shock when Danny did that. Flinching at the gunshots. Looking at the body. He was still amazed that Klinder hadn't shot him right away, as soon as he entered the room. Kyo had said Klinder couldn't kill him, only Danny could. But until he saw the raw fear on the doctor's face, as if Klinder were looking at death himself, he didn't really believe it. God knows he must have killed enough strangers in his day.

He could say the *D* word; he didn't hesitate shooting Kyo. Why couldn't he pull the trigger?

Jesus. That was what the look on his face meant! Klinder was afraid of pulling a Wu! He was terrified of disappearing for good! And what did that mean?

Christ, Mike thought. Holy Christ!

The bastard liked me. He really liked me.

And Mike thought he understood something else as he watched Donna looking at his gun on the table. Something even more shocking. When Danny shot Klinder, Mike hadn't just feel appalled. He felt relieved. As if their tried-and-true roles were reversed. As if Danny had finally bailed *him* out. He was amazed at how relieved he felt. He realized now it was because he couldn't do it. He had pointed the gun straight at Klinder's face but he couldn't do it. Just like Klinder, he couldn't pull the trigger. Even after Buffalo. Even after watching Kyo die. Because in the end he felt the same way about Klinder that Danny felt about Uncle Louie.

He was all he had.

Donna's shoulders slumped and she made an ugly sound in her mouth. "Shit. I'm so stupid. I thought . . . if I ever met a Corrector, I could talk them out of it. If anyone could, I could. I thought: I'd been there." She looked at him. "But I've never been anywhere you are."

"No," he agreed. "You haven't."

"Mike? Do I get any say in this?"

"No."

"If I run . . . ?"

"I'll catch you."

"No matter how many people you butcher, you can't stop us."

"I can try."

She grabbed the gun off the table and stood, pointing it at his chest. "Don't move!"

Mike looked at the gun.

"Don't smile at me, you fucking creep!"

He could tell: she hadn't done this before.

He stood. The gun followed him.

"Stay there!"

He took a step toward her, ignoring the shivering gun, his eyes locked on hers.

"Mike—don't!"

Between his second and third step she tried to pull the trigger twice. By the time he felt the barrel against his chest, she had tried once more. He watched as she closed her eyes and one tear drifted down her cheek. He took the gun and watched her collect herself, watched her cross her arms and rub her biceps as if she were chilled. She opened her eyes. She wouldn't look at him. But, finally gazing out the window at the drifting floes of ice, she said, "I don't know if I can ever forgive you for that." She sighed. "That ... that was the worst moment of my life."

"This is mine," he answered, clicked off the safety and, before she could turn, shot her once behind the ear.

All the Ice Cream
in the World

D aniel realized he hadn't had a bite all day, so, up the road, he stopped at a diner-gas-groceries-ice-live bait place. Something familiar about the pumps. Red cherries on top of them.

A bell above the screen door rang as he entered. One old waitress in a pink uniform behind the counter. Beer posters everywhere: breasty young women holding sweating bottles. And a beautiful young boy in the corner playing an old shuffleboard game. He wore a red T-shirt and blue jeans three sizes too big for him; they sagged, revealing his black boxers, and crumpled over his shoes. It made Daniel happy to see the boy enjoying himself. He sat and ordered a cherry pie and a coffee. Black.

"Can I heat that up for ya?"

"Yes, ma'am." Old ladies with southern accents always made him want to say *ma'am*.

She poured his coffee and asked, "How about a scoop on it?"

"Sure."

"What's your favorite?" she asked with relish.

"Butter pecan."

She slid open a freezer under the counter and a cloud of frosty air lifted up between them. "You're in luck," she said, bending over to scoop. "We got all the ice cream in the world."

Daniel clinked his teeth against the coffee cup. Her black name tag read *Emma*.

After a time she asked, "How's the pie?"

"Delicious."

She smiled proudly. "Best you ever tasted, I bet."

"Yes."

She was rinsing the ice cream scoop when Daniel asked, "How's the fishing 'round here?"

She whacked it hard a couple of times against the sink. "They say it's good. Can't stand the thought myself."

"She's a full-tilter," a young voice behind him said.

Daniel turned to look at the boy. But he was concentrating on his game. Sliding the stainless steel puck over the sawdust and the burnished wood.

"Mind your own business, Dwight," the waitress said.

"Full-tilter?" Daniel asked.

The waitress leaned in close to him. "He makes up words. Not right in the head. If I didn't keep an eye on him he'd wander right out into traffic. He means *full gospel. We don't believe in taking life. Abortion. Capital punishment. War. It's all the same sin.* God made everything sacred."

After a moment Daniel said, "Cows?"

"Well..." she said.

"Fish?"

"Sure, fish too. Why not? They got as much right to live as we do. It's not like we have to eat."

"You sell bait," he said.

"I been meaning to take that sign down. But . . . it's too close to the road."

There was a sudden jangly noise from the shuffleboard. "I won!" the boy said.

"You always win," the old woman said, rolling her eyes. "You want a sandwich or something? We got everything but fish." She smiled and wiped her hands on a dishrag. "House rules." She leaned over the counter and rested on her elbows. "Tell you the truth? I couldn't fry a fish to save my life."

Daniel looked at her face. She blew a stray strand of gray hair out from over her eyes. Green eyes. She must have been a looker in her day.

"I used to gut 'em, clean 'em, cook 'em. Every day. Fish, fish, fish. Lord, how I hated that smell."

"You're a vegetarian?"

"No, sir. I just object when it gets personal. Ever since the day I saw him pull the hook right out of a bass's mouth"—she showed him with her hands, the index finger curled into the hook and shoved between the "Okay" sign on her other hand, then pulled away—"ripped the poor thing's lip off. My husband?" She shook her head. "See, he was on a mission. He had to catch the big one. But that bass was too darned smart for him. 'Old-timer,' I used to tell him. 'You've met your match.' Didn't stop him. He'd go traipsing off like he owned the place to the worst part of that stream—"

"—Emma?—"

"Treacherous. You know what I'm saying? Awful currents. 'Stay out of the current,' I'd say. I kept warning him and warning him, but did he listen to me? No, sir. I was just an old worrywart didn't know nothing—"

"—Emma?"

She blinked several times. "What?"

"He's there."

"Who's there?"

"Your husband."

"Where?"

"At the stream. He's still trying to catch that fish."

She was quiet a long time. She wiped the counter with a rag. Finally, she harrumphed and said, "Figures."

The Last Bullet

~ ~ ~

Mike didn't remember leaving the restaurant.

He came awake sitting at the edge of the Detroit River, watching a pair of mating ducks below him. The green-necked male viciously snatched the female by her neck from behind, mounted her briefly, came, then rolled off of her into the water like a man off a woman. It took about five seconds.

Five. Jive. Alive.

Mike pointed the gun to his heart and pulled the trigger.

Click.

He looked at it. He brought it back to his scalp just above the ear and pulled the trigger.

Click.

Pressed it to the base of his neck. And pulled the trigger.

Click.

None of the clean shots worked.

He put the gun in his mouth and pulled the trigger.

Click.

He checked the gun. No bullets. He was all out.

He counted the shots. He'd been in the last party of the raid and he hadn't done much shooting. The guard on the seventh floor of the compound. Somebody called Jacob in communications. The man who had wounded Dot on level twelve. Dot again when she begged him. Sean. Then Donna who wasn't Donna.

She got the last bullet.

He walked over and stood under the Noguchi fountain in Hart Plaza—a huge ring held up by two angled aluminum buttresses—it reminded him of an old satellite design. The silver shafts were perforated at intervals by holes. It was dry now, off season. He kept hoping someone would turn it on and he could bathe in the cold downpour.

But nothing happened. Mike covered his head with his hands. It didn't matter who he killed. *They were never going to let him go.*

Then he saw a couple in love, walking arm-in-arm through the plaza—oblivious to his attention, their eyes locked together, their breaths mingling above them. He wanted to corner them and make them listen. He wanted to tell them about love. Not to bother. It wasn't worth it. Nobody knows anybody. Everyone's a fucking stranger. You may think you love him and you may think you love her but it doesn't matter. In the end you'll find a way to make each other miserable.

What the fuck was he thinking? He didn't know anything about love.

He saw a black mounted cop in his police-issue leather jacket on a brown horse. Mike approached him, smiling. The man smiled back. The horse snorted clouds and shuffled sideways when Mike got close. Cold duty, he thought.

"You lost?" the policeman asked.

"Yes," said Mike. "What's his name?"

"Gabriel." He smiled and stroked its mane. "Been together ten years now."

"Horse years?"

"Beg your pardon?"

"That's an old horse."

"He's twenty. But he's good as new. Aren't you, Gabe?" The cop patted its neck, which seemed to settled the creature. "Nothing like a horse's love. You give them a little and they triple your investment."

"What do you do when you catch a . . . criminal?" Mike asked.

He had the cop's attention now. "Why?" he asked good-naturedly. "You know any?"

"You take them to jail, I guess. 'Book 'em'?"

The cop nodded. "That would be procedure. Only we don't have much call for that these days, thank god."

"What good is a cop then?"

The man looked at him as if he were crazy. Mike got that a lot.

"It's the best job in the world. Watching out. Taking care of people. Minding the peace. It's what I've always done."

"But there's no crime."

"So?"

"So what do you do?"

"I told you. Watch. Take care. Mind the peace."

Mike noticed the row of medals above his badge. Ribbons, stars, and a spread of black wings.

"What if somebody came to you and said, 'I'm a murderer. I just shot a woman I liked in the back of the head. She didn't feel it. It was a clean shot. Her brains were spread all over the window like spaghetti.' "

The horse snorted. The man petted him again and looked out over the river. "You'd be surprised. I get that a lot." The cop smiled at Mike. "This is hypothetical, right?"

Mike nodded.

"Well, then. I'd say: go to bed. Get some sleep. You've had a bad dream. Lotsa people do." He looked down at Mike, salt-and-pepper mustache twitching. "Or I'd say, go to the library."

"The library?"

"Yessir. That's where I go when I need some answers. Hasn't failed me yet."

Mike chuckled to himself and thought: the library. Now why didn't I think of that? That's where Danny always went. He noticed the cop's holster was empty. "Where's your gun, officer?"

The man took his time replying. "Haven't needed one for years." The cop leaned down and looked at Mike directly, unruffled and confident, accustomed to belligerence from drunks or troublemakers. "And I haven't come across anything I couldn't handle without one."

Mike respected him. "The library?" he asked.

The cop relaxed, sat back in the saddle and pointed over his shoulder. "That way. You can't miss the lions." The cop held out his hand. "I'll take your gun, if you don't mind."

Mike stared at him.

"The one in your left pocket."

Mike pulled it out and handed it over grip first. It felt good to get rid of it. To lose that option.

"Thank you, sir." The cop stared down the barrel and sniffed. "Don't remember the last time I saw one of these. But you never forget the smell." He inspected the gun, then put it in the empty holster on his hip, and snapped it shut. "You won't be needing it, right?"

"No," said Mike. "I'm done."

"Good. Guns are a world of trouble." The cop regarded him. "You see Sam? Tell him Gabriel says 'Hi'." A gentle smile.

"Sam?" Mike asked.

"At the library," the cop said. Then, with a click of his tongue, he coaxed his mount into a dawdling walk.

How?

e's looking for you, Emma," Daniel told the old, dead waitress across the counter. "Every day he wakes up and goes back to the hole and calls your name. I heard him."

"You heard him?"

"Yes, Ma'am."

She nodded for a long time. "Sounds just like Henry. Stubborn old coot."

"Ten miles back. The hole by the skids."

"I know about skids," the boy said.

"I know where it is," said Emma.

The shuffleboard jangled and the boy pumped his arms in the air. "I *won!*"

She smirked. "Imagine that."

"Emma?" Daniel said.

"What?"

"Don't you . . ."

"Oh, honey, that was years ago. I got a place of my own now. Made a new life. I'm not some fish stuck in a hole. I've moved on."

They were so close to being together. All the man wanted was a chance.

"Besides," she said, "the roads."

Daniel questioned her with his eyebrows.

"Truckers plowing through here like there's no tomorrow. Speed limits be damned. They try to make it from Orlando to the Keys in one last leg and they don't give a hoot what gets in their way. Animals. Pedestrians. And these kids. Hopped up on dope. In their speedsters. And at night there's all the creatures."

"Wolves," Dwight said. The boy was looking at him intently. Deliberately he raised one tiny finger and pointed it at Daniel.

"Skeeters," Emma said with a shudder. *"Come summer, those skeeters like to wanna eat you alive.* Then there's all the crazy people. With guns."

"Strangers," the boy said. "Candy."

"He means danger. No, sir. That highway just isn't safe anymore."

Daniel stopped eating. "He's ten miles up the road. He wants to apologize. I could drive you."

Silence.

"Emma?"

"Mister, I don't know you from Adam. For all I know you'd take me down the road and have your way with me and no one would know the better. That's two-fifty."

A great sense of defeat descended over Daniel as he paid the bill.

"It's the worst road in the world, I tell you. There's just not enough law to keep track of all the speeders. Heck, I'd have as much chance if I laid down in the middle of it and let them squish me like a possum. No, sir. I'll take my chances on the inside, thank you."

The boy giggled. "It's cold. You think the blacktop's hot, but it's cold." He laid a hand against his cheek.

"He knows," Emma indicated the boy with a tilt of her head. "First-hand he knows. What you want for dinner, Dwight?"

"Ice cream."

"What's your favorite?"

"Chocolate chip."

"Well, whatddaya know. We got lots of that." She smiled and winked at Daniel. "We got all the ice cream in the world."

He leaned over the counter and saw, under the frosty pane, one tub of chocolate-chip ice cream.

One tub.

Daniel got up to leave, thinking: somewhere, anywhere. Julie could be ten miles from him and he'd never even know it. How would he find her? How? He could be walking right past her in a crowded mall and they'd miss each other. Or maybe—the thought burned him—maybe she had simply moved on. And it wouldn't matter how much he needed her or wanted her. He'd be stuck forever with this impossible desire.

He opened the screen door. The bell above him rang and he watch-ed it shiver. The shuffleboard jangled and the celebrating boy shouted, "I won!"

Horrified, Emma said, "You're letting all the bugs in!"

Why?

You couldn't miss the lions. Mike turned the corner and there they were: Like sphinxes stationed on both sides of the thirty white marble steps to the front doors of the library. The winter sun made their much-abused stone hides golden and pocked. Passing one as he ascended, Mike grazed his hand over its long, winding tail—sandpaper.

Inside: quiet. Marble floors and high ceilings. The solemnity of a mausoleum. He strolled to the fiction section and drifted till he got to mysteries. Plucking a blue-spined book off the shelf, he searched for a place to sit down. There were black leather chairs next to some newspapers hung on racks like sheets out to dry. An old man holding an empty pipe was sitting in a square of light reading a sports section. Mike settled in, the leather cushed and he cracked the book at random.

It was a summer book. An easy read. It relaxed him. Someone was chasing someone else who had done something awful and if he wasn't found soon something worse would happen. After a few pages he came upon an odd line.

Just what do you think you're doing, Michael?

Odd because, as far as he could tell, it had nothing to do with the story. He reread the preceding paragraphs just to make sure, and nope—no "Michael." He had appeared without any preamble. He read on a few pages and confirmed it: the question was indeed a nonsequitur. Was it a typo? Sloppy editing? Or had he forgotten he'd already seen the name? He'd always been terrible at names. There was a hole in his ample hard drive of memory that refused to save them. Maybe Michael was a nickname he had missed? Or did the author mean the one-armed CIA guy?

Then this:

No, we mean you.

No, we mean you? What the fuck was that? He rescanned the page. It had nothing to do with anything. It was smack-dab in the middle of a paragraph describing how drugs were smuggled into Philadelphia. Was the author losing it? Playing games?

Mike got up, walked over and put the book back in its gap. He reached for the next one on the shelf. Opening to the first lines, he read:

We must love one another, yes, yes, that's all true enough, but nothing says we have to like each other. It may be the very recognition of all men as our brothers that accounts for the sibling rivalry, and even enmity, we have toward so many of them. No, we don't play games, Michael.

Mike snapped the book shut and looked at the cover. Peter De Vries, *The Glory of the Hummingbird.*

He reread the last line. It had to be some in-joke. Maybe the writer was being cute. Danny used to say how much he hated that cheap self-conscious stuff. Anybody could do that.

Mike shelved the book, then ran his fingers over the spines of the hardcovers, choosing a red one. A story collection by Gene Wolfe. *Castle of Days*. He thumbed it open and read:

"You may have been oppressed by demons," the small man said. "Or revived by unseen aliens who, landing on the Earth eons after the death of the last man, have sought to re-create the life of the twentieth century." And we don't make jokes either, Michael. Just what exactly are you trying to do?

He yelped and dropped the book as if it had burned him.

He looked at his hands. He scanned the library. The old pipe man was staring at the book where it had landed. Across the way, behind a glass, two teens—a boy and girl—were sharing a computer, surfing.

Silence.

The book—its blood-red cover garish and disturbing—lay at his feet.

Feeling as though he were being watched, Mike bent over, picked it up and read:

You are an intelligent man, Michael. Why do you refuse to grasp the obvious?

He dropped the book and looked over his shoulder. Outside the window a scarlet, tubular bird feeder glistened in the sunlight. A hummingbird hovered over one of the nozzles, occasionally dipping its curved beak inside to feast. Watching him in profile, with one eye.

"Okay," Mike said.

He picked up the book and strode over to the glass. The bird ignored him, which was odd; he'd always found birds to be the most skittish things.

"Okay," he said. "Let's talk."

"You all right, mister?" It was the pipe man.

"Are you doing this?" he asked, holding out the open book.

"Doing what?" the old man said, his forehead full of ridges.

"Never mind," said Mike. Then he read:

No need to speak. We can hear you.

Who are you? he thought.

Us, the book replied.

He swallowed. How are you doing this?

You will not think us rude, we hope, if we suggest that you couldn't begin to understand?

No, he thought.

But that is not really the question foremost in your mind, is it?

No, he thought.

You'll need another book for that. May we suggest science fiction? The section behind you. Any book will do.

Mike reshelved the blood-red book, and grabbed something paperback with a golden spaceship on its spine. By someone with the unlikely name "Spider Robinson." After he sat back down in the leather chair the first words he read were:

Pain shared is lessened. Joy shared is trebled. Thus do we defeat entropy.

And then:

What is your question, Michael?

It pissed him off that they could read him so well, pull out a question that he didn't dare ask, yet couldn't quite escape. It had been floating below the surface of his thoughts ever since he touched the hummingbird.

Where's Julie? he thought.

That was the question.

She would understand if anyone could. She had understood about his stepdaughter. How it killed him to watch her suffer like that. How he would have given anything to spare her, to put her out of her misery. It wasn't fair. No child should have to endure what he'd gone through in Buffalo.

You see? He'd tell her. That's why. That's why I killed your son.

She would understand. He felt sure she would.

Where's Julie? He thought. Then he looked at the book in his hand.

The answer was astounding.

Julie is home.

At that Mike nearly dashed out of the library. But he noticed the red-and-white sign above the door to the reading room: QUIET PLEASE. STAY, MICHAEL. YOU STILL HAVE QUESTIONS.

"Are you trying to impress me?" he said aloud. "I'm impressed, you omnipotent pricks."

When the sign did not change he turned to the book.

Unfortunately, you will not be able to see your lover for some time. You will have to accept that.

I will, will I? he thought.

Yes.

Why?

That is always the question. Julie is alive and well. Take heart. She will join you someday.

He thought: I'm supposed to find that reassuring? But thinking it, Mike realized: he did.

Most people do, he read. *Why did you kill the young one?*

Mike smiled and hated himself. Donna? She wasn't that young. Besides, it got your attention, didn't it?

The SF novel went on for paragraphs—an amusing, pun-filled story about a bartender whose odd clientele included leprechauns, robots, and pookahs. But no answers. The aliens seemed to have temporarily vacated the premises.

Pookahs.

Harvey, he thought. This is a scene from *Harvey!*

He read on. Nothing for a few lines, then:

You misunderstand. You have always had our attention. You are not using it wisely.

For no rational reason the words on the page suggested revulsion.

Are you threatening me? Fuck. You. What are you gonna do? What else can you possibly take from me?

Sit down, please, Michael. We don't make threats. Forgive the repetition, but we don't play games, either.

What's this, then? he thought, shaking the book.

The most efficient way to communicate without misunderstanding. We thought, perhaps, this way would be less disturbing than the last time.

They meant the red bullet room. Mike shuddered, recalling their choir-boy chorus. They were right: this was better. He wondered how the alien's words on the page could sound like a voice. A cool and soothing single voice. That was quite a trick.

You are obsessed with "how," Michael. That is not the question.

You say . . . Julie is home and well. Can I see her?

No.

Why the fuck not?

She's alive.

Somehow, until that moment, Mike hadn't really understood just how big the gulf between him and Julie was.

He did now.

He slumped into the black leather chair. Why did he believe the book? Why didn't he presume this was an hallucination? A virtual dream. Why did he believe the birds when it was the last thing in the world he wanted to believe? He checked the window. The hummingbird was gone. The old man was waddling toward him in his baggy brown suit, holding his pipe by the bowl.

"A sad book?" he asked.

Mike looked down at the paperback in his hand. "It's the saddest book I've ever read."

"History?"

"Science fiction," Mike said, holding it up so he could see the cover.

"Ahhh. Well. You follow anything to its logical extreme and it can get pretty depressing. My name's Sam."

Mike took the offered hand and shook. The old man's suit was way too big for him, its sleeve rustled as he pumped the soft, warm hand. "Gabriel says 'Hi.' "

The old man smiled. "A fine old stallion."

"I'm Mike. I'm dead." They stopped shaking.

The old man sat gingerly on the fat, black armrest beside him. This sudden closeness didn't bother Mike. Sam smelled wonderful. The comfortable lived-in scent of old people. "Funny, I don't think I've heard that word for years. It's like a phone number that's on the tip of my tongue and I can't—" He looked at Mike's face. "We all are, son. It's quite an adjustment. Took me—ohh—three years to get used to it."

"My lover..." Mike began, but he found he couldn't finish.

"Yes?"

"My lover..."

"Yes, I know. I lost my Alice. Feels like somebody reached right into my chest and took my heart out. You can't dwell on that stuff, son. You gotta have hope. Any day now I'm hoping Alice will walk through those doors." The man tapped the empty bowl against his saggy, wrinkled palm. "Then there's the next stage. After so long, you wonder whether or not you'll even recognize her. Or if both of you will have changed so much you won't remember how to be together. Stuff like that. But I trust her. I'm sure it'll be worth the wait. Hope, you see? What was *your* wife's name?"

"Julie," he answered, staring at the cover of the book, not really seeing it. "She wasn't my wife."

After a moment the man said, "I find a hot cup settles me when I get in a state. Would you like some tea? I promise you: it's superb."

This little gesture of courtesy nearly sent Mike over the brink. He swallowed and ground his teeth together.

The old man laid a hand on his shoulder. "I think you better see the Keeper," he said, depositing his pipe in the pocket of his suit. "She's a good egg. But, ah...words to the wise? If she offers you something to drink...pass."

A memory of something sour pressed itself into the old man's features and, for a moment, Mike could see every wrinkle his face had ever earned.

The D Word

Why not end it here? Daniel wondered.

It was a gorgeous fall afternoon. The kind of day they used to burn leaves. He loved that smell. Why was the smell of decay so beautiful?

He was standing outside the diner staring at the pumps. Red cherries. The *Live Bait* sign. He seemed to have been standing there a long time, though he couldn't recall what stopped him and couldn't say what prevented him from moving forward. He noticed he'd left his keys in the Volvo's ignition.

Daniel walked out into the middle of the highway and looked both ways. One way the two-lane blacktop went straight as far as he could see. The other way it bent and disappeared under a canopy of palms. He realized Frost was wrong. It didn't make any difference which way he chose. It would all be the same. People missing each other or finding each other. It didn't matter anymore. Not here.

In the distance he heard the clank and snort of an eighteen-wheeler shifting gears.

Daniel concluded: It was a mistake, this virtual earth the birds had made. An insane proposition carried to its illogical extreme. What if life lacked mortality? It was like asking: what if light lacked color? What if love lacked emotion? What if brothers weren't related? It was like any of the heavens conceived by anyone other than the original landlord. It depended on what you left out. Life without hunger. Life without anguish. Life without ignorance. But life without just about anything wasn't life anymore. A world without loss was a world without meaning. *Why couldn't the birds see that? Were they so pleased to provide humans with their deepest desire— immortality—that they hadn't thought through the consequences of granting that wish?*

The hulking truck approached the bend a hundred yards away. He could see it through the hanging palm fronds.

Daniel looked down and leaned over his belly to see his feet were resting beside the double-yellow lines. He took a long step sideways until he stood smack-dab in the middle of the lane. Follow the yellow-brick road. He laughed at himself. A grown man on a country road on a golden autumn day having an existential crisis. Sparring with a foe he couldn't speak to, couldn't understand, couldn't even see.

Don't you get it? He thought. You can give us everything about life except what makes it worth living.

And what was that? He wondered. What was that?

The silver-grilled truck emerged from the trees, approaching fast.

Daniel surprised himself at the conclusion he reached: the *D* word. Death. That made all the difference. Not choice. Not eternity. Not even love. Everything mattered because everything was temporary, fleeting, evanescent. Those were the boundaries that defined the game. House rules. Without death nothing matters.

Strange. All this way to discover: our deepest dream was a nightmare. The payoff of every religion on the planet was bogus. To live forever spoiled everything. The *D* word is what made life precious.

And for a time Daniel felt a wonderful certainty. Because he knew: this wasn't life. He didn't want this. He wanted no part of this.

The truck's grille had a silver slash down the middle and chrome goggle headlights embedded in its white fenders. Its horn blew twice.

Daniel wanted that other place. The place where things were missing. Where people left and never came back. He thought of his barber, Rachel. He thought of his mother. Or the pictures of her. He thought of his wife and son. That was life. That was what he wanted. The place where people lie, and hurt each other, and trains go off rails, and planes fall out of the sky, and children learn fear, and women are raped, and earthquakes swallow towns, and friends let you down, and every day, every minute was a wonder, every second was a miracle. Not because it was good, but because it was real. And it ended. Twenty hours of agony-transition and there was Sean, erupting out of Julie's belly, covered with cheese and blood, still connected to his mother by a twisty white cord like those balloons you get at the circus before you blow them up. His brother lying next to him, or hurting him, or snickering at him, or mortified by him—but there, dammit. There.

He wanted that. He wanted a place where things mattered. Where things ended.

The trucker's horn was blaring continuously now. Daniel could almost read the logo on the grille.

He had lost Julie.

He had lost Sean.

He had lost that bastard Mike.

Everyone that mattered.

Who was left?

Daniel looked at the onrushing grille, thinking, pull the plug. Press the armageddon button.

The truck's brakes were hissing and the eighteen wheels were screeching and smoking on the blacktop when Daniel felt himself grabbed by a little hand and spun and tugged off to the side of the road. He could feel the draft on his face as the truck whooshed by. And looking at its retreat he saw the trucker stab his arm out the driver's window, giving him the finger.

A little voice said, "It doesn't work that way, mister. You'll just come back."

Huitzilopochtli

For as long as he lived Mike would never forget the little woman and the house full of hummingbirds.

The old man drove him silently to a suburb of Detroit: Royal Oak. On the way Mike caught himself staring at Sam's hands on the steering wheel. Beautiful hands, he thought. Kind hands.

They arrived at a dilapidated green house with an unmown lawn. One of those real eyesores, property value depleters. Still there was something cozy about the house, set back from the road, hidden by a row of wild, untrimmed bushes, mailbox overflowing with unanswered mail, grass overgrowing the slate stones that led to the screened-in porch. It smelled like the jungle: decay. A humming sound everywhere as if someone were weedwhacking the garden.

Mike waved good-bye to Sam in his black Lincoln, then walked up the broken, wooden steps and saw a yellow stickie over the doorbell: *OUT*

OF ORDER. When he knocked on the screen door dry flakes fell like faded shards of emerald to his shoes. The door, like the rest of the peeling house, hadn't seen a paintbrush in years.

She came out of the shadows wearing her rainbow muumuu house-dress—reminding him of a nun on holiday. A midget. Fat toes poking out of her yellow flip-flops. Bulging arms. A round, doll face with black bangs and a tattoo between her eyes—something he had only seen before, in Marrakech: an upside-down teardrop rising to the sky. Her eyes were simply black, but there was nothing frightening about them.

"Come on in," she said.

The screen door creaked open and banged shut behind him—a friendly sound. The porch was crammed with stuff: a tattered couch, yellow newspapers in tottering stacks, towers of old shoe boxes. Did she ever throw anything away? Red bird feeders of all shapes and sizes hung like wind chimes in the corners. Great messy visual. He'd have to use that.

Mike smelled cat litter as he stepped across the threshold. All the windows were open in the living room, the dining room. Though it was the height of summer, there were no screens anywhere.

He felt as if he had walked into an aviary. The house was full of hummingbirds. Like swallows at play, the birds were engaged in an elaborate game of tag. He paused, worrying that they might bombard him, but he noted her nonchalance and followed her to the kitchen in the back, the streams of green washing past his peripheral vision.

"Lemonade?" she asked.

"Sure," he said, sitting at the kitchen table.

The house appeared to have its own climate. Mike didn't mind that it was winter when he'd left Hart Plaza and it was August here. Nothing surprised him anymore. Apparently, the birds had different rules about weather.

The kitchen was full of shade and flitting birds who lit up like fireflies when they passed through the bright afternoon light that streamed in from the open windows. It was a hummingbird dogfight. Flits of color swooping and looping. The buzzing, not quite musical sound of their wings dop-plering as they passed. How come they never collided?

An enormous black cat strolled into the kitchen like it owned the place, padding over the red-and-white checkerboard tiles, stepping deli-cately, Mike noticed, only on the red ones. The cat regarded Mike with contemptuous yellow eyes.

The little woman was stirring a pitcher full of lemon slices with a wooden spoon. The satisfying tinkle of ice and knock of wood on glass.

The cat was doing an infinity swirl around Mike's legs, pressing its smooth weight against his shins. He asked, "Aren't you afraid he'll get the birds?"

"Sebastian? Nahh, Sebastian loves those birds. Don't you, boy?" The cat looked up at her. She giggled. "Besides, he has manners."

Sebastian. The name sounded familiar. Then the cat leapt onto Mike's lap and sat down facing him, poised as a sphinx. It felt like someone had dropped a sack of warm clay on his legs. The cat stared with those yellow eyes, the pupil slits hard as daggers, as if to say: you're mine.

The Keeper handed Mike a plastic glass with a pattern of sunflowers. It was so cold it bit his fingers. He expected to taste perfection: perfectly sweet, perfectly sour lemonade. He was shocked and practically choked when he swallowed. It was perfectly awful. Oh, it was bad. Bad in ways that he had never imagined. It had no redeeming qualities.

"I've seen you before," he said. She was leaning back against the sink, crossing her arms. "In an airport, I think."

"It's possible. I fly a lot. I'm in the resettlement business."

He couldn't place her accent. He wanted to say British, but that wasn't it. It was earthier, slangier. And her voice was strangely low for a woman of her stature. She shooed a few birds off the countertop. They admired the bird dance for a while: the black cat and him. She was right. It wasn't that the cat wasn't interested. But he was reigning in his impulses, as if he were subject to a higher law than appetite.

"Isn't that the strangest thing you've ever seen?" She meant the birds.

"I thought I saw a flying saucer once. When I was a kid."

The Berber teardrop between her eyes was a dark, rusty gold. "They're not flying saucers, sweetie."

"What are they?"

"You're not gonna believe me."

"Try me."

"Bubbles. The flock flies in 'em. That's how they cross space. Perfect recycling vessels. Absolutely no waste. They're masters of entropy." She noted his face and added, "Told ya."

The sudden turn in the conversation made him self-conscious. Mike looked about the room. The light. The birds. The cat. The lemonade in his hand catching his pulse, concentric rings collapsing from the outside in, like the opposite of a pebble dropped into water. "Where am I?"

"Close your eyes and put your hands over them. Like this." She made the peekaboo gesture.

He obeyed. And for a moment he didn't know where he was. He only knew that he was no longer in the Keeper's kitchen.

We see the impossible in stages. Working our way slowly through familiar perspectives and inadequate metaphors until language fails and we see the thing itself.

First, he seemed to be standing at the bottom of a hollow sequoia tree. Mike had been in such a tree in a rain forest in Washington state. Hollowed out by fire and enterable by a tall notch in its trunk.

"Keep yer eyes closed. Gotcher bearings?"

He nodded.

"Now look closer."

He did. He saw then it wasn't really a tree, or if it was, it was the tallest tree on earth. The hollow of a giant beanstalk that stretched up as far as he could see. The walls seemed to pulse and shimmer as if the stalk were twisting ever so slightly in the breeze. Finally, through some trick of mind or shift in perception, Mike saw that he was at the bottom of a huge funnel cloud, a twister, but the sides were swirling in slow motion, and the walls were coated with hummingbirds, their wings flapping, their breasts of many colors facing the center, pulsing in and out as they breathed. It almost made him nauseous to watch the twisting tunnel, the hovering birds, and to hear the incessant low-level hum as the tubular cloud arched and coiled above him like the stem of a plant on the ocean floor.

"What is it?" he asked.

"Let's call it a living library."

"Where is it?"

"Think of it as a tether to the mother ship. If one could see it, and no one can—its dimensional position is beyond you, like the wings of a hummingbird—but, if one *could* see it, it would look like one helluva mushroom cloud over Miami, Florida."

Well, that answers everything, Mike thought. What a relief. I'm in Miami.

The Keeper giggled and he got the impression that she overheard his thought.

High, high above him he saw a silver dot in the center of white haze. He remembered. "That's them! That's the UFO I saw. The mother ship?"

"It's not a ship, Michael. I told you. It's them."

He removed his palms and squinted and blinked as his eyes adjusted to the light of the Keeper's kitchen.

"What are they doing?"

"Saving you. Collecting data. Storing it."

"Digital?" he asked.

She shook her head and swallowed. "They're way beyond ones and zeroes, sweetie. Binary is kid stuff to them. What's the opposite of entropy?"

After a few moments, he answered, "Life?"

"No. Information." She indicated the kitchen with her arms but she meant the world around them. "Information is forever."

The cat was purring on his lap like the grumbling of a door on its hinges.

She set down her drink and walked past him into the dining room. "Come," she said.

There are certain people who expect to be followed, who collect devotees as a whale gathers parasites. Mike stood and the cat dropped to the floor. He followed.

Sebastian, he thought.

The Keeper stood before an old mahogany buffet with huge drawers. Each had two pewter handles shaped like upside-down question marks. She could barely reach both of them with her tiny, fat arms. The drawer squeaked open and released the smell of graham crackers dipped in chocolate—his favorite. Mike expected to see white linen or stitched doilies, but what he saw was a type of mausoleum. Dead hummingbirds filled the bottom of the drawer, neatly lined up in rows, each lying on its back. "I started with shoe boxes, but I ran out." Before he could warn her, she touched one on its glowing crimson neck. "This was the first."

She showed no reaction to the touch, and he wondered if she was immune to the birds' magic. "Found him flopping around in the sink. I kept finding them on the windowsills, on the ground. It's the century plant." He looked at her. "I'll show you later. It's in my garden. Supposed to blossom every hundred years. Has these spears like asparagus. Hummingbirds love red flowers. But they go loony for the century plant. The blossoms are red and very potent when they ferment."

"Ferment?"

"Rot. It gets the poor bastards blasted. So they go smacking themselves against the cabinets, the walls. Had to take off all the screens on the first floor, didn't I? But still I'd find them staggering about like Pentecostals. I think some of them can't take the bargain."

Baahgin, she called it.

"With the aliens," she said, noting his confusion. "Most are volunteers. They're a generous species. And the aliens give them their heart's content of pure nectar. But the rest come here and drop some oblivion. Can't say as I blame them. It's a tough mission."

"What mission?"

"Save the people."

Papal, she pronounced it.

The Keeper shut the drawer and led him back to the kitchen where she hoisted herself and sat on the edge of the stainless steel sink. He returned to his seat. The black cat landed on his lap with an oomph.

"Know anything about hummingbirds?"

"Not much," he admitted.

"I reckon not. Closest earthly analogy to the aliens. Smallest bird in the world. Life span: five years. Some migrate over the Gulf of Mexico. Nonstop flight: one thousand, eight hundred and fifty miles. Practically a light-year for them. Spunky little dinkos. Burn up calories like a marathoner. Gotta eat twice their body weight every day. Which means they eat all the time. Which means...?" she prompted.

"They're starving?"

An approving smile. "Bingo. That's how the aliens saw it. No wonder you're their favorite. You're hungry all the time, aren't you? You just don't know what for." She reached down behind her into the sink and retrieved a little green bird. Holding it in her fist, she blew softly into its face, and Mike could see the tiny feathers acquiring and relinquishing colors as they rippled. "You *papal.* You're a bunch of monkeys with free will. Monkeys, each with a fist full of peanuts, paw stuck in a jar. You can be free and hungry. Or stuck with all the peanuts you need. And hungry." She smiled. "Which would you prefer?"

Mike smiled at the paradox. And he was getting used to the detours. Once you didn't expect linearity, it was possible to ride with it. "I'd rather not be hungry."

She flicked open a brown-paper lunch bag and deposited the bird with a *thuck.* She got down and walked over to the freezer. Opened it and placed the bag inside. A cloud of frosty air exhaled behind her head as she turned to him. "Do you know: they don't use names?"

"The birds?"

"And the aliens. Something else you have in common. It would never occur to them to give labels to their brothers."

Brothers? he thought. "Why don't I remember your name?"

"You have a learning disability about names."

Yes, he thought, like Teflon. "Who are you?"

"What do you think?" she asked.

He smiled nervously. "I think I had some bad mushrooms in the jungle."

"Ah, drugs. The life-is-a-chemical-gumbo-answer. I've never been a big fan of materialism." She smiled. "And vice versa."

There was an infinite pause. The birds, he noticed, had all roosted. The room had grown very quiet.

"Devils?" he asked, finally. Not exactly frightened, but on the verge of it.

"Dualism. The magnetic-pole-theory-of-reality. You do so cling to those either-ors, don't you?"

The cat purred on his lap. Pet me, it seemed to say. Mike stroked the cat's thick coat and felt a knob under the fur. Gently, he parted the soft blackness to reveal the pink skin and a nasty mouth of stitches beside the spine. Poor boy. The cat protested with whiny growl, but didn't move.

"Sebastian?" she said. "You wait your turn. Maybe it's a combination, Michael. Maybe you're a good man tempted by demons. Or a bad man tempted by angels. Perhaps I am the governing intelligence of the alien's biotechnology. The onboard AI, if you will. Or perhaps I am a glitch— a ghost in the machine—a renegade consciousness. Or perhaps I am an intelligence ungoverned by your laws or their laws. Perhaps I am a law unto myself."

The lemonade, he thought. That sure broke the rules.

"Possession. Hallucination. Miracles. They're just labels. They're all stories."

"Stories?" he asked.

She sighed. "Take Abraham and Isaac. The idea of sacrifice. It's a human construct. An attempt to explain suffering. To mend a mystery. Pain for pain. Unnecessary, unless one believes in a bad god. That's what happens when you force your god stories on other cultures. They don't fit. Bound to be a misunderstanding. Maybe that's all reality is. A consensual misunderstanding."

"You've lost me," Mike admitted.

"Not yet," the Keeper said. "You ever hear of Huitzilopochtli? Now that's a mouthful. Aztecs believed that dead warriors were reborn as hummingbirds. And their god Huitzilopochtli demanded human hearts and blood for nourishment. Now, I ask you—where's the logic in that?"

"Who are you?" he asked again. More politely this time.

She did a fair Popeye imitation. "I yam what I yam. I am your brother's keeper."

"I'm being punished. This is hell."

"You think so?"

"I coveted my brother's wife," he admitted miserably.

"Yeah, and you fucked her too, didn't ya?" She stepped over, met him eye to eye and slapped him hard across the mouth.

Mike held his palm to his stinging lips.

"Feel any better?"

"No."

"I thought not. Sebastian? Bite him."

The cat snarled, pounced, and set his teeth into Mike's wrist.

Nobody's Father,
Nobody's Son

Daniel turned and saw the boy from the diner standing beside the road. The boy who had saved him from the truck.

"Hi, Dwight. Did you win again?"

He smiled proudly. "I'm on a rock."

The boy was holding something with both hands. Like a karate student about to bow.

"You shouldn't be out here on the highway. Emma will worry."

"I snuck out." His eyes smiled. "I remember the accident. She doesn't think I do, but I do. White car. Right over there by the snake." He pointed at a yellow curve sign. "I saw him coming but I wasn't fast enough. Knocked me right out of my shoes."

"I'm sorry."

"Do you remember yours?"

"My what?"

"Accident."

How could he know? Daniel looked down the highway. "No. Maybe. There was a tree."

"Here," the boy held out his fist. "Hold me for a second."

His hand received the hummingbird. A tiny, fragile thing; it weighed almost nothing in his palm. Its heart beat like a miniature drum roll. A picture flashed inside his mind, like an image made visible by lightning. It didn't make sense. Daniel felt as if he were inside a mirror looking out at his own face. Except the mirror was dripping. Then . . . blackness.

"Not like that. You gotta make a fist."

Daniel made a fist and had the strange feeling that he had known this boy all his life. But the memories were like the signal from a radio station that wouldn't quite tune in: staccato fragments, snippets of images, words and faces—essentially noise.

"That's me," Dwight said. "Where's yours?"

"What?"

"Your birdie."

"I don't have one."

"That's impossible."

"Is it?"

The boy looked up into the sky as if he were watching a passing jet or a UFO. Daniel couldn't bring himself to follow the boy's rapturous gaze. Such a beautiful face, he thought. His parents must love him. A sudden, cool shade covered the day, softening the shadows around them.

"He's not on our team," the boy was saying.

Finally, Daniel looked up. A big, white cumulus blocked the sun, a glowing yellow nimbus at the edges. Calendar art, he thought.

"Where's his birdie, then?"

Daniel looked at Dwight's face. Such a sad, crazy boy.

"That's not fair." The boy looked at him and smirked. "Well, that sucks. *They say: You gotta remember.*"

"Remember what?"

"The accident."

Daniel felt a sudden chill. As if something was about to drop on his head. "Why?"

"Them's the bricks. That's just the way it works." Dwight cocked his head to one side, listening. "They say they would gladly spare you the memory. Well, it can't be worse than mine and I remember. Except the man's face." He looked at Daniel. "I don't like that part."

Daniel knelt beside the boy. "You can talk to them?"

He smiled. "Yup. They like the way I taste."

Daniel shuddered. "Tell them something for me?"

"Sure."

"Tell them: Nothing could be worse than this."

Dwight looked to the sky again. "He says, 'nothing could be worse than this.'" His brow crinkled. "Oh. They say they heard that." There was a pause. Apparently a long monologue. The boy scrunched his eyebrows, listening. "No, he can use me. I don't mind. No...no...sure. Just let him out, would ya? He wants to go home." Then Dwight turned to him, cupped both his hands over Daniel's palm and the bird, and whispered, "Ask them nice and they'll let you go."

"Why?"

"It's crowded where they come from. They say *please* a lot."

"Okay," said Daniel, not understanding. "Thanks."

"Yer welcome." It was a singsong voice. Something he learned by imitating adults. His mother, maybe.

"Dwight!" Emma was calling from inside the diner. "Where'd you get to?"

"I better go. She'll miss me. She's a warrior. I'll see you later." The boy saw the look on Daniel's face and added, "I mean: I won't see you later. Okay?"

"Okay," he managed to say.

Dwight walked away, swimming in his baggy jeans, the shoelaces on his ruby-red sneakers undone and dragging, back past the cherry pumps to the diner, looking very much, he thought, like the little boy he'd once been before it was all taken away. Daniel felt a greater emptiness fill him than he had ever felt before. It was as though he had been stripped of everything that mattered. He had nothing else to lose or to give. He was nobody's lover, nobody's father, nobody's son.

That was when the miracle occurred.

Death Is for Keeps

The black cat Sebastian released Mike as quickly as he had bitten him.

He leapt off his lap and strutted gingerly on tiptoes over the red squares, out of the room. Holding his wrist, Mike saw a puncture in the skin where the face of his watch used to be. As shocking as the bite had been, it hadn't hurt that much. Still, he was shaking.

The Keeper looked at him and repeated his thoughts. "Shaking. Baking. Taking. Calm down, Michael. I promise you: that's as bad as it gets."

"That fucker bit me!"

"Gotta let him have a taste now and then. Feel better?"

"No," he said. "I thought you said he was tame."

"I never said he was tame," she giggled. "I said he had manners." The Keeper went to the sink and ran some water. "Where'd this idea of torture as purification come from? Guilt? Appeasement? To give suffering some sense of justice? Meaning? Not from me, I assure you."

She brought over a damp, red dishrag from the sink. "Hold still," she said, dabbing at the wound. "You think God cares about fucking? Do you have any idea how many organisms boff each other every millisecond?" She applied a clear plastic Band-Aid to his wrist. It felt as though Sebastian had left a fang under the skin, like the broken tip of a pencil. "What?" said the Keeper. "She's got nothing better to do than keep score?"

She? Mike thought.

She smiled. "You were expecting, what? Charlton Heston? A burning bush?" The Keeper placed a hand under his chin and inspected his face. She smelled good enough to eat. "What do you want, Michael?"

He thought about it. The question was ordinary but the intensity with which she asked it wasn't. It felt important.

"Last chance," she coaxed.

"I want Danny." He had surprised himself. He wouldn't have expected that to be the answer.

"He's dead, sweetie," she said gently, removing her hand. "Death is for keeps."

"He's the closest thing I ever had—" Mike couldn't finish.

She could. "To a home. Yes. So... what you're really saying is: You want to go home."

"Yes."

"Well, that's my specialty," she said. "Say it, sweetie."

He looked into her eyes and was startled to discover that she was really a very beautiful woman. He wanted to take her in his arms. It didn't matter that she wasn't his type. He would have gone to bed with her in an instant. "Home," he said. "I want to go home."

"Again." The word lifting musically on the second syllable.

"I want to go home."

"One more time."

"I want to go home. Please."

"See? All you have to do is ask nicely. Maybe you ought to read the letter now."

"What letter?"

"The one in your wallet."

He looked down at the floor. "I know it by heart."

"No, sweetie. The other letter."

How could she possibly have known about that? Folded inside the letter from Julie was another letter which she had included in her kiss-off. Thin blue onionskin stationery smudged with black ink: Danny's handwriting. The last straw. Apparently the reason she ditched him. Mike had read it once that first time. And never again. He hadn't thrown it away, though. He just never reread it. It hurt too much.

The Other Letter

Jan. 4, 1991

Dearest,

Something you said the other day has been bothering me. So I decided to write you about it. I know I don't do this often enough. Just as I never tell you enough how much I love you. You will just say you don't deserve it. And, frankly my dear, I get tired of hearing that. Someday, I hope, you will understand.

You will say I'm naive. But I'm not really. You always say it's impossible for me to believe the worst of others. But I know what people are capable of. Just because it surprises me, doesn't mean I can't deal with it. And you should know that no matter what you've done in the past, no matter how many times you've hurt me, (we both hurt each other—this isn't news. This is what marriage is: Hurting each other, forgiving each other, and moving on. I sound so wise, don't I?) No matter what: I love you.

Some people have the ability to choose who they love. I'm not one of them. I fall in love and stay in love and like a whipped puppy I keep coming back for more. I don't deserve a lot of credit for it. I'm not a particularly evolved virtuous person. I don't have any choice in who or how I love—it just happens.

I hope this is clear. You're stuck with a man who will love you till the day you die. I also like you but that's another letter.

I'm between classes. The usual piles of papers to correct. Two committee meetings this morning—awful stuff. The usual hard feelings, petty politics and maneuverings for advantage. Are there any other happy English professors? I'm the only one I know. Outside on the common, bundled students tilting forward against the windchill. It's brutal out there. Days like this make me wonder why we live in Michigan. But I love it too. And I love my job. *And the young minds I get to touch. It's an honor, really.* The morning light is crisp and golden and it's cozy in my office, but if I move close to my window I can feel the cold struggling to get in.

Anyway, the reason I'm writing this is to respond to something strange you said the other day that I can't get out of my head. "There are no heroes anymore. They've been replaced by stars."

Strange, because it sounded like you were quoting my brother.

And Mike never said that to me.

Well, I've got to say I think you're wrong. I think you're cynically buying the values of our media while pretending to reject them. The world has gotten smaller. There are no

more secrets. And every other news story is some exposé
about the failings of our leaders or celebrities: this basketball player does crack, that politician had phone sex—after
a while you start to believe that it's all a sham. Everybody's
just putting on an act but, really, under the skin, they're
phonies, hypocrites, slimeballs. Not heroes.

I couldn't disagree more.

Heroes haven't disappeared. They've just gotten
smaller.

And I think heroism is overrated. You've said heroic virtue is demanded when one considers the truly rampant hor-
rors and tragedies that occur daily, from genocide to
accidents. A world, you say, it would be criminal to bring a
child into. That's a cop-out. And I'm not talking about our
disagreement on kids. Yes, I've always wanted a son but
that's another letter. We'll figure that out in time. There's
no hurry. What I mean is: It's all very well and good to adopt
a stance of fierce dismay and register sympathy for
thousands of strangers you can't do anything to help. But
all that does is depress you, or make you feel superior. Or
justify passivity. Like I said: a cop-out.

Here's what I think. What is needed in a cruel and ter-
rifying reality isn't heroic virtue—how often do we get that
chance? What's needed is heroic courtesy. A personal response to the world we bitch in and cut people off in, and
curse and snub and cheat and gossip in. The world we create.
I don't believe it just happens by itself. It's our responsibility. It's up to us. And I believe with all my heart that the
bottom line ought to be something smaller than kindness
even. Courtesy. Courtesy lubricates and sustains our soci-
ety, leavens the world from the inside out. I don't think Mike
ever understood that.

And yet what do we value? Movie stars who kick ass.

Quick comebacks and prime-time sarcasm. The brave sol-
dier who takes out five enemies with a grenade and rescues
his wounded buddy on the battlefield. Sports heroes who can
leap higher than anyone—dunk, and smack and hit and kick
and bodycheck. We admire violence. I think it says a lot
about how powerless we feel: how much we revere muscles
and fitness.

But violence, despite what we see on the news, is exceptional. It wouldn't be news if it wasn't. It seems to me that
most of life is little moments, tiny thoughtless habitual vir-
tues that make it bearable, that make civilization possible—
not extraordinary acts that make headlines. Most people are
good. If they weren't it'd be chaos.

Just today, I was feeling particularly glum for the usual
reasons and this total stranger approached me at the phar-
macy and said, "You dropped this." She was a teenager with
that Goth thing, nose ring, black fingernails and lipstick—I
guess they have to find *something* to shock their parents—
and if you didn't look beyond the frightening aspect of her
makeup you'd never see the sweet, well-mannered child
there. She casually handed me the box of Band-Aids that I
had dropped. She didn't even smile when I thanked her; just
nodded and went on her way. Well, see, to me, that's special.
She didn't have to do that. Fifteen seconds to make a
stranger's life just a little easier. Who taught her that? Not
the newspapers.

You say you cannot trust anyone. You say the world is a
horrible place. Well, perhaps. But to me it's a better place
knowing that dark girl is walking around in it, throwing
away courtesy that will never make the six o'clock news.
That is my hope. That the little things we do and say and
even think, these tiny accidental miracles of grace and goodness will make the difference between a living hell and some-

thing else—I won't call it heaven. I never believed in heaven.
But I've always believed in you.

Love,

D

Somehow, during the journey of years it had spent folded in his wallet, in his back pocket, the letter had become a new thing. It was as if Mike had never read it before. The black ink and the blue paper glowed between his hands, like a slide held up to a candle. How could he have missed it? It was perfectly obvious to him now.

Danny was talking about them. Him and Julie.

He wasn't naive.

He suspected. He was forgiving her. Something Mike could never do. That would be when the tears started. Mike cried for a long time.

When he was done, Mike felt the Keeper breathing on his shoulder. "Time for the powwows," she said.

Contact

"Higher," the Keeper called from below, her upturned face smiling between the boughs of green maple leaves.

Mike struggled up another limb of the tall, gray tree until she looked like a doll wandering about her overgrown garden, sniffing the red blossoms of the century plant, carefully stepping over the many dead birds, picking them up one by one, putting them in her straw purse.

"If I break my legs, it's your fault."

He heard her giggling beneath him.

He hadn't done this for years. And he remembered the joy and fear of climbing trees: the tingly body knowledge that he was one slip away from falling. He recalled how Danny had always stood safely on the ground, watching, letting his big brother take all the chances.

"Remember, Michael," she called. "Mind your manners."

It was only later that Mike realized those were the last words the Keeper ever said to him.

He was higher than the rooftops now and the view was wonderful. Perfect clouds in a blue sky. The green roofs of the quiet neighborhood basking in a sunny day. A black flock of birds in the distance, roiling, coming closer. He found a comfortable *V* and straddled it. Immediately, he felt the childhood thrill of the ideal hiding place—safe and secluded as the world flowed on beneath you. The leaves whispered; the branches swayed. The maple had a separate rhythm, an easier, shallower current than the depths below. How different the world looked from up here. How quiet and peaceful. It was like flying.

It must be what birds feel.

And thinking that, they arrived. The tree was surrounded by flitting tufts of rainbow as the hummingbirds swarmed, a cloud of shimmering confetti he glimpsed between the gaps. It was something you only saw in a Disney movie: this much color and choreography. Their invisible wings roused a mild turbulence that fanned the leaves into shivers, and cascaded gently across his face.

"I want to go home," Mike told them, as the Keeper had instructed.

And he felt it: contact.

Their voices seemed to emanate from a hidden speaker just beyond the reach of the branches: a chorus of a dozen boys fed through a swirling reverb. Though they spoke in perfect unison, their words shivered and echoed like bells in an empty church.

"*Home?*" their chorus replied. "*Is this not an improvement?*"

"No," he said and snorted a mild laugh.

"*But you have everything now.*"

"I never asked for everything. I want life."

"*We've done our best to approximate it. What has been lost in the translation? Your hunger? Your pain? A brief lifetime of desperation and desire?*"

A wave passed through the cloud of birds, and Mike felt a strange emotion wash over him. An inadvertent condescension. As if they were parents dealing with the unreasonable tantrum of a willful child.

"That is, for many humans, the state of living. To be starving and not to eat. What is the loss in losing that?"

He shook his head. "It's not the same."

Looking at the enclosing limbs about him, Mike felt, suddenly, as if he were in a cage. "It's a prison. A playpen. Or is it a zoo?"

"There are no bars. There are no locks. We wish you could enjoy yourself. We enjoy you."

No, Mike thought. You *need* us.

The thought stopped him. He could feel it. They needed humans for something. But what? The clues had to be in their emotions that flowed into him like a scent. He asked himself: what did he feel when they spoke? He came up with a very scary conclusion. He felt hunger.

Hunger for what?

"You do not understand. People are our favorites."

Good god, he thought, maybe they're Catholics.

He remembered the fasting place. The Lenten ache of giving up your heart's desire for forty days: chocolate—the preferred drug of childhood. He imagined that they lived in perpetual deprivation—surrounded by a gourmet's feast they couldn't allow themselves to eat, forbidden by some innate code to satisfy their greatest appetite. No chocolate. And all that fucking fish.

Then Mike remembered something Danny had said to him at the compound. Right after he had killed Klinder. "Shooting fish in a barrel."

The fish, Mike thought. The sucker.

The sucker they had caught that summer in the stream. The one they put in the rain barrel.

Uncle Louie had cooked it and served it to them for supper.

He didn't tell them till they were finished eating.

Mike showing nothing at the dinner table. Staring at the man.

Mike holding Danny's head over the toilet as he vomited.

Uncle Louie saying, "It's a *fish*, for chrissake! It's not a pet!"

Mike saying, "Shuttup, shithead."

He shook his head and thought: pets.

People are their favorites.

To be starving and not to eat.

Christ. They *ate* humans.

"We would never eat you. That would be rude."

Rude? he thought. Yeah, *I'd* say that would be rude.

"It is true, we enjoy reading you. Especially the parts about us. But we would never devour you."

Reading? Did they say *reading*? Why did it sound like *eating*? And why stifle it? Because once they eat us, he thought, we're gone. Because they can't have their cake and eat it too.

Their silence told him he was on the mark.

"Dot was right. We're your Twinkies."

"Twinkies?"

"Yeah, Twinkies. They're so stuffed with preservatives they last forever."

"Preservation is not exploitation."

Their smugness annoyed him. They were like a circus audience demanding the same tried-and-true death-defying acts over and over. Fans addicted to the same characters. Sequel after sequel. And nobody gets hurt. Nobody really dies. Not even Spock. Feeding on the thrills that cost them nothing to watch. Voyeurs relishing prime-time stunts safely from the bleachers. They're just like us, he thought. We all know we're going to die. Yet all our popular myths refute it. The afterlife. The resurrection. The comeback. The close call. We act as though we are going to live forever. It's all a show. And we're the stars. Death is what happens to other people. Meanwhile, the dream is preserved on celluloid. Or digitally archived. To be watched and relished over and over and over. Reruns. We sit in darkened rooms, sharing the same lies. And the stars live. The stars live forever. Tamed and immortal.

"We have no desire to tame you."

"You've no right to tamper with our lives. Or our deaths."

"Is your life so perfect it cannot be corrected?"

Something was going on. "For instance?" he asked.

"You think pain-fall down is funny."

He felt a repugnance in that phrase. "Yes."

"Why?"

He thought about it. The funniest home videos. The pratfalls. Chaplin. Keaton. Slapstick. Why are stumbles so comical? They're not, of course, when they happen to you. Why? Because they only show the survivors?

"I don't know why," he told them. "It's just always been that way."

"In a world of no fall down, you have a lost a lot of laughter, but also a lot of pain."

Mike realized then: it was absurd. He was sitting in a tree having a philosophical debate with a crowd of complete strangers. Aliens who didn't believe in death: the bedrock of his reality. Foreigners who shared no frame of reference with his culture. It was hopeless. They'd never understand. They had no common ground. It was like his shoot in Morocco. He had never felt so surrounded, yet so isolated and alone.

Mike sighed a defeated and exhausted sigh.

It would take a miracle to bridge this gap.

Look Is for Free

A nd just like that, as he stood beside the two-lane blacktop on a sunny day in Florida in a virtual world created by hummingbirds, the miracle happened.

Daniel knew who he was.

He hadn't thought his way to the idea; it had landed on him as if it had fallen from the sky. It was a gift.

After everything had been taken from him, there was only one thing left. He was nobody's father, nobody's lover, and nobody's son. But there was one thing he was sure of. In the end it was the only thing he knew.

He was a brother.

No one could ever take that away from him.

No matter how much he hated Mike. No matter how much Mike hurt him. He was family. That was all that was left.

That was who he was. A brother.

The aliens would never understand that. That closeness. That belonging.

How could they? They were tourists from another world.

Daniel smelled a distant sweetness, a scent of citrus wafting through the moist, warm air over the highway. He held Dwight's sleeping hummingbird and took a long, close look at the tiny face. He was surprised to see its closed eyes had thick, almost cartoon lashes. He didn't know birds had them. For some reason, Daniel was reminded of Mike's strange shoot in Morocco, perhaps the most fascinating story his brother had ever told him.

Mike had flown from Casablanca to Marrakech in the evening. In the morning, after scouting locations, he wandered off from his hotel to the market square. Del La Fina. The "Place of Death." Dubbed so because it used to be an execution ground—the emperor staged daily beheadings; the heads were posted on stakes around the square. Now it was the most hallucinatory farmer's market he had ever visited. First he smelled the saffron. Then the smoke. Then he heard the clang of cymbals and the cacophony of competing languages—French, Arabic, Berber mixed with tourist Dutch, Spanish, Italian, English.

Acrobats in pink silk somersaulted about him. A snake charmer emptied a cloth bag of three miniature diamondbacks, who curled into anger and rattled their tiny tails. A black cobra flicked its tongue at the dark face of the handler in the maroon cloak and black skullcap, who kept them cold in a Coleman icebox to slow their metabolisms so they'd be sleepy and less likely to strike. A white-bearded dentist who looked like an overweight smurf in a white bathrobe sat at a cardboard table laden with the teeth he pulled—hundreds of teeth, some still fresh with tendrils of bloody root and skin: evidence in lieu of a diploma. Veiled women with thick, black eyelashes and laughing eyes walked by arm in arm—the men did too. Yet during the whole shoot Mike never saw physical affection displayed between grown men and women. Everyone touched: men kissed each other's cheeks, children were hugged and corrected, but not once did he see a man and a woman nuzzle, hug, hold hands or kiss.

Strange. Beggars every thirty yards, sitting on the ground, holding out their filthy hands and practiced plaintive faces for the tourists.

To be starving and not to eat.

And the smoke of skinned goat heads on the grills, the tang of ripe dates in waterfall displays that threatened to topple over. Pyramids of vivid green limes and deep orange clementines. Nuts. And herbs. And corked potions in tiny glass bottles that could spell you a long life, a lover's hand, a husband, a baby, a good job, a better bike. Fortune-tellers who only serviced women; apparently men had no future. Bikes and motorcycles and little yellow taxis streaming everywhere, spewing gray exhaust in a chaotic dance where every orbit was respected—amazing no one ever got in an accident. Had this been Manhattan, people would be out of their cars and swinging at each other.

And the muezzin on the top of the minaret chanting out the call to prayer: "There is one God and Mohammed is his prophet…" The call Mike had mimicked and taught to Sean. Abundant silk and leather, wood and silver, cut and beaten, hammered and polished into useful human things: necklaces, bracelets, bells and lamps and jewelry boxes. Walking canes studded with brass and jade and ivory and inlays of red and orange amber, and some of them were hollow, their spines were hidden swords. And the souk shopkeeper saying: "Come, come! Come in, my friend! Look is for free! Look is for free!"

That was what the birds were like, Daniel concluded. Tourists. They were passing through. Browsing. Sampling. They didn't understand. It didn't cost them anything. Look is for free. He wished he could explain that to them. But it was his brother's story. Actually, Mike would have told it better than he could.

Daniel knelt beside the road, holding Dwight's hummingbird in his closed palms, repeating the magic words that seemed to be everything he needed: I am a brother. I am a brother. I am a brother. He realized it was a strange sort of prayer. He didn't remember the last time he'd done that: knelt and prayed. But he felt grateful, very grateful, and he had to thank someone. Somewhere. Not that he wanted to repeat the trip. Once was enough. Once was plenty. It had been a long journey to discover the terrible beauty of death. But worth it, he concluded. He had found himself along the way.

His only regret was that he wouldn't be able to tell anyone about it. It'd make a helluva book. It'd be a book you could enjoy; not one of those books you had to study. Though you'd probably have to read it twice. Like life, it wouldn't make sense the first time through. And you wouldn't be the same person after the first time. It took two people to understand it. The book he'd never write. He'd call it *The Impossible Bird*.

"Please," he said. "I'm ready. Let me go."

And he remembered.

Communion

—   —   —

Mike understood then: he hadn't a clue who he was dealing with.

"I want to know," he said from his perch in the tree. "What you're like. That's the only way I can understand."

The birds were surprised. *"You want to understand?"*

"Yes."

"You won't understand." Sadness.

"I'll try."

"You won't." Deep sadness. Why did they project sadness?

"Please," Mike said. "Help me." And he felt the temperature of the day change as if a cloud had blocked out the sun. It cost him a lot to say it, for it meant he had to trust them. And that was the last thing he wanted to do. But he needed to know there was a reason for all of this. He could take it if there was a reason. It didn't even have to be a good one.

"What do you call yourselves?" Mike asked, suddenly realizing they hadn't been introduced, feeling a belated embarrassment.

"We have no names."

That's right. The Keeper had mentioned that. "How do you tell each other apart?"

"We had much the same problem," they said in that strange, swirling chorus. *"You all look alike to us."* And immediately, Mike could have sworn that the whole flock was stifling a laugh. Nothing was said, but their emotions seemed implicit in the air.

"What do you eat?"

"Same as you," they answered. *"Starlight."*

Starlight? He thought. Well, sure, sunlight. Which feeds the earth and sea, which feeds the animals and plants. Which feed us.

"What do you look like?" He almost regretted the question as soon as it had left his mouth, for he felt a stab of dread left over from his youth: vague memories of aliens who exposed themselves as grotesque nightmares. Slimy and tentacled. Horned and slithering.

"Rub your eyeballs, please."

"What?"

"Close your eyelids first!" A tense yet tender parental reminder.

He did. Closed his eyes and knuckled his eyeballs and saw the fireworks dancing, neurons igniting his optical nerve, streaks and comets orbiting each other in wacky loop de loops, leaving tracers in their wakes that glowed and dissipated like—

"Fireflies!" he said, and felt a warm smile wash over him.

"Something like that. 'Fire Tails,' we call them. They are beautiful, are they not?"

"Yes," Mike said, recalling summer nights when he and Danny chased them in the backyard with canning jars.

"We are beautiful."

Funny. He had never heard anyone say that about themselves.

"Danny and I poked holes in the lids," he said, feeling the need to explain the memory. "So they wouldn't die."

Silence.

"But they died anyway," he admitted, recalling the litter of brown bodies that huddled on the bottom of the jar in the morning.

"Some things cannot be helped."

He scanned the iridescent curtain of hummingbirds that ebbed and flowed about him like a Moroccan rug hanging in the breeze. Beautiful, abstract patterns that must have meant something to somebody. Not him. He felt useless and stupid: the wrong man for the job. "I could ask you a million questions and I still wouldn't understand."

"We are very different, Michael. And we've only just started talking."

He sighed. "Maybe I don't need to understand. Maybe I just need to hear your story."

"Our story?"

"What it's like to be you."

He could tell: the thought excited them. *"Communion. We can do that. But it won't be..."* A pause, as if they had to consult with one another. *"It cannot be a perfect copy. Is 'almost' good enough?"*

"What do you mean?"

"We can supply an analogy. But it won't be us. Michael? We would spare you the experience. You should brace yourself."

He was so tired of everyone's indirection. Their almost clarity. "Just do it," he said.

And they did.

Falling

Falling

Oh My God He Was Falling

The world was burning all their wings were frying in the air like cellophane in a bonfire their beautiful green land reduced to cinder and ash and molten rivers of lava and the children the ones with wings too weak to catch the currents who had to ride upon the backs of their mothers couldn't breathe the scorching air couldn't hold on kept falling

falling into the great fire below and their calls and their cries and the agony of the mothers who had to watch them fall listen to their cries could do nothing to stop their descent and the mothers who gave up then stopped beating their massive wings folded them over their chests and dropped into the flaming abyss one dark lost look to the others in the flock then gone falling falling to be roasted on their burning world Oh how it hurt to lose their freedom and flight and their home gone a world they had always known as solid stable true and how to stop it stop the falling stop the falling stop the falling

Falling. Falling. Falling—

"—stop it!" Mike yelled, nearly losing his grip as he collapsed to the *V* of the trunk.

After a long while they said, *"So. You see?"*

Dragons, he thought, shuddering. Dragons.

"Something like that, yes. But much, much smaller."

Mike trembled as their memory receded, taking deep, deep breaths to steady himself. He had never felt that much pain and sorrow in his entire life. He could hardly believe it was possible. Finally, he said, "I'm—I'm so sorry."

And the world seemed to freeze. The birds hovered in the air in their strange combination of frantic motion and vivid stillness. It reminded him of the starched and rippling stars and stripes the astronauts saluted on the moon. And the silence was so rich and deep he felt as if he had jolted a jury box with a startling confession of guilt.

No—not shock. He felt it: gratitude. That simple, thoughtless human courtesy of apologizing for something you didn't do had stunned the aliens.

"Thank you," they said.

"What'd I say?"

"Thank you. No one has ever asked before."

"Oh," he said. "You're welcome." Then he thought: no one? Had no one ever understood them? Had no one tried? Not even Klinder?

"No. He was too full of fear. The Wing Man thought we were the gods who eat your children. He thought: contact. We could not make him understand communion. Or even courtesy."

"I'm sorry," Mike said, trying to imagine how lonely they felt. And felt again their shocked, pregnant silence, like an inrush of breath, a gasp at something astounding. "That was so awful. The children. The fire. The falling..."

"You have a similar story."

"Hell." Was this why they chose earth? Flight and falling and hell?

"Partly. Yes. And the birds."

"You never experienced that before? Death? Losing your friends and family. Your...flock?"

"And our mother."

"Your planet?"

"Yes."

"And you...never wanted anyone to feel what you felt then."

"YES," and it was so loud it was almost orgasmic.

The next question was the hardest one. For it meant he had to go somewhere he never wanted to go again. No place in his life had ever made him feel so weak and small. And to go there he had to do the opposite of the shrinking trick: he had to get bigger. Mike had to hold his deepest fear, contain it somehow, and not let it overwhelm him with anger and grief. It was, perhaps, the bravest thing he'd ever done.

"Buffalo?" he asked.

The flock of birds in unison turned away from him and showed him their backs. A great wave of shame passed over him like a gust of wind.

"We apologize for that. We did not intend to bring pain. The Wing Man said he would use the doubling trick and you would feel nothing when we tasted the place of tears. He promised: you would not remember."

"I remember everything," Mike said, trying hard to keep the bitterness out of his voice.

"We know that now. We didn't then. Daniel remembered too much, as well. Though it went easier for him. We are sorry, Michael. And we have tried to make up for it."

"How?"

"This," they said. The flock turned back around, paused in the air again, and spread their wings wide. They meant this virtual world they had created. The whole schmear. *"We did this for both of you. You and Daniel."*

"You did it for us?"

"Yes. It is what you asked so nicely for."

"We asked?"

"The words. 'Barrada. Nikto.' We would save you. Spare you everything. Especially your endings."

"Our deaths?"

"Yes. That is why we never gave you your birds."

"Because they contain our deaths?"

"Yes. They contain everything. We would not have you remember."

After a long minute, Mike said, "Thank you. But . . . it is a gift I must refuse."

He wished Danny was here. Danny would have explained this better than he could. He would find a way to tell them how wrong it was. He was a teacher. He could explain anything to anybody. Even a child.

"Do *you* have any questions?" he asked, feeling their wide-open curiosity.

There was a pause. Then a reluctant speech. *"An abundance. You are, by far, the strangest creatures we have ever met. Yes . . .* (a silent discussion seemed to ensue). *Yes. We do have two questions that we have carried a long time. Please, if you would be so kind. We would be most grateful."*

"Shoot," said Mike. "I mean—go ahead." And after a moment: "Any time you're ready."

It is difficult if not impossible to describe the impact these two questions had on Mike. True, they no longer shocked him. He was growing accustomed to their strangeness; he had even attained a comfortable truce with their telepathy, the odd way their thoughts rang inside him like songs he was listening to and, simultaneously, singing along with in his brain. The way impressions and images slid into his consciousness, as if by osmosis: strangely familiar facts whose source he could not trace. But he was not prepared for this.

The birds asked, *"Why are we here? What are we to do?"*

Simple questions. Child questions. Questions everyone has asked in one form or another. And it hurt Mike to realize that they were just like him. Stuck without answers. They had mastered entropy, gathered boundless stores of knowledge, crossed aeons of time and oceans of space, skimmed galaxies and swum vast corridors of emptiness. He saw the flock in his mind, a glowing funnel cloud of sparkling lights, twisting and winding through the darkness like a magical strand of rope, feeding on light, transmuting it and discharging it through their glowing tails; they had searched lifetimes for what? For what? They didn't have a clue.

"We did not intend to bring pain."

"I know," he said covering his eyes with one hand and waving off their apology with the other. "I really wish I could help you out there, kids, but—ah, hell . . ." He gave a small, dark laugh. "The truth is you're asking the wrong guy. I make it up as I go."

"As do we," they said.

Kids. He had called them kids.

Mike realized then, the hummingbirds were children. Young by some tally he could not hope to grasp. He knew it. He imagined they were all sitting together around a cozy campfire. Surrounded by a night of stars. Waiting for him to tell them a bedtime story. He hadn't done that in years.

"Listen to me," Mike said. "Please."

And he told them a story that cost him a lot to tell.

And Mike told his story in the same way they thanked him when he was through: without words. And all the birds flew away but one. And he was left where he started. A grown man with no answers sitting in a tree as the wind played in the leaves, watching the white clouds slide by slowly in the perfect blue of a late summer day. The Keeper was nowhere to be seen. She must have gone inside.

Mike took one last look. It was a perfect world they had made. That was why it was so terrible. He had to show them.

It was all visual: his story. He was a filmmaker after all. And he used his vision to give them a piece of his past that had haunted him all his life. That he had never forgotten. No words. Just pictures.

This is what he showed them.

Danny and him in bed.

A hot summer night.

Lying on sweaty sheets.

Naked. Together.

Sucking each other's cocks.

Pleasure. Stimulation. Kid stuff. Curiosity. Smells. Warm and hard. And sounds. Feeling guilty about it later. Never talked about it. Wouldn't. Years later, Danny asked him if he remembered that summer they found the fish in the stream and kept it in a barrel. The sucker. It was their code. Sure, he said. He remembered. But he knew the question Danny wasn't asking. About the night that summer when two boys explored each other's bodies. "Why hadn't it worked?" Pleasure. But no fulfillment. Trying to get closer to their best friends. Playing adult games they didn't understand. A dry rehearsal of love. Unable, finally, to bridge the gap between them. Because curiosity wasn't enough. Neither was need. Because they were kids. Because they were straight. And that meant they couldn't love that way. They were looking for something they couldn't give each other. It was impossible.

Julie, he thought.

The word felt strangely detached. Like it belonged to someone else. Something that meant something a long time ago. Was this healing? He wondered. Letting go? Her words. Memorized and folded and carried in his wallet for years. Her name. It didn't hurt to think it anymore. Surely, there was something miraculous about that?

Do you see? he asked the birds, after he had showed them his childhood secret. We're not yours to save. We don't belong here. You can't have us and we can't have you. We're not made for each other. That's why it's wrong.

Please, he thought. Please let us go.

Let us go home.

The green bird flew into his hand and laid down on its back, its wings lightly tickling his palm. One tiny eye regarded him, and then it shut.

Gently, Mike made a fist around the nearly weightless body.

And he remembered.

Michael?

S uddenly it was dark.
Very dark.
And the road was wet.

Even with the wipers slapping double-time he could barely see past the windshield. It was like driving through a waterfall. Daniel hunched over the wheel, trying to get a better view of the road ahead. He was laughing at something Sean had just said in the backseat: his favorite line from *The Andromeda Strain*: "Helluva way to run a hospital!" A bit of comic relief he'd repeat whenever a crisis had reached an unbearable peak of chaos and suspense. One of the few times they allowed him vulgarity. And Sean relished it as any boy would.

Daniel glanced at Julie and caught her liking him, his easy laugh. It gave him pleasure. Her new blond bangs were still wet and they made her look younger. He recalled her saying, just two weeks before, "I've never met anyone as good as you." Him feeling proud and embarrassed.

They whizzed past a diner/live bait shop in the rain. He could just make out the red cherries on top of the pumps. He glanced in the rearview mirror and saw Sean giggling at his joke and thought: that's my life, right there. That's the best thing that's ever happened to me. This beautiful boy who loves birds and Cheerios dashed with powered chocolate, and hates homework. Daniel felt that fierce joy that would sometimes overtake him: the joy mixed with fear that only parents felt. He knew there were monsters in the world—sometimes they were invisible, impossible to identify—but they would have to go through him to get to this kid. He'd do anything not to let him down. To give him the family he himself had never had.

Even if he was somebody else's son.

He felt Julie's hand slip gently over his and was, as always, a bit shocked. To understand that she admired him, respected him. Even though he knew she couldn't desire him as he desired her. He recalled the impossible promises they made each other, that every young couple makes. Big words like *forever* and *always* that only the young have the audacity and blind faith to risk. But it was okay. He made her feel safe. That was enough.

That was plenty.

Mike had always held Daniel's life in contempt. Like it was a self-imposed prison of conformity and timidity. He never said it outright but Daniel knew he wondered: what kind of life have you saddled Julie with? This middle-class dream is fine for you—you like it. But it's killing her.

It may have looked that way from the outside. But on the inside it was, if not comfortable, comforting. There was something sad and desperate about Mike's thirst for experience and drama. Always wanting to go somewhere, see new things. Living out of hotels. Taking chances. Sure, it was exciting, but what about this? What about a boy who told bad jokes and a wife who admired you and occasionally touched you like she meant it? And there was always the chance he'd finish that Faulkner paper; he might even present it at a conference. And tomorrow they would be a day closer to home.

Home?

They'd been to Disney World, for chrissake. Sean's dream vacation. Their feet were sore and they were exhausted, but Sean had his picture taken with Donald Duck and had a new stash of valuable souvenirs to put untouched into his attic collection—including a Davy Crockett coonskin hat and a bow and arrow set from the lost boys' island.

His private hoard against time. Toys that would never break or get lost. Gifts whose value could only grow by standing still.

This is what happy families did. It was dark and it was raining but they would get to a motel soon, slide under warm, dry sheets and sleep and dream and wake up together. A family. Mike didn't understand that. Put their lives side by side and who was to say which was better? It wasn't perfect; it wasn't heaven; but it was enough. It was more than many got.

Then a sheet of fog swallowed the road, the headlights punched into the mist and swelled into a yellow cloud within the cloud. Daniel took his foot off the gas; the engine slid into a coast; the rain relented momentarily as if they had slipped under the cover of an overpass. When they emerged from the cloud, the waterfall returned with new force.

That's when he saw it.

There was something in the road, something white and red and small caught by the headlights.

What on earth was that boy doing there?

Why would his parents let him out in this storm?

Dwight, get back inside.

Daniel swerved and the car started to skid and the world blurred. What would Mike call it? "A swish pan." For a second, it was like Dorothy caught in the twister in Kansas—the whirlwind spinning past the window—everything swirling as the headlights swung round and round and round. Darn, he thought, not sensing any danger, merely feeling helpless as he waited for the world to return to order. Then the big gray oak appeared out of nowhere leaning toward them like a huge Louisville slugger.

Snapshots.

Julie's hand braced on the glove box.

A row of pennies sliding from one side of the dash to the other.

Julie screaming, *"Michael!"*

Through his side window: A soaked white child, looking back over his shoulder.

An awful thump.

The barefoot boy flying up and disappearing over the roof.

The steering wheel spinning violently.

His thumb bent out of its socket.

Julie's head caroming off the ceiling.

Michael?

The yawning takeoff feeling as the wheels left the ground.

A boy's forearm becoming an *L*.

Michael?

And right before the impact, Sean screaming, *"Dad!"*

Then the feeling of flying and the gray bark trunk coming at him like the surface of the moon until he could see every crack, every flake, and every valley in between.

Before the darkness: One question that echoed like a call down a deep well.

Michael?

Michael?

Michael?

Danny!

One shot. That's all he needed.

One last shot and he was out of here. Free. Kiss the jungle good-bye. Get off this fucking treadmill. Board. Pitch. Shoot. Cut. Okay—he was drunk, but this time he meant it. He would start over. Move to the mountains. Live with Pauline. She'd make him crepes. She'd smile at him and say stuff like, "You silly fool. Why do I put up with your nonsense?"

Look in her eyes, you idiot. Anyone can see she loves you.

He would get out of ads and shoot features. Shorts, maybe. He'd make the movies he'd always wanted to make. Real movies. Movies where he wouldn't have to leave out . . . what was the word? There had to be a word for all the essential things. Things that'd never get past the initial studio pitch. But he couldn't think of it. Maybe Danny could.

Go to bed. Don't you answer that phone.

Danny would visit the location. And they'd get back what they felt when they were young. The easy closeness of best friends. The acceptance. That's what he wanted. His brother. Before they grew up. Grew apart. Grew into their own lives. Maybe Julie was just a symptom of that. Wanting to share it. Have what Danny had. Be what only Danny could be. His brother never knew how much he envied the order of his life: the wife and kid. Family. The tenure—the normalcy he never got close to because he always pretended to scorn it.

Don't. Don't get on the helicopter.

He was stuck in the jungle. The wrap party. It was storming outside the tents. Fucking monsoon. He was drunk on some godawful paste from some plant the Wyoompee women chewed and spat into wooden bowls. Looked like humus and spinach dip. Really drunk.

His stomach turned at the memory.

There was a call. A phone call on his cell phone. Bad connection. Emergency. Some PA at his production house in LA calling. Lotsa hiss. There's been an accident. Didn't make any sense. What was he saying? An accident? A car accident! Fuck! His brother in a hospital in Florida. Critical injuries. Brain-dead. What the fuck? His sister-in-law messed up, but okay. His nephew dead. Killed instantly. What the fuck? Insisting that they take the chopper. Now. Right now. Overruling their objections. It isn't safe. What about the rain, the fog? Fuck the fog. Had to get to the hospital. You're drunk. Fuck you, Juan! Wait till morning, boss. It can wait. Fuck you, Jim!

Somebody! Anybody! Stop him!

The chickenshit Brazilian pilot said he wouldn't fly. Oh, yeah? Grabbing the key grip's gun again and putting the barrel to the shaking pilot's head. Saying, take me, motherfucker. Take me home. Now. Or I'm gonna keel this cheekin.

Then they crowded on the chopper like a fraternity in a phone booth. Wouldn't let him go alone. They loved him. His friends. Juan, Jim, Art, and Pauline.

No. Get her off. Get her off! Get her off the fucking chopper, you fucking, you fucking you fucking, fucking, fucking

Then something about the chief. Just as they were taking off they found the fucking munchkin had climbed onto the landing whatchamacallits. Hanging from the runners. Insisted on joining them. The translator shouting: he says he's your friend too. The pilot yelling something in Portuguese about being overloaded. And Pauline calling out,

That beautiful voice.

"Too much weight! Too much weight!"

Too much. Wait.

Rising into a foggy cloud the chopper began to yaw over at a sickening, impossible angle from which there was no recovery and Pauline reaching for his hand, reaching for his hand. His last word screamed as the rotors broke off and macheted through the trees and the chopper tipped upside down and Pauline fell into his arms and the dark jungle swallowed them.

"Danny!"

Home

Two dead men found themselves lying in a pale, moonlit field of wheat.

Side-by-side, on their backs, as if they'd fallen from the black sky above.

Together they watched the stars.

There was a piano playing softly somewhere and the melody coasted over the field like birdsong, unhurried, plaintive, as if every phrase were a question. It was a tune Mrs. McNulty used to play next door, on hot summer evenings just like this when she left the windows open: Satie's "Gymnopedie No. I." One of the few pieces of music they could agree on.

The brothers didn't look at each other. They were reliving their deaths. And the memories reverberated in their minds as if they had each awoken from their worst nightmare, shivering and glistening with a sheen of sweat.

What next? their bodies seemed to ask. What now? The chilling final details of their endings echoed in their blood irrefutably except for one impossible fact: somehow, they had survived.

For a moment they had to remember to breathe.

Still, they were silent. Perhaps they thought they were still dreaming. Perhaps it was like the awkwardness of waking up next to a stranger after a night of sex—an experience only one of them had had. Or the odder estrangement: finding the person you thought you knew well was somebody else. Perhaps it was the blunt fact that no one really rehearses for this moment; it is totally impromptu. Or, perhaps, they knew this would be the last and most important conversation of their lives and they simply did not know where to begin.

A wavering voice asked, "Danny?"

The piano played a few more bars.

Daniel wouldn't say his name. He wouldn't give him that.

Mike looked at his brother. "I'm sorry."

"Fuck you."

"I am."

"Fuck you!"

After a moment Mike said, "You shouldn't swear. It's not polite."

Daniel sat up and turned to his brother. "You think this is *funny*? You prick! You moron! You fucking, fucking, *fucking*...!" There weren't enough obscenities for what he felt and he gave up and laid back down.

Shush, the wind in the wheat seemed to say.

Daniel's whole face moved as he asked the only question left. "Why?"

Mike couldn't look at that face for long. He closed his eyes and thought: that's what the hummingbirds said. "*'Why?' That is always the question.*" He felt he had to give Danny something. He couldn't leave him with that question. There had to be some way to explain himself. But how?

Mike noticed his fist lay over his heart, but, instead of a heartbeat, he felt a soft lump in his hand. He sat up, and opened his fingers. The hummingbird had a scarlet ascot. His hummingbird. What had Klinder said? "That's me." Maybe that was it. Maybe he had to show Danny his story as he had shown the birds. Perhaps then he would understand. He remembered touching the woman's hummingbird in the locker room. Feeling her death. He wondered what he would have learned if he hadn't let go. If he'd stuck it out. And waited for the whole story to download. Maybe that's what Danny needed: the whole story.

Mike held the green bird out to his brother. "I'll show you mine if you show me yours."

Daniel's was in his fist. He noticed it was a different bird than the one Dwight had given him. Its breast was purple. Did he really want Mike to know his secrets? Did he deserve that? After what he had done? Why should he do him any favors? Why? That was the question.

Wait a second. Wait, just a second . . .

A thought was humming on the edge of his consciousness. It burst into clarity and he understood. Mike didn't know. What had Klinder said? "Mike doesn't know about me." And Mike didn't know about Sean. If he had he couldn't have killed him. And Daniel recalled what the birds had told Dwight. "You have to remember. They would gladly spare you the memory." They meant recalling his death would hurt. And it had. Especially Julie's last word.

For a long minute Daniel contemplated the cruelest thing he would ever do.

"What are you smiling about?" Mike asked.

Daniel held out his bird. "You sure?"

Mike nodded.

They exchanged birds.

The memories filled them instantly, swamping them like tidal waves. Lifetimes of laughter, fear, pain, joy, disappointment, hope, loss, with none of the comfort of chronology, the buffers of boredom and waiting, sleep and distraction. They absorbed each other's memories at the speed of light, at a pace which only a creature who lived in a whirlwind blur of awareness could appreciate. They had the experience, then they experienced the experience like the aftermath of a long fall—feeling the scream there'd been no time to voice, wondering how anyone could possibly survive this astonishing thing called life. The journey left them breathless and woozy, and the highlights continued to prick at their brains like the trailing sparks of fireworks: flares of pain, most having to do with the woman they had loved, making love to a familiar stranger, someone other than themselves. Their bodies shuddered and twitched; their mouths made noises they had never made before. And they discovered that there is a safety in the private self which, once violated, can never be reassumed. They didn't have to guess or pretend or excuse anymore. They knew. Who they were. How they lived. How they died. Somehow, this knowledge of the other was even worse than remembering their own deaths.

"Jesus," Daniel said.

"Christ," said Mike.

A long silence followed that could have been a minute or an hour. Nobody was counting. The piano no longer played and the bleached wheat stood still as if all the wind had been taken from the world.

Daniel heard his brother sobbing. He had expected to take some bitter satisfaction in this weird exchange. He was amazed to find there was none. He felt numb.

"He was my son. I killed my fucking son!"

Daniel didn't cry for himself or his brother. Strangely, the fresh hell that lingered and disturbed him most wasn't Mike in Buffalo, or Mike with Julie or even Mike's last word. It was Mike's stepdaughter in the hospital. He had forgotten that his brother knew what it was to watch a child die.

Mike was covering his eyes with a hand, wiping the tears. Kyo had warned him. When he had asked how Danny and Sean had died. "Trust me. You don't want to know." Why hadn't he listened to him?

"You killed our dad!"

Daniel was silent.

"How could you do that?"

Daniel shrugged.

"Danny, you never stood up to anyone in your life! How could you kill Klinder?"

"I hated him. It seemed like a good idea at the time."

There was something frightening about Danny's calm. Mike had always thought of himself as the brave one, the strong one. Not anymore. How could Danny handle this? Then it occurred to him that his brother had had more time to absorb this pain. It was, after all, his life. "And that boy in the road! Jesus, we're *both* killers."

Daniel nodded.

"This is truly, truly fucked up."

"Amen." Daniel was stuck with a new knowledge that seemed to douse most of his rage and leave him adrift, with no safe harbor. He had always been the injured party. He had always conceded his fate to forces outside of his control. There was a comfort in victimhood that he'd never understood before. But now that all his losses were settled, the arguments were over, the evidence cataloged, the judgement remained uncertain. Life was an accident. But living was a choice. Now he realized that it was up to him to decide.

Jesus, Mike thought, and he had *asked* for this? The aliens had warned him. They wanted to spare him this truth. It was too much. "It's too much."

"I guess we don't get to decide that," Daniel said.

"I screwed up everything I touched." There was no pity in Mike's words. Only wonder and pain. "Everything."

"Look who's talking," Daniel said.

"What?" he asked at this absurd suggestion of guilt.

"Me too, Mike. I could have been..."

"Don't," Mike said fiercely.

"Better," Daniel concluded.

"Stop being so goddamned nice!"

Daniel snorted. "I'm not nice. I'm done with nice. I wanted those memories to hurt you. And they did."

"I deserved it."

"Maybe. But that doesn't make it right." He looked over at his brother. "You know, I suspected Julie and you, but...I never really knew."

"It's not your fucking fault, okay? It was me!"

"No, Mike. You don't get to do that anymore."

"What are you talking about?"

"Sticking up for me. Watching out for me. Playing the bad guy. Taking all the chances and the blame. That's kid's stuff. That's over."

"Danny..."

"Would you shuttup for a second? This is hard enough." Daniel braced himself with a deep breath. "I'm saying I didn't know you loved her. I thought you were just..."

"Fucking around?"

"Yeah."

"No." Mike gave a wet sigh. "Not that time."

"Then I'm sorry."

"*You're* sorry?"

"For keeping you apart."

There was a long silence when both brothers wondered, in their own way, if this endless reckoning would ever end.

"Danny. Does 'sorry' really help?"

"No," he admitted with sad smile. "But it's a nice gesture. Why didn't you...?" Daniel's question dissolved in his mouth.

"What?" Mike asked.

"I don't know. Something else..."

Mike shrugged. "I don't know. Why didn't *you*?"

"I don't know," Daniel said. He shook his head. "Helluva way to run a hospital."

Mike smiled. He'd never understood the joke before. He did now.

"Hey, Mike?"

"What?"

"Fuck you," he said halfheartedly.

Mike closed his eyes and nodded. "Okay."

They lay there holding each other's birds, too exhausted to do anything but look at the stars.

Then, together, Mike and Daniel felt something.

It was as if, for once in their lives, they had shared exactly the same experience and they didn't have to argue about it. Something had stopped hurting. They felt a cool night breeze on their skin and smelled the pungent, reassuring fragrance of burning leaves. No, it still hurt. Maybe it would always hurt. Like grief. It never goes away; it just gets smaller. Or maybe you get bigger. But now they knew they weren't alone. They held each other's story. Not bits or pieces. Not just their half. There was nothing left unsaid. For the first time they knew the whole schmear.

All their lives they had been missing something. And they had grown around that void, taken it for granted, until it had defined them. Become something very empty, yet very hard. Like a hollow stainless steel ball bearing in their chests they had carried through the years. It had to do with the mom they never knew, and the father they never had. But now the missing thing was gone. And somehow, someone had replaced it with something better. Something that belonged. It was a new feeling for them. As if someone had laid down in their open suitcase while they were packing, to let them know there was room, that they could fit too.

It felt like home.

"At least . . ." Mike began.

"What?"

"At least Sean got the father he deserved. I probably would have botched that too."

"That's very nice of you, Mike."

"Shuttup. It's true."

Daniel smiled an evil smile. "I know." Then he looked back to the stars. "But you really missed out on something. It was an honor, raising your son."

"Our son," Mike said.

And Daniel cried.

The stars seemed brighter now. Closer.

After a time Mike said, "We could stay here forever."

"Let's not, okay?" said Daniel.

"Okay."

Daniel was looking at the hummingbird he held in his hand. "You want yours back?"

Mike looked at Danny's bird. "You want yours?"

"Nahh, keep it."

"Cool."

After a moment, Mike chuckled.

"What?"

"Nothing."

"No. What?"

"Just..." Mike laughed again. *"Hummingbirds?"*

"Yeah," said Daniel, grinning. "Who'd have thunk?"

After a minute Mike spoke to the black sky and the frozen stars above them, "Any time you're ready..."

"I'm ready," said Daniel.

"I was talking to them."

"Oh."

The ghostly stalks of wheat stood perfectly still. Like no wheat anyone has ever seen.

"Maybe we're forgetting something."

Daniel said, "The magic word?"

Mike smiled and shouted, "Gort!"

Daniel smiled. "Barrada!"

"Nikto!"

And when that didn't work, the fathers exchanged a last look, a last smile, and said the magic word together.

Mike and Daniel whispered, "Please!"

And they were dead dead.

Tell me, what else should I have done?
Doesn't everything die at last, and too soon?
Tell me, what is it you plan to do
with your one wild and precious life?

—MARY OLIVER, "THE SUMMER DAY"